Lips of an Angel

What if you could know how your story ends

right now?

Adam Alexander

Dedication

For Annie
My Angel, with real wings.

For everyone who has felt love, loss or longing.
For the broken hearted, the bereaved and the lost.
For the deeply content, who love all of life,
The ones who grab life with both hands.
For those hanging back in the shadows
Looking for that glimmer of hope.
For the remembered
And the forgotten.

This is for you.

Acknowledgements

This was a challenging genre to write, and during the last part of the book, I became all consumed in my writing. I sometimes think my family must wonder if my head has a front side.

Thank you, Annie, for waiting patiently for the next book from your favourite author, and for being the medical consultant. Thank you for your constant encouragement, your unwavering belief in me, and for being my unsung hero.

As always, I've borrowed stories and experiences I've heard along the way, so to those whose experiences and stories I've drawn on, thank you for being part of the journey.

I believe that we're all part of this story, and I hope that this touches you in some small way.

Chapter 1

Riley waited outside the ward. She could hear the mother's sobs, but it was the father's unreserved wailing that reduced her to tears. What parent has the strength to watch their child die?

To Riley O'Connor, death was both beautiful and tragic. There were always the distraught and the bereaved. The lost and the hopeless. That was the tragic part. But death brought with it the hope of a new life.

Tommy Williams was twenty-one, and had just written his final exams at college, Riley had heard the boy's mother saying to the doctor.

As Theresa Williams looked at her disfigured son lying on the hospital bed, memories of Tommy's entire life began to play inside her head like a slide show on repeat with no stop button. She tried to fight the echoing words that repeated endlessly in her mind. *Your entire life flashes before you before you die.* But what if you can't see it? What if you're already dead?

Outside in the hallway, Riley adjusted her hair, a habit she was hardly aware of doing. She removed the band from her pony tail, slid it up onto her wrist, and pulled her blonde, almost golden hair tightly back into a pony once again, before sliding the band back in place and wrapping it around the thick strand three times. She watched through the window as Alistair, Tommy's father, stood beside his wife, sobbing. He was a burly man and looked to Riley as someone who probably worked with his hands. His skin looked like it had endured the warm summers and the cold winters unprotected for hours on end. Tough as he was on the outside, Alistair Williams was broken. There was nothing he could do to save his boy who lay motionless on the bed in front of him, connected to machines that rhythmically pumped air into his lungs. He stared at the blips and the numbers that seemed to repeat the same pattern with each shrill second.

Theresa remembered the moment she first held the tiny baby in her arms. It was right here, at this hospital. Alistair was so proud. She remembered his words to her.

"Now we really can call you Mother Theresa," he had said, beaming, stroking his newborn son's head.

"You call me that and I'll make sure this is your one and only child. By me or any other woman," she'd said. They laughed.

"What are we going to name him?" Theresa had asked.

"I want to name him Thomas, after my late dad," Alistair had said. "To honor his memory. He'll be Tommy for short."

"Tommy," Theresa had repeated. "I like the sound of that." She'd looked down at the newborn, nestling at her breast. "Welcome to the world, Tommy."

The face in front of her now was so disfigured that it hardly resembled her son. His eye sockets were swollen. A huge gash ran down the right side of his face. They'd cleaned him up after surgery, but he still looked beat up and swollen.

"He was a star student," Theresa Williams said through her tears.

Doctor Cairns nodded. Theresa found herself reading the name on the stethoscope that hung around his neck. Litmann. All in capitals, with a distinctive cursive capital L.

"He'd already been selected for the honors program," she said, still looking at the mesmerizing L, tracing its flowing shape with her eyes, from the top all the way to the end. Alistair squeezed her shoulder and bit back the involuntary urge to sob. Inside, he felt like all the tears within had been cried out, that every bit of emotion was lying on the bed next to his son, yet still the surges of sadness swept over him relentlessly like waves against the shore in a torrential downpour, beating at his very soul again and again. "I told him a thousand times that bike of his was a death trap," Theresa continued, "but he never listened. He'd always leave the house, and rev that bloody engine loudly, knowing I was listening, and my heart stopped every time I heard it fade away, praying, *bring my son home to me*. And when he came home later that day, he'd tousle my hair and say, *See, Mom, everything's ok*."

Until a truck shot a red light right in front of him.

Theresa and Alistair were called as the boy was wheeled in to the ER, hardly recognizable. Doctor Cairns and his team fought for hours trying to save Tommy, but there was too much damage to his brain. Not even his helmet could withstand the impact. It had shattered as soon as he hit the side of the truck leaving a deep gash down the left side of his face, and orbital blowout fractures to his left and right sockets. Tommy Williams had more broken bones in his body than he had textbooks and notepads in his bookshelves from his three years at university. After calling Tommy's parents, the hospital receptionist was told to call Riley. Tommy's record showed that he was an organ donor.

Tommy had signed up shortly after his twenty first birthday. He never thought it important enough to tell his parents. He was twenty-one. He was bullet proof. He still had his whole life ahead of him. And the really attractive brunette sitting at the organ donor promo table on campus had something to do with his willingness to sign up. Tommy wanted all of life or none of it. He and three friends had signed the organ donor forms some time between the endless string of frat parties and the Dean's annual address, which

Tommy attended wearing dark glasses, nursing a nauseating headache, staring blankly in front of him, hoping he'd survive the man's endless monotonous drone. He hoped he'd get the brunette's number, but in the end it was the girl who managed to convince Tommy to do something noble with the last gift he had to give on this earth. He didn't have to think too hard about joining the Organ Donor program. If his organs could save another life in the event of his death, he was in.

Now Riley waited in the hallway, her hands shifting from the pockets of her red overalls branded across the back with the hospital's emblem, to being folded across her chest, and back to her pockets again. Inside the ward, the distraught parents were grieving, unaware of the difficult road ahead. Dealing with grief can last a lifetime. Theresa and Alistair hadn't even taken the first step.

"Did you know your son is an organ donor?" the doctor asked.

"What?" Alistair's eyes widened. "He's a what?"

Cairns handed Tommy's parents a copy of Tommy's organ donor forms. Theresa and Alistair looked at each other, confused.

"He never said anything..." Theresa studied the page. "He signed this on the twenty sixth. Just after his birthday."

Doctor Cairns gave them a moment to take in the news.

"What does this mean?" Theresa asked. "You're going to cut him open and ... and ..." She couldn't say the words. She couldn't face the thought of her son's body being stripped of its organs. "No, never!" Theresa protested.

"It was your son's wish. He was brave. And selfless," Cairns tried to reassure them. This was Riley's cue. She took a deep breath, and stepped into the room, hovering the doorway.

Tommy's parents stared at the piece of paper, then at each other. This time it was Theresa who broke down and cried uncontrollably, while her husband held her tightly. He pulled away for a moment, and looked at his wife tenderly.

"If it's what he wanted..."

"I know," she sobbed. "I know, but he's my baby. My boy."

The family mourned against the backdrop of the blips and bleeps of the monitors and the rhythmic pumping of the ventilator that kept him breathing and his body technically alive. Tommy had been brain dead for several hours now. Theresa and Alistair both knew that their son was never coming home.

"We're ready for you," the doctor nodded to Riley after a long while.

"Are they absolutely sure?" Riley asked from the doorway and repeated the ritual of adjusting her ponytail. Her baggy overalls hid her slim and shapely form.

Cairns looked over at Tommy's parents. They looked across to Riley, holding on to each other, then back at the doctor. God knows what they must have been thinking at that moment, Riley thought. They nodded at Cairns, and the doctor relayed their consent in turn to her.

What parent has the strength to watch their child die?

But even in the face of despair and grief, Riley brought hope. Tommy's mother sank into a chair beside her son. Alistair stood behind her, holding onto her shoulder, while Theresa clasped his hand tightly, her expression vacant. There were no more tears, only emptiness.

"Mr and Mrs Williams?" Riley spoke softly from the doorway. "I'm so sorry for your loss." They both looked up, and greeted her silently. Theresa's lip began to quiver. Tommy wasn't dead. Not yet. Riley pulled up a chair from the corner of the room and sat beside Theresa. "I know this isn't easy for you, but I thought this might bring you some comfort."

Tommy's mother looked at Riley through red eyes, and his father drew closer. Any comfort at that moment would be welcome.

"Tommy joined the organ donor program. I know it isn't easy, but can I tell you about the lives your son will save today?"

Alistair and Theresa looked at each other for a moment, fresh tears welling up inside both of them. Tommy's mother nodded, unable to look at Riley. Tears dripped from her cheek onto her knee forming a damp pool on the fabric.

"There's a twenty three year old girl not too far from here who was born with a heart condition. Her own heart is close to giving in. Remember how you were at twenty three?" Both grieving parents smiled briefly. Tight, pursed lipped smiles, wet with tears. "Without a heart transplant, she won't survive the week. Tommy's heart will give a twenty three year old girl the gift of life. Tommy will help a dying girl to live. To meet a man, and get married. To have children and start a family. There aren't too many people in the world that can give someone that kind of gift."

Both parents wept until eventually Alistair held his wife gently by her shoulders and looked into her eyes. She shook her head, unwilling to let go, but his silent gaze, begging her to release him, reduced her to sobs that rocked both of them as he held her.

"Let me say goodbye to my baby," she pleaded. "Give me some time to say goodbye before you take him," she begged.

"Take as long as you need," Riley whispered. She stepped out of the room with Doctor Cairns, leaving Theresa and Alistair alone.

Theresa rested her head on her son's chest, and Alistair knelt beside her, taking Tommy's hand. She felt his heart beating, and let her tears fall on his skin. The mechanical sounds of the respirator reminded her that he would not return to her. She pulled back, and brushed the hair from Tommy's forehead.

"Goodbye my beautiful boy. Mommy loves you." Theresa kissed the boy's forehead.

Alistair leaned in and enveloped the boy in his arms, raising his torso from the bed. His words were lost in the sounds of his sobs, which returned with a fresh supply of tears.

"I miss you already, my boy. My beautiful boy."

It was a long while before Alistair opened the door. He looked reluctantly across at Riley and nodded.

Doctor Cairns called to the ward sister, and soon afterwards, the porter arrived. He was a young man, early twenties, with a friendly face. The porter followed Cairns and Riley into the ward. Alistair drew his wife to one side, and held her.

"Mr and Mrs Williams," Riley said. "May we take him now?"

Through their tears, clinging to each other, Tommy's parents nodded. Doctor Cairns and the nurse disconnected Tommy from the ventilator and attached a ambubag, which the nurse squeezed to simulate the breathing motion. Riley and the porter wheeled the bed out of the room, while the nurse walked beside them pumping the breathing device, leaving Theresa with her face buried in her husband's chest. The two of them clung tightly to each other, as if each was the other's driftwood in the ocean in which they were both drowning. But neither of them were anchored to anything.

Riley followed the transplant team across town shortly after 8:00pm. She was greeted at the entrance to the hospital by a woman in her early fifties, wiry from substituting cigarettes for food, and tense as a steel cable supporting a heavy bridge. Betty stubbed out her cigarette as she saw the team in red overalls approaching, her eyes fixed on the small cooler box that swung like a pendulum as the bearer walked with purpose from the emergency parking bay.

"Is it here? Is that it?" Betty asked, her voice scratchy from lack of sleep, lack of food and an excess of nicotine.

Riley nodded. "Come with me, Betty," she said as she wrapped an arm around Charlotte's mother.

"I can't believe it's really here. I'd given up hope completely. And when they called again, I was just preparing myself for another let down, like all the other times," Betty said as she looked at Riley for confirmation.

"This time, it's real, Betty, I promise you."

Riley's' team went ahead of her to the theatre level while she and Betty made their way to the ward where the staff were already wheeling the bed down the passage as they approached. The girl on the bed was pale, and rolled her head feebly to look at her mother.

"You're getting a new heart, my baby," Betty said, changing

direction and moving with the bed, wedging herself between the two nursing staff at either end. The wheels squeaked rhythmically as they pushed Charlotte into the elevator.

"Please sign these," Riley interrupted Betty, handing her a clipboard. "Here, and here, and then initial each page and sign the last page in full." Betty scribbled furiously and handed the clipboard back.

"Now it's over to Doctor Horowitz and his team, and your daughter is going to have a brand new heart. She's going to live, Betty. Charlotte is going to live."

"I'm sorry ma'am. You can't cross the red line," one of the theatre sisters said.

Betty looked down at the line beyond which only medical personnel were allowed. She stopped, and watched as her daughter's bed was wheeled out of sight, before she flopped down into a chair, and broke down in tears of relief.

"I can't believe this is really happening," she said over and over again.

Riley waited with Betty and finally managed to persuade her to leave the row of chairs outside the operating theatre and get some coffee. Waiting at the closed theatre doors, watching every time they swung open as theatre sisters and doctors moved in and out, as beds were wheeled in, and the hallway filled up with more anxious friends and family, none of it helped Betty's anxiety.

Being in the coffee shop seemed to ease her tension a little. The movement and conversation of the people around them distracted Charlotte's mother for a while. As she looked around, Riley noticed a man she'd seen before. A young man, wearing a grey hoodie, always with his head turned away from her, but she'd definitely seen him before. People have a unique signature to the way they move, the subtle lines that make up their form, even if concealed in a baggy top, or a hoodie like this one. Was it here at this hospital, or one of the others? She couldn't remember. She remembered seeing him a few days ago across town. Was this a coincidence? Riley herself had been at two hospitals that day. People get bounced from one specialist to another, it could be coincidence. Maybe she was being paranoid.

Riley left Betty outside the operating theatre after sitting with her for another hour. There was no word from the operating room, which was good news. It had been a long and emotionally draining day. Dealing with death was never easy, but giving people hope helped make sense of the tragedy.

It all happened so suddenly, she thought as she watched the headlights move endlessly past her while she drove through the evening traffic to meet up with her friends. People take life for granted. Tommy thought he had his whole life ahead of him, and Charlotte was about to give up on hers. In an instant, life changed for both of them. One life sacrificed, another gets a second chance.

The bar Riley's friends had chosen was a sophisticated and elegant one in the business district, amidst glitzy corporate office blocks and expensive restaurants. She pushed through the glass double doors and searched the crowded room. Around her, people in suits and high heels chatted and drank, seated in comfortable dark leather sofas, or on high stainless steel stools around glass and chrome cocktail tables. Riley managed to fit in with the crowd wearing her tight fitting denims and black top with angel wings in Swarovski crystals across the back.

"There you are!" Eleni said, dropping lightly from her barstool onto her high heels to greet her. She was a subtly beautiful girl, with dark hair and a strong nose, a feature of her Greek heritage. She kept herself slim by waking up before the sun every morning to get an hour at the gym before work. Her skin was a healthy shade of olive brown, evidence of the amount of time she spent outdoors on weekends. Her bare arms were perfectly toned, just the right balance between inner strength and outer feminine elegance.

"Hey. Sorry I'm late, Riley said apologetically. "I had to wait till it was safe to leave in case I got called back." They hugged, and

Riley moved around the small, high table to greet her friend. "Hi, Jenna."

Jenna leaned forward and gave her a perfunctory hug, not letting go of her glass. Jenna was slightly over her ideal BMI, but dressed as if her excess weight didn't matter. She wore short skirts, high heels, and most often, too much make up.

"What's that you're drinking?" Riley asked. "Looks good. Get me one will you? I need to pee." Jenna shook her head mouthing something only she could hear as Riley headed through the crowded space to the restrooms.

The men's and ladies' rooms shared a common hand-wash basin, a wide, shallow beaten copper bowl with several sensor-activated spigots emptying into it from all around its circumference. A handsome man in a blue suit eyed her as she passed by, but Riley ignored him. He continued washing his hands, but followed her with his eyes as she went back to join her friends at their high table.

"So?" Eleni asked. "How was your day?"

"You know how these things go," Riley began. "Tragic, unnecessary death on the one side, grieving parents that wrench your heart out. And then relief and … I can't explain … gratitude for want of a better word, on the other, for getting another chance."

"God, I could never do your job, I don't know how you cope," Eleni said, placing a hand on Riley's shoulder.

"It was heartbreaking. This twenty one year old guy, gorgeous, I mean really beautiful young boy. Motor bikes, I tell you, deathtraps." Eleni shook her head empathetically as Riley spoke. "The parents were broken. How do you ever get over that? How can you ever get over losing a child?"

"You don't," Eleni tried to comfort her. Riley shook her head, trying to clear the memory from her mind.

"That's why I'm never having children," Jenna said. She was already half way through her third G&T, and the ugly side of her was seeping through her carefully applied layers of make-up. "That and the fact that I'm never carrying a baby around inside this body for nine months."

"Sometimes I'm inclined to agree with you," Riley conceded. "But not often. This is one of those times."

"Ha-ha," Jenna said with no expression. "Oh, I wanted to show you what *I* got today." She leaned over and picked up a small Barnes and Noble bag, in which were three thick paperbacks. She pulled one out and placed it on the high table. Riley was still trying to get the images of her day out of her mind. Jenna's lack of interest wasn't uncommon, but today it was a welcome distraction.

"What's that?" Riley asked, picking up the book, and turning to the back cover to read the blurb.

"It's the new Angels and He-Men romance trilogy," Jenna replied proudly.

Sounds like utter crap, Riley thought. "Oh, looks interesting," she lied.

"That's the first one in the series," Jenna pointed at the book. "It's a bit like City of Angels, but with a lot more romance."

"And sex," Eleni chipped in. "Jenna wouldn't read it if it didn't have lots of sex. Like, a *lot* of sex, with a bit of plot in between."

"Oh, fuck off," Jenna waved a hand. She snatched the book from Riley and leafed through it, stopping at the last page, which she began to read in silence. Riley picked another book from the bag and turned to the back cover.

"Are you reading the last page of the book?" Eleni asked in disbelief. "Before you've even read it?"

"Sure," Jenna said looking up innocently. "I always do."

"What?" Riley joined in. "How can you do that? Doesn't that kill the story for you?"

"No," Jenna replied. "Where's your drink?" she pointed to Riley.

"I don't' know, where's that waiter?"

"That *hot* waiter," Eleni smiled.

"Yeah, whatever," Riley looked around, saw a waiter in the distance, and waved. The man in the blue suit had joined a group of good looking young men near the bar, and raised his eyebrows at Riley, but then realized she was looking at the waiter behind him. The waiter raised a hand in acknowledgement from the bar counter, and indicted that her drink was on its way. Riley waved a thumbs-up.

"I can't wait till the end of the book to find out what happens," Jenna said to Eleni. "I can't wait that long. I don't mind reading the story if I kinda know how it ends."

"You're like my mom," Eleni said. "Except with her, it's tennis."

"But your mom's like, seventy," Jenna said.

"Seventy four. She watches tennis all day. If you walk into her house, you have to talk over the TV, and god help you if you want to have a conversation while her favorite player's playing. She won't watch a game live. She waits till the game's over, and she knows what the final score was, and if he won, she'll watch. If he didn't, she won't watch the game."

Riley laughed. Her mind returned to the two sides of life she'd experienced that day. As much as it was her job, she could never harden herself to the pain people went through. The face of the grieving father as he sobbed right before they wheeled his son away. She'd never get that out of her head.

"Why?" Jenna asked, her mouth wide open.

The hot waiter arrived with Riley's drink. "Here you go," he said, placing her drink on a small blue napkin in front of her. Riley returned from her thoughts and smiled politely.

"About time," Jenna chided. "You owe her a phone number for making her wait so long."

Eleni laughed, and Riley shook her head. "You can ignore my friend," she apologized.

"You can bring her friend another one of these," Jenna pointed to her nearly empty glass. "And your phone number."

"Sure," the waiter said, and disappeared abruptly.

"*That* hot waiter," Jenna pointed.

"Yeah, yeah," Riley waved her off. "I told you I'm off men."

"How can you be *off* men?" Jenna asked like a rejected Jehovah's Witness. "We *live* for men." She held two upturned palms in the air as if worshipping her god.

"You maybe, but not me." Riley sipped her drink, her eyes closed, trying to get the image of the grieving parents to go away. "Fuck, that was a long day," she said, overriding the direction Jenna wanted to steer the conversation.

"You're gonna die a virgin," Jenna waved a finger at her.

"For fuck sakes, I'm not a virgin, Jenna!"

"Alone then," Jenna corrected.

"After this last relationship, I swear I'd prefer to die alone. I'm over men, they're fucking useless, lying shitbags," Riley said.

"Present company excluded," the hot waiter appeared over Riley's shoulder and cleared Jenna's now empty glass. "Your drink's coming," he said.

"Sorry," Riley apologized sheepishly. "I didn't mean you."

"You keep that up and I'll come too," Jenna smiled seductively. The waiter flashed a perfunctory grin, and disappeared back to the bar. He'd heard it a dozen times every night from women who thought so much of themselves and so little of him, that he wore his sensitivity like elephant skin.

"Love that fucking man bun," Jenna said.

"You love anything on a man," said Eleni.

"She loves *everything* on a man," Riley corrected.

"And you, Riley? You've become like a frikkin' nun," Jenna said.

"I'm not celibate," Riley insisted defensively. "I'm just off men."

"Come on! The best way to get over a man is to get under another one," Jenna suggested.

Riley had had enough. "So, what's been happening?" she turned to Eleni.

"Work, work, work," Eleni replied. She brushed her long, dark curls off her shoulder. "But it's all good. Can't complain. Boss is nice, people are nice. Work is nice."

"Jesus spare me," Jenna said, dominating the conversation once again. "I'd die of never ending career boredom."

"Yeah, well, some of us have to work, Jenna, we can't all live off trust funds," Eleni said cuttingly.

"Ouch," Riley tried to diffuse the situation. Jenna was already pouting.

"Has he tried to contact you again?" Eleni asked.

"What? Oh. Yeah, a few times but I blocked him." Riley smiled. "You don't do that to a person. To *me*."

"It was a pretty shitty thing to do," Jenna rejoined the conversation. "Well good riddance. You don't deserve to be treated like that."

Eleni's mouth dropped. Jenna seemed to have done a complete about turn.

"He was pretty hot though," Jenna continued.

"Anything with a dick is hot to you," Eleni bit back.

"Mmmm." Jenna's eyes searched the room for the waiter with the man bun.

"Didn't you ever suspect?" Eleni asked.

"Now that it's over, a lot of things make sense," Riley said. "Like the way he always used to cancel on me last minute. Never wanting to commit to long term plans. He never wanted to meet my mom."

"That's a big red flag," Eleni said.

Riley nodded. "I couldn't see it while we were together but after I found out he was married and told him to fuck off, it all started to add up. I should call his wife, but I couldn't do that to her. I feel sorry for the woman."

"But if you don't he's just going to do that to someone else," Eleni insisted.

"That's not my problem," Riley said, flaring her fingers. "I'm not the man's conscience. Karma's a bitch. He'll get what's coming to him, but not from me."

"Do you really believe in all that?" Jenna said, returning her attention to her friends. She had made eye contact with the man in the blue suit at the bar, and kept looking over at him.

"What, Karma?" Riley asked.

"Karma, Buddah, Allah – call it whatever," Jenna swiveled the ice around in the bottom of her glass.

"Uh oh, she's getting drunk depression," Eleni warned. "She's about to get deep."

"I definitely believe there's a spiritual world," Riley began, but Jenna interrupted her mid sentence.

"When my dad died, I was sitting in the church, listening to the priest doing the service, reading from the Bible and all that, and I didn't buy any of it. It was like he was selling hope for the bereaved, and saying nice words that people wanted to hear. Needed to hear. But I really don't believe any of that…" she circled a hand in the air, "…stuff. I went to see a medium afterwards, to see if maybe he had something better to tell me, you know? Like tell me where my dad was. That was probably the most freaky thing I've ever done." She sat forward, leaning on both elbows. "This guy, right, he calls himself Angel Martin. I got his number from a friend at the salon. So I go there, expecting, I don't know, like you find fortuneteller gypsies in caravans. I was expecting moons and stars, and the guy to be wearing a robe or something. Nothing like that," she waved a hand in the air. "The guy's wearing jeans and a T-shirt, like he's just come back from the Seven-Eleven, and there's nothing, like, spiritual about his place at all. Ok, he has a little bowl of salt at the door, and he made me rub my hands in it. But then, he sits me down at his table, and there's no mood music or anything. He just takes my hands, and off he goes. Telling me things about myself he could never have known. He was talking to me and some spirit he says has been my Spirit Guide, just like I'm talking to you now, like its something he does every day. I'm telling you, it was weird."

Eleni straightened immediately. She'd been brought up Greek Orthodox all her life, and although she didn't consider herself strictly observant, what Jenna was talking about was Occult, and it was evil.

"What did he tell you?" Riley asked, unaware of the way Eleni was looking at Jenna.

"Well for one thing, he told me about my dad, and that he suffered a lot before he died, but that he was happy now."

Riley thought about her own parents, taken from her at an early age. She was six when they died. Although she had few memories of them, she thought about them often, but to her they were more like characters in a fairy tale, people she knew about, and had heard about, but Riley had to make believe they were real. She had grown up without them, but missed the idea of having parents of her own.

"And then he told me about me and my mom," Jenna continued. "About our relationship and the way we're always fighting, which is also completely true. It was like he'd been in the room listening to us fighting. Mom's always calling me a lazy bitch, and telling me to get off my ass and get a job," Jenna looked up with her mouth agape for a moment before continuing, "Like I need to, right?" She shook her head, and then her expression changed from pouting to mysterious. "And then he said that he saw tires."

"Tires like car tires?" Riley asked.

"Yeah. And get this. Three weeks later, I got a puncture in one of my tires from driving over a nail, like this big." She separated her thumb and forefinger to show the size of the nail, and exaggerated just a little. "And a few weeks after that, I got a flat while I was driving to get my nails done, but I didn't realize it, and my tire just disintegrated. I had to pull into the nearest service station, and get someone to help me put the spare wheel on."

Eleni stared at Jenna enviously. After Jenna's father had died, her fortunes had changed entirely. Her father had left Jenna and her mother a sizeable trust fund, and as soon as Jenna turned twenty-five, she was given a monthly allowance that was more than Eleni was earning after three years as a junior Advertising Account manager. Eleni's day started at 5:00am, and ended after 7:00pm, and then she still had to come home and take care of household chores, load the washing machine, empty the dryer, do her own ironing, clean the kitchen. She had bought her own car after saving up for the deposit for a year. Jenna's trust fund had set her up in a fully furnished apartment in an expensive neighborhood, with a new BMW parked in the basement, and a monthly income that meant she never had to work a day in her life. Ever. Jenna had nothing to concern herself with but getting her nails done, choosing what hair style she wanted from week to week, and shopping for new items of clothing while getting other people to change her tires when she had a flat, do her laundry, and clean her apartment. Eleni shook her head, trying to put aside her jealousy. She couldn't hide the feelings she had towards the subject of Jenna's conversation – mediums and talking to spirits.

"Wow, you've got to give me his number," Riley couldn't help saying.

"Sure," Jenna said reaching for her phone immediately.

Riley glanced across at Eleni, and saw the expression on her face. "Let's not have this discussion," Riley said to diffuse the tension between Eleni and Jenna. "Talking about religion or politics is sure to break up the party."

"You *are* a fucking nun," Jenna insisted. "There, I've sent you his number."

Eleni still looked uneasy.

"Am I interrupting?" a man's voice said from over Riley's shoulder.

"Not at all, come and rescue me," Jenna smiled seductively. Riley turned to see the man in the blue suit. His cologne was powerful, and pungent, like cinnamon carried on a breeze of lemon. He turned to Riley. "Hi," he said to her.

"I'm Jenna," Jenna said loudly, trying to attract the man's attention, but his eyes didn't stray from Riley.

"I'm Grant," he said extending a hand to Riley.

"Grant? I've just had a bad break up," Riley said holding both hands in the air as if in surrender. "And I'm not interested." She dropped to her feet from her bar stool. "That's my cue to leave. Ladies, it's been a long day and I need a little me time." She slid a twenty-dollar bill into the middle of the table, gave Eleni a kiss on the cheek, and waved at Jenna, then turned and made her way to the door.

As she walked away from the table, she heard Jenna call out

loudly behind her, "Night Riley."

"Bitch," she cursed under her breath.

Riley entered her apartment on the eighth floor. She flipped the lights on as she closed the front door behind her and set her keys down next to an old photo frame on the white chest of drawers in the tiny entrance hall.

Her first port of call was the kitchen, where she poured herself a glass of Chardonnay from an open bottle in the refrigerator. Next, she kicked off her shoes in the living room and put on a Crimson House CD. She moved through to the bedroom, where she dumped her handbag on the bed. Before long the sounds of running water filled the apartment, accompanied by the sweet smells of lavender and vanilla. She turned off all the lights, leaving her in the warm glow of the candles she placed around the bathroom. Riley shed her clothes, let her golden hair hang loose, and slipped into the steaming hot water, sliding down till her face was just above the mountain of bubbles. Soothing Jazz played in the background.

Some days she could deal with the exchange of life and death, and some days it became more than she could bear. The haunting echo of Tommy's father's sobs filled her mind, as she held her breath, dropped her head below the bubbles and sank beneath the water where everything was quiet. The water blocked her ears so she could hear nothing but the sound of her own heartbeat. Her hair floated around her, and tickled her face. Beneath the water, it was warm, and peaceful.

One of her patients on death's door had told her she'd seen an angel shortly before she'd made a miraculous recovery with the help of an organ transplant. She'd told Riley the angel she saw was nothing like the pictures you see of angels. This one was over eight feet tall, and spread his body over hers, hovering there, holding her through her fear of death, telling her she was gong to live. The woman had told her it was Archangel Michael.

Riley wasn't sure what she believed about angels and the

afterlife. She'd formulated her own idea of spirituality in spite of Aunt Sal's total absence of anything religious. Riley was convinced that there must be something spiritual, something supernatural, but she never really allowed herself time to explore that world. She wondered about it now, suspended under the warm water, with her eyes shut tight, in this vacuum of silence. Sometimes she thought she could feel a presence, but she'd never paid it much attention. People needed her. There was not much time or energy left for herself at the end of a day like today.

When she surfaced, she allowed the water to drip soothingly down her face.

She reached over the rim of the bath to retrieve her wine glass. It had been a hell of a day. Sometimes after an emotional day like today, joining the girls for a couple of drinks would take away the tension, but not tonight. She just wanted to be alone. Jenna had killed the party for her. She had a habit of doing that. Jenna wasn't known for her consideration towards others. If she had to put a label on Jenna, Riley would class her as self-absorbed, self centered and conniving.

She thought again of Tommy's parents and what they must be feeling right now. Their entire world torn apart, like running a giant earth mover through a field of beautiful flowers, brutally turning the whole thing upside down so the earth swallowed all the beauty that was once on the surface.

Sometimes she wished she could remember her own parents. At times like this, Riley wondered what they would have done had they been alive and that was her in Tommy's position, but they'd been gone so long, and Riley had endured so many days like today, that they were a distant memory, like a sunrise she'd seen years ago. She knew the feeling, that there had been warmth, and bright colors, but the memory was far from vivid. She was six years old when they died. She remembered only moments of her childhood, precious moments with them that she'd give anything to have again. She remembered her mother's gentle face, and warm smile. She remembered her dad leading her around the garden on the pony he'd hired for her sixth birthday. He had dark hair. Lots of it.

Riley smiled. They seemed to be the only memories she had of her mom and dad, and still she missed them terribly. Riley could only imagine what Tommy's parents must be going through now, in the empty wake of losing their only child after twenty-one years.

She found herself saying a prayer for Tommy, and his parents. "Give them some comfort," she whispered. The wine was cool compared to the steaming water that enveloped her. She let her tears run down her face, and drip into the bubbles, making a muted thump each time they fell.

Riley had never committed herself to any form of spirituality. She saw the science of life almost every day. Sickness and injury cured by doctors. Sickness that eluded cure. The rhythm of life and death. It wasn't a mystery to her. People live and people die. She didn't need religion to help her make sense of it all. Still, she was intrigued by Jenna's story. Maybe she'd pay Angel Martin a visit.

After a long while, the water now lukewarm, she rose and stepped out of the bath. Wrapping a towel around her, she turned to look behind her and for a moment she could swear she saw angel wings reflected in the water. Two perfectly formed wings with feathers of pale grey.

"Must be the wine," she said, before blowing out the candles.

Chapter 2

Ethan sat in silence holding his mother's hand. She wore black. Everyone wore black except the priest who was adorned in a flowing white robe with colorful images of doves and crucifixes embroidered on the sleeves. Carol, Ethan's mother sniffed again, and dabbed a tissue to her eyes beneath the black veil. Ivan, his father, sat beside her, stone faced, his emotions a close reflection of Ethan's. Unfathomable grief mixed with bottomless rage. Carly's death was senseless and tragic. Where were the police? What were they dong to bring Carly's killer to justice?

"Dearly beloved," the young priest began. He was not much older than Ethan, who watched him through eyes red from days of endless tears. *Carly is gone*, he kept thinking. *Carly is gone*.

The last few days had been a blur, from the moment he'd received the call from his mother. She could hardly speak. He kept on repeating, *"Mom?"* till she'd eventually said, "Carly's been shot. Your brother is dead." He remembered the feeling of shock and disbelief. He never went through denial, just disbelief and emptiness.

Ethan ran his hand along his closely cropped beard. He wasn't paying much attention to what was going on at the altar. Sitting there in the church he felt like a fraud, having never set foot in one for as long as he could remember.

The service seemed to drag on, and the longer he sat on the mourner's bench, the more restless he became. He felt like he'd been made to sit in the naughty chair, right in front so everyone could see what a bad Catholic he'd been. Looking behind him, Ethan saw rows of pews filled with tearful people, some of whom he knew well, and others, Carly's college friends, whom he'd never met. There must have been in excess of two hundred people.

After the service was over, Ethan escorted his parents outside into the sun where he stood in the courtyard that flanked the stone building, feeling emotionally vacant, like the last drops of his being had been sucked out of his body. He left his mom and dad in the company of his uncle and aunt, while he moved away and stood alone under the shade of a tall oak tree that must have been at least a hundred years old. He lit a cigarette and stared down at the fallen leaves on the ground. Ethan Lynch noticed the priest joining those outside, and turned his back as the man in the white robe moved towards his parents lest he try to make eye contact. The last thing he felt like at that moment was empty words of consolation from a man whose god he didn't believe in.

"This is fucked up, man," Dan said, joining Ethan under the tree. He placed a heavy hand on his friend's shoulder and stood silently with him. Ethan nodded.

"He shouldn't even have been there," Ethan said, drawing on his cigarette. "They were supposed to be meeting at Carly's dorm to work on a project, but Nathan was having car trouble. He wasn't even supposed to be there."

Dan nodded in silence. There were no words of comfort he could find to make Ethan's pain bearable, nothing he could say that would make the death of his brother anything besides excruciating.

Abe joined them in silence, exchanging glances with Ethan and

Dan. He lit up a cigarette in solidarity.

"I wish he'd just stayed at the dorm," Ethan said, "and met up with them the next day in the library. Why'd it have to be him? Why Carly? This whole thing was so random."

"I know," Dan said. He waited till the cloud of smoke around him dissipated before breathing in.

The random chance of it all plagued Ethan's mind. If Carly had arrived a minute later, or hadn't stopped at a red light, and had arrived there a minute earlier, he'd still be alive. If Nathan's car hadn't packed up that day, Carly would still be alive. If that deranged gang lord hadn't decided to open fire on whoever his real target was at that particular moment in that particular street, Carly would still be alive. It was as if Carly's death was orchestrated, planned by some cosmic power, manipulating all the pieces and the players so that Carly ended up in that very spot in the fifteen seconds it took for the drive by shooting to happen.

"Fuck!" Ethan exploded, drawing stares from everyone, including the priest. His mother excused herself and came over to his isolated spot. She held him, and they sobbed together.

"I miss him too," she said through her tears. "I miss him so much."

"Me too, mom," Ethan managed. Dan wrapped them both in his arms, and held them. He wanted to tell them that Carly was in a better place, that this was all part of God's plan, but he knew Ethan wasn't ready to hear that right now.

Abe stood silently beside the huddle, not sure what to do with himself. He placed a hand awkwardly on Ethan's shoulder, and then withdrew it again, turning instead, and pacing a small circle while Ethan and his mom took comfort in Dan's embrace.

Dan and Ethan agreed on most things except the topic of religion. For Dan it was simple, having spent every Sunday in church with his family for as long as he could remember. Ethan had a different view of the things he couldn't see. Every time Ethan stepped into a church he felt like a fraud, and today was no different.

When the formalities at the church had finally been concluded, the mourning continued at Carol and Ivan Lynch's home in the suburbs. They lived well, and the home was a reflection of Ivan Lynch's success. He'd started his own business years ago, when Carly was still a baby, and from its shaky foundation, Lynch and Associates had grown into a well known, successful enterprise. Ivan had brought in one of the architects he worked with to remodel a house originally built in the sixties. He had transformed the old farmhouse with its tin roof and steel frame windows into a modern work of art, with black aluminum window frames, exposed steel trusses and raw brickwork. The floors were glossy Italian marble. But despite its architectural appeal the place felt empty and cold, even when filled with their friends, family and many people they didn't know.

Ethan Lynch looked around at his childhood home with mixed feelings now that the tears seemed to have all been cried. He'd moved out as soon as he could, choosing a small apartment in the city over his room in his parents' luxurious home. He didn't visit often. Saw his parents maybe three times a year.

Ethan hovered in the entrance hall for a moment recalling his formative and adolescent years. And the distinct absence of his father throughout most of them.

People drifted towards him offering their sympathy, and after a few drinks, Ethan found it easier to endure the endless stream of condolences.

"I wish you a long life," he heard from behind him. He turned to see Abe giving Carol and Ivan a long hug. It was a welcome change from the endless repetition of empty words, *I'm so sorry for your loss,* that he'd heard so many times. Ethan found a safe corner to escape the attention of people he hardly knew, and relatives he hadn't seen in years, where he remained in the company of Abe and Dan.

It was beginning to get dark by the time most of the guests had left. Ethan moved over to his parents, who were sitting in the living room with the last of the visitors.

"Mom, Dad," Ethan said. "I'm going."

Carol stood up and hugged Ethan as if she was never going to see him again. Ivan stood, and hung back for a moment. He waited until the boy had finished saying goodbye to his mother before stepping forward.

"Bye, son," he said. Ivan was never sure what to say to Ethan. It felt as if every word was awkward, even simple greetings.

Ethan turned and left the house, followed by his two close friends. They climbed into Abe's car, which was parked some distance away.

"Let's go," Ethan said. "I need to get away from here." He cast a final glance at his parent's home as they drove past. His face was contorted from the anguish he felt inside, cut up about losing Carly. But as deep as the pain of his brother's death, so deep was the sense of loss he felt when he thought about his father.

Abe chose the Leprechaun, a popular bar on a busy street in the center of town. Ethan was thankful for the loud noise. The whispers and the gentle condolences he'd heard throughout the day were killing him. Too much time to have to deal with his grief. Too much time to have to face the pain. He needed to escape the confines of his own mind. He needed to not think. The louder the noise the better. Inside the bar, they found an unoccupied wine barrel that served as a tall drinks table.

"You two keep our spot, I'll get us some drinks," Dan said, leaving Abe and Ethan at the barrel while he disappeared into the crowd around the bar counter.

"Tell me some good memories you have of Carly," Abe tried to break the silence. Ethan looked around him at the people in the bar. None of them had just lost someone close. None of them seemed to have anything to worry about. No horrible and gut wrenching trauma that had just uprooted their lives.

"Carly was just one of those guys that could do no wrong," Ethan began, talking loudly over the din of conversation and the music around them. "I hardly remember a time when mom or dad had to come down hard on him. Not like me, Jesus, they were on my case since forever." Ethan studied the stains and grooves in the wood on the top of the barrel, running his finger along a monogram of the letters GD that somebody had carved. "Look. God was here," he said to Abe. "Isn't that how you guys write it?"

"We don't call him by name," Abe nodded. "We refer to him as *Hashem*. It means, *the name*." Abe could see Ethan wasn't in the mood for a deep discussion, even though he'd brought up the topic. "But that could have been Gary Daly too."

Ethan nodded. "Man, I haven't seen Gary in years. I wonder what's happened to him."

"He moved to Australia years ago. I saw on his Facebook page he joined the army there. Fought in Iraq. That must have fucked him up," Abe said.

"Drinks! Finally," Ethan said thankfully as Dan arrived carrying a tray laden with three whiskeys, three beers, and three vodkas. He handed out the shot glasses first.

"To Carly," Dan said, holding his glass up, and waiting for the others to join.

"To Carly," they repeated.

"Taken from us far too soon," Ethan added before downing his Vodka.

"To Carly," Ethan said again, and immediately raised the whiskey glass. Dan eyed him apprehensively, but Abe nudged him with his elbow.

"To Carly," they echoed. Ethan downed his, but the others only sipped their drinks.

"Best baby brother ever. I'm gonna miss you, buddy."

"Ok," Abe said sternly, standing. The other two looked at him. "So I know this is a tragic day, but I say we've mourned enough for one day. Not meaning any disrespect at all," he looked at Ethan who raised a hand in acknowledgement, allowing Abe to continue. "But tonight, I say we celebrate *life*."

"Amen to that," Dan replied quickly, relieved at the prospect of raising their spirits out of the gloomy cloud that had dogged them all day.

"I can drink to that." Ethan took the beer glass.

"To life," Abe said. "*L'chaim!*"

"What he said," Ethan repeated.

Before long, they'd drained their glasses several times, and were on the fourth round of beer.

"What's happened to that girl you were dating?" Ethan asked.

"Didn't work out," Dan said. "Too old."

"What her?" Abe asked.

"No, me." Dan replied. They laughed loudly. "And you, Ethan, when you gonna get a girlfriend?"

"I haven't got time for a girlfriend," Ethan replied. "And I haven't got time for all that crap too." He put on a woman's voice, *"When you coming home? What you doing? Honey, I've got to work late…what d'you mean you gotta work late, come home now!"*

Dan laughed loudly.

"He just hasn't found the right girl. You'll meet the right girl when you're ready. You're not ready," Abe said, hearing his own mother's voice in the words he'd just spoken.

"Not ready you are, foolish one," Ethan put on his best Yoda voice. "Meet the right girl he will, when ready he is."

"Maybe," Dan slapped him on the back. "But it still doesn't get you off the hook. You need to stop living like a hermit and meet someone. Get a girlfriend. Stop eating microwave dinners."

"Maybe later. I'm not ready for a relationship," Ethan said defensively.

Abe put a hand on Dan's forearm. *Leave it.* Dan nodded.

"So a Catholic, an Atheist and a Jew walk into a bar," Ethan said to change the subject.

"And?" Abe said.

"And now it's your turn to get another round." Ethan pointed to Abe. He was talking loudly, and his words were beginning to slur.

"This Catholic's got work tomorrow," Dan said. "I have to make sure I wake up in the morning. You two go ahead."

"I can't either," Abe said. "I have to be at work too. Yom Kippur's coming up, I have to get a lot of work in before I take off."

Ethan screwed up his face at Abe. "What's that, like another Jewish holiday?"

"If I only take one Jewish holiday off a year, it'll be that one. It's the most important one. The day of Atonement," Abe tried to explain but Ethan waved him off.

"Well, *I've* got a few days off," Ethan said, looking at his watch. It was nearing 11:00pm. "I'm gonna stick around for a few more." He raised his nearly empty glass.

"Can I call you a cab?" Abe asked.

"You can call me whatever you want, but nah. I'm good," Ethan said.

"I'm gonna take a walk too," Dan said, rising.

"You sure I can't call you a cab?" Abe asked. Ethan declined again. Abe stood, and embraced Ethan. "Really sorry about Carly, man," he said one more time.

"Yeah," Ethan nodded. He'd long since passed the point of tears. There were no more inside him. Instead, the rage he'd suppressed was beginning to surface once more. He'd put thoughts of Carly to rest until the mention of his name had come up again. "Yeah," he said once more. "Me too."

"See you, Ethan." Dan's girth was almost double that of Ethan's, and he reached over to give his friend a hug before he and Abe headed for the door. Ethan watched them move through the crowded room until they were out of sight.

"See ya," Ethan waved long after they'd disappeared from view.

Rage. For days he'd suppressed the mounting anger silently boiling inside him after the initial shock of his brother's senseless death. He'd waited patiently beside his grieving parents as the police had asked them questions, and told them that they would do everything they could to bring the perpetrator to justice. But four days later, they'd still heard nothing more from the investigating officer, Detective Morris.

The expression on Ethan's face changed the moment his friends left him on his own. The corners of his mouth turned south, and his face was possessed by a dark scowl.

It was common knowledge that two gangs ruled the area where Carly was gunned down. The Eighth Street Crushers and the Dragon Kings. The other casualty of the shooting was a nineteen year-old with a Dragon Kings tattoo on his back. It didn't take a genius to figure out who killed Carly. What were the cops doing? How hard could it be to find the Eight Street Crusher who pulled the trigger? If the cops weren't going to do anything about bringing Carly's killer to justice, Ethan would find the son of a bitch and kill him himself. He abandoned the wine barrel and made his way unsteadily through the crowd to the bar counter.

"Beer, please," he shouted to the bartender, a twenty something hipster with a long brown beard and equally long hair. Still tending to other customers, the barman nodded and raised a thumb in his direction.

Ethan slumped heavily onto a recently vacated barstool as a couple that had been eyeing his wine barrel quickly weaved towards it. The long-haired bartender slid a pint over and waited while Ethan dug in his pockets. Almost instinctively, Ethan looked around for someone with whom to raise his glass, but then remembered his friends had already left. He found himself halfway through the motion as the man sitting next to him looked up in his direction. Ethan felt a shiver down his spine for a moment. The man's face was partially concealed beneath his grey hoodie, but as he turned his head, Ethan found himself looking into eyes so pale they were almost white against the man's toffee colored skin.

"Cheers," the man volunteered before Ethan could recover from his momentary shock.

"Um...cheers," Ethan said after a while and tapped the man's glass. "Jeez, sorry, man, I was just..."

"No sweat, man, I get it all the time. My eyes, right?"

"Uh huh," Ethan breathed, relieved that the stranger had mentioned it first. The man seemed to be staring right through him. His appearance was striking. His skin was smooth, his face angled.

Looking into those pale eyes was unnerving. Ethan chose rather to study the rows of backlit bottles behind the bar.

"Archer," the stranger waved. "But people call me the Oracle."

"Ethan," he reciprocated, daring again to look into those pale eyes. "People call me Ethan." He laughed loudly at his own joke. Archer smiled. "Why Oracle?" Ethan asked.

"You feeling brave?" Archer said. "If you are, I'll tell you."

Ethan's inhibitions were well submerged beneath several pints of beer. "Sure," he said.

"Give me your hand," Archer said.

"What?"

"Give me your hand," Archer repeated, extending his own.

Ethan looked around self consciously, and slowly placed his right hand in Archer's. The Oracle closed his pale eyes and dropped his head.

"I'm sorry about your brother, man," he said. Ethan pulled his hand away as if he'd just touched burning metal. "Carly, right?" Archer continued.

It was as if Ethan had taken hold of a live wire with both hands and thousands of volts tore through his body. He stared, wide eyed. "How did you know?"

"That's why they call me Oracle, man. I see into people's lives. It's a gift and it's a curse."

"Yeah," Ethan said, regarding the man with the pale grey eyes suspiciously. He found himself holding onto his own hand, keeping it from touching this man. "Carly was my brother. He was killed in a drive-by shooting on Thursday. The funeral was today."

"I'm sorry man," Archer said again. "Like I said, it's a gift and it's a curse. If you don't want to talk about it, that's cool, I understand, I didn't mean to intrude. I just saw your pain, and I can't ignore that shit. It's like, bam, it's right there." Archer flared the fingers of both his hands. "As soon as I touch someone, it happens. I see into their past, sometimes into their future."

"It's ok. I came here to drink my anger away."

"You angry at who?" Archer asked.

"The cops. It's been four days, and they've done nothing to catch Carly's killer. Everybody knows who it was, but the cops aren't doing a damn thing. They're too shit scared to go into gang territory."

"That what they said?" the Oracle asked.

"Nah. It's what they *didn't* say."

"You gotta let them do their thing, man. It takes time, they'll find the guy."

"You saw that in my future?" Ethan asked sarcastically.

"No, I just know cops, gangs and vigilantes." He emphasized the last word. "It never ends well for the vigilantes. I seen this shit before. Just don't be doing something stupid."

Ethan's head was beginning to feel light. It was a better feeling than the heaviness that had weighed him down over the past four days.

Although Dan and Abe had been with him throughout the day, Ethan hadn't been able to open up and talk about Carly. Not to them, anyway. Maybe it was the familiarity that made him feel reserved, but this stranger, Archer, seemed to already know about his pain, so he felt more comfortable talking.

"Still doesn't make it any easier," Ethan said. "They shot him in cold blood. He was just a kid. Still had his whole life in front of him."

"Every life has a beginning, and an end. Even before we're born, the end of our lives is already marked out. If it wasn't by this shooting, then Carly would probably have died some other way at the exact same time."

Ethan suddenly felt sick. "What are you talking about? Carly wasn't even supposed to be there," he said, raising his voice.

"Listen," Archer placed a hand on Ethan's forearm and leaned in. "Not everyone can speak to people from the other side. I do. I speak to them every day." He could see the way Ethan was looking at him. The Oracle had seen this look many times before. Disbelief. Skepticism. "And I promise you I'm not crazy. I can just be minding my own business, and some voice pops into my head, saying some shit about some dude I don't even know, and two minutes later, that same dude comes over to talk to me, and I already know everything about him."

"So how does that make you an expert on life and death? How come you know so much about when somebody's supposed to die?" Ethan asked.

"Because I seen it once. I saw the angel who carries the book."

"What book?" Ethan couldn't help being intrigued.

Archer looked around, making sure nobody was within earshot. "Every person on this earth has a book. The story of their life here on earth. The book is already written. And there's only one angel I've ever seen who carries a person's book with him. If that angel was here now, and I was talking to you, he'd be holding your book. The whole story of your life."

Ethan screwed up his face in a caricature of a frown. "Are you saying that everybody's life is predetermined? That everything I'm going to do has already been written, like some movie script?"

"Not *everything*, man, no," Archer said. "Just the important things. Like significant events in your life. It's not like everything you're going to say, and everything you're going to do is scripted in advance. No," Archer shook his head vigorously. "What would be the point of living?"

"Yeah, my thoughts exactly." Ethan's frown eased.

"And the two most significant events in a person's life are the day they're born and the day they die. Those two are always in the book."

"Have you ever seen it?" Ethan asked. "Someone's future like that. In their book."

"Like I said, once. Only once."

"And?"

Archer hesitated. "I seen a man's death in the book moments

before it happened."

Ethan straightened. "You did?"

"I was in a hospital with my friend. He'd broken his arm in a skateboarding accident. Actually it was no accident, he was trying to do something really stupid. There isn't a word for that. If you break your arm doing something that stupid. It ain't no accident." Archer had his hands in the air, ready to explain the entire act, but stopped. "Lets just say that trying to skateboard from a roof to a stairway railing to the street is just asking for trouble. So anyway, I'm there in casualty with my friend, and I know my angels, man. I know Jackson's angel, I see him all the time. He's a big dude, nothing like Jackson, which isn't weird. But anyway, like I said, I see his angel every time me and him are together, and that's, like, almost every day. But then suddenly, his angel disappears and I see this other angel, and he was different, man. Not like the others."

Archer paused for a moment. Ethan was leaning forward, mouth open, listening like a child watching his first superhero movie.

"You believe in this stuff, right?" Archer asked.

"What? In angels?"

"Yeah," Archer said. Ethan wanted to hear the rest of the story, and would have said anything for the Oracle to go on.

"Truthfully? I'm not sure. You don't get taught to believe in angels when you're a Catholic. I mean there were angels, back in the day, but we … I mean, Catholics … pray to Mary, because we believe she can talk to God for us."

"Yeah, I know that," Archer said dismissively. "But what do *you* believe?" He tapped a finger gently on Ethan's chest.

"I don't know. I can't honestly say." Ethan was overcome with the same feeling of guilt from earlier that day, when he was sitting in church at Carly's funeral. Knowing that the people around him expected him to believe in the Catholic faith just like they did made him feel hollow, like an imposter. "I don't know," he said again. "And I've never told anyone about that, you're the first. My parents still think I'm a good Catholic."

"What are you?" Archer asked.

"In between religions. An Atheist," Ethan offered.

"It's ok, man. Rather be what you are. There's no sense pretending to believe in something you're not. Who are you fooling in the end?" Archer's words were simple yet profound.

"I guess. But they think … how do I tell them? It's like their whole life. Especially now with Carly …" He couldn't say the word. "… now that Carly's gone. They're clinging to their faith more then anything. Its what keep's them from falling apart. Especially my Mom. Her religion has been her entire life."

"That's their thing. It doesn't have to be your thing," Archer said. "I mean, honestly, imagine that angels, god, buddah – whatever you believe in. You expect your god to be all powerful, right?"

Ethan nodded.

Archer continued. "So, if you're lying to yourself about what you believe in, don't you think your god knows?"

Ethan was silent. He suddenly felt exposed.

"So," Archer said, breaking through Ethan's inner conflict, "I asked you that because I can't be telling you about angels and spirits if you don't believe in that stuff. This is real. To me, talking to angels is like talking to you here in front of me. I see them. I hear them."

"I believe you," Ethan said. He felt a wave of cold prickles washing over him, like he was standing on a stage where the whole world could see him, and he'd forgotten his lines. He felt vulnerable. His beliefs were one of his most deeply kept secrets, hidden from the world, out of fear of hurting people he loved. Acknowledging that he believed in something so removed from the faith he was brought up on felt like betraying the very foundations of his life, even though he'd lost faith in those foundations years ago.

"So I was in the hospital with Jackson, right?" Archer's face was animated, making his eerie pale grey eyes seem even more enchanting. "And suddenly his angel disappears and I see this new angel who I've never seen before. This one was a different kind of angel entirely. He had a different aura about him. A different glow. And he had a book under his arm."

"Jackson's book?"

"No. It wasn't his. The book was about some other dude. Now this is all strange in itself because I don't see other people's angels unless I'm with them. Like with you now, I can see your angels, but not them." He pointed to a group of people at the bar a short distance away. "I'd have to touch one of them, physically, like hold their hand, before I can communicate with their angels. It's like they have to let me in, you know?"

Ethan nodded eagerly, like he was learning the rules of some new game he desperately wanted to play.

"Then this angel literally opens up the book, so I can see the dude's name, and turns to the last page," Archer pointed his right index finger into the palm of his left hand, "where it says this guy is in a car accident, and dies, and the date on the page was that same day, and then I looked at the time."

"And?" Ethan couldn't help asking.

"The time on my watch was 3:48pm, and the time in the book was 4:33pm."

Ethan felt another cold shiver. He wanted to know what happened next, but at the same time, he already knew what Archer was going to say.

"I left Jackson, and went to see if this dude was in the hospital, and as I'm standing there, I can see this whole team of doctors crowded around this one bed, and I knew, that's the guy. So I asked one of the nurses if that was him. I asked for him by name, because I saw it in the book."

"And it was him?"

Archer nodded. "The nurse didn't say much. I wasn't family, but from the look on her face it was bad. All she said was that it was a car accident."

"So what happened?" Ethan asked.

"The doctors tried to save him, but he didn't make it. The doctor called time of death at 4:33pm."

"Ok, now I've got goosebumps."

"I kinda had them same goosebumps for days afterwards. I've been trying to find that same angel again since that day." Archer shook his head. "Never again like that one time. I've seen him, always with a book, but he's never shown it to me like that one time."

"Can you see my future?" Ethan asked.

Archer shook his head. "It doesn't work like that. I get images, pictures, mainly of things, but not events. Like I might get a picture of a football, and pain, and I know you're gonna hurt yourself playing football, but I don't get dates and times. That book..." Archer was momentarily lost in a vivid memory of that day at the hospital. "That's the only time I knew what was going to happen to the minute."

"So what can you tell me about my future?" Ethan asked.

"That's usually my cue to get out of here," Archer said, dropping off the barstool to his feet. "I can tell you that you blame yourself for Carly's death. That you're very angry." As Archer spoke, Ethan went into immediate denial, but deep within he knew the man spoke the truth. He'd felt the symptoms of all those things but hadn't put a name to the feelings. Archer continued. "I can tell you that you need to let go of all that guilt and anger and let the police do their thing. But that's all I got. Your angels aren't very forthcoming. Might just be the place. Maybe they don't like it here." Archer circled a finger in the air.

"Yeah, maybe." Ethan looked down, feeling very self-conscious. He became aware of the music again, and realized that he had hardly noticed the noise around him while he'd been listening to Archer's story. The stranger with the pale eyes had made him confront the mixed feelings he had about church and religion. He couldn't really talk about it to his parents, or even to Abe and Dan. Archer had excited him with his talk of angels and a world the stranger seemed to know so well. "Would it be weird if I came to speak to you some time?" Ethan asked.

"Sure, man, no sweat." Archer reached into his back pocket and pulled out a card, which he handed to Ethan. "Here's my card."

Ethan studied it for a moment, and read it out loud.

"Oracle Archer." Beneath the title was Archer's number, and the words, *I speak to Angels*.

"Call me," Archer said. "Nice meeting you man. Sorry about your brother."

"Yeah." Before Ethan had time to say anything else, the Oracle had moved through the crowd, and he caught a glimpse of the man's grey hoodie before it disappeared amongst a group of people entering the bar. Ethan found himself staring down at Archer's card, repeating the words, "I speak to Angels." He was soon distracted by the group of people who had just entered the room and were now gathered next to him at the counter. One of their party, a young man with a long hipster beard, tried to attract the barman's attention.

"My cue to leave," Ethan found himself repeating Archer's words as he too left his barstool to the newcomers, and moved through the crowded room to the exit.

Today was one he'd remember forever but wanted to forget. It was long past midnight when he stepped out into the fresh night air. Finally alone, he could no longer avoid confronting his own feelings. Conflicted about so many things, from his feelings during the church service, to the anger he felt at the injustice of his brother's death, Ethan Lynch hadn't allowed himself to deal with how he really felt about losing his little brother.

As he walked, he relived memories of their childhood. Fragmented moments that merged into a mosaic of memories. Playing together in the yard when they were both kids. Memories of protecting his little brother against the older kids at school. Talking secretly about mom and dad in the back seat of the car, while their parents sat up front. Memories upon memories of their time together. Realizing that those were the last memories he'd ever have with Carly made him weep. He allowed the tears to flow, wiping his face on his sleeve. It was cold, but he walked on with his jacket slung over his shoulder. He wanted to feel it. To feel the cold biting at his skin. To feel pain upon pain.

"I miss you, buddy," he said through his tears, and then to himself as he walked he repeated over and over, "My brother is dead. My little brother is dead," until, overcome with grief, he dropped to his knees and sobbed uncontrollably.

Chapter 3

Riley woke to the sound of a hooter blaring somewhere in the street below. For a moment she panicked, thinking she'd slept through her alarm, but realized after a while that it was Saturday. She wasn't working, although she was still on call. She closed her eyes and tried to return to her deep slumber. In her half-awake state, she remembered the good looking man in the blue suit, and wondered what would have happened if she'd allowed him to engage her in conversation. Then she relived the day she discovered her ex-boyfriend was married, and pulled her pillow over her face, shoving the man in the blue suit out of her mind entirely.

"Fucking asshole bastard," she said to no one. Her pulse was racing now and there was no hope of returning to her peaceful sleep. She checked her phone, and scrolled through screen after screen of inconsequential social media posts from three different platforms before finally throwing the covers aside.

After pouring herself a mug of coffee, she slid the glass doors open, and stepped out onto her tiny balcony eight floors above the noise of morning in the city below. It took a while before she powered through the feeling of surfacing from a coma, assisted by a second cup of coffee.

Her phone rang. It was Aunt Sal.

"Hey," she answered, looking out over morning in the city. "I was just thinking about you last night."

"Why didn't you call," Sal said. "I was awake. Anyway, that's not what I called for. I'm just checking in on my favorite niece."

"It was late. Thanks," Riley said. "Had a tough one yesterday." Riley told her aunt about the Williams case. "It's times like that I miss mom and dad."

"I miss them too, hun. Every day," Sal replied. "Otherwise you good?"

"Otherwise I'm good," Riley smiled. She wasn't really. She hoped her aunt wouldn't notice.

"I'm not even going to ask if you met someone?"

"Jesus, Sal, really?" Riley couldn't check herself. "Sorry."

"It's ok," Aunt Sal said, but Riley could tell she'd upset her.

"I'm sorry, Sal, I didn't mean it. I mean, after …" she couldn't bring herself to say his name. "No. I'm giving myself a break." She was lying. She had no intention of putting herself back on the board.

"Ok," her aunt said. Riley could tell there was something she wanted to say, but wasn't. "You take care, Riley."

"Hey. I love you Sal."

"Love you too, hun."

Sally hung up. Riley stared at the phone with mixed feelings. Sally was more than an aunt. She was Riley's surrogate mother. She'd raised her since the age of six. Riley would call her again later. Smooth things out. Then Riley noticed the message from Jenna and the contact card her friend had sent her the night before.

Angel Martin.

Riley stared at the name for a long while before saving the contact, and typing a message.

Hi Martin. I got your number from Jenna. She said she saw you a while ago. I was wondering, when I can come and see you?

She left her phone on the kitchen counter while she went through to the bathroom to shower and throw on some weekend clothes. Martin had replied by the time she returned, saying he'd just had a cancellation so he could see her later that morning, otherwise he wouldn't be available till the end of the following month. Riley said she'd be right over and asked for his address.

Martin lived in an apartment not far from Riley's. The Uber dropped her off outside the building a few minutes before her appointment, and she was about to press the button alongside Martin's apartment number at the front door, when she noticed the worn handwritten note stuck to the panel.

Don't buzz if you're early.

With her finger poised above the button, Riley hesitated for a moment. She dropped her hand, and looked around not sure what to do. Should she wait? Should she come back?

She looked at her watch as the seconds ticked slowly by. Still a few minutes to go, but not much to do except stand at the top of the steps at the doorway, and wait.

Finally her watch showed that there was one minute to go. She moved closer to the door, and brought her face up to the panel, eager to press Martin's buzzer exactly on the hour. Finally with less than ten seconds to go, she flexed her fingers and was about to press the button when she heard the loud electronic buzz as the latch was unlocked from the inside, and the door popped open just a fraction. Riley stood with a finger resting on the button.

"Damn he's good," she said to herself before going in.

Riley climbed the four flights of steps, and found Martin's apartment, where the door was wide open. A bowl of coarse salt sat on the floor in the opening.

"Please rub your hands in the salt," a deep voice said from inside.

What are you, psychic, she wondered to herself.

Riley immersed her hands in the bowl of salt and rubbed the

grains against them.

"Riley?" Martin greeted her as he approached from the living room.

Riley straightened. "Yes. Hello."

"I'm Angel Martin. Come in." Martin stood at the door, an unassuming, regular man in his late forties, with dark skin, a rounded belly and a friendly face with a few days of stubble on his chin. He ushered her through to a table against the window.

The room was modest. It was small and cluttered, yet not untidy. The living room consisted of a small sofa and a wall mounted TV, a single speaker, and the table by the window. Bookshelves filled the rest of the room and were crammed full of books in some sections, while others contained ornaments – miniature statues of angels, feathers, angel wings, crystals, and decks of cards.

"Are we doing a Spirit reading or a card reading for you?" Martin asked as he followed her to the table.

"Umm," Riley hesitated. "I don't know. This is my first time."

"Let's see where this takes us then, ok?" he suggested.

"Sure."

"Please sit." Martin pulled a chair back for her, and Riley lowered herself into it, perching on the edge, looking through the window uneasily.

"Can I get you some water?"

Riley nodded. Martin moved to the kitchenette, which was beyond an open archway, and returned moments later with two empty glasses and a bottle of still water.

"Water from the mountains," he said as he poured two glasses. "Unaltered. Pure, straight from the source." He drank deeply from the glass, and then said, "So tell me a little about yourself."

"I thought you were supposed to do that," Riley smiled.

Martin chuckled. "Please," he said again. "It helps to get in tune with you first. I won't tell you anything you already know."

"Ok. My name is Riley. I work in the medical field. I'm a transplant coordinator."

Martin's eyebrows rose. "A transplant coordinator? What's that?"

"When people who signed up as organ donors die, my job is to get the organs from the donor to the recipient."

"So you deal a lot with death," Martin observed.

Riley nodded. "And life. The other half of death is life. Sometimes more than half. One organ donor can save many lives."

"Family?" Martin asked. "Anyone who has crossed over?"

"Crossed over? You mean died?" Riley asked.

"No. I mean crossed over to the other side. Very few spirits die. Most cross over," Martin explained.

If only life could be that simple, Riley thought. In her world, people died every day. Families grieved. Lives were torn apart. Of course people die. The notion of downplaying death to simply passing on to another life was a myth that people who can't deal with death cling on to. But this wasn't a debate. Riley let it go.

"My mom and dad died when I was six. I hardly knew them," Riley said, smiling fondly at the few memories she could conjure up of her parents. "I've known some people who I wish would ..." she paused and looked up at Martin, "... cross over, but only the good ones seem to die."

"Ok, let's start there." Martin reached forward and gently wrapped his hands around Riley's fingers. "Let's start with those people who have hurt you so deeply."

Riley had seen families and loved ones waiting in hope for someone on the operating table or in ICU to make it through. Many times she would watch as a couple sitting opposite each other would clasp hands, bow their heads, close their eyes, and pray to an invisible god. But Martin looked at her, and spoke to Riley as if discussing the football.

"I'm getting a D," Martin's eyes were fixed on Riley, but not in an uncomfortable way. His voice was gentle and soothing. Warmth sparkled in his eyes as if reflecting a bright inner light flickering inside him. "He hurt you. He cheated on you."

Riley nodded.

"Dean."

Riley nodded again. How could he know this?

"And you still feel betrayed by what he did. So much so that you won't let anybody in. I'm getting a picture of your heart. It's bleeding, like it's been cut deeply, and you've protected it by enclosing it in a fortress. You've surrounded it with barbed wire and broken glass to prevent anyone else from getting near."

Tears welled up in her eyes, and cascaded down her cheeks. Riley looked at the table and nodded.

"And that's become your whole world. Keeping your wounded heart in its fortress."

In ten seconds, Angel Martin had told her more about herself than she cared to acknowledge. He squeezed her hand a little, causing her to look up into his warm eyes.

"You of all people should know better," Martin said. "The way to heal a bleeding wound is not to keep it locked up in its own prison. That way it might never heal, or if it does, it will heal with a scar, and it might never work the way it used to before."

The Angel's analogy made perfect sense to her. She felt her spirit rise, as if a huge weight had been lifted from her shoulders.

"Most of the time, people don't even know they're hobbling around with a broken soul," Martin said. "The heart is the symbolic center of the soul. Not the physical heart in the body. The spiritual heart. The one that pumps, not blood, but light, or darkness. In your spirit, there is only light or darkness. The wounded heart bleeds light that should be spreading throughout your soul. Instead of spreading light, the wounded heart allows darkness to seep in and overshadow you. Heal the tear in your heart, and let the light inside you spread to your soul once more. There can be no room for both light and darkness inside your soul. Only one or the other." He let go of her hands for a moment, and immediately, Riley felt as if the power in her soul had depleted. She wanted desperately to feel the light that Martin seemed to emanate flow into her own soul through the touch of his hands once more. Was she imagining it? Did he really have a tangible power? He weighed both hands as if they were the arms of a scale, one rising while the other fell, then the opposite, several times. When he touched Riley's hands again, she felt it. Like an electric charge, coursing through her being, spreading from her fingertips to her very soul. Could he heal her heart?

"So how do I mend the tear in my heart?" Riley asked.

"Cast aside the darkness. Remove the thorns that surround you."

"How?" Riley asked, holding on to Martin's hands a little more firmly than before.

"Close your eyes," he instructed. He closed his eyes first, and Riley followed. "Now, breathe in." He breathed in deeply, and waited to hear the sound as Riley did the same. "That's the light going in. Now breathe out." Both exhaled, long and slow. "That's the darkness leaving you. Breathe in." They repeated the motion. "Breathe in only good and positive feelings, positive emotions." They held their breath for a moment. "Love. Peace. Forgiveness. Now breathe out." As they breathed out, Martin said, "Let go of anger and fear. Breathe in light, love, freedom." They breathed in again, one long and slow breath. "Breathe out fear, anger, self destruction, darkness."

Riley felt warmth inside her. With her eyes closed she could picture her heart, surrounded by thorns and sharp pieces of broken glass. There was a cut deep into the tender flesh of her heart and rays of bright light radiated from the hole. As she breathed in and out with Martin, his soothing voice like a mantra, guiding her, the hole closed, and the light now contained within her heart glowed brighter and stronger. The broken glass melted away, and the thorns transformed into welcoming green grass and bright flowers. She felt whole again.

"What do I do about Dean? Do I just forgive him? Let everything he did to me go? Just like that?"

"Has holding on to the anger and the hurt from his betrayal done you any good at all?" Martin asked.

His words were simple truths that Riley had heard many times in different circumstances, but never applied to herself, never thinking she needed to heed them.

"No."

"Let me say this then," Martin said. "You can hold on to the anger and bitterness for as long as you want to. But know that holding on will only prolong the tear in your spirit's heart. You cannot begin to heal until you have let them go. As long as they are inside your soul, they will eat away at your heart, and will open up the wound more and more. It's your choice."

Riley felt that she'd been given more than her money's worth. She'd expected a simple fortune telling, a stranger's words lighting up the path to her future. Instead, she was beginning to find her very soul.

"You have some very interesting spirits around you," Martin continued, hardly giving Riley time to digest his earlier words. "There's a young man with you. Tommy. Do you know Tommy Williams?"

Riley felt a shiver. She nodded.

"He says to thank you for what you did for him and his parents when he crossed over. He didn't get a chance to say goodbye to them, but you helped them deal with his passing. You gave them comfort and strength to let go. He says if it weren't for you, he'd still be trapped in a body kept alive by a ventilator. He says his parents would never have been able to afford to keep him alive but they would have sold everything they had to pay for a machine that would have done no more than keep his heart beating while the rest of his body was already dead. He says you saved more than just that girl the day he died. You saved his parents too."

Again, tears rolled down Riley's cheeks. "Thank you," she said in a soft voice, momentarily letting go of Martin's electric hands to wipe the tears.

"I get the feeling you're an angel too," Martin smiled. "Do you want to know something?" He looked up at her, his sparkling eyes welling with tears of his own that he couldn't hold back. "There's a long line of them."

"Of what?"

"Of people waiting to thank you." Martin looked through Riley, into the distance beyond her. "People you've touched without knowing. People who want to pay tribute."

"To me? But I'm just the coordinator," Riley said, humbly. "The people who should be thanked are the ones who saved others by donating their organs."

"That's not what they're all here for. You brought comfort to those left behind where they couldn't say goodbye. They all watched as you consoled their family and loved ones, every last one of them. Your job title may be coordinating organ donations, but the work you do goes far deeper. It takes a special someone to do what you do for the people you touch. You bring comfort to people in their deepest, darkest moments. You bring light."

Martin mentioned one name after another, as the multitude of spirits that gathered around Riley spoke through him, thanking her for what she'd done when they crossed over, until the gathering of spirits finally diminished and only two remained.

By this time, Martin had moved the tissues from the windowsill to the center of the table, and Riley had emptied half the box.

"There are two spirits with us now. One is your guide, and the other I'm not sure. He's not saying much. Your guide is a woman, not someone you know. Her name is Haniel. She says she's the one you've been talking to you in the bath. The one you asked to bring comfort to Tommy's family. She says she tried to tell you that you already had, but you may not have seen her wings in the water."

Riley went cold. She felt the goose bumps rise all over her body. "I thought I was seeing things," she said. "I saw angel wings reflected in the water. I thought I was imagining it."

"Haniel is smiling. She hoped you noticed. And she says to listen to the angel in front of you." Martin seemed to break eye contact with the angels to look directly at Riley. "I'm not just saying that, this really is her." He stared beyond Riley again. "The angel beside her is male, really huge, maybe one of the archangels. I think he just wants you to know he's around. I don't know his name, but

I think you can call on him if you need to. He carries a book, but I have a feeling that what's inside the book is only for you to see."

Martin's words were lost on Riley. She'd experienced so much in the last hour, far more than she expected when she asked Jenna for this man's number, that she hardly registered his last words. The world beyond the one she knew, the world of spirits and angels that she had refused to acknowledge for so long, seemed so real now that she could no longer pretend it didn't exist. She felt like a child on her first day at school, standing at the threshold to a world of knowledge, aware only of this new world's existence, but no more beyond that.

Martin released Riley's hands, and immediately she felt the change in energy as he moved away. She wanted to grab on to him and draw on that energy.

"That's our time, I'm afraid." He rose, and moved to Riley's side, offering her a hand. As they walked to the door he said, "You'll find, now that you're aware of your angels, they may try to communicate with you more. And you'll know when they've been around, because angels leave a calling card."

"A calling card? Really?"

"Yes," Martin nodded. "You'll see a feather. One single feather."

"That's it?"

Martin smiled. "There's a lot to think about, I'm sure."

"You're right about that. There's so much to deal with."

"Call me if you want to see me again. I'm sure I can find some time to squeeze you in. Please take the stairs on your way down, not the elevator." He motioned down the passage towards the stairwell door. Riley remembered taking the stairs up to Martin's apartment when she arrived. Did he not want his visitors to meet each other as one left and the other arrived?

"Is that so I don't see…"

"Yes," he interrupted. "Your visit is yours only."

"But how did you know I'd take the stairs?"

He said nothing. Martin simply smiled warmly. He motioned again to the stairs.

"Ok. Thank you," Riley said as she left Martin standing in the doorway and made her way down the passage. She heard the loud electronic buzz as he opened the front door for his next visitor.

"Oh, Riley," he called after her.

"Yes?"

"Don't close your heart to the next one who knocks at your door. You're supposed to let him in."

"Easier said than done," she returned his smile before disappearing through the doorway. On the way down the stairs she thought of her mom and dad. She'd been overwhelmed by all the people who had spoken to her. *Next time,* she told herself. *I'll ask him next time. When there isn't such a queue.*

Riley emerged on the street as if re-entering a world from which she'd been absent for ages. It felt like a lifetime had passed in the hour she'd spent in Martin's tiny apartment four stories above. She felt wiser, and older, while the world outside hadn't changed at all.

Instead of going home, Riley took a walk along the busy street, and found an inviting patisserie where she could process her thoughts and try to make sense of everything Martin had told her about herself.

Over a steaming cup of coffee and a crispy pastry that came straight out of the oven, she allowed her mind to retrace her session with Angel Martin.

Haniel.

Do you hear me when I think, or do I have to talk to you, she wondered. She dared not speak out loud, nor whisper to herself in public. But there was no parting of the heavens, no revelation to answer her question. The tiny patisserie continued to serve up freshly baked delectable pastries and hot coffee as people breezed in and out, each time, ringing the bell above the door.

How do I just let go of the pain Dean caused me?

Martin's words returned to her as if he were still holding on to her fingertips. *Breathe in love and freedom. Breathe out darkness and anger.* Breathe out resentment, she added.

Riley closed her eyes, and breathed in a long slow breath. As she did, she tried to imagine herself filling up with light, and the weightlessness of freedom. Freedom from the burden she'd been carrying around with her. The anger and bitterness over what he'd done to her. As she breathed out, she tried to imagine all that hurt and bitterness floating away, carried on her breath, dissolving into a faint mist. The more she repeated the process, the lighter she felt. The weight of her anger lifted, leaving a freedom she hadn't experienced for so long. If she could let go of this anger forever, she felt for the first time that a less complicated life might just be possible.

Dean was no longer allowed to rob her of her own freedom to live. *Breathe in love and light.* Dean no longer had dominion over her feelings. She was capable of love, but she wouldn't allow anyone to get too close to her for fear of another betrayal. *Breathe out the bitterness.* She saw Dean in front of her, his back turned, disappearing on her breath. The more she breathed in, the more she was aware of the absence of bitterness, and the presence of warmth. The more she breathed out, the more she became aware of a new freedom, a void inside her which had been occupied by Dean until that moment. She began to release him from her life. She began to realize that although she had been the one who had broken it off with Dean, she was the one still holding on to him. To the idea of him. He turned out not to be the man she thought he was, but Riley was still in love with the man she wanted him to be. And for that she had hated him. For destroying her ideal, for making her realize that the life she'd dreamed of wasn't possible. Finally, Riley let go of the real feeling she had harbored. A longing for something beautiful, embodied in the man that she wanted Dean to be. She breathed him out one last time before she finally allowed herself to be completely free of him. Yes, he had lied to her, but that wasn't his real crime in Riley's eyes. His real crime was promising her something that she now realized she wanted desperately, and then taking that promise away from her.

Riley opened her eyes. She felt a lightness about her. A freedom.

Dean was finally gone. She'd let him go. The noise around her suddenly became real again, and Riley realized she'd been so focused on her own breathing, on letting go of Dean, that she'd become completely unaware of the buzz around her. People sat at the small, round tables crammed into the tiny store, talking, and clinking cutlery on plates, and cups on saucers. People browsed at the counter, stooping to select the pastries, croissants, Danishes and cakes, pointing at the ones they wanted while the young girl behind the counter filled brown paper bags, and collected cash. The coffee machine hissed as the young man poured one cup after another. It sounded like a train station in peak hours. Riley's mind turned to the other things Martin had said.

Haniel.

She had a guide, an angel, and Martin knew how to communicate with her. Riley felt an insatiable desire to communicate with Haniel. If she knew what to tell people before their loved ones died, she could bring them comfort. Maybe Haniel would tell her more now that Riley knew she was there.

She left the little patisserie feeling energized. As she walked, a feather floated gently in the air, drifting first this way, then falling the other way, repeating the descending dance until it landed at her feet on the sidewalk. A perfect white feather the size of her finger.

Angels leave a calling card, Martin's words echoed in her head. She picked it up and continued walking, holding onto the feather as if it were some precious relic.

As she walked, Riley dialed Jenna.

"Hey," Riley greeted her friend as she answered. "You'll never believe who I just saw?"

"Hey." Jenna sounded like she'd been crying.

"Are you ok?" Riley asked.

"No," Jenna sniffed. "No. Not at all."

"What happened?"

"Grant," she said sadly.

"Who's Grant," Riley asked.

"That guy from the bar the other night. Remember? The one you wouldn't talk to?" Jenna sniffed again.

"The guy in the blue suit?" Riley said. Jenna burst into tears. "Do you want me to come over?"

"Yes, please," Jenna managed before she hung up.

Riley arrived at Jenna's apartment about twenty minutes later. The concierge let her in and she rode the elevator up to the fourteenth floor and pressed the doorbell.

Jenna opened the door without a word. She wore a silk dressing gown, and her face was dark with mascara that ran down her cheeks from her puffy eyes, making it look like she'd just come back from a Halloween party. Her hair was wild.

"What happened?" Riley asked.

"That fucking asshole!" Jenna cursed, retreating into her apartment. Riley followed as Jenna poured herself a fresh gin and tonic. She offered Riley, who declined with a single movement of her head.

"You got some coffee?" Riley asked, moving to the kitchen. Jenna's apartment was opulent, situated in an expensive neighborhood that attracted the wealthy. The kitchen was Italian marble, and the appliances were German. Riley filled the kettle and switched it on. It was one of those fancy ones where you could control the temperature of the water. She didn't ask Jenna, but set two cups down on the counter. Her friend plonked herself down on a leather and chrome high chair on the opposite side of the counter. "So what happened?" Riley asked.

"After that night at the bar," Jenna said, "he called me."

"You gave him your number?" Riley asked.

Jenna looked at her and nodded. Her eyes were red and swollen with tears. She emptied the best part of her drink in a single sip. Riley moved the Gin bottle along the kitchen counter, far away from her friend.

"I met him for drinks last night at the same bar," Jenna confessed. "He seemed ok. Told me he worked at a law firm near here," she pointed vaguely over her shoulder with one finger. "And we talked a lot. I invited him back here after, and we had a few more drinks."

Riley looked over Jenna's shoulder. The living room had a view over the whole city. Floor to ceiling glass in white powder coated aluminum frames. There were two empty wine glasses on the coffee table and two empty bottles.

"We drank, and we talked, and then he kissed me, and we went to the bedroom." Jenna looked up. "And it was all great until I woke up this morning."

"What happened?" Riley asked.

"He was gone. Not even a note, a thank you ma'am, nothing." Jenna shook her head sorrowfully. "But that's ok. I can handle that. I wanted to go to the mall today, and my car keys were gone, and my wallet was missing from my purse. Then I started looking around. My gold necklace, my rings, my diamond earrings. Everything. Gone!"

"What?" Riley said, her eyes widening as she spoke. "Have you called the police?"

Jenna nodded. "It's not a priority case, they're very busy right now and they said they'll send someone around as soon as they can," she replied, imitating the tone of the officer that had taken her call earlier.

"Your car?" Riley asked.

"Gone," Jenna said.

"Jesus, Jenna! I can't believe this!" Riley said. "That bastard!"

Jenna broke down in tears. "I feel so violated. I feel like such a fool!"

Riley came around the counter and slid Jenna's drink away from her. "I think you've had enough of those," she said. "Come on." She led Jenna to the living room and set her down on a white leather and chrome sofa, and then retrieved the two cups of coffee from the kitchen. Riley couldn't help feeling like she'd dodged a bullet. What if that had happened to her? "Did you get a last name?"

Again Jenna shook her head. "Just Grant. That's all he said. I don't know anything more about him. I don't even know if he really does work at the law firm. I'm sure that was a lie too."

"Bastard," Riley said. Jenna curled up in Riley's arms, and cried. Riley was grateful she was wearing black, or there'd be mascara stains all over her clothes.

Jenna never showed her own vulnerability. She always put on a façade, making as if everything in her life was perfect. It should be, Riley thought. She was set for life. She never had to work. She didn't have to deal with the problems most people had to face. Making enough money to pay rent. Living on the brink of the bank balance, hoping to make it till payday without running out of food, or money. Life was a game to Jenna and people were merely props. Jenna was bored of life at the age of twenty-six.

"He'll get what's coming to him some day, I promise you that," Riley said, stroking Jenna's tousled hair.

"You think?" Jenna said without looking up.

"Karma's a bitch," Riley reassured her. "You can't escape that. Some day, some time, what he did to you will come back to bite him. You'll see."

"Hmm," Jenna mused sorrowfully, still unable to move her head from Riley's lap.

Chapter 4

Ethan waited impatiently on a hard wooden bench in the foyer of the police station. There was little activity in the room except for the occasional shuffling of pages by the Duty Sergeant, a man in his late forties who wore an expression that heralded authority, self- importance, and an equal degree of boredom and dissatisfaction with a life that had taken him on a different path to where he thought he'd end up by now. His rank in the police force was testament to his lack of leadership material, and frustration at his own ineptitude had caused him to accept a position that allowed him to vent his pent up anger on anyone who crossed into his domain. Today that included Ethan.

Lynch rose and approached the Sergeant for the third time.

"Is Detective Morris going to be in this morning? It's been almost an hour."

The Sergeant looked up from his paperwork deliberately, and glared at the young man.

"I called him. Twice. He said he'd be here. Twice. Maybe he got delayed. Maybe he's chasing a suspect. Maybe he's following up on a lead. Maybe he stopped to get ice cream. I'm not calling him again." The Sergeant stared at Ethan for as long as it took the young man to back down.

Ethan was fuming inside, and returned to the bench, clenching his fists by his sides, cursing under his breath. As he sat down, Detective Morris appeared in the doorway looking worn.

"Detective Morris," Ethan called out, crossing the foyer.

The detective looked his way, and acknowledged him with a reluctant dip of his chin.

Morris had worked homicide for the last three years, and he'd seen Ethan's kind before. The kid had an air of desperation about him, like he was trying to deal with his tragedy by seeking justice, and in Morris' experience, that never ended well.

"Ethan, is it?" he said.

Ethan nodded. "Yeah. I wanna know…" he began, but Morris held up one hand to stop him, and placed the other on Ethan's shoulder.

"Let's talk in my office."

Morris led the way, his temperament and pace worn down by his years. He was approaching fifty, but inside he felt a lot older. This job had sucked the life out of him slowly. He was no longer the energetic, idealistic, enthusiastic cop he was when he first joined the force.

"Sit," he said, motioning to a chair, while he rounded his desk and slumped heavily into his own seat.

"Please tell me you know who did this? Please tell me you got the guy," Ethan said.

Morris nodded, but his expression wasn't one of confirmation.

"We're working on witnesses and leads."

"But you *know* who did it?" Ethan asked again.

"It isn't that easy, son," Morris said wearily. He took a deep breath as if to summon the energy it was going to take to explain this to a novice. "In that part of town, you've got two gangs, the Dragon Kings and the Eighth Street Crushers. The kid who was gunned down with your brother was a member of the Dragon

Kings. So it doesn't take a genius to figure out that the hit probably came from the Crushers, but all we've got right now is a theory based on a process of elimination and we're working leads to get solid evidence. We don't know who pulled the trigger, and until we know for sure, we can't make an arrest. You don't want to make waves with those gangs unless you're one hundred percent sure, because you only get one chance to bring a guy in when you go into that territory. Mess it up, and they won't let you get near anyone again. They'll start shooting the minute they see you coming."

"So what are you saying? That you can't find the guy who pulled the trigger because you're afraid of them?" Ethan's mouth dropped in disbelief.

Morris' patience was wearing thin. "That's not what I'm saying, Ethan," he said defensively. "Now I know you must be cut up inside, and angry, but hear me out."

Tears welled up in Ethan's eyes before he could fight them back. He was cut up, and angry. He felt cheated and helpless. Cheated out of the years he should still have had with Carly, and angry at whoever stole his brother from him. Morris continued.

"Let justice take its course. We'll get this guy. We know how to get information out of these people, and we'll get it. Just don't expect it today, because that's not how it works. Getting information is like baking a cake. You gotta let it do its thing before you try to pull it out of the oven, because if you try to take it out too early, it turns to mush. We got our informants, and we're working our leads, but you can't rush the way we get our information. Nobody's walking away from this, I promise you." Morris sat back in his chair and let the silence hang in the air for a moment. "We're gonna get the guy who killed your brother, you have my word. But this is police business. Don't get involved. Let us do our work."

It wasn't what Ethan wanted to hear. He had hoped they'd have found out who pulled the trigger by now. Was the detective spinning him along, or were they really working the case the way he said they were? It was hard to know whom to believe.

"Promise me, Ethan. Don't go doing anything stupid, ok?" Morris warned.

Ethan stared at the grain in the wood of the detective's desk. After a long while he nodded reluctantly. "Ok," he said finally. "Ok. But you have to promise you'll keep me in the loop. I want to know when you've got the guy."

Morris picked one of his cards from the box in his desk drawer and handed it to Ethan.

"It's an active investigation, Ethan. When I have something I can tell you I will, but you're not law enforcement. That's my card. There's no need for you to come all the way down here if you want to know what's going on, just call me, ok? Any time, just call me. I've got your number," Morris tapped the folder in front of him marked C Lynch. "As soon as we have a suspect behind bars, you'll be the first to know, I promise. I'll tell you what I can. Understand that I can't share information with you during an ongoing investigation, but I'll tell you what I can."

Ethan nodded and tucked the detective's card into his shirt pocket. It wasn't what he wanted to hear, but he got the feeling that was all Morris was going to say. They hadn't found the killer, and it looked like it was still going to take some time before they did. The detective hadn't been forthcoming about how close they were to catching the guy, and to Ethan, that implied that they didn't have any leads or suspects. He rested his forehead in the palm of his hand and nodded.

"Yeah, I understand. Thank you for your time, Detective."

Ethan stood up to leave.

"Don't do anything stupid, Ethan," Morris warned again. "I don't want to have to bring you in. Not while you're still mourning your brother."

"I said I got you," Ethan shot back, before turning to leave.

"Right now, you're a victim," Morris called after him. Ethan stopped without turning his head as the detective continued. "Don't end up on the wrong side of my sympathy."

Ethan left the station feeling more frustrated than when he had arrived. If the police knew which gang started the gunfire, why hadn't they arrested anyone?

He slipped into a Starbucks on a busy street and ordered himself coffee with a double shot, hoping that being around people would ease his discomfort, but instead he found himself unable to sit still. He was edgy, and the caffeine made him more restless.

Ethan found himself walking aimlessly in the mid-morning, gazing into shop windows, watching people as he passed them by. Nothing had changed in their worlds while his had a gaping hole in the middle.

They teach you everything in school except how to deal with death. They should cover that, Ethan decided as he passed a glitzy office, probably belonging to a law firm, he thought, before looking up at the name on the building. Yep. Lawyers. Through the glass he could see the expansive reception area, with lavish seating arranged in circles. Each cluster had a custom made sofa, semi circular in shape, in front of which was a round stainless steel and glass coffee table, and some casual chairs, each one probably more expensive than his car. There was no-one in the lobby except for the receptionist. Ethan sneered at the opulence before moving on. He found himself at the intersection of Main Street and Eighth.

The Eighth Street Crushers, he thought. Eighth Street stretched all the way from this part of the city to the slums, from the business district, through some pricy neighborhoods, and eventually led to the densely populated and less desirable gang territory. Ethan glanced at the street sign for a long moment before tossing his coffee cup into a bin, and drifting along Eighth Street, away from the business district.

Before long, the last of the habitable neighborhoods was behind him. Everywhere he looked he saw litter and disrepair. Graffiti covered anything within human reach. Where the business district had shop windows displaying desirable merchandise, and inviting places to eat and drink, these grimy windows were protected by metal shutters and rusty burglar bars. Instead of glitzy buildings with glass facades and opulent interiors, this area had functional doorways protected by security gates. Paint was a luxury. Glass windows at street level were cracked, or boarded up. Everything about where he was screamed unwelcome. People didn't walk in the streets, but instead, groups of people, mostly men, gathered on steps and in alleyways, and Ethan suddenly became aware that he was the main attraction. A white boy in a poor black neighborhood. He suddenly realized he was in danger, but too late.

"What you doin' here white boy? You lost?"

The voice came from a man in a torn shirt leaning against the wall. His friends turned to see who the man was talking to. Ethan suddenly found himself confronted by three unfriendly faces, looking at him the way a predator in the zoo would a visitor who dropped into its cage by accident. He felt the blood drain from his face, and his mind went numb, paralyzed by fear and panic. He froze, unable to move, despite everything inside him telling him to run.

"My brother was killed," he began, "somewhere near here."

"We don't do no family discounts," the man sneered. His friends laughed, moving in closer.

"This was a mistake," Ethan said, backing away, hands raised apologetically, but he bumped into something solid and immovable behind him. He turned to find himself staring into the steel expressions of two more men who had somehow closed in at his rear. "I'm sorry," he found himself turning, looking for a way out, but the wall of unfriendly bodies boxed him in.

"You ain't as sorry as you gonna be," the first one said, striking Ethan so hard across the face with a clenched fist that he spun, and fell against one of the men behind him. Bewildered and terrified, he struggled to break through the pack of men, but a sharp stabbing pain spread from his abdomen as the leader of the gang landed another jarring punch to his ribs. Ethan screamed involuntarily, and dropped to his knees.

The gang moved in closer, kicking him over and over again. Ethan curled defensively, trying to shield his face with his arms, but his body exploded in agony with each blow. He arched backwards as a kick landed hard against his kidney, exposing his face, and then he saw the toe of a boot heading straight towards him. His head jerked back, and Ethan lost consciousness.

When he came to, he was in an ambulance, looking up at a paramedic over an oxygen mask. His eyes felt heavy, and the taste of blood was strong in his mouth.

"Where am I?" he asked. "Am I in an…"

Ethan drifted off again as the morphine kicked in.

Billy, the paramedic, secured the neck stabilizer, and shook his head. He'd seen this inhumanity all too often, and it was beginning to affect the way he saw the world. He was supposed to be impartial, but who could separate their emotions from such a grotesque and violent act?

Billy was a big man. Obese. But he avoided the word. He had a kindly face, and an equally kind demeanor. Still, the first thing anyone who didn't know him saw was his size, and most people would treat him as if he had some sort of scourge, avoiding any contact if possible, and when contact became unavoidable, they would extricate themselves from conversation as quickly as they could. Those that knew him would say that as big as Billy was, his heart was twice the size.

"Patient's stabilized," he called out to the driver. "Think he's got an orbital fracture, a few broken bones, possible punctured lung. Those animals worked him over good."

"What was he doing in this neighborhood anyway?" the driver asked.

"Fucked if I know," Billy replied. "Fucked if I know."

"What have we got?" the doctor at the ER receiving bay called as he and two others approached the ambulance.

"Male, late twenties, multiple contusions, possible orbital

fracture, definitely some broken ribs, and possible punctured lung. I've given him 20 milligrams of morphine," Billy explained.

"Thanks, Billy. We'll take it from here."

"He had this in his pocket." Billy handed the card over.

"Thanks." The doctor noticed the police emblem, and handed the card to one of the interns. "Get this to the front desk and ask them to call Detective Morris on this number."

"Yes, Doctor," the intern said obediently, and ran ahead of the gurney into the hospital building.

Billy watched as they wheeled the victim into the ER. His work done, he and the driver moved off to the smoking area, an enclosure just off the parking bay, where they depleted their cigarettes in silence.

"I'm going to get some coffee", Billy said to the driver, stubbing his cigarette butt in the ashtray.

"Yeah," his partner said, falling in behind him.

They entered the hospital, and followed the passages and hallways to the staff pause area.

"Riley!" Billy said with a smile as they entered. "What are you doing here? You got a thing happening?" His smile immediately turned into a concerned frown.

"Hey, Billy," Riley rose from the sofa and came over to give him a big hug. "Yeah," she said as she pulled back for a moment. "Horrible case. Guy with a brain tumor, fifty six years old."

"Sorry," Billy said, and brought Riley close again. She rested her head on his shoulder, and stayed there for a long moment.

"Thanks," Riley said. She wiped her cheeks and said, "Got to get all the tears out here where the family can't see me. If I start they'll start."

"Yep," Billy agreed with a somber nod.

"And you?" Riley asked.

"Just brought a guy in from lower Eighth Street. White guy. God only knows what he was doing all the way down there. Badly beaten. Probably one of the gangs."

"Poor guy," Riley said. Her phone vibrated. "I'm needed," she said. "Gotta go. Take care of yourself, Billy."

"You too," the paramedic called after her as she disappeared.

Riley read the message on her phone as she moved through the hospital corridors. She looked up and froze. She'd seen that man before. His grey eyes looked ghostly against his dark skin, almost transparent. He looked away as she caught his eye, as if he were pretending not to have noticed her. *Strange*, Riley thought. She'd seen him a few times before, probably here at the hospital. It wasn't unusual, she reminded herself as she continued to the ward.

"Haniel," Riley said to herself. "If you're there, help."

She paused outside the ward and gathered herself. This was the difficult part of her job.

"Mrs Giardelli? I'm Riley from the transplant team."

Mrs Giardelli looked down and nodded. Riley's greeting had the same effect as the toll of the final bell on her husband's life.

Archer watched from a distance as the two women spoke.

"Where is he?" Detective Morris said angrily as he approached the desk, flashing his badge. "Ethan Lynch, the assault victim, brought in earlier today?"

"He's in 19E," the nurse replied after looking for the patient's name on the monitor in front of her. "He's just come out of surgery, I'm not sure just how lucid he's going to be."

Morris grunted. "I've already called his parents, they're on their way over here. He awake?" The nurse nodded. Morris moved off down the ward, studying the numbers on the doors. He stopped outside room 19.

Ethan Lynch looked badly beaten, and Morris heaved a deep sigh. As much as he wanted to give the kid a tongue lashing, he realized that Lynch probably realized his mistake, and didn't need reminding. Especially in Morris' current mood. The detective's wife had often warned him about his temper. She'd told him on many occasions that she wasn't going to talk to him because he was in a "mood", and she'd talk to him later when he was more approachable. The woman possessed wisdom beyond her years, Morris thought. Anyone else would have left him by now. But she understood him more than he understood himself. Today he was in one of those moods, and remembering her words made him pause a moment. He took a deep breath, and entered the room.

"Ethan," he greeted the deflated man.

"I know what you're going to say," Lynch replied. His lips were swollen, and his words sounded like he was slurring.

"What were you thinking?" Morris said, shaking his head, his hands on his hips. Ethan opened his mouth to speak, but the detective held up his hand. "In a way this is a good thing," he said. "You can't interfere in my investigation while you're in a hospital bed. Part of me wants to have a word with the doctors and see if they can keep you in here until this is all over."

Ethan didn't say anything. He felt humiliated and bruised, both inside and out.

"Listen, kid, you're not the first one, alright? Did you get a good look at them? The ones who did this to you?"

Lynch nodded painfully.

"Can you describe him for me?"

"There were five of them. One of them had steel caps on his shoes, with some sort of design on the end. He was the leader. Young guy. Black. Scar here." He tried to touch his cheek with his right hand, but winced. "On his cheek. Tattoo of a crow on his forearm."

"That's good, Ethan. We can ID the guy from your description. Do you want to press charges?" Morris was scribbling in his notepad. Ethan nodded. "Good. Anything else you can tell me? Like why you went down there?"

Ethan shook his head slowly. "No idea. Just wandering. Ended up there. Big mistake."

"You don't say. You just remember that." Morris shook a finger at him.

"Sure."

The awkward silence was broken by the frantic cries of Ethan's mother. "Ethan!" she bellowed from the doorway. She hurried over to him with open arms, tears running down her cheeks. She had no more words. She just cried tears of gratitude and relief as she took hold of his hand.

"Mom, Dad," Ethan said.

Ethan's father followed closely behind. He was in his own world, wanting to blow up at his son for being such a fool, and at the same time wanting to hold his boy close, and tell him he loved him.

"What were you thinking, Ethan," he said as he stood behind his wife, looking down at his son. Words were still his enemy. Just say the words, he thought to himself, but in the company of the detective he felt inhibited.

Morris waited until they'd greeted their son. "Mr and Mrs Lynch," he said, standing. Ethan's father shook his hand. Mrs Lynch nodded, wiping her cheeks with the back of her hand.

"Thank you for calling," Ivan Lynch said.

"It's a good thing the boy had my card in his pocket. Keep him out of trouble," Morris said to Ethan's father. It wasn't a pleasantry. It was a warning. Ivan Lynch nodded, and Morris left.

"Ethan," his mother said. "What were you doing down there? You know it isn't safe."

Ethan waited till he saw the detective cross past the window to the ward, and was well out of earshot.

"The police weren't doing anything, Mom. I thought I'd…" he paused, realizing how futile his excursion into the ganglands proved to be. "I thought I'd see if I could find anything out. It was stupid," he said looking down.

Ethan's mother brushed hair from his eyes.

"My beautiful boy," she said.

Ordinarily Ethan would have reared back, and pulled himself away. It was a conditioned response from school days and bullies sneering at kids whose mothers kissed them goodbye at the drop off. But here, he warmed to her gentle touch, something he'd denied himself since high school. Maybe it was his vulnerability that allowed him to give in. To feel loved.

"Promise your mother and me you won't try something like that again, Ethan. Your mother's been through enough. We can't take this any more." Ethan's father was worn, and broken inside, but still put on a strong face. Next to his wife, he had to or she'd crumble. Without his strength, she'd have given up long ago.

Ethan nodded.

"I know, dad. I know." He looked up at his father and said, "Sorry."

They sat in silence for a long while until something caught Ethan's eye, a movement, someone passing the window to the ward.

"What is it?" Ethan's father asked, following his son's gaze.

"I know that guy," he said, pointing.

"Who?"

"The guy who just walked past. I met him at a bar the other night, with Abe and Dan."

"Want me to call him?" Ivan Lynch asked, standing quickly, not waiting for Ethan's reply. "Excuse me," he called politely. The man turned.

"Yeah?"

Ethan's father was mesmerized momentarily by the man's pale grey eyes.

"Um, my son says he recognized you from the bar the other night. Wanted to say hi."

"He in there?" Archer pointed to the ward. Ivan nodded. "Ok, sure."

Ivan Lynch returned to Ethan's bedside as Archer entered the room.

"I remember you," he said approaching the opposite side of the bed. "Damn. You looked a lot better the last time I saw you." Archer placed a hand on Ethan's and breathed in deeply, as if he was surprised by something.

"We won't talk about that," Ethan tried to avoid the subject. "You visiting someone in here?"

"Looking for someone," Archer said.

"You didn't see this in my future when we met last time, did you?" Ethan tried a smile, but his face hurt.

His parents exchanged glances. Mediums and spirits were not part of their religion, but this wasn't the place to come down on their son.

"Nah," Archer replied. "I think you must have done something you weren't supposed to."

"It works like that?" Ethan asked.

"Like what?" Carol Lynch asked skeptically, trying to follow.

Archer suddenly felt like he was in the spotlight unexpectedly, and spoke to Ethan's parents. "Last time we met, I said that everyone's life has a beginning and an end that's already marked out. That, and other main events in your life. He's asking me how come he could do something that I couldn't see in his future."

Ivan Lynch frowned. Carol looked down, unsure about whether to avoid the conversation and pretend she wasn't in the room.

"I wasn't looking to see his future, but even so, even if I could and this wasn't in it, he made this happen by doing something he wasn't supposed to," Archer replied. Noting the apprehension on their faces, he added, "Hey, look, I'm not trying to offend anyone here, ok? I just told him the way I see the world."

Ivan nodded. Carol sat upright, stiffly.

"So can you see my future now?" Ethan asked, aware of his parent's skepticism, but ignoring it anyway. "Will the cops get the guy who killed my brother?"

"Like I said, man, you gotta leave this to the police, and I mean it man. Stay away from the Eighth Street Crushers, they'll kill you next time."

"That your opinion again?" Ethan rolled his head to look through the window into the hallway.

"I know the gangs. I know what they can do. And yeah, I see something in your future. Something dangerous heading your way."

A cold shiver ran down Ethan's spine. Maybe Archer was

referring to what had already happened to him. Maybe his angels' clairvoyance was running on a delay.

"What?" Carol wanted to know despite her first response to this man and the spirits he believed in. "What danger?"

Archer looked down at Ethan. He saw fear in the man's eyes. "I can't say. I just get a picture of something unavoidable. Something ugly."

"What could be more ugly than what he's already been through?" Carol asked.

"I can't say," Archer repeated. "That's not how this gift works. I don't get specifics. I get feelings. Images of things that represent something. Not snapshots of the future."

Ethan was beginning to regret asking Archer to come in. He was hoping for reassurance and comfort. Instead, he felt more fearful now than before. What could Archer mean?

"Can you tell your angels to throw in a good word for me, at least?" Ethan asked hopefully.

Archer smiled. "Sure. Never hurts." He withdrew his hands from Ethan's suddenly. "You take care, man. I gotta go."

"Thanks, Archer. I still got your number. I'll call you some time, ok?"

"Sure," Archer said on his way through the door.

They watched the man with the eerie grey eyes leave the room.

"You believe any of that?" Ethan's mother asked.

"You can see he believes it, and yeah, I think I might too," Ethan said.

"He says you're going to be in danger," Ivan repeated. "I wonder what he means."

"I think his angels are just late. I've already been in danger. I'm not going near that place again. I'm fine," Ethan reassured his parents, who were still processing the fact that they'd just been in the same room as a medium.

Archer walked briskly to the exit. What he had seen at Ethan's bedside disturbed him, but he couldn't tell the young man in the hospital bed. How do you tell someone who is recovering from a near-death experience that it won't be his last? Archer's mouth was dry. This gift could be a curse. He didn't ask to see into Ethan's future, but he saw something he couldn't ignore. Ethan was in imminent danger, but from what, he couldn't tell.

He stopped for a moment, and stared down the corridor as the woman he had seen earlier walked towards him. And then he saw the angel with the book, following her. It *was* her. She was the one who channeled the angel. Archer took a deep breath and moved towards the girl.

Riley looked up, straight into the eerie grey eyes of the man she was sure had been following her.

"Hey!" she called, quickening her pace as she moved towards him. This time, the stranger didn't try to run away. Riley caught up to him, and confronted him, hands on her hips. "Have you been following me?" she asked firmly.

"Look, it's not what you think," Archer tried to explain.

"What is it then? I've seen you here a few times now, watching me. Why?" she demanded. "Why are you following me?"

She wouldn't believe him if he told her the truth, but he had to tell her. Archer held his breath, desperately searching for the words in the fractions of a second he had to think.

"Ok, ok. You're not going to believe this, and I'm sure this is going to sound really outrageous. And crazy. And you're gonna think I'm weird," he stammered.

"No weirder than I already think you are for stalking me." Riley said.

"I'm not stalking you," Archer protested. "I'm looking for someone else."

Riley's head jutted forward an inch, silently demanding an explanation.

Archer closed his eyes as he spoke, like an ostrich burying its head in the sand to avoid danger. "The angel with the book – I'm looking for the angel who carries the book, and I think he's bound to you. Somehow." Archer opened his eyes slowly, hoping Riley would have evaporated but she was still there, staring at him with her eyes wide open, as if she'd seen the angels that surround Archer for herself.

"The book that tells the end of a person's life?" Riley asked in disbelief. She'd never heard of this angel before and now two different people had mentioned him in the space of two days.

Archer was taken a back. "You know about him?"

"Somebody told me yesterday," Riley said.

"Who?"

"Angel Martin," she replied.

Archer had heard the name before, but was trying to remember from whom or where. "Have you seen him?" he asked.

"No. Martin said he saw him. Have you?" Riley asked.

"Yes. Once before. Here. He spoke to me."

"Can you see him now? Is he here," Riley asked the man with the grey eyes.

"Not right now, but he was earlier. 5:58."

"What's that?"

"Somebody's dying today. At 5:58," Archer explained.

Riley looked at her watch. "That's just over an hour from now. Come with me."

She led Archer to Ward B. They stood outside one of the rooms, and watched through the window as a man in his late fifties lay unconscious on the bed, attached to a ventilator and a number of machines. The ventilator pumped rhythmically, simulating the breathing motion of the man in the bed.

"Mr Ghirardelli. He's an organ donor. That's why I'm here. We're waiting for the family to sign the consent forms."

Archer checked his watch. Still a long wait till 5:58. Maybe the angel would appear again now that the one who channeled him was here.

"Do you mind if I wait with you?" Archer asked. "I won't get in the way, I promise."

"If you see him, you tell me," Riley instructed. Archer nodded rapidly.

Archer waited outside the ward while Riley went inside and placed a hand on Sophia Ghirardelli's shoulder. The woman looked up at Riley, and nodded tearfully, several times. She didn't say the words, but she would let her husband go.

Sophia stood, and rested her head on her husband's chest one last time.

"My heart," she whispered. "Wait for me on the other side, my love. I'll see you soon."

After a long while, Sophia pulled away, allowing her hand to linger gently on her husband's for a moment. She closed her eyes, breathed deeply, and nodded, holding out her hand. Riley slipped her the clipboard containing the consent forms, which Sophia signed without hesitation.

"Are you married?" Sophia asked unexpectedly.

"No," Riley replied.

"Thirty two years," Sophia said distantly, as if recalling every one of those years in that moment. "He was my first love, you know."

Riley nodded. They'd been married longer than she'd been alive. There are no words of comfort that would ever take away the pain. She knew that. Silence and solidarity were all she could offer.

Sophia wiped a tear from her cheek. "I would stay here with him forever if it would bring him back," she said. Again Riley nodded. Sophia continued. "But he's already gone. My husband has already gone, and I'm alone, even though I'm right beside him. He was a strong man, you know? My Antonio. Strong inside. He came from nothing, and he fought. He made a good life for us."

"You have children?" Riley asked.

Sophia nodded. "Yes. They live in Italy now. In Milan. Our son is a fashion designer. He has a factory there. Our daughter went over to help him. They were planning to come over next month to say goodbye, but Antonio..." She paused, allowing the tears to flow until she could speak again. "He wouldn't have wanted them to see him like this. The tumor took him earlier than we had expected. Than the doctors led us to believe. When you're young, you think that you have all your life ahead of you. You never stop to realize that there's a limit to the amount of time you have here. Would you do things differently if you knew you didn't have as much time left as you thought you did?" Sophia asked Riley unexpectedly.

"Maybe," Riley said without thinking. "Sure, of course I would."

Sophia placed a hand on Riley's. "Don't wait until somebody turns your timer over, and the sand starts running down. You have time now," she said.

Riley nodded. "I will, Mrs Ghirardelli."

"Be good to my Antonio. Treat him with respect. It's how he lived his life. With respect for others."

"We will, Sophia, I promise."

With a final nod, Sophia gave the go ahead.

Moments later, Antonio Ghirardelli was wheeled out of the ward. Archer looked at his watch. 5:36pm. Riley followed the gurney, and Archer fell in behind her. As they neared the operating theater, the transplant team joined Riley.

"You can't cross the line," she said to Archer as they reached the red line at the entrance to the operating theatres. Archer nodded, and backed away as the transplant team wheeled the donor around the corner and out of view.

As Riley disappeared, Archer froze. The angel holding the book appeared alongside Riley for just a moment.

"It's him," Archer said to himself, and looked at his watch again. It was 5:47pm.

Some time after 6:00pm, the swing doors opened, and a man carrying a yellow medical cooler box left the operating theatre, speaking into his phone. As the minutes ticked by, another man from the organ donor team walked through the same doors carrying a similar yellow medical cooler box. Riley emerged just before 6:30pm, and walked straight over to Archer.

"He died at 5:58pm," she said. "Can we talk? About this angel?"

"Sure," Archer replied without hesitation.

"I've got some paper work to do. Meet me at the coffee shop in half an hour?"

"Let's take a look at you, Mr. Lynch," the Doctor Jansen said, examining Ethan's face. "How do you feel?"

"Sore," Ethan replied. "A little stupid."

"Hmmm," the doctor approved. "Only Superman and Chuck Norris can handle bad guys like that single handedly," he laughed.

"Chuck who?"

The doctor continued examining Ethan. "Before your time, kid. I'm going to prescribe you something for pain. You're good to go, young man," he looked up at Ethan's parents. "Just make sure he doesn't try anything heroic again, ok?"

"Sure," Ivan said.

"Ok, doc," Ethan agreed.

"He needs an antibiotic too, it's on the script. Make sure he finishes the course," the doctor looked up at Carol, who nodded.

Ethan swung his legs over the edge of the bed and took the prescription from his mother's hand.

"I'm not dead, you know. I'm right here."

"Ethan," his mother began but he interrupted her.

"I'm ok, mom. I can take care of myself."

Ivan placed a hand on his wife's shoulder. *Let the boy be.*

"Ok, but if you need anything," she continued.

"Sure mom," Ethan conceded.

He stood, winced, and hobbled to the pile of clothes on the chair.

"A little privacy?"

The three of them walked towards the exit a few minutes later.

"Are you sure we can't give you a ride home?" Ivan asked.

"It's ok, Dad, I'll take a cab," Ethan insisted.

"You sure?" Ivan asked again. From the look on Ethan's face his father could tell that asking any more was going to be a waste of time. Ethan was as stubborn as he was. "Ok. Call if you need anything, ok?"

"Yep," Ethan said. Lately he couldn't stand to be around his parents. They over-compensated for the loss of their youngest child, and Ethan was beginning to feel suffocated. "I'll call if I need anything," he said, hoping it would make them leave. "I promise, ok? I'm going to pick up my meds at the pharmacy and then I'm going to catch a cab home. It's ok. You can leave me, I'm fine."

"Come on Carol. The boy wants to be alone." Ivan put an arm around his wife's shoulder. Carol nodded, and reached up to kiss Ethan one more time.

"Call if you need anything," she said.

"I will, Mom."

Ethan watched his parents disappear slowly down the corridor before he joined the line at the dispensary. He hardly knew what to say to them any more. They seemed to have aged a hundred years in the days since Carly's death.

He still felt the burning injustice in his gut. Bruised and banged up as he was, he still didn't want to let it go.

The pharmacist was an elderly man with a professional expression on his face, framed by neatly styled grey hair. He looked like the poster face for a family planning clinic. A kind of benevolent, grandfather figure. He cable-tied the prescription in a small metal cage.

"Please pay at the check out," he said, handing it to Ethan over the counter.

"Thanks," Ethan said. The poster face nodded professionally.

With the small metal cage in his hand, Ethan went over to the cashier and waited in another line. He hadn't been waiting longer than a minute when a pretty young woman about his own age joined the line behind him, holding an energy drink and a Mars bar. She wore overalls that made her look a bit like a paramedic, and her hair was pulled back into a pony behind her head. Still,

Ethan thought she was a pretty girl.

"Looks like you're in for a long day," he smiled at her.

The woman nodded. "It's already been a long day, and its set to be a long one still," she replied. She had a captivating smile, Ethan thought. Pretty eyes. The kind that sparkled and seemed to change color as you looked into them. "Looks like you came off your bicycle at high speed," the woman said.

"Oh, yeah. No, not a bicycle. I got mugged," he said. "Eighth Street. I was in the wrong place."

The woman made a face. "What were you doing down there?"

"Took a few wrong turns," Ethan looked down. He pointed to the energy drink. "Only reason why I've ever needed energy drinks and chocolates was late night partying and having to work the next day. But not for a long time now. What's your excuse?"

The woman smiled. "Nothing so exciting. Just work."

"What kind of work would that be?"

"I'm a transplant coordinator," the woman replied.

Ethan couldn't hide his surprise. "That's not something you hear every day."

"I do," she smiled.

"My name's Ethan." He wasn't sure whether to shake her hand, it seemed so formal. Instead, he held onto his metal medicine cage.

"Riley."

"Good to meet you Riley," Ethan said, still unsure whether or not to extend a hand.

"You too," she smiled.

"Next please," the cashier's voice interrupted them. Ethan waved his cage.

"Gotta go."

Riley watched as Ethan moved off to pay for his medication. He smiled back at her one more time before he left the pharmacy. He was slim and athletic. Neatly cropped beard. Might even have been her type, but with all that bruising…

"Next please."

Riley approached the cashier, and caught a glimpse of Archer heading past the pharmacy on his way to the exit.

"Crap," Riley whispered. He was supposed to meet her at the coffee shop. She paid for her energy fix quickly, and ran after him.

"Hey!" she called.

Archer was almost at the exit. He turned, and waited for her to catch up.

"Hey," he greeted her as she arrived. "Sorry, I couldn't wait. You in for a long night?" he asked, pointing at her energy drink.

"Jesus, not you too. What's with everybody and my energy drink today?" Riley cracked open the can and took a sip. "There was a guy in front of me at the pharmacy. Same thing." Riley saw Ethan outside the hospital, waiting. "There. Him. He also had something to say about it."

Archer looked up, and his mouth opened.

"It's him."

"Yes, I know," Riley replied, but Archer held up his hand.

"Not the guy. The Angel."

"The Angel with the book?" Riley asked.

"Yeah. And he's with that guy," Archer said, pointing.

"With Ethan?" Riley asked.

"You know him too?"

"*You* know him?" Riley asked, surprised.

"Yeah," Archer continued.

"Can you see the book?" Riley asked.

"Nah," Archer said. "He's just there, hanging around Ethan, but I can't see. Come on."

He grabbed Riley's hand, and pulled her towards the exit. The glass doors slid open, and they stepped outside. There was a slight chill in the late afternoon air.

"Ethan!" Archer called. Ethan turned, expecting to see Archer, but his smile broadened when he saw Riley alongside him.

"Archer," he greeted the man, and then his attention turned to Riley. "You know this guy?"

Riley nodded. *He was stalking me for months and we just met today,* she thought. "Yeah, we did some work together."

"You part of the transplant thing?" Ethan asked Archer.

"Uh…no, not really. I um… helped her out with a reading."

"Oh," Ethan said.

"So you two know each other?" Archer asked, waving a finger between Ethan and Riley.

"We just met in the pharmacy," Ethan said. "But I didn't really get a chance to introduce myself properly." This time he extended a hand. "Ethan Lynch."

"Riley O'Connor," she said. As she took Ethan's hand, her face went pale.

"What?" Ethan asked. "You look like you just saw a ghost."

"I think I just did." Riley turned to Archer. "I can see him."

"Well hello," Ethan waved a hand in front of Riley's eyes. "I'm right here."

"The angel with the book?" Archer asked.

Riley nodded. "The book's closed."

"The book?" Ethan asked Archer. "The one you told me about?" Archer nodded. Ethan turned to Riley. "You can see him too?"

Riley nodded, wide eyed. Her mouth was still agape.

"Will somebody please tell me what's going on?" Ethan demanded.

Riley let go of Ethan's hand as if it was suddenly burning her flesh.

"He's gone," Riley said, suddenly disappointed.

"Yeah," Archer said. "I can't see him either."

"Will somebody please tell me what's going on?" Ethan's tone was aggravated and impatient.

"I just saw the angel with the book," Riley said in a voice that was a barely a whisper.

"So?" Ethan pressed.

"I've never seen an angel before in my life. Ever." Riley replied.

A silver car pulled up at the entrance to the hospital.

"I think that's my ride," Ethan said, checking his phone. "Yep. That's me."

"Nice meeting you," Riley said again.

"Yeah, same here." Ethan moved to the cab, and climbed in painfully. He waved as the car pulled away, and watched as Riley and Archer continued their conversation without him.

"Can we talk?" Riley asked.

Archer looked at his watch. "I'm supposed to meet someone, but I'll tell him I'm gonna be a little late." He pulled out his phone and sent a message while Riley waited for him. "Ok. I got a few more minutes. I could use some coffee."

"Already got mine," Riley wiggled her energy drink in the air.

They went back inside the hospital, and stood in line at the cafeteria where Archer ordered an Americano, and then took a table by the window next to an old couple who must have been in their late seventies. The man had a thinning crop of wispy grey hair combed over his balding head. A walking stick balanced against his leg, which was bandaged from the knee down. His wife's hair was white as snow, and she looked to be perfectly healthy. Odd how the women usually age better than the men, Riley thought. The couple made her wonder what she would be like at that age. Would she ever find someone to share her life with?

"You ok?" Archer asked as he slid into his seat. He set his coffee cup and the tiny milk jug down on the table.

"What?" Riley realized she was far away. "Oh, yeah, I'm fine. So how did that happen, Archer?" Riley asked excitedly. "I saw him. With my own eyes. I saw the angel with the book."

"Well I know for myself I only see him when you're around. I been seeing angels since I was a kid, but never seen that angel before until that day in the hospital." Archer cradled his coffee in both hands, watching the steam rise from the top. He made a ceremony of pouring milk slowly from the small stainless steel jug, and watching the colors swirl until it was just the right shade of brown. "Ever since then I've been hanging around hospitals trying to see him again, but I'd only see him sometimes, and it wasn't always in the same hospital. Then I figured he must have some connection with a person, so I started noticing who was around when I saw the angel. And that led me to you. I think he needs two people, connected in some way, before he lets himself be seen. But it doesn't work both ways. Like I can see him when you're around, but you can't. You need your own someone. And I think your someone is Ethan."

Riley thought for a moment. "You think so?"

Archer nodded. "I been following this angel for a long time. Had plenty of time to try to figure him out. Like I said, I see angels all the time. But this one is different."

"What now? What am I supposed to do? Do I go find this guy so I can see the angel again?" Riley asked.

Archer leaned forward and Riley found herself mesmerized by his pale eyes. "To be honest, Riley, I don't know. I don't know why I get to see the end of people's lives before it happens. It hasn't changed anything. I haven't been able to do anything for the person once I knew they would die. Both times, the person I was told about – they were in a place I couldn't even talk to them. So I don't know what I'm supposed to do with this. I only just figured out that the angel and you are connected. Maybe its not for *me* to figure out."

"What do you mean?" Riley asked.

"Maybe he's not my angel. Maybe he's yours," Archer suggested. He cradled his coffee cup again, and brought it to his lips.

Riley felt a chill running through her body. "I don't…"

"Maybe the reason I can see the angel around you is because you and the angel are connected," Archer said.

"Why can't you see him now?" Riley asked. "If you can see him around me, how come you can't talk to him the way you can talk to other angels?"

"Like I said," Archer shook his head slowly. "I'm trying to figure this angel out. He's different. I get to talk to the other angels. This one never said a word to me."

"Do you think I'll see him again if I'm around Ethan?" Riley suggested, a smile creeping across her face.

Archer shrugged, turning both palms heavenward. "I really can't say. It might be a one-time thing. When it comes to angels and the spirit world, we know very little except what they tell us themselves. I know that people cross over. I know that angels speak to us. I know that there's good and evil. I know that Karma's real. Very real. Beyond that I actually know very little. I'm in tune with them. I can speak to them. But more than that..."

"Damn!" Riley said loudly enough to draw the attention of old couple at the next table.

"What?" Archer asked. He had a habit of raising his eyebrows each time he took a sip of coffee.

"I didn't get his number."

"Who, Ethan?" Archer asked.

Riley nodded. "Yeah. I'm not in the habit of giving my number to guys I just met." Her mind went to Jenna and her latest random hook-up.

"You've just come out of a relationship where you were lied to," Archer said. He wasn't asking. He knew. Riley felt suddenly exposed.

"Forget about it," Riley said, folding her arms.

"I'm just trying to help," he said.

Riley felt compelled to explain. "He lied to me. Made me believe I was everything to him. Made me believe he loved me. Meanwhile he was married, and it took me two years to find that out. He made me his emotional slave. I don't know how I could have let him do that to me. I'm not that weak."

"Not now," Archer said, reaching forward to take her hand. Riley was hesitant, but allowed him to take it, remembering the electricity she felt when she touched Martin's hand. Maybe this would be the same. Archer continued. "But back then you were insecure, and vulnerable."

Riley pulled her hand away and rubbed it as if he'd just burned her flesh.

"How could you know that?"

"Haniel," he said.

"You're talking to *my* angel?" Riley said indignantly.

"More like she's talking to me," Archer said.

Riley looked over her shoulder. "I thought you were on my side."

"She is. That's why she's telling me about you. To help you," Archer explained.

"I don't want to talk about it. I'm so over him," Riley said. Her eyes were fierce with fresh, raw emotion.

"No you're not."

Riley hugged herself tightly with both arms, staring into Archer's eerily pale eyes that pierced her exterior and bore into the very depths of her soul. She felt as if her hidden emotional self had been laid bare in front of this stranger, exposed, with nowhere to hide. It was as if every secret fear, every hidden scar that she'd convinced herself had been healed, dealt with, sorted, was laid out on the coroner's table, and she could do nothing to conceal her deepest insecurities.

"Why are you doing this to me?" Riley asked, burying her face in her hands. "I can't deal with this right now."

"You don't want to deal with this. You've been avoiding the truth. Refusing to admit what you really feel."

Riley tried to hold back the tears, but her shoulders were shaking as she sobbed into her hands.

"What?" Riley said, glaring at Archer through reddened eyes. "What am I not admitting?"

"That you're still in love with him."

The words hit her like a bucket of cold water. Everything inside her froze, as if time itself had stopped. She could hear the beating of her heart inside her head, pounding like a huge clock, ticking in slow motion.

"What did you just say?" she whispered.

"You hated him for what he did to you," Archer said. "You threw him out when you found out how he lied to you. You've convinced yourself that you're over him. You've closed the doors to your heart. You've convinced yourself that you're better off without him. That you deserve better. That you're never going to be lied to again."

Riley nodded rapidly as Archer spoke. *This* was her truth. This was the closure she'd reached finally after months of anger.

"But before you discovered his secret, you loved him, and you've never stopped loving him," Archer said. Right there, in the canteen, the place she visited almost every day, the stranger she'd only just met had exposed her soul.

"I hate the bastard for what he did to me," Riley said in a voice barely loud enough to be a whisper, her eyes brimming with tears.

"You hate the action of his betrayal, but you still love the man. You're angry with him. You feel betrayed by what he did. But if it weren't for the lie, you'd still be together. You'd still love him."

"But I hate him," Riley insisted. "I hate him for lying to me."

"I know," Archer nodded.

"And I hate him for making me his fool," she continued.

"I know," Archer said again.

"But you're right," she looked up at Archer through strands of hair that had fallen over her face. "What we had was so good and I hate him for ruining that."

"You're *angry* at him for ruining that. You're still in love with him," Archer corrected. He had the demeanor of a sage. Endless patience, a gentleness to his words, damning as they might have been.

"How can I still be in love with him?" She thought she'd let all her anger go. All that light and breathing she'd been through after seeing Martin, she thought she was finally done with the pain of Dean's betrayal.

"You won't let anyone else in," Archer said.

"Because I don't want to be hurt again," Riley said defensively. Martin had told her the same thing.

"Because you're still in love with him," Archer insisted.

Riley was silent. This was a new revelation.

Archer continued. "Because you still feel that letting anyone else in would be a betrayal of your love for him."

Riley shook her head. "No. That's not true."

Archer looked at her silently without blinking. His eyes were like a lie detector.

"Is it?" Riley asked herself. "Am I really still in love with him?" As she voiced the question, she felt a warmth in her heart welling up like lava from a volcano, rising up and up until there was nowhere to go but over the edge and down the outside wall. She felt the tears streaming down her face. Riley sobbed for a long while before she was able to speak again. "I loved him so much," she said through her tears. "He was my everything."

Archer simply nodded. His job wasn't to analyze, or diagnose. His job was simply to repeat the message the angels told him. Haniel hovered behind Riley, smiling at him.

"Now she can be free," Haniel said to Archer before she vanished from his sight.

"What am I supposed to do now?" Riley asked. "Am I supposed to go tell him that I still love him? Beg him to come back after he lied to me?"

"No," Archer said. "You won't ever let him back in. You said so yourself. You deserve better. But you couldn't move on without acknowledging your feelings. To love someone even though they've hurt you is a gift. Not many people have the strength to live that way. It's easier to shut someone off. Close the doors. But the only person you're enclosing in a prison when you do that is yourself. You have to open the doors again, let the light back in. But acknowledge your true feelings. They exist within you. All you have to do is acknowledge that they're there and give them free reign. You don't have to live a lie. Just acknowledge that your love for him still lives."

"And then?"

"And then your heart will be free," Archer splayed both hands, palms up.

"What do I do about Dean?" Riley's conflicting emotions tormented her. How could she feel anger, and acknowledge love, and then just let it drift into the ether?

"You do nothing," Archer replied. "You deserve better. Just be honest to yourself. Then let him go."

Riley shook her head. "That's easier said than done." She looked at Archer for a long while, staring into his pale eyes as if they would help her through her confusion, but she found no more wisdom, only that she was mesmerized by their unique appearance. She closed her eyes, and thought of the angel with the book once more. Anything to divert the conversation away from Dean and her own feelings for him. "How do I see the angel with the book again?" she said. "If he's connected to Ethan?"

"Ethan found us both once. He'll find you again," Archer said simply, as if they were certain to bump into each other like kids in the school playground. "Here, take my card, just in case." He handed her a card, and Riley read the line out loud, looking at the Oracle.

"I talk to Angels?"

Archer smiled. Riley looked through the window as the late afternoon sun balanced on the horizon.

Chapter 5

The sun was just setting as Abe took a last sip of tea. The small family gathering had just finished a light supper.

"Thanks for dinner, Mom, that was great, as always." Abe played absent-mindedly with the napkin on his lap.

Yetta, Abe's mom smiled, crinkling the corners of her eyes. "For you, my boy, it's always a pleasure." She began to clear the table, and drifted between the dining room and the kitchen of her small apartment.

"Anything for you my boy," Rivki mimicked her mom, and pinched Abe's cheeks. "Always for you my boy, never for me."

"Of course for you, Rivki," Yetta called from the kitchen.

"Yeah, yeah." Rivki pushed her chair back and took as many condiments as she could to the kitchen in one load. Abe sat at the table and smiled at his uncle Leon, who gnawed on a piece of *challah*.

"Thank you, Sis," Leon called, wiping his mouth. He glanced at his watch. "That's it, 6:04pm. Time to starve." He dropped the rest of the bread on side plate, and held up his hands.

"It's twenty four hours," Abe smiled. "You'll live."

"Twenty four hours and thirty seven minutes," Leon corrected him. "According to the Beth Din."

"Why don't they just make it like it's supposed to be. Sunset to sunset."

"Just in case," Leon waved a finger. He pushed the empty plate away from him. "Just in case. So they add on a couple extra minutes. To be extra blessed while you fast."

"Sure," Abe said. Leon smiled.

"You get the day off tomorrow?" Yetta asked Abe between trips.

"Yeah," her son replied.

"Good," said Yetta. "It's better to fast when you're not at work."

"What time's breaking of the fast tomorrow?" he asked.

"Six forty one," his mother replied. "And we're expected at Sylvie's at seven."

Abe rose and placed his napkin on the table. "Ok, Mom, I'll see you there at seven. What are you doing tomorrow?" he asked his sister.

"I don't know. Sleeping. Watching movies. Staying in my PJ's all day, that's for sure. You?" Rivki removed the pony from her hair and went through the ritual of fluffing out her wild, dark locks before pulling them tightly back and replacing the pony again.

"I don't know," Abe began.

"Me, I'm going to shul in the morning," Leon interrupted. "Me and your mom, right Yetta."

"Uh huh," she called from the kitchen, amidst the clatter of crockery in the sink.

"Come to shul with us," Leon urged.

"I don't know, uncle Leon. I don't understand a word of Hebrew. Except for Shalom, and maybe Yom Kippur."

"Ah," Leon waved a hand dismissively. "So read the English."

"Yeah, so read the English," Rivki goaded. She knew where Abe stood when it came to the religion of his parents. Abe glared at her.

"I'm going to head home now if that's ok, Mom?" Abe said loudly so his mom could hear from the kitchen.

"Sure, but wait, I'm making you something to take with you," she called.

"I'm ok, really," Abe protested, but Yetta insisted.

She came bustling through from the kitchen. "Here," she said, handing her son a brown paper bag. "Take this. There's some chopped herring for the fridge, and some *kichel*, and some *bulkes* for you to break the fast tomorrow."

"Mom, I've got plenty..." he began but Yetta spoke over his protest.

"My boy's gotta eat. Do it for your mamma." Yetta placed a hand on her bosom. The guilt trip. Hardly subtle. "Rivki, this is for you." Yetta pinched her daughter's cheeks. "Before you accuse me of favoritism. And you," she turned back to Abe. "When are you going to find a nice Jewish girl and settle down? There's no one to cook for you, no one to look after you."

"I can take care of myself, Mom. And I'm still looking for a nice girl, I just haven't found the right one yet."

"Look at you," Yetta stood squarely in front of her son. "You're young, you're handsome." She looked him up and down. "Maybe a bit thin."

"Oh stop it Mom," Abe objected, but Yetta carried right on.

"You're a catch. A real catch. Isn't he a catch?" she turned to Leon.

"A real catch," Leon concurred.

"Make your mama happy before she dies."

"Oh please!" Abe protested once more, but she ignored him.

"Here, take your food. Fast well. Then eat something nice." She thrust the brown paper bag in Abe's hand.

"And me?" Leon threw up his hands. "What am I? Chopped liver?"

"Yeah, I'll make you one too."

"Thanks, Sis." Leon eyed the discarded piece of bread on his side plate.

"Sure."

"Thanks, Mom," Abe said, taking the bag. He kissed his mother on the cheek. "And thanks for dinner."

"That's my boy."

"Night, Mom," Rivki said, slipping into her coat.

"You're leaving too?"

"Abe's going to walk me home," she said, kissing her mother on the cheek.

Abe stepped into the cool night air with his sister on his arm.

"She'll never stop, you know. Until you find a nice Jewish girl and settle down," Rivki said.

Abe enjoyed the feeling of his little sister holding onto his arm. It made him feel responsible, and mature. Needed.

"One day. Not now. Not yet. I haven't found …"

"…the right girl, yeah, I know you keep saying. But have you looked?"

They stopped walking, and Abe turned to her for a moment. He opened his mouth to say something, but changed his mind, and dismissed it with a wave of his hand.

"What?" Rivki pressed.

"Never mind."

"Abe! What?" she asked again, tugging on his sleeve.

"I'm not looking for a *Jewish* girl. I'm just looking for a girl. A nice girl."

"Mom won't be happy," his sister warned. She took his arm and they continued walking.

"Mom's not the one that's going to get married some day."

"So you fasting this year?" Rivki changed the subject.

"I don't know," Abe said. "I have this dilemma every year." The fast had begun, and with it, the annual debate he had with himself every year. Was he going to fast? Did he really believe in all of this anyway? "The last time I set foot in a shul was for Yitzi's bar-mitzvah. And the last time before that was for Joanne's wedding."

"I went on first night Pesach this year," Rivki said.

"Really?"

His sister nodded. "It's not so bad. You should come with me.

We'll go tomorrow."

"Jeez, I don't know. I sit there like a schmuck listening to everybody mumbling in Hebrew and I seriously don't know what the hell is going on. You women have it easy. You sit up there in the gallery, and you can chat to each other while us men do the praying. Sitting in shul won't save my soul, sis."

"Yeah, I suppose you're right. You walking me all the way home?"

Abe smiled at her. "Sure. Like I'm gonna let you walk alone."

"I'll never walk alone," she said, knowing what was coming next.

Abe sang, "You'll never walk alone," and breathed in deep before he belted the refrain again at the top of his voice in the empty street, "You'll never walk alone!"

"You could be a baritone," Rivki smiled. "Oh that reminds me, I bought you a new scarf. Your old one is looking a bit sad. Like really sad."

"Really? A Man U one?" Abe smiled.

"Of course."

"You're the best." He wrapped an arm around her shoulders and squeezed.

"I know," Rivki smiled as they walked.

Abe unlocked the door to his apartment on the third floor about an hour later. The walk was relaxing, and spending time with Rivki was rare these days. Their jobs kept them busy during the week, and they usually spent weekends with their own circles of friends. They'd gather at one or other relative's house for the major Jewish festivals, but apart from that they didn't see much of each other.

"I've got to invite her over more," Abe thought as he locked the door behind him. He hung the red and white scarf Rivki had given him on the coat hook and admired it proudly. Next, he moved instinctively to the kitchen where he opened the fridge and stood there looking into it for a long while. Should he? Shouldn't he? He wasn't hungry at all. He was just used to grabbing something to snack on while he lay on the couch watching TV or reading a book. Rivki was fasting. His mom was fasting. He unpacked the chopped herring from the brown paper bag and put it in the fridge before closing the door.

Abe found himself reading on the sofa, wondering about why he was actually fasting. He stopped thinking about food, and read for a while, but his mind kept coming back to his own hypocrisy. He wasn't a bad person, yet this time of year always left him feeling guilty. It was all supposed to be about wiping the slate clean of one's sins, but a sin is only a sin if you believe in the law that makes it so. The Ten Commandments were universal principles of life. Most religions believed in the value of life, respect for parents, monogamy and dedication to one deity. Had he sinned since the last fast? Sure, he thought. He must have. He'd blown off steam here and there. He'd told a white lie or two to cover up a mistake. Said he wasn't feeling well in order to avoid some social engagement he really didn't feel like going to. Skipped a day or two of work, calling in sick when he wasn't really. But in the main, Abe was a forthright and honest person who loved his parents and lived a decent moral life. Had he sinned? Did he need to beg for forgiveness? Was this at all necessary?

A whiskey would be good right about now, he thought, but then his mind returned to his family, all of them fasting.

"Oh for crap sakes," he mumbled to himself. The guilt of betraying the family got the better of his desire for something to snack on, and something to drink. He flipped out the lights and made for his bedroom where he climbed into bed, throwing his head down hard against the pillow. He'd see how he felt when he woke up. There was no need to test the wrath of a god he had difficulty believing in just then.

Riley arrived home late. After her meeting with Archer, she'd responded to an emergency that had taken her across town. Her premonitions were never wrong. She knew she'd need that energy drink. The chocolate she'd bought earlier was supper on the way home.

She poured herself a glass of wine, slumped into the sofa, and placed her heavy boots on the coffee table.

"Jesus what a day," she said to herself. The trauma of death wasn't plaguing her mind as much as the angel she'd seen around Ethan Lynch. It was too late for a phone call so she texted Archer instead.

It's Riley. Can I come see you tomorrow?

It was a while before Archer replied.

Only after 12pm.

Riley had a day off the next day. That would give her chance to sleep in, and be fully rested by the time she saw him.

Ok, 12? Where?

He sent her the address.

After a slow start to her day, Riley took a long shower before breakfast. She slipped into a pair of tight fitting denims and a top that clung to her shapely contours, and left the apartment at 11:30am. She found Archer's place a few minutes before her appointed time, and waited until exactly midday before ringing the bell. Martin had taught her how to behave around mediums.

"Yeah?" Archer's voice crackled through the intercom.

"It's Riley."

"Come on up. First floor, apartment 108."

There was a loud buzz and a clunk as the door unlocked. She made her way inside, and climbed the rickety staircase. The inside of the three-story apartment block hadn't seen a fresh coat of paint in over two decades.

Riley made her way down the hall, and passed several doors till she found apartment 108. She knocked.

"Come on in," Archer said, opening the door. He stood aside for her to enter. His place was different to Martin's. No coarse salt at the door. It looked like a teenage gamer's lounge more than a medium's place of work. A game console lay on the coffee table, and the TV screen was frozen on an image of a battle zone in a futuristic dystopian landscape.

"Take a seat," Archer motioned to the couch. Riley placed her handbag close to her and sat on the edge of the sofa. "Can I get you some coffee?"

"Thanks."

"Cream and sugar?"

"Yes, please."

He poured two cups of cheap instant coffee and sat diagonally opposite her, placing one next to the game controller on the coffee table.

"So, your angels are unique, I have to say." Archer looked at Riley, and she found herself mesmerized again by the color of his eyes. She could never get used to it. They reminded her of a wolf.

"You can see them already?" Riley asked.

"Just the one. Impatient, that one, I'll tell you that. Been wanting to talk to you since you knocked on my door."

Riley made a surprised face. "Talk to me about what?" she asked.

"We're gonna find out. Give me your hands." Archer sat forward and reached across the low table. He balanced on the edge of his seat, rested his elbows on his knees and took her hands. Riley found herself staring into those pale, eerie eyes, but as she did they took on an apologetic expression.

"You have to let it go," Archer began. "You have to stop looking for the angel with the book. Your angel, Haniel, says to stop searching for him. She says he will show you the future, and no one should know the future. Not theirs, nor anyone else's."

Riley felt icy prickles running through her body, the kind of feeling you get when you've been caught doing something you shouldn't be doing.

"But then why does the angel with the book want to show himself to me? Why shouldn't I know the future?" Riley objected, feeling deflated.

Archer shook his head. He was just the messenger, relaying a message meant in part for him.

"Because the moment you know the future, you'll try to change what you don't like, or you'll try to make it happen and do something you wouldn't have done, and mess it up anyway," Archer explained.

"But what if he shows me something?" Riley protested. She had a connection to this angel, she was convinced. She wanted to communicate with him. To communicate with an angel directly, not through a medium.

"He might," Archer said. "I'm not sure how this angel works. I don't know if you have to ask him to show you, or if he just swoops in and shows you. And if he does show you, to what purpose?"

"You saw the future. You saw someone else's future. He showed it to you," Riley said.

"The first time he showed it to me. The times after that I asked him. I wanted to know what future he was going to show me."

"So why's it different for me?" Riley was devastated. Yesterday, she'd hit the biggest emotional high of her life, seeing an angel with her own eyes, and now she felt more deflated than she'd ever felt before, being told that she shouldn't ask him about the future. "Can I ask him about anything else?"

Archer waited a moment, and nodded. "Ask him for advice. For wisdom, she says. Just don't ask him to show you what's in the book, or you'll want to change it, and that could ripple into the future, and have a devastating effect."

"What? That sounds a bit overboard."

"She says one small change to the events of tomorrow could have a major impact on the future of the world." Archer let go of Riley's hands, and she immediately sat back. Archer mirrored her movement. "What if you knew that JFK was going to get shot that day?" he asked. "And where the shooter would be. You'd have stopped it, right? Or if you knew about the tsunami that hit Phuket on December 25th. You'd have warned someone, and maybe saved thousands of lives, but what would the knock on effect have been ten years into the future? Some engineer who was supposed to die that day lives to invent something that destroys an entire continent? Or a child that wasn't supposed to have been born becomes a mass murderer and wipes out your own family? She's not wrong, Riley. We should both listen. The angel with the book is a door that shouldn't be opened."

"What are you going to do if he opens his book for you again? Not look?" Riley pouted.

Archer opened his mouth to say something, but changed his mind. "I never told anyone about it. Except you. And I've never tried to interfere."

Riley wondered what she would do if she knew someone's future, and had the chance to change it. Would she remain silent? Maybe her angel knew her better than she knew herself.

"I'd probably try to change it if it was bad. Like really bad. And it was about someone I knew." Riley's eyes drifted to the untouched coffee cup.

"You kinda do that every day. Change people's future," Archer observed.

"There's balance in what I do," Riley reached forward and scooped up the coffee cup, cradling it in both hands, allowing the warmth to permeate through her as if it were a life force to recharge her soul. "One life ends, another gets a chance to go on."

"As long as you don't play god," Archer said.

"I just play the messenger and delivery girl. I don't get to decide who lives and who dies. Thank god. That's a responsibility I don't ever want to have to bear." Riley stared into the distance beyond Archer contemplating what she might do if she did have to make that decision. Deciding who lives and who dies. It was responsibility that people shouldn't have to carry. But in her line of work, it was someone's job. Donors and recipients were matched, and recipients on the list were moved up and down depending on the severity of their condition. The more critical ones were shifted up in priority, and those priorities changed by the minute. Mostly it was an algorithm that decided who got a chance to live. Tom, her boss, managed the list. Riley and her team fetched and delivered. Agnes did the paper work.

"I see things in people's future," Archer said. "Like I can see in yours – you have to let someone in."

"You're the second person who's told me that, you know."

"They don't call me the Oracle for nothing. But this time it's not coming from me," Archer said. "This is Haniel."

"She still here?" Riley looked down into her coffee. "I thought she'd left. Then it's the second time she's tried to tell me the same thing. I'm not deaf you know," Riley said over Archer's shoulder.

"She's behind *you*, not me," Archer smiled.

"That's not funny."

"It's the truth, she's right there." Archer pointed over Riley's shoulder.

"Whatever. She's told me that before. When I went to see Angel Martin. That I have to let someone in. Or be ready to let someone in." Riley went back to her relationship with Dean, one that should never have gone past the first date, but she had been so desperate to get a boyfriend so that Jenna would stop trying to match her up with every stranger they met. Whenever they were out together Jenna would latch on to the first half-decent man they encountered. It turned out to have devastating consequences. Riley had fallen for him hard, and he'd lied to her about one thing. She'd been enraged with him when she found out he was married, and she threw him out. It was a wise decision, she told herself at the time. To end it suddenly. To throw the lying, cheating bastard out and have nothing more to do with him. And while she was filled with anger towards Dean for what he had done to her, there was no room for anyone else.

Archer continued, unaware of what was going on inside her head. "See that right there is wisdom, not the future. She hasn't told you that you're going to meet someone, or who he is. It is going to be a *he*, right?" Archer raised his eyebrows.

Riley smiled. "Yes, it would be a he. I'm done with that one asshole, not all men," Riley lied.

"Admit that you still love him, Riley."

She stared at him for a moment. Then she nodded slowly.

"I still love that bastard." She had never let go of Dean. She had never given herself time to heal the scar inside left by his sudden absence.

Archer smiled. "Now you're ready to open yourself to meet someone."

Archer's phone vibrated. He ignored it.

"Aren't you going to get that?" Riley pointed to the phone.

The medium glanced at the screen. "It's Ethan."

Riley's face lit up. "It's ok, take it."

Archer picked up the phone.

"Yeah? … I'm good, man, you? … Uh huh." He looked directly at Riley. "Why don't you ask her yourself, she's right here with me?"

Before Riley had time to object, Archer thrust his phone in her hand. She looked at Archer for some sort of briefing that wasn't forthcoming.

"Hi," she said unsteadily after a long silence, glaring at Archer.

"Hey," Ethan said. "This is an unexpected surprise. To catch you there with Archer, I mean. I just called him to ask him if he had your number. I was going to ask if you want to meet up for coffee some time."

Coffee, Riley thought. The modern day blessing for first dates and blind dates. *What did we do before Starbucks*, she wondered fleetingly.

"Uh," she looked at Archer, who nodded slowly, hypnotically with those pale eyes, causing her to mirror his action with her body and then her mind. "Ok, sure," she said before she could decide whether she wanted to let someone else into her life or not. "Yeah, what the hell."

"What the hell?" Ethan said playfully. "Am I a *what the hell*?"

"It's a long story," Riley said. "I'll tell you over coffee."

"I'd love to hear it," Ethan's tone had changed from playful. "So, I know most people communicate with the dead through mediums, but just so I don't have to go through a medium to talk to you, can I get your number?"

Riley smiled and gave it to him.

"When's good for you? Thursday?" Ethan pressed.

"Uh. Ok." She thought for a minute about her work schedule. "I'm on call, but Thursday."

"10:00am at the Starbucks on Upper Seventh?"

"Yeah. That works for me." It was near the hospital. And it was Starbucks. And she knew the place well enough. If he turned out to be a creep, she'd have the hospital as an excuse. Eleni would be on call as the emergency exit. "See you then."

She handed Archer's phone back to him. "What are you doing?" she chided him.

Archer raised his eyebrows, and dropped his chin an inch. "You gotta be open to letting someone else in, Riley. This is *Letting Someone Else In* practice."

"Urgh," she dismissed him.

"Haniel says you gotta do it."

Riley was texting on her phone.

"What you doing?" Archer asked.

"Exit strategy," Riley said, typing rapidly.

"What?"

"Eleni. My friend. She's on standby for Thursday."

"I don't understand?" Archer said, palms raised.

"If the date goes south, or I get a bad feeling I give Eleni a missed call under the table. She calls me back. I pretend it's an emergency, and I split," Riley smiled.

Archer pursed his lips pensively. "So that's how it works."

"Sad but true," Riley said. "I've got no time for assholes, liars, and relationships in general. I'm only doing this because you said."

"And Haniel," Archer corrected with a pointed finger.

"Yeah, and her. Shit," Riley said reading a new message on her phone.

"Emergency?" Archer asked.

"Kind of. Jenna's having a thing on Friday, and she's invited me and a plus one."

"That's an emergency?"

"It is. Guess she's gotten over Grant, then. I'm going to be the only one minus a plus one. And Jenna can be a real bitch." Riley thought of how she'd ended up with Dean because of Jenna's constant pressure, and this was going to be another of those occasions. She thought of asking Archer for a moment, but decided it wasn't a good idea.

Archer's pale eyes were silently compelling her to consider something she was vehemently against.

Chapter 6

The Starbucks on Upper Seventh Street was humming by the time Riley arrived on Thursday morning. She'd taken time to make herself look pretty. Her blonde hair hung below her shoulders, and she wore a pair of tight denims and a tight fitting black T-shirt. She found Ethan sitting at a table, dressed in a casual jacket over a T-shirt, with denims and a pair of shoes that were flashy yet casual.

"Ethan," Riley greeted him as she approached the table. He looked up and made no effort to hide his surprise and delight at the way she looked.

"Wow!" he said. "You look..." he searched for the words, "...amazing." Ethan stood and gave her a friendly kiss on the cheek.

"You clean up pretty good too," she said. His face was still bruised, but the swelling had gone down. Without the disfiguration around his eyes and cheeks, he was a good-looking man.

"Thanks. Pity about the make up," he said, pointing at the bruising.

"It'll heal."

They ordered coffee at the counter and returned to their table while the baristas went about preparing it. Ethan waited till Riley was seated before he lowered himself gently into the chair opposite her.

"Thanks for meeting me," he began. "I know we only said a few words at the hospital, but after I left and the whole way home, I couldn't stop thinking about you. There's something about you that I found intriguing. Magnetic. I had to meet you again, and...I don't know... it sounds corny, but I had to find out more about you."

Riley blushed. "Oh, I'm just me," she said. "Nothing intriguing."

"To you maybe," he smiled. "So tell me. You said your *what the hell* was a long story over the phone?"

"Bonny and Clyde?" The barista called from the counter.

"Oh. That'd be us," Ethan smiled.

"Bonny and Clyde?" Riley laughed. Ethan shrugged and left her for a moment to get their coffee. He returned and placed the one marked Bonny in front of her.

"Bonny and Clyde?" Riley asked again, reading the name scribbled on her cup. "Didn't they both die?"

Ethan made a face. "It was a spur of the moment thing. Where were we? That long story?"

"You don't miss a thing do you?" Riley looked down. She didn't like talking about her past relationship, especially now, after Archer had made her realize that she still loved Dean.

"I've just come out of a long relationship," Riley began. "I was really in love with him." She couldn't believe she was actually saying the words. But they felt right. Honest. Truthful. "And it ended because I found out he was married."

"Ouch!" Ethan made a face.

"Yeah," Riley agreed. "What about you?"

"Wait, that's it? That wasn't a long story at all. Where's my long story?" Ethan asked, turning his palm upward in expectation.

He took a sip of his coffee, and Riley watched the way he narrowed his eyes. She could almost taste the way he relished that first sip.

"It *was* a long story," Riley said. "We were together for almost two years. He had me believing he was a different person for all that time. That's a long time to believe a lie."

"And you don't hate him? That's admirable." Ethan wondered if he'd have the strength of character to not hate someone for stringing him along for two years.

"I did at first," Riley began, "but Archer helped me realize that I couldn't move on until I admitted to myself how I really felt about him."

"And that is?"

"That in some bizarre way, I'm still in love with him." Riley surprised herself. She'd only just met Ethan, and she found herself talking about feelings she'd hardly made sense of herself. Somehow she felt comfortable around him.

"Wow," Ethan couldn't help feeling a little dejected. If she still had feelings for this ex of hers, maybe this would be their one and only date. Yet something else inside him set his mind at ease. He brought a curled finger to his chin and leaned forward just a little. "Really? After he lied to you like that?" He watched the way she nodded. She was very beautiful. The last time he'd seen her, she was wearing her work overalls, no make-up, and her hair was pulled back in a pony. But here she was with her hair cascading down her shoulders like an angel, and she looked more beautiful than he had anticipated. He felt somehow connected to her. Like she was someone he'd known for a long time. "How do you get over that? How do you deal with loving someone like that?"

She smiled. "I'm not sure. I've been told to acknowledge my feelings, and let him go. I'm not so good at either right now. Jeez, I'm talking a lot. What about you?" Riley changed the subject, feeling a little uncomfortable, finding herself suddenly in the spotlight as if she were lying on the sofa in a psychiatrist's rooms. "What's your emotional baggage, seeing as how I'm sharing all my deepest darkest secrets with a total stranger?"

"Well, not a total stranger. We have met. Three times now. By this stage in our relationship you should be leaving your toothbrush at my place," Ethan chuckled.

Riley laughed loudly, and cupped a hand over her mouth. "Sorry," she apologized, waving a hand, still laughing. "That just ...I wasn't expecting that."

Her eyes sparkled when she smiled. Ethan watched for a moment, fascinated. "My emotional baggage? You sure you wanna know?"

"I've seen everything, believe me. The floor is yours." Riley sat back in the low leather chair, and sipped her coffee slowly. As much as she'd been avoiding men, she found this one charming, even though he wasn't trying to be. Maybe that was why she found him charming. He seemed to be an open book.

"Carly, my younger brother was killed two weeks ago. Murdered. On Eighth Street," Ethan began.

"Oh my god, I'm so sorry," Riley leaned forward and placed a hand on Ethan's knee without thinking. Looking down, she suddenly wondered if he'd think she was being forward.

"It's been hard, and to be honest, I'm angry. Still angry." Ethan's mind went back to those first moments when he heard that his brother had been killed. He felt the numbness all over again. It was one of those moments when reality suddenly crushes the superficial. When what's really important overshadows what we think is important. He remembered looking around the office at everyone else around him, as if time had frozen for that moment. His boss had been standing by the window, going through a project report with one of the PM's. Sandy was on her way to fetch a set of plans from the A1 printer. And his mother was on the phone, telling him his brother had been shot and killed. Ethan was aware that he had drifted off as he heard Riley's words breaking into his momentary trance.

"What happened?" Riley asked.

Ethan brought himself back to the present. He found comfort in the girl's sparkling eyes. They emanated kindness. "He was supposed to be meeting his study group at his dorm room," Ethan told her, "and one of the guys couldn't get there, so they moved the meeting to his place on Eighth Street. As Carly was getting out of his car, some..." Ethan paused, filtering his next words. "He got caught up in a drive by shooting. Some rival gang member happened to be right there, at that particular moment, and Carly got caught in the cross fire." Ethan's eyes welled up with tears that ran down his cheek and disappeared into his beard.

"I'm so sorry for your loss," Riley said. Ethan pinched a thumb and forefinger to the bridge of his nose, and took a deep breath, trying to fight back the tears. He couldn't speak. All he could manage was to hold up a hand in apology momentarily. "It's ok, there's no need to pretend its all fine," Riley comforted him.

"I tried to stay strong, for my parents," Ethan said after a while, recovering enough to go on. "Let my anger drive me. But that almost got me killed. I went down there. To Eighth Street..."

"You went to confront the gangs?" Riley asked.

"I went to see if I could find out anything. Somebody has to have seen something. The cops aren't doing anything. Carly's killer is still out there. And he's going to get away with it. Cops are afraid of the gangs. Or the gangs have the cops in their pockets. Either way, they're not doing anything to catch Carly's killer." Ethan tried to mask his outburst with a smile. "I tried to do something about it." He looked down, feeling ashamed. "I didn't get anywhere."

"I can't imagine what you're going through. But whatever you're doing isn't going to bring him back," she reassured him.

"I know," Ethan said quietly. "I know." There was a pause. "So that's my emotional baggage." Ethan looked up, feeling a little embarrassed, and tried to cover it up with a brave face, although his eyes were still glistening with tears. "Pretty deep for a first date, huh? Are you sorry you asked?" He forced a smile, and wiped his eyes once more.

"Not at all," Riley said. She drained her coffee in one long sip.

Her gut feel about people was usually on point, and she'd only ever been wrong once. Ethan seemed authentic. He didn't try to cover his insecurities. He spoke his about feelings. And he cried on a first date. That was new. He didn't feel embarrassed about showing his emotions, he owned them. All of that was a good sign. "People are so obsessed with the superficial. I know when I'm with my friends, the conversation is usually so pointless that I find myself ready to gnaw my arm off to get out of there." She smiled warmly. "It's not often I get to talk about life with someone."

Ethan returned her smile. She was right. His own conversation was usually superficial when he was with people he'd just met. Even around Abe and Dan, he didn't talk about things of consequence, until recently. Carly's death had turned everything upside down. It had brought about a realization that there were more important things in life than those that occupied all his time, his thoughts, and his conversation. "Tell me about your job? It must be pretty tough," Ethan asked.

"It's not an easy job to do." Riley looked away as she spoke, giving Ethan a chance to explore her beautiful face. "Definitely not for the faint hearted. I deal with death every day, and I give people second chances every day. Somebody dies, somebody else gets a chance to live. Sometimes more than one person. It's the real side of life." Ethan studied her as she looked into the distance. "People put so much energy into the material things in life. Bigger houses. Expensive cars. Working their lives away to make more money." For a moment Ethan felt exposed, as if she were talking about him. He was one of those who wanted a big house, a nice car, and a healthy bank balance. "But death doesn't choose its victims," Riley continued. "There's no preference and there's no escape. Rich, poor, good, bad. Nobody knows when their time is up." Riley thought about the angel with the book. *He* knew when people's time was up. He was the only one who seemed to know, and now she wanted to know, despite Haniel's warning. "When it's over, nobody remembers you for how much time you spent at the office, or how hard you worked." Ethan found himself thinking about his father as she spoke. "Your family grieves because they miss you. Kids wish their dads had spent more time with them. Parents wish they'd spent more time with their kids. *That's* what life is all about. It's not about how popular you are, or how many friends you have. When people die I get to see what really mattered. Their lives are measured by the people they leave behind, not by the things they've done."

"That's deep," Ethan said. He thought about Carly, that bright, beautiful soul. His family missed him. He hadn't yet had a chance to make something of his life. He still had a year to go to finish college. Yet he was missed. So much. "That gives me some comfort," Ethan said.

"Really?"

Ethan nodded. "Knowing that his life had meaning, if you put it that way. I loved him. Fuck, I loved him." Ethan shook his head, and then looked up apologetically. "Sorry, I didn't mean to…"

"…It's ok," Riley interjected. "You can say what you want to around me, I'm not prissy."

"Thank god, because I'm more irreverent that's for sure. My family's Catholic, and I'm definitely not," Ethan confessed.

"I'm not very religious," Riley said. "My folks died when I was very young, so I was brought up by my aunt Sal." She smiled fondly. "That's one brave woman, I tell you that. Raised me up as her own kid. She's not very spiritual, so I found my own definition of god over the years. I believe there's a higher power, somewhere, but I don't believe in the same the God that the Christians or the Jews believe in. Or any other god for that matter. I've always been fascinated by angels, and the world of spirits."

Ethan noticed how the corners of Riley's mouth curled into a smile as she spoke.

"And that stuff is real," Riley continued. "You can't deny it when you speak to angels and they tell you about your life through a stranger, and they know more about you than you ever thought you knew about yourself. Have you ever been to a medium and had a reading?"

Ethan shook his head. "I bumped into Archer in a bar. The day of Carly's funeral, actually. That's the closest I've been to one of them. I have to say, I was intrigued, and when I called Archer...to get your number...I was going to ask him if I could see him."

"I went to one. Angel Martin he calls himself," Riley said. She looked deep in thought as she spoke. "He told me about my life, and about my angel."

"The one with the book?" Ethan asked.

"No. He's a special one. My angel is Haniel."

Ethan nodded. Whatever that meant.

Riley continued. "Since I went to see Angel Martin, I feel like I can access them easier. My angels. I ..." Riley looked at Ethan uneasily. "This is gonna sound crazy." She waited for him to make her continue.

"It's ok," Ethan said. "I think I can take it." He smiled warmly.

"I saw her. My angel. One day after a really shitty day at work. It was emotional as hell. I saw her wings in the bath water, reflecting as clear as a mirror. It was beautiful. I thought I was seeing things, but then I saw Angel Martin the next day and he told me Haniel had been trying to comfort me."

"Wow," Ethan said. "I just got a shiver. For real."

"I told you it was weird," Riley said, a little embarrassed.

"No, really," Ethan reassured her. "I don't think it's weird. To tell you the truth, I'm not sure what I believe in. I know what I don't believe in." His hand went to the small cross he wore around his neck, part of his being, but an accessory more than a religious artifact. He never took it off. Most times, he wasn't even aware he was wearing it. "It's weird, isn't it?" he looked into Riley's eyes. "Things like this." He motioned towards the artifact around his neck. "I wear it, but I don't believe in it."

"Why *do* you wear it?"

"My parents gave it to me when I was twelve. At my Confirmation. Catholic upbringing. I wear it because they gave it to me. I stopped believing in that stuff long ago, about the time I realized there was no Father Christmas." He gave a warm smile, reminiscing about family and Christmas. As much as his dad was often absent, he had always been around for Christmas. "But if I'm honest with myself, I think I've been searching for something to believe in."

They looked at each other for a long while. Riley was intrigued. Ethan wasn't like any of the men she'd met. He was open. Real. He didn't need to pretend to be something to impress anyone. He seemed to be happy with who he was, even in the midst of the turmoil he must be going through. To lose a brother so young, and so suddenly, and not be bitter with the world or angry with god. And to be so open about what he believed in.

"Hey, um," Riley began. "This is going to sound a bit forward, but are you free tomorrow night?"

Ethan raised his eyebrows, unable to hide his surprise.

"What? Um. Sure. What for?" he said.

"One of my friends is having a thing at her place, and everyone's bringing a partner. If I arrive alone, I'm going to feel like a spare wheel. Wanna be my plus one?"

"Ok," Ethan said, not certain of what he'd just let himself in for.

"My friends can be a little crazy, I'm just warning you."

"I can handle crazy," Ethan said bravely. Inside he was suddenly a mix of excited and nervous. He liked this girl. He had from the moment he first met her. "Do you think they can handle me?" he asked, pointing to his swollen, bruised face.

"I'll just tell them you said something I didn't like and this is how I handled the situation," Riley smiled.

Ethan laughed. "I like a girl who can handle herself," he said. He found himself staring into her eyes. They drew him inside. For a moment he was completely mesmerized, and unable to say anything at all. Riley seemed to be caught up in Ethan too.

"So, tell me about your crazy friends," Ethan said eventually to break the silence. He could swear she had moved a few inches closer to him, drawn like a floating magnet to a solid metal mass.

"Oh, yeah, I shouldn't be saying this but you don't know what you've just let yourself in for. Eleni is my favorite friend. But don't tell anyone that, because it'll piss Jenna off."

Ethan held up two fingers. "Promise," he said.

"She's cool, you'll like her. Everyone likes her. And you'll like Blake, her boyfriend. He's a nice guy, I think the two of you will get along well."

"Uh huh," Ethan said, making mental notes of names. He'd forget everything by tomorrow.

"Then there's Jenna. Beware of Jenna," Riley warned.

Ethan cocked his head to one side.

"Jenna is opinionated, and she believes that the entire universe was built for her. Don't ask me how come we're still friends, but we're about as different as two people can be. As much as she is hard work though, when she's your friend she'll fight tooth and nail for you."

Ethan nodded again, adding Jenna to his mental note pad.

"But then every now and again she has a speed wobble, and she becomes a real bitch."

"Ok," Ethan said.

"She hasn't got a boyfriend, but I'm sure she'll arrive with some older, helluva wealthy daddy figure tomorrow. I don't think I've ever seen her with the same guy twice. She's like a black widow. She leaves a trail of corpses. Except sometimes she's the collateral damage." Riley thought of Jenna's recent encounter with Grant and wondered if there was any justice in the world, if Karma really would catch up to him. Guys like Grant who prey on weak willed women deserve a special place in hell, she thought.

"I'll steer clear of Jenna," Ethan suggested.

"She'll question you worse than the Spanish Inquisition," Riley cautioned. "You won't be able to avoid her. She's going to grill you, just be warned. Tell her we've just met, that's all. Don't tell her we're just friends, or she'll berate you that I'm not important enough for you. I told you – she fights for her friends. Most of the time without being asked to."

"Ok. Anyone else going to be there that I should know about?" Ethan asked with trepidation.

"Those are my closest friends. I'm sure Jenna will have a lot of other strays that she's just met and wants to impress."

They'd been talking for over two hours when Ethan eventually kissed Riley on the cheek and said goodbye. He would meet her at a rooftop bar close to Jenna's place on Friday for a drink before the party, and they'd go from there.

Abe stood next to a buffet table laden with food in a room filled with friends and family, all talking loudly to one another. Two large round tables occupied the living room of the ornate house, around which plastic chairs had been crammed for the occasion, and most of them were occupied by Sylvie's friends and family. He popped a small canapé made of *kichel* and chopped herring into his mouth, when his phone rang. "Hey, Ethan," he spoke through a mouthful of food. "What's up?"

"Sounds like you're at a party?" Ethan said.

"Breaking of the fast at Aunt Sylvie's," Abe explained.

"Oh yeah. Sorry, I forgot it was a Jewish holiday," Ethan apologized.

"It's ok," Abe said. He was planning his attack on the buffet as he spoke. "The holiday was yesterday till this evening. The fast is over, I'm not going to be struck down by lightening for talking on my phone. Now we're eating like there's just been a famine."

"Did you fast?" Ethan asked. Abe wasn't known for observing Jewish traditions.

"I did, actually," Abe said. "Surprised myself. I wasn't going to, but I woke up at about eleven this morning, and by that stage there was only eight hours of the fast left, so I thought, *what the hell*."

"Ok," Ethan said. "Whatever floats your boat."

"So what's up?" Abe had an empty plate in his hand, which he placed on the table alongside a platter of baked salmon, and began to dish up a delectable, pink slice. He moved to the collection of salads next in line.

"I think I just met the girl I'm going to marry," Ethan said.

"What? Don't talk shit?" Abe said. Aunt Sylvie glared at him from the opposite end of the table. Abe smiled apologetically and turned his attention to a salad of fresh greens, sliced avocado and papaya, topped with caramelized nuts that was begging to be added to his plate.

"I'm serious. I met her at the hospital yesterday."

"You picking up girls at the hospital now?" Abe asked, dishing up some of the papaya salad. "That's a bit desperate." Abe moved one step to his left.

"Thanks for the flowers, by the way. Remind me next time you're flat on your back."

"Sorry, Ethan. I didn't look at my phone the whole of yesterday," Abe apologized.

"You *were* taking this seriously," Ethan said. Abe had now moved on to some fried fish, which he added to his plate using a pair of shiny silver tongs.

"Like I said, I surprised myself. So you met her at the hospital? What is she – a nurse?" Abe asked, moving on to a platter of smoked salmon.

"She's a transplant coordinator. Hectic job."

"A what?" Abe asked. His plate was now running out of real estate. He headed for a table on the patio, away from the din of the family gabble.

Ethan explained Riley's day job.

"Jeez," Abe remarked. "Sounds like a hell of a job. Is she pretty?"

"Very."

"And you like her?" Abe found himself smiling, enviously.

"We've only had one date, but she asked me to go with her tomorrow to some party at one of her friends," Ethan said.

"Good sign," Abe said. He took a bite of the baked salmon. "Mmmm," he said loudly with a mouth full of food. "This is so good."

"Am I interrupting supper?" Ethan asked.

"Nah, don't worry about it. I'll go back inside when we're done talking. Its family, I'll see them again. This is more important.

Ethan's finally found someone."

A group of kids came bounding through the doorway to the patio laughing loudly, followed by two Beagles.

"I get a feeling about her I've never had with anyone before," Ethan said. "She's got her head screwed on right. She's just...I don't know, I can't explain it. Like I just know. Does this sound weird?"

"For you, yes," Abe said, watching the kids playing in the garden outside. "You're the eternal cynic. I don't remember any woman you've met that you haven't immediately found something wrong with. The last one was too clingy. The one before that was too fake. The one before that..."

"...I get the point," Ethan interrupted. "And yeah, you're right. There's always been something. But not with Riley."

"Riley, huh?"

"Yeah. Riley O'Connor," Ethan said.

"Irish?" Abe plunged a fork into a piece of smoked salmon.

"Somewhere I guess. Doesn't speak in an Irish accent."

"I love that Irish accent," Abe said. "I think I'm going to make that my goal in life. To marry a girl with an Irish accent."

"Isn't your family, like, full on Jewish? Won't your mom have something to say if you don't marry a Jewish girl?" Ethan asked.

"Jeez, you and my sister both. Enough already." Abe looked around self consciously, as if the kids playing on the jungle gym, plus the two bounding Beagles were listening. "I think I'm in the middle of a religious crisis, man. You know I dropped shul the day after my bar-mitzvah, and I haven't been back except under duress, but today got me thinking."

"Really? You? I never would have thought."

"Yeah, I don't know, man," Abe toyed with another piece of smoked salmon on the plate. "Either I am or I'm not, you know what I mean? But I've been sitting in no-man's land pretending to be one thing for the last ten years, and I've either got to drop it and behave like I really feel inside, or I've got to take it on for real."

"I can't see you becoming all religious, my friend," Ethan said.

He made a face as he realized why he'd just said that to Abe. He was afraid of losing his friend. He didn't want him to become different. The observant Jews he'd worked with were a world within a world. Living one set of beliefs within a world that held a different set, endeavoring to ignore the one around them while they tried desperately to hang on to a five thousand year old religion that hadn't evolved with the times. He didn't want Abe to become one of those. "Just promise me you're still shaving your sideburns. And you're not going to tie string to your belt."

Abe laughed. There were people in his family like that. Ethan had seen them on occasion. "You don't have to worry about that, man," Abe said. "But today just messed with my head. So you going to this party with the new girl?"

"Yeah," Ethan replied. "Tomorrow. I get to be the new guy, paraded in front of her friends like a race-horse on show."

"Just don't snort on any of her friends," Abe laughed. "So you asked her parents yet?"

"Who?"

"The girl. Have you asked her parents if you can marry her?" Abe questioned.

Ethan laughed. "She doesn't have any, they both died when she was little."

"That's a bummer," Abe laughed. "Guess you're gonna have to pay for the whole wedding then."

"I swear, Abe, sometimes I think you have no soul."

"Just kidding, Ethan. Hey, I gotta go. I better go join the family inside or they're gonna come looking for me."

"Enjoy your dinner, Abe," Ethan said.

"Yeah, see ya." Abe hung up, picked up his plate and went back inside to join the *balagan*. There was a frenzy of conversation in the small space. Uncles sitting around one of the tables, pouring whiskey, talking about golf, football, and business. Aunts and grand parents huddled around the other, rapidly exchanging words about who was doing what with whom and to whom. Gossiping about whom they saw where, and what they were wearing. The kids that had been playing outside were now inside, running between all of them, laughing loudly and calling to each other. And somewhere in between all of them, the male Beagle was trying to hump the female. The buffet table looked like it had fallen victim to a swarm of locusts. The baked salmon was reduced to a small puddle of oil. The smoked salmon platter was now two lemons and a piece of parsley. There was still plenty of *gefilte* fish.

"Abe, where've you been, come join us." Rivki scooched a chair over and made space between her and their mother. Abe dragged a chair into the empty space and joined the circle of women and their gossip. Rivki slipped an arm around Abe's as he picked at his plate, and she joined in the conversation. He felt a sense of warmth. The kind that comes from having a place to belong. Whether he believed in his mother's religion or not, he belonged. There probably wasn't a single person at either of the two tables that really believed and observed properly, yet they were all here, celebrating this ritual. He took a deep breath, and smiled at Rivki as she spoke over the loud din to get her little piece of airtime.

This is family, Abe thought. It was as if the religion was secondary. For all of its rules and limitations, it was the rituals that kept the family together. If it weren't for these occasions, he'd probably never see most of the people in the room. He gave Rivki's arm a squeeze with his and wolfed down the rest of his dinner. There was still the dessert table to be decimated.

Riley spent a long time getting herself ready for Jenna's party. Longer than she ordinarily would have. Putting the final touches to her make up, she stood in front of the mirror in the bedroom, and put on a pair of earrings, studying the way they fitted in with her look. She felt an unexpected excitement knowing she would be seeing Ethan again. As she thought about him, she froze suddenly, staring at the image in the mirror. Someone was behind her, yet she felt peace, not fear.

It was the angel with the book.

She turned slowly, so as not to spoil what she was seeing. Her heart raced in her chest.

"Are you real?" she asked.

Now facing him, she could see the angel, hovering in front of her. He was taller than she was by over two foot, with locks of light brown hair, and a full beard. He wore a white tunic, and a white, flowing robe covered the rest of his body. Extending high up behind him was a pair of wings comprised of small grey feathers. And under his arm was a book. He reached for it, and presented it to her.

Riley stretched forward to touch it, but it was always just out of reach. Slowly the angel opened the book, and Riley's heart pounded in her chest with excitement.

"Whose story is this?" she asked.

The angel said nothing. Instead he showed her the open page, on which was an image that made Riley smile. It was a picture of a man and a woman kissing, entangled in each other's arms. She couldn't see their faces, but at the foot of the image was a time stamp. 7:53pm.

"Who's in the picture?" she asked.

The angel closed the book, and faded into nothing. As quickly as the angel had appeared, Riley suddenly found herself standing alone, one arm outstretched to where the book had been. She covered her mouth with her hand, and stood there for a moment, her heart racing. She had just seen an angel on her own, for the first time. And she had seen something about to happen in the future, the very near future. She checked her watch. It was 7:12pm, and almost time to leave.

Riley stopped for a moment and stared at the floor beneath the mirror. A single grey feather lay at her feet.

Riley O'Connor arrived at the rooftop bar just after seven thirty. Ethan was already waiting for her, elegantly propped up on a chrome stool at the bar, stirring a cocktail with a short straw. A second concoction stood alongside his. He looked over his shoulder as she entered, and came over to greet her. Riley smiled.

"Hey," he kissed her on the cheek. "Wow, you look amazing."

Riley wore a short, black, tight fitting dress that complemented her figure. He caught a whiff of her perfume. It was like breathing in a field of roses and jasmine.

Riley flushed. "You look pretty good yourself," she said. Ethan wore the same jacket as the previous night, but a different pair of denims and a button up shirt open at the neck. She lingered for a moment to breathe in his cologne.

"Thank you. I hope you don't mind, I ordered you a drink," he said as they moved to the empty seats at the bar counter. The rooftop bar Ethan had chosen was situated in an upmarket area. Behind the bar counter, bottles were evenly spaced against the backlit mirror, their shapes enhanced by the LED strip lights that framed each one in miniscule luminescent points.

"Not at all," Riley lied. She preferred to order her own drinks. She looked around her to take in the other patrons. There was a couple not far from them at the bar, and several more seated opposite each other at the tables lining the edge of the rooftop, against a low balustrade of waist-high clear glass, looking out over the city.

"This place makes the best Mojito in town. The bartender's a mixologist. You've never tasted one like this before." Ethan handed Riley a bubble-shaped glass, unaware of her apprehension. She smiled as she took it. Fresh mint leaves and a bashed lime floated inside. Her apprehension abated.

"Cheers," Ethan said, tapping her glass. His eyes were brown, and intense. There was a determination about him, Riley thought.

They took a sip before Ethan led her to an empty table at the edge of the bar, overlooking the city lights. Riley watched the couples they passed, and glanced at her watch. None of the ones at the tables out here were close enough to each other to be the people she saw in the book. Maybe the couple at the bar counter?

"This place is lovely," Riley said. "I haven't been here before."

"It's new," Ethan explained. "The company I work for did the interiors for the whole building."

"You worked on this?" Riley asked, becoming more impressed with this new man.

Ethan nodded. "I did a lot of the interior for this bar, and one of the offices on the second floor. You have to see that place. It's a tech marketing company. They wanted something wildly creative."

He motioned to a table, and she chose a seat that offered her a clear view of the couple at the bar counter.

"Wow," Riley said. "I really love this place. And you were right about the Mojito. Best I've ever had."

Ethan hoped she'd be saying that about him too. "I'm glad you like it. You never know, ordering a drink for someone you've just met. I took a chance. I know some women don't like that."

You don't know how right you are, Riley thought. "Well, you did ok."

"Just ok?" Ethan smiled.

"Mmm," Riley smiled. That smile looked like a flirt, Ethan thought. There was a playful warmth about it, accompanied by a particular sparkle in her eyes.

"So, Ethan Lynch, are you ready for this?" she asked.

"To meet your friends? Sure," Ethan said bravely.

"If you say so," she laughed.

"Are they really that bad?"

"Not all of them." Riley said. "Just some." She smiled at him over her bubble shaped glass, and Ethan watched her lips as she sipped her drink. "It's really beautiful up here." Riley looked out over the lights of the city. "I love being up high, looking out over the city. It's always been one of my favorite places to be."

"Me too," Ethan said. "Ever since I was a kid. Grew up in apartments, and spent many long hours staring out the window. Watching the people below. Wondering who lived in all the windows around me. Watching the sun set between the buildings. Until my dad started his own company and we moved into a house in the suburbs."

Riley smiled. "I'm the opposite. I grew up away from the city, in a house. Never got the chance to be up high till I started college. My dorm was on the second floor, but I'd go up on the roof often, when I needed to take a break and get away from everything. Find some space to be on my own. I used to love it up there. And then studying stopped and life began, and all that blurred into days and days of … stuff." She played with her glass as she spoke. "Your job sounds interesting."

"What, me? It's ok. I guess. I enjoy it, but it's not as glamorous as it sounds. When we did this place, for example, there was a team of about fifteen, and I just did the dog work, really. Did the drawings for the designs the senior guys came up with. It's going to take a few more years before I get to do the interesting stuff. I want to be taking client meetings, getting the brief, designing the concept, and handing it to a team to execute." He looked at her with a smile. "But that's still a few years away. You must have some stories to tell?"

"I do, but they all have two sides. A happy one and a sad one. Sometimes tragic. I don't think you want deep and sad stories tonight."

"Tell me about some of the happier ones then," he said.

Riley drained the last of her Mojito. "This was really good."

"Told you it would be," Ethan looked at his watch. They still had a few minutes before 8:00pm.

"Last week I gave a twenty three year old girl a new heart," she said, looking at Ethan with a warm smile as she remembered the look on Betty's face. "This week I gave a twenty one year old girl a chance to live a normal life. She had a degenerative kidney disease. She was confined to bed, and she literally had hours left before her kidney packed in. She was on the transplant list, but kept being bumped down. There were three times where we'd scheduled the transplant, and then another more urgent case took priority. Her family were preparing for the worst. They knew it was just a matter of hours. And then the miracle they'd been waiting for happened. A donor kidney became available, and I got there as fast as I could, got her in that O.R. before the kidney could be reassigned. When she woke up – I can't describe what it's like to give someone a second chance at life. Imagine knowing you're going to die, and there's nothing you can do to stop it, and then literally minutes before you know you're going to die, someone shows you a miracle, and you get to live."

Riley was smiling, and her face exuded a kind of deep-rooted contentment and joy that Ethan rarely saw. He'd encountered dozens of people in his line of work, on the surface content with life, but none this happy. Clients spending millions on new offices, new restaurants like this one. There was an emptiness in their eyes when he met with them. They concerned themselves with building things that were beautiful on the outside, but there was no love to what they did. It was all business. Risk and return. Calculated. But with Riley, her love for what she did radiated from her smile to the sparkle in her eyes.

"You're an amazing woman, Riley," Ethan said, catching her by surprise.

"Really?"

"I don't do this often, but…" he moved to the empty chair next to her, took her glass from her hand and placed it on the table, leaned forward, and kissed her. She drew herself towards him, as if he was the place she had always wanted to be. She tasted sweet, and Ethan felt her quick breaths against his skin.

As they pulled apart for a moment, Riley smiled and was about to say something when her eyes widened.

"Oh my god," she whispered, looking over Ethan's shoulder. She flipped her wrist and glanced at the time. It was 7:52pm.

"What? I'm sorry I shouldn't have…"

But Riley placed a finger gently on his lips, still staring.

"Shh. It's not you at all. It's the angel with the book. He's here right now."

"Really? Now?" Ethan felt his heart drop.

"He's right here. Right behind you, holding a book. I can see him, as clearly as I can see you."

Riley's face was beaming, and Ethan felt dejected once again.

His advance had just been overshadowed by a presence with whom he could never compete. Just as quickly as the angel had appeared, he was gone, and Riley blinked. She squeezed Ethan's hand hard.

"Ethan. I saw him again. I saw the angel," she said excitedly.

"Yeah, I gather," Ethan said flatly, trying to smile, but it wasn't convincing. Riley hardly noticed.

"Oh my god, I can't believe this," she said, hand on her heart. "Do you know what this means? I've seen him three times now."

"I guess it means you can talk to angels?" Ethan said flatly.

"Not any angels, just this one," she corrected him, "I went to a reading with Angel Martin, and I honestly never had any yearning to see angels. I knew that angels existed, and I was happy to let Martin tell me what my angels were saying, but I never in my wildest dreams thought I'd be able to see them for myself. This is huge, Ethan." She thought again about telling Ethan what she'd seen earlier, how the angel had predicted that they would kiss, but decided against it. "This is the most significant day of my life."

Again, Ethan forced a smile. He had just braved their first kiss, only to be completely dwarfed by the appearance of this angel. He was about to check his watch and suggest that they get to the party, when Riley surprised him by throwing her arms around his neck, and kissing him passionately, more so than a moment ago. Riley wasn't looking, but if she had checked her watch again, it would have read 7:53pm, the exact moment the angel had foretold that they would be wrapped up in a passionate embrace.

They spent long moments in each other's arms kissing, and Ethan's ill feeling about the angel's interruption dissipated quickly.

"I've never met anyone like you," Ethan said between breaths.

"Me neither," Riley replied. She kissed him so hard their teeth collided. "Sorry."

"It's ok."

"I feel like I've known you forever," Riley said.

"I do too," Ethan said. He looked at her for a long moment, one that made him feel giddy. "It's the strangest thing. It's like we're meant to be here. Together."

Riley was about to tell him what the angel had predicted, but instead kissed him once more, and said, "We should get to the party."

"I guess," Ethan conceded.

They left the bar joined at the hip, Ethan's arm holding Riley close, and Riley clinging tightly to him.

"Nice place," Ethan said, as the concierge opened the door for them.

"Yeah," Riley said. "Evening, Hamish," she greeted the concierge. He was an old man, in his seventies. Hamish smiled warmly at her, and waved her towards the elevators.

"He's been here since they built this place," Riley explained as the entered the elevator. As the doors closed, Ethan drew her close and they kissed until the doors opened on the fourteenth floor.

They heard the thumping of the music as they walked down the hallway towards Jenna's apartment. Riley pressed the buzzer and Jenna answered moments later, shrieking loudly.

"Hi," she sang, drawing out the word into a long, shrill chorus as she hugged Riley. "Is this…?"

Riley nodded. "Ethan. Jenna," she did the introductions. Jenna took Ethan by the hand.

"Come on in. Everyone's already here."

Ethan followed her in, and Riley trailed behind.

"Everyone, this is Ethan, Riley's new boyfriend," Jenna announced at the top of her voice.

"Hey, easy," Riley tried to stop her, but everyone in the room had already heard Jenna's announcement and was looking at Ethan.

"Sorry," Riley caught up with them. She took Ethan's hand and spoke in his ear, over the music. "See? I warned you about her."

Ethan smiled. "I'll play the part of your boyfriend," he reassured her. Riley shook her head. She'd often wondered why she maintained her friendship with Jenna, and this was another one of those times. Riley glared at Jenna, but her friend ignored her. It was Jenna's way. It had always been her way. Stealing people's thunder. Putting them on the spot. Anything to draw attention to herself. She seemed to have completely forgotten about crying on Riley's shoulder just a few days before.

"Come on. Let me introduce you to Eleni and Blake." Riley led Ethan away from Jenna and into the crowded room. "You'll like them."

She found Eleni and her boyfriend by the drinks cabinet, and everyone introduced themselves.

They spent most of the evening with Eleni and Blake. The four of them made good company. The girls let the men ask about each other's work and sports interests, and eventually they found themselves laughing and talking most of the night away. The host occasionally drifted to their corner, but largely left them alone until she reappeared towards the end of the evening. She had had a good many drinks, and was louder than usual. Jenna curled an arm tightly around Ethan's neck, and stood on tiptoes to get her mouth close to his ear.

"Fuck with my friend, and you fuck with me!" she warned.

Ethan didn't try to hide his surprise at the unexpected confrontation.

"I'll take that as a warning," he said to Jenna.

"You do that," she said, pulling away, and then left the group again to mingle elsewhere.

"What was that about?" Riley asked.

"She just threatened me," Ethan said. "I think."

"Did she give you the *don't fuck with my friend* thing?" Blake asked.

Ethan nodded.

"Oh, I got that too," Blake laughed loudly.

"Then I don't feel quite so shit scared right now," Ethan smiled at Riley. She returned his smile and whispered in his ear, "I think I have an emergency I have to attend to." She pulled Ethan away from Blake and Eleni, and led him down the small hallway and into Jenna's bedroom, where she pressed herself hard up against him.

"There was something very important we were discussing before we had to come to the party," she said, kissing him once more.

Ethan didn't have a moment to reply with a witty response. He held her tightly, and they kissed passionately in the privacy of Jenna's room.

They left the party after midnight. Ethan accompanied Riley in a cab to her place, and they sat huddled in the back seat as the car moved through the empty streets.

"Quite a party," Ethan said.

"Yeah. That's Jenna, I'm afraid. You survived her though." Riley patted his shoulder.

"She wasn't that bad," Ethan smiled. Jenna's last warning in his ear still bothered him. He was sure she was just mouthing off, but he couldn't tell if she was actually serious.

Riley's mind went back to the angel. She thought about telling Ethan what she had seen before she met up with him at the bar.

"If you could see what was going to happen to you in the future, would you want to know?" she asked instead.

"I don't know," he thought out loud, surprised by Riley's question that came out of nowhere. "I don't think I'd want to know. If I knew what was going to happen to me, and it was something horrible, I'd try to avoid it. Like if I knew I was going to be in a car accident one day, I'd stay at home. Or take the train. Anything to keep away from the roads. I think if you know your future you have the power to change it. Don't you?"

Riley recalled the warnings she'd heard from Haniel about knowing the future. Her brief encounter with the angel shortly before meeting Ethan at the bar came to mind too.

"Maybe knowing the future is more like a guiding beacon. Maybe if you know what's going to happen, but you can't change it, it just helps you deal with it better." She wondered though. She knew that two people would be kissing at 7:53pm, but it didn't really help her to know. She never imagined that it would be her, and she'd done nothing to bring about or change what she'd seen. If anything, Ethan, who hadn't seen the future the way she had, made it happen. Riley convinced herself that it was a good thing to know the future, despite Haniel's warning.

"I still wouldn't want to know. If I'm going to die, I don't want to know it's coming." Ethan said.

Riley pondered for a moment, then changed the subject, and spoke instead about the party, and about Eleni and Blake. The angel had given her a glimpse of the future, and it had happened just the way he'd told her it would. Whether or not Ethan wanted to know his future, she certainly wanted to know hers.

She would ask the angel with the book if she ever she saw him again. She wanted to experience it once more. She'd been selected out of millions of people to see this angel, and she felt like she was almost living in parallel world, where everyone else could see one dimension and she could see a completely different one. A dimension that shed light on normality.

She nestled her head on Ethan's shoulder for the rest of the ride home, and held his hand tightly.

Ethan smiled, resting his head on hers, breathing in the scent that emanated from her hair as if it were a sacred perfume, feeling inside that as crazy as it might seem, they were made for each other, that their union was intended right from the moment they were born. And from the way she was clinging to him, it looked like Riley felt the same.

Riley watched the cab pull away as she unlocked her apartment door and disappeared inside. She took the elevator to the eighth floor, unaware that she was still smiling, feeling light, and bursting with energy. Dropping her handbag next to her bed she kicked off her shoes and slumped down on the mattress, bouncing briefly on her back, and called Eleni, even though it was almost one in the morning.

"Are you crazy?" Eleni whispered as she answered the phone.

"Are you still awake?" Riley asked.

"Yeah, well even if I wasn't..." Eleni began.

"Isn't he amazing?" Riley asked, rhetorically.

"I think he's your someone," her friend said. "The two of you just looked so right together."

"Didn't we?" Riley said. "I know we've only just met, but I have such a good feeling about him. Like this is the one. This is my guy. Am I being silly?"

Eleni yawned. "Is there ever anything logical about love? Love makes you do stupid things."

"You're not being very helpful," Riley said.

"Just don't go running off to Vegas to get married or anything. I'm expecting a big wedding," Eleni said. "And I want to be maid of honor."

"Not so fast," Riley cautioned. "I like him a lot, but let's not be too hasty."

"I get a good feeling about him too. I think the two of you will be good together." Eleni yawned again.

"Am I keeping you up?" Riley asked.

"No, I was going to answer the phone anyway," Eleni said.

"Fine. I just wanted to hear what you had to say about him," Riley smiled. "Goodnight."

"Sweet dreams."

Riley hung up the phone and drifted off to sleep, lying diagonally across the bed. She woke dreamily some time around 3:00am, wriggled out of her clothes, and slipped under the covers.

Chapter 7

When the alarm broke her slumber at 6:00am Riley woke feeling disoriented for a moment. She'd been dreaming about the angel, but her dream felt so real. She was following him through a field of wild flowers somewhere she'd never been. She could actually smell the freshness of the outdoors, and the scent of the morning dew on the grass. In the distance she saw something small and dark. The angel led her towards it. The closer she came, the more the object looked like a person, lying in the grass, curled up, with its back to her. It looked like a man, and he was wearing Ethan's jacket, but then her alarm woke her from her dream. She lay awake, trying to recall the last moments, trying to imagine Ethan waking up from his sleep in the long grass, and calling to her. She would fall into his arms and they'd kiss in the wild flowers, but the dream had ended. She lay under the covers for a long while, trying to recreate the dream but eventually had to throw the duvet aside and drag herself out of bed.

Sitting at the kitchen counter over a cup of coffee and some toast and peanut butter, she spoke out loud. "Can you hear me?" she asked, looking around. "Can I call you?" There was silence, and Riley was thankful she was alone. She'd look pretty stupid talking to herself if anyone had been watching. "How does this work?" she asked again. Since her monologue was going unanswered, she tucked into a piece of her breakfast, and carried on talking with her mouth full of crunchy toast. No one was paying her any attention anyway. "I was hoping to see more of the future," she said sipping her coffee. "If you wouldn't mind. I mean, I thought it was pretty cool. To see what was going to happen. And I've never done that before. Looked into the future. Hell, I've never even seen an angel. Until you. Are you even here?" She looked around again. "Can you even hear me?" There was a long silence.

Breakfast was finished, and Riley moved her empty plate to the kitchen sink. "I've gotta get to work now, so, see you? Maybe?" She let her words hang in the air, but still there was no sign of the angel with the book. "Ok then." She lingered at the door, but still nothing.

Riley locked her apartment and took the elevator down to the basement, where she climbed into the SUV, which was branded with the city's Department of Health emblem. She turned the key in the ignition and the big machine hummed instantly.

Her drive to work was usually a slow progression, an exercise in gaining ground, inch by inch. She'd realized a long time ago that she couldn't fight the traffic, so the best thing to do was tune into some good music and enjoy the commute.

At one intersection, after about twenty-five minutes of slow going, the light turned green, and the queue of cars ahead of her began to move slowly.

"Come on!" she urged, as the car before her took a while to get going. As it did, the light turned orange.

"Damn!" Riley cursed. The car in front of her crossed the intersection, and Riley figured if she punched it she could shoot across the junction, just as the light turned red. She made a quick decision, and floored the accelerator. The car lurched forward seconds after the light turned red. Instantly she regretted her decision. From her right, a car came tearing through the intersection, and Riley T-boned it, sending the other car spinning, and crashing into the traffic light.

"Shit!" she cursed. "Shit!" Riley hit the brakes. She left the SUV in the middle of the intersection and ran to the other car.

The red Ford was billowing steam from the engine. Its windshield was shattered and through the side window, Riley could see a person compressed between the airbag and the seat. As the airbag deflated, Riley saw the driver more clearly. It was a young woman in her early twenties with long black hair. She was conscious, and disoriented. Immediately, Riley went to open the door but it was locked. She hammered her fist on the window. As she did, she noticed a crowd gathering around the scene, and she swallowed hard. This was her fault. There was no disputing that. And there were dozens of witnesses, all holding their cell phones out in front of them as if they'd been primed like a flash mob.

"Somebody call 911!" Riley yelled to the crowd. A young man began to dial immediately. "Can you open the door?" Riley called to the girl in the car. "Are you ok?" She hammered repeatedly on the window, calling again and again as the girl inside lolled her head, and gazed at Riley, still disoriented. She looked around her, and took in the shattered windshield, and the bent traffic light right in the center of the Ford's bonnet, saw the steam rising from the engine, and realized what had happened. She tried to move, but the seat belt had pulled tight, and she had to push herself back in her seat a few times before the tension lock released. As she moved, she cried out in agony.

"Can you open the door?" Riley demanded loudly, pulling again and again at the door handle. She felt a sharp pain as one of her fingernails splintered and cracked under the door handle. The woman inside reached for the door from the inside, and opened it. "Thank god!" Riley breathed, and yanked the door open, immediately leaning inside. The girl's face was already swelling from the impact of the airbag. "I'm going to unclip the seat beat, ok, but don't move if anything hurts. Can you move?"

The girl tried to shift her legs, and winced, holding her ribs. "It hurts," she groaned. "I think it's broken". She placed her feet on the ground, holding her broken ribs tenderly. Riley took her hand and helped her stand. A palpable wave of relief swept over the spectators.

"She's ok," Riley heard one voice saying, and several others chorusing, "Thank god," as she helped the unsteady girl to the sidewalk, and sat her down. The girl was bleeding from a cut in her arm, probably scratched when the airbag deployed. As Riley stood back, she noticed some blood on her sleeve.

Riley felt ill. If she'd only waited at that traffic light instead of rushing, this would never have happened.

"Dammit!" Riley cursed, reprimanding herself, but as she spoke the words, she felt as if she was being pulled back, as if everything she'd just experienced was reversing in fast motion. The accident victim was back in her car, slumped against the airbag. Riley was back in her SUV. Then she was moving quickly backwards, watching the moment of impact in reverse, then travelling backwards, with street lights, traffic and buildings whizzing past in front of her until she was back in the basement of her apartment, then walking backwards up the stairs until she was standing at her apartment door, not locking it, but unlocking it, and then moving backwards to the kitchen sink, where everything suddenly reverted to normality.

Riley stared around her. She was in her kitchen. Exactly where she'd been before she left for work. In front of her was the empty plate with crumbs of toast and a smudge of peanut butter, and next to it was her empty coffee cup. What had just happened? She looked around her and found herself staring into the face of the angel with the book. He was holding it open, and Riley understood immediately. He wasn't *telling* her what was going to happen in her future. He'd just *shown* her.

"That's going to happen to me today?" Riley asked, a feeling of desperation and helplessness overcoming her. "I'm going to do that?" she said in disbelief. The angel remained still in front of her, holding the book open. Riley looked down at her hand, outstretched towards the open page. Had she touched it? Had she touched the book, and lived her future? Then the angel vanished and left Riley in a deathly silence. It was as if all the noise in the entire city had been sucked into a vacuum in that moment, and the absolute lack of any sound echoed loudly in her ears.

Riley rested both hands on the sink, and breathed heavily for a moment. It felt so real. She was there! Right there, standing over that poor girl in the red car, with plumes of steam coming out of the engine. She'd heard the hiss of the airbag, felt the heat of the engine, and broken a nail trying to pull the door open, even got blood on her shirt. She looked at her sleeve but the blood was gone, and her nails were still intact. There was no way she could leave the SUV parked in the basement and take the bus. It was part of her job, being able to deliver donor organs as quickly as possible. Riley picked up the car keys and stared at them as if they were some vile disease.

She drove to work overly cautious. Traffic was fairly heavy, so she didn't need to worry about her speed, but she left bigger gaps between her car and the ones in front. She looked more than twice in each direction when she approached an intersection. But her heart began to pound in her chest when she approached the traffic light she'd seen in her earlier vision. The light had just turned amber, but instead of flooring the accelerator as she had in her vision, she slowed, and stopped at the red light. The accident was so vivid in her memory. Cars began to cross the intersection in front of her, and Riley found herself looking for the red Ford, but there was no sign of it by the time the light turned green. She wondered what the vision was supposed to mean. Was it a glimpse of her future? Was it a warning? Was it supposed to have happened *today*? What if it wasn't today? What if what she saw was some time in the future?

Hooters blared behind her and Riley realized she was holding up the line of cars. She waved a hand in apology and moved forward slowly, expecting at any moment that the red Ford would come barreling through the intersection.

"Morning. You look like you've seen a ghost," Tom said as Riley walked into the office on the third floor. He was older than her by about fifteen years, greying at the temples in a way that makes men look inexplicably attractive, and was just on the comfortable side of athletic.

"Morning Tom," Riley said. "I think I did." She went over to her desk in the tiny office, dumped her laptop bag on it and stared out the window, which overlooked the parking lot of the hospital. It was already packed full of cars, and she watched as visitors circled and hovered trying to find a parking space.

"So?" Tom said, standing behind her, holding a wad of files against his chest in one arm while sipping coffee with his free hand. "Did you or didn't you?"

"You're not going to believe me if I told you," Riley said.

"Fine," Tom replied, leaving Riley to her window while he went over to Agnes' desk and dropped the files on top of it. Agnes was older than Tom, the mother hen of the office, keeper of order, but not law.

"Thanks," Agnes lied.

Riley couldn't keep this to herself any more.

"Ok," she said turning to face the other two, "I'll tell you, but promise you won't think I'm going all weird?"

Agnes looked up and Tom turned to face her, leaning against Agnes' desk. Riley noticed Agnes' eyes drop in the direction of Tom's behind for a moment, and smiled.

"Do you believe in angels?" she asked. Agnes shrugged, and Tom raised his eyebrows.

"I'm interested, let's put it that way," Agnes said. "Got a million books on angels at home. Read them all, but ask me what I believe?" She held her hands up in the air. "Not sure. I hear about them, and you watch those people talking to people on the other side who've crossed over, but I don't pay it much attention. I'm an atheist, I'll tell you that straight with no apologies. My parents were both like, heavy Christians, dragged me to church till the day I moved out of home, and I've never been back. Never believed that stuff, never will. But spirits and angels – I dunno. Maybe."

Tom shrugged. "I'm Greek Orthodox," he said. "We're not supposed to." Tom was in his early forties. He wouldn't call himself a religious man, but he was born Greek and therefore was part of the Greek Church by default. Most Greeks found it obligatory to be in Church at least once a year at Easter, and there were a handful who went each Sunday, whether as a result of their belief, or as a tribute in return for absolution. For Tom it ran deeper. He'd been deeply moved at his Confirmation, and although he didn't make the weekly pilgrimage, he still held his reverence for his god in high regard. The people at the office knew him as a good man, although not spiritual.

"Alright," Riley began. "A couple of weeks ago, me and my friends were talking and Jenna mentioned this medium she'd seen who told her stuff about herself that nobody could have known. And things about her future."

Tom squinted his eyes and folded his arms defensively. Even at forty, he felt guilty for entertaining the discussion that the pastor at his church would have cut off immediately as a gateway to the Occult.

"So what did he say about her?" Agnes asked.

"It wasn't so much what he said about *her*, but I went to see him a few days after."

"Oooh?" Agnes perked up, leaning forward. She clasped her fingers under her chin. Agnes' bookshelf at home was filled with everything mystical. Crystals and healing. Angels. Metaphysics. Psychics and spirits. Around her neck, she wore an amethyst on a long chain that she'd bought at a psychic fair a few years ago, and she thumbed it subconsciously as she listened. Tom was skeptical.

"He calls himself Angel Martin. To cut a long story short, he said he saw, literally every person I've ever touched. People who have died whose organs I placed," Riley continued.

"I've got prickles," Agnes said, rubbing her arms.

"He mentioned them by name, almost every one of them. He couldn't have known who they were unless…"

"Unless they spoke to him," Tom added. He dropped his arms, and held on to the edge of Agnes' desk.

"But that's not the very weird part," Riley waved a hand.

"There's more?" Tom was visibly surprised.

"Yes. He said he saw an angel he'd never seen before, one carrying a book, and then later on I met this other guy, Archer, who's been following me around the hospital for months."

"Woah," Agnes said, holding both hands up like a traffic cop at an intersection. "Someone's been stalking you? Here?"

"Kinda, but not exactly. Listen," Riley implored. Agnes replaced her hands under her chin and Riley continued. "He says he also saw this angel with the book, but only around me."

"Ok, you're right," Tom said, pushing himself off Agnes' desk, and wheeling a chair around from his own desk into the middle of the room. "I am beginning to think you're a bit weird. I can call psychiatry for a consult."

"Oh shut it, Tom, I want to hear the rest," Agnes chided. Both her and Tom looked expectantly at Riley.

"Alright, so this guy, Archer, said he only sees this angel with the book when he's around me, and he tells me he can see the angel, and that someone is going to die at 5:48."

"He told you that?" Agnes asked. "And then?"

Tom was in a state of flux. His religious dogma called this the work of the devil.

"And then I took him to one of my donor patients that was at death's door. The time of death was called at 5:48."

"Oh god, I've got frikkin' goose bumps again," Agnes rubbed her arms vigorously.

"And then just after that, I was still at the hospital, and I met this guy, Ethan."

"Another medium?" Agnes asked.

"No," Riley smiled. "He'd been beaten up on Eighth Street."

"Oh. Ok," said Agnes.

"And Archer was there too, and when I was with Ethan and Archer, I saw the angel with the book. I saw him with my own eyes."

"You saw an angel?" Tom asked.

"I did, I swear to you. It was late afternoon, and I saw him. He was big, like eight feet tall, long flowing hair and a beard, and wings, oh my god, they were beautiful." Riley looked past the people in the room. She could see the angel vividly in her mind, as if he were standing in front of her at that moment.

The room was silent for a long moment.

"And then I saw him again this morning, and he..." Riley searched for the word "...he showed me my future. It was like I was in a movie of my own life. I had a car accident because I shot a red light."

"What, now?" Agnes asked.

"No, in my vision."

"You had a vision of your future?" Tom asked.

Riley nodded. "It was real. It was so real. I hit this red car, and there was a girl with long black hair, and I T-boned her car, and she was bruised, and had broken ribs. So when I did drive to work today, I drove extra careful."

"And you didn't hit anyone?" Agnes asked, one hand over her mouth, the other rubbing her crystal.

Riley shook her head. "So when you asked if I'd seen a ghost, Tom, I kinda had seen one. A real one."

"Jeez," Tom said slowly. "That's..." He searched for a word.

"That's frikkin incredible," Agnes interjected.

"Yeah," Tom agreed. "Incredible." His words were more cynical.

"I know, right?" Riley said. "I'm not sure what's happening to me. I don't know what I saw exactly, if it was something that was going to happen today, or some day in the future, or just a warning not to shoot red lights."

"You still look pretty shaken up. Come on, let's get you some coffee," Tom said, hoping to change the subject. "We've still got work to do today, you know." He pointed to a stack of files on his desk.

"Yeah, I know. Sorry," she said.

"It's ok," Tom replied, walking with Riley to the small kitchen that was some distance along the hall.

"You think I'm weird, don't you?" Riley asked as they walked down the hallway. Although Tom didn't speak openly about his beliefs, Riley had him pegged for a conservative.

The third floor of the hospital was largely consulting rooms and admin offices. People walked the hallway in both directions. Patients seeing doctors. Doctors and hospital staff moving between the wards on the lower level and their rooms.

Tom shook his head, conflicted inside. "Nah," he said. "Not at all." The spiritual world was supposed to be a gateway to the devil himself. Opening yourself up to spirits and talking to people who had crossed over was opening yourself up to possession by demons. But Riley? He'd worked with her for years. Talking to angels? That didn't fit. Angels were supposed to come from heaven. Spirits from hell. How could she be talking to both of them? Together. It didn't make sense. Like so many contradictions he'd heard over the years. Stories that people had told him of their own experiences that contradicted so many of his Church's religious teachings. "You saw what you saw."

They stood in silence as they waited for the kettle to boil.

"We didn't offer Agnes any tea," Riley said.

"She drinks that herbal tea," Tom said. "Same tea bag every day. Maybe just take her some boiling water for a refill."

Tom waited as Riley poured herself a cup of coffee, and then took the kettle full of hot water with her as they left the kitchen to head back to their office.

Riley didn't see the woman running down the corridor as she turned the corner from the kitchen into the hallway. The woman bumped into Riley, knocking the kettle from her hand. She screamed as she fell to the linoleum floor, covered in boiling water from the kettle.

"Shit!" Riley cursed. "Shit!" Then Riley froze, cold shivers running throughout her entire body. She'd spoken those exact words earlier today. In her vision. She saw Tom stooping over the woman, scooping her up to her feet, moving her swiftly down the hallway. Riley heard noises, and saw motion but took in none of it. The woman's face. It was the woman she'd seen in her vision. The same woman. It was her.

"Riley!" Tom's voice broke through her stupor. "Call ER now! She's badly burned. I'm taking her down there now. Call them!" Tom was some distance away from her, moving towards the elevators. Riley nodded, and ran to her office.

"What just happened?" Agnes looked up as Riley burst through the door.

"Fuck!" Riley cursed loudly. She was pale. "Call ER, now. Please. Tell them Tom's on his way with a burn victim."

Agnes called and gave ER the heads up. Putting down the phone, she stood, and came around to put a comforting arm around Riley's shoulder.

"Will you tell me what's going on?" she asked.

"It was her. The same woman from my vision this morning. I was bringing you hot water for your tea, and she bumped into me, and I spilled boiling water from the kettle all over her." Riley was pale.

"She's here? At the hospital?" Agnes asked. Riley nodded. They stood in silence for a long while.

"That's what your vision was about," Agnes said.

"What do you mean?" Riley asked, still dazed. "In my vision I crashed into her car."

"In your vision you hurt her badly. Your vision was showing you that you were going to hurt her somehow," Agnes said.

"You think that's it?" Riley asked, snapping back to the present.

"Your vision was about you crashing into her car, but when you came to work, you changed that because you were driving carefully. You stopped it from happening. But I think your angel was showing you that you were going to hurt this poor person one way or the other, whether it was in a car crash, or bumping her on her head, or spilling boiling water over her," Agnes suggested.

"So I didn't change the future by not running that red light," Riley said slowly.

"My opinion?" Agnes said, releasing her comforting hold on Riley's shoulder. "The future is the future. You can't change the future. It's going to happen, even if you stop one thing from happening, something else will happen, and the thing that was going to happen will still happen."

Riley screwed up her face.

"You get what I mean," Agnes said. Riley nodded. Silently trying to make sense of everything she'd experienced over the past few days. Before her session with Martin, she'd only had a mild interest in the world of spirits and angels. She would listen to the stories she'd heard with keen interest but nothing beyond that. Now, in just a few days she'd visited one medium, spoken to another, discovered her own angel, Haniel, and actually seen the angel with the book who foretold the future.

Archer had been able to see the future of other people. For him, the angel had shown him a page in a book that Archer could read, and it showed him the time of someone's death. Archer never knew who the person was, just that someone was going to die. Maybe that was a good thing, Riley thought. That he didn't know who was going to die. Could he stop it if he did? From what Archer had said, the people who had died were terminal in some way or other, and there was no way he could interfere with the future, as she had done today.

But the angel had shown Riley her own future in a very different way, she thought. Archer saw a number on a page. Riley actually lived a moment in time as if she were really there. It felt so real. It *was* real. Wasn't it? Did that future really happen, and did she travel back in time or was it a projection of her future?

Riley's mind was spiraling rapidly. What part of her day today *had* been real? Why had the angel shown her the future in such a clear and vivid way?

She had to find Archer. And Martin. Between the two of them, they would surely know.

Later in the day, Tom returned to the office, and Riley bolted out of her chair.

"Is she going to be ok?" Riley asked. Tom held a hand up and spoke calmly.

"She's going to be ok. I took her to the ER, and they immediately referred her to the Special Burns Unit. She was lucky the accident had happened here, otherwise she may not have had immediate access to specialized treatment, and the burns might have left scars. As it happens, the nurses at the Burns Unit said there's a good chance there won't be any permanent damage."

"Oh thank god," Riley said, hand on her chest. She could feel her heart thumping.

"They've given her something for the pain. She's going to be ok," Tom said. Riley breathed a huge sigh of relief. Agnes gave her a reassuring glance as their boss sat down at his desk. Sensing her uncertainty, Tom added, "It was an accident. You're not getting fired." He smiled warmly at Riley who nodded, but was still visibly apprehensive. "It happens," Tom said, but Riley still wasn't comforted.

As Tom and Agnes went back to their work, Riley thought about the angel and the future. At first she'd been excited that she could see the angel, and that she might get a glimpse of the future, but now she wasn't so sure. Maybe there was a reason Haniel had cautioned her about knowing the future.

No good can come of this.

"I need to take a walk," she said. Tom looked up.

"Take as long as you need, Riley," he said.

"You want me to come with you?" Agnes asked.

"I'm fine. Just need a few minutes alone."

Riley sat quietly in the tiny atrium. It had been built as a place for reflection and peace, a tiny enclave of sanctity within the constant activity of the hospital. It was furnished with a single cast iron bench surrounded by colorful beds of Begonias. The morning sunlight crept across the windows a few floors above her head.

No longer sure about whether she wanted to know the future or not, she wanted the guidance of someone wiser. Martin and Archer. They'd know what she was supposed to do with this gift that was turning into a burden. What was she to do if she were to learn that her future held some tragic events that couldn't be avoided? Was that not the point of being shown the future? To be able to rectify it if the future meant someone was going to get hurt? Riley didn't understand, and subconsciously spoke to the angel.

"What am I supposed to do with this?" she said in the silence of her mind, picturing the angel in front of her. As she looked up into the glass that framed the Atrium, she could see his reflection, hovering just a few meters away, on the other side of the pane. She wasn't sure if it was her own imagination or if it was really him. "What am I supposed to do with this?" she asked again. Her eyes were drawn to the book beneath his right arm, and as she gazed at it, the angel took the book in his hand and held it out to her.

Her day was uneventful until the late afternoon when it was time to pack up and head home. She looked at her watch as she slipped her laptop into its cover. It was 4:38pm.

"See you tomorrow," she said as she left Tom and Agnes, and walked down the corridor. Her heart was heavy from the incident that had plagued her day. Her feelings about the angel still swung one way and then the other within her. She took the spiral stairway that stretched up from the center of the voluminous concourse on ground level all the way up to the third floor. She descended, looking down at the people below, taking each step one at a time, her mind absorbed in her own internal conflict. She didn't notice Ethan until she was on the ground floor. He approached her from the reception desk holding an enormous bunch of red roses.

"Ethan!" she greeted him, surprised.

"Hey," he said.

"Are those for me?" she said as he handed her the flowers. People passing by looked at the two of them with admiring smiles.

"These are for you," he said. They stood there for a moment, and then kissed, oblivious of the people around them. A woman in a blue dress crossed the lobby to the elevator and stopped to speak to a man who was waiting there.

Riley was about to say something when she felt that familiar feeling. The feeling of moving backwards rapidly. Taking the flowers, but in reverse, watching them go back into Ethan's hands. Walking backwards up the stairs, ascending back to the third floor, walking backwards down the corridor, into the office, zipping her laptop away in reverse. Every moment of her day rapidly playing backwards until she was in the atrium, alone, with the morning sun shining brightly through the windows two stories above her head.

"What the hell..." she said, feeling everything around her, trying to establish what was real. She *was* in the atrium. Through the glass in front of her she could see people moving up and down the hallways like a never-ending tide. The angel was gone. Had she seen him or imagined him?

Riley returned to the office, bewildered and dazed. This had been a day like no other, and she found it difficult to focus on her work. Tom and Agnes noticed that Riley had been physically at her desk, but mentally absent. They said nothing, given the traumatic events of the morning and attributed her state of mind to the incident with the boiling water. Eventually Riley couldn't take it any longer.

"Tom, do you mind if I head home? I'm finding it hard to get anything productive done today," she asked.

It was already after 4:00pm. "Sure," Tom agreed quickly. Both he and Agnes had noticed that Riley seemed distracted by the way she'd approached her work throughout the day.

Riley packed up her things, and slid her laptop bag into its cover. She didn't look at the time. If she had, she would have noticed that it was 4:38pm. As she walked down the spiral staircase that filled the voluminous space in the hospital lobby, she argued with the angel in her head.

"I don't want this," she said silently to the angel, wondering if he'd hear her. Images of the woman in the car wreck and the burned woman in the hospital corridor returned vividly to her mind. "What am I supposed to do with this?" she asked herself. "I don't want this."

As she stepped off the spiral staircase, she looked up to see Ethan crossing the glossy, white lobby towards her carrying a bunch of red roses.

"Ethan!" she greeted him, but her voice wasn't filled with surprise as it had been in her earlier vision. Instead, her entire mood was subdued, dampened by what she'd experienced following her vision. Roses today, but what if tomorrow there's something horrible? Something unavoidable? *I don't want this,* she said inside her head. *I wish I'd been surprised by him, the way I was in the vision before. I wish I hadn't known.*

"Hey," he said.

"Are those for me?" she said without thinking, hearing the words echo in her head the moment they left her lips. Ethan handed her the flowers. Riley noticed the people passing by, watching the two of them with admiring smiles, as if in slow motion. She'd seen the woman in the blue dress in her vision before. *She's going to turn away again and talk to the man by the elevator.*

"These are for you," he said. They stood there for a moment, and then Ethan wrapped an arm around Riley's neck gently, pulling her towards him. She allowed herself to be held, kissed, despite the knowing looks from the people around her.

"Can we get out of here?" Riley asked.

"Sure," Ethan smiled. She took his arm and squeezed tightly.

"What's wrong?" he asked as they walked. He sensed something was off. Riley didn't seem upbeat as she had been on their last date.

"Not here. Take me somewhere we can drink. And talk."

Ethan regarded her questioningly. "Everything ok?" he asked.

"Nothing you need to worry about," Riley reassured him. She kissed him on the cheek as they walked.

They took a short drive to a nearby bar, a pub on a corner whose entrance was on a narrow street, with cars parked half way up the block.

"So, are you going to tell me what happened?" Ethan asked.

They entered the bar and took a small round table by the window. The bar area was newly renovated, with a highly polished wide bar counter of light wood, and beyond that was a dingy, cramped dining area, with dim lighting and old, square tables arranged in rows. The two sections looked like they belonged in different buildings.

Ethan left Riley holding her roses at the table as if they were a precious relic, while he ordered from the bar, and returned with two frosted glasses filled to within an inch of the brim and topped with an even foam.

"*Now* are you going to tell me what happened?" he asked. "Cheers." He tapped his glass against Riley's. "It's that angel thing again, isn't it?" he asked.

Riley nodded. "I don't even know where to start."

He listened as she told him about the way her day began. When she reached the part about spilling boiling water over the woman from her vision Ethan had his hand to his mouth.

"For real?" he said. Riley nodded.

"But that's not the end," Riley continued. "After that, I saw you greeting me at the bottom of the stairs with a bunch of roses."

Ethan was completely lost for words. He pointed a finger at his own chest.

"You saw me?" he said after a while. He pointed to the flowers. "With these roses?" Riley nodded. "I almost didn't get them. It was the last bunch and another guy had them in his hand, and he was about to buy them, and then he put them back again, so I snatched them up. That's so…" he searched for the word, "…freaky. That you saw me there with the roses. It was a spur of the moment thing. I was going to call you, and then I thought I'd surprise you and try catch you before you left the hospital, and the roses…I only thought of that when I saw them in the gift shop on my way into the hospital."

"I don't know what to make of this, Ethan," Riley said. "If you think its freaky, can you imagine how I feel? I'm totally freaked out."

Ethan moved his chair closer to her, and leaned his head against hers.

"I don't really care how freaky your angels are," Ethan said. "As long as they like me, because I kinda like you, and I'd hate for them to hate me."

She turned to look at him. "Is that your idea of a compliment," she said.

"Yeah, it is," Ethan said. "About the best you're going to get out of me tonight."

Riley buried her head in her hands for a moment, rubbing her face vigorously as if trying to remove an ink-blot from her forehead. "Fine, I'll take it. I don't know what's happening to me. I don't even want this. I was curious at first, but I didn't think I was going to be one of them."

"One of who?" Ethan asked.

"Those people who speak to angels. That's not me," Riley said, waving a hand in the air.

"Maybe you do speak to them. When you're helping people," Ethan suggested.

Riley thought for a moment. "You can't help it. When people are dying. And when someone gets a second chance. You can't help but feel connected to the other side."

"Did you ever wish you could speak to angels?" Ethan asked.

"I don't know. Maybe. Not that I remember anyway. Maybe I did," Riley conceded.

"I'll bet you did."

"You think?" Riley asked.

"I just don't think your angels would talk to you like this if you didn't open yourself up to it first." He ran his fingers through Riley's hair as if mesmerized by a strange and unfamiliar feeling that fascinated him. "I'm not an expert on spirits and angels, but it's just how I imagine it would be. Good spirits don't take over your body unless you ask them. Bad ones get in there without your permission."

Riley smiled. His words were reassuring. "You don't think I'm crazy?"

"I've seen bat shit crazy," Ethan said, glass in hand, pointing one finger in Riley's direction. "You're not crazy."

"Who was bat shit crazy?" she asked.

"Hmmm," he began. "You're not supposed to talk about ex's with your girlfriend."

"Your girlfriend?" she looked at him, suddenly alert, and oblivious to her dilemma about her angels and what it was doing to her mind.

"Yeah. My girlfriend." He pulled her head closer and planted a warm kiss on top of her hair.

"I like the sound of that," Riley said, allowing her head to linger close to his for a moment.

There was something about Ethan that made Riley feel comfortable. She'd heard somewhere as a kid, maybe from her mom, or from a book she'd read: *You'll know your friends better in the first minute you meet them than you'll know your acquaintances in a lifetime.* She felt that way about him. He was a gentle soul in torment, dealing with the trauma of having lost his brother, but even though he was angry at the police for dragging their heels, he was kind and gentle to her.

"You do?" Ethan smiled. "Because that just slipped out. I mean, not that it wasn't supposed to. It was. Eventually. Not right now."

Riley giggled, and they kissed as people around them, oblivious of how the world had just turned into a happier place for her and Ethan, carried on their conversations about work, and football, and government and social media.

"So do you want to do it the way you were going to do it?" Riley asked, her forehead against Ethan's, and her arms wrapped loosely around his neck.

"What? Ask you to be my girlfriend?" he asked, suddenly aware of the people around him.

"Yeah," Riley teased. Without blinking, Ethan reached behind her, took hold of the roses, and raised them till their scented petals tickled Riley's chin.

"Riley, will you be my girlfriend?" he asked. With their faces so close together, Riley looked like she had one huge eye in the center of her forehead.

"Yes," she laughed. "I will be your girlfriend, Ethan."

"Then these are for you." She released his neck and drew back just enough for him to present her with the flowers a second time.

"It's so much better when you don't know what's going to happen," she said, taking hold of the roses and breathing in their scent. "They're beautiful."

"Just like you," he said. Riley flushed. She wasn't used to being complimented. Not after the last relationship. All the sweet words Dean had said to lure her in. He'd told her she was beautiful and how much she meant to him at first. He'd told her about the life they were going to build together. They'd shared dreams and secrets. And when Riley had discovered it was all a lie, she'd bricked herself in, just as Martin had described to her. She'd built a wall around her, distrusting anything any man would say to her. If a man had told her she was beautiful, she'd brush it off as a lie, something men would say to get her into bed. Her initial response had become an automatic defense, one she had to consciously shake now. Ethan wasn't like Dean. He wasn't like anyone she'd ever met. He felt like her other half. Her soul mate.

"You ok? What's wrong?" Ethan asked.

Riley shook her head. "Nothing," she smiled. "It's nothing. Just thinking of the young woman I burned," she lied.

"It was an accident," Ethan reminded her gently.

"I know," she said. "I know." Dean's voice was telling her this guy was just like all the others. That he'd eventually lie to her. Disappoint her. *What did she think was going to happen*, his voice echoed in her head. *That this guy was different? That he loved her with no hidden agenda? Don't be ridiculous!*

"You look like you've seen a ghost." Again, Ethan brushed her hair from her face tenderly. "Are you sure you're ok?"

Riley mustered everything inside her to shoo the imaginary voice of Dean away. She focused on the handsome young man in front of her. The one who wanted to be her boyfriend. The one who had brought her flowers. The one she saw in her vision. Maybe the vision had happened for a reason. Maybe it was telling her something deeper than just the future. Maybe it was telling her that he was the one. Yes, that was it. Her vision wasn't just a glimpse into the future. Her vision was a confirmation that Ethan was going to be the man in her life. A good man. A man who was capable of love and honesty and openness.

"I've never been happier," Riley smiled. She forced the memory of Dean back in her mind, and kissed Ethan until all she could smell, and feel and taste was every sensation of him, until all the happiness she imagined she felt came flooding back in a rush of endorphins and hormones.

"Take me home," she whispered.

Abe woke with a start in the small hours of the morning and sat bolt upright in bed.

"It was just a dream," he told himself, placing a hand on his chest to calm his rapidly beating heart. "It was just a dream."

"Do you want me to come with you?" Ethan asked over breakfast, which he'd cooked up for his new girlfriend. It was a man's breakfast. Functional. Desperately in need of a woman's touch. Riley sipped her coffee and smiled. Devoid as it was of elegance, he'd made it for her, and that made it special.

Ethan's apartment was becoming of a young designer. He'd

used his creative talents to turn a low-rent apartment into something trendy. He'd chipped away at the plasterwork on the wall in the living room to create a mural in relief, using the depth of the plaster, and the contrast of the underlying brickwork to produce an image of a person walking down a busy street. The darker shades were created by the exposed brickwork. The lines that gave the picture its depth and form were etched into the plasterwork, so that the shadows of the white wall created the buildings and the cityscape. It was simple, yet highly effective. He'd painted other walls in bright shades of primary colors so that the interior was vibrant wherever you looked.

"I think I should go alone," she said.

Earlier that morning, Riley had contacted Angel Martin, and Archer, and asked them if they'd both meet with her to figure out what this thing was with the angel who carried the book. They didn't need much convincing. Martin had called her back a few minutes later, having shifted some of his clients around, and Archer seemed to be permanently available, and had agreed instantly.

"Where are you meeting them?" Ethan asked. He squeezed some ketchup onto the side of his plate, and then used his fork to combine it with his scrambled egg, turning it into a kind of pink cottage cheese.

"My place," Riley said.

"You're meeting two single men at your place, and I shouldn't come?" Ethan asked. His tone said he was joking. His expression said he wasn't. "Are you sure I can't be there?" He took a fork and scooped up some of his pink scrambled egg.

Riley shook her head. "I think this is all about me and the angel. I need to know what it is. I promise I'll tell you after." She placed a reassuring hand on his.

"Ok," he said reluctantly. He couldn't shake a feeling of discomfort.

After Riley had left, Ethan washed up, and stood in the living room of his empty apartment. He realized that for a short time, while Riley had been around, he'd forgotten his grief. She had helped him forget. He went over to the bookshelf by the window, and picked up a picture of himself and Carly, taken a few years ago at the school football field. In the background, there were kids in football gear, and cheerleaders standing idly, chatting. The picture was taken one day when Ethan had come to watch a game that Carly was playing. They'd lost horribly.

Ethan smiled, looking at the picture. Carly was good, but he wasn't cut out for football. The two of them had arms locked around each other's necks and his brother was smiling broadly. Carly didn't care how crap his team had been all season. He just enjoyed being out there, playing together with his team, winning or losing, it was all the same to him. He was a special kid. Ethan felt a pang of guilt at allowing himself to forget about his brother while he was preoccupied with his love life.

Had the police gotten any further with their investigation, he wondered. Was Carly's killer still out there?

Ethan touched his face subconsciously as he remembered his journey into Eighth Street, and the beating he got. He dialed Detective Morris.

"Ethan, how you holding up?" Morris said as he answered the call. Morris had just arrived at his desk. He hovered at one corner, and picked up a folder.

"I'd feel better if I knew you were closer to catching Carly's killer," Ethan said. He perched on a high chair at the kitchen counter. The same one Riley had been sitting on just a few minutes earlier. He stroked the marble counter where her hands had been.

"Look, kid, it's not as easy as you think. People in gang territory don't talk," Morris said. The usual activity continued at the station around him. People sat at desks, working on computers, talking on telephones, or fiddling with files. There was little sense of urgency. "We know someone must have seen something, and we're still looking, but right now, it's a little tricky."

"What do you mean, tricky?" Ethan asked.

"I mean Knuckle Head Ed tricky," Morris said, opening the folder. In it was a sheaf of paper, and clipped to the top sheet was a 5 by 7 picture of a man's face, bald, dark complexion, scars running down both his left and right cheeks that looked like they were decades old, and a single gold earring in the shape of a skull in one ear. The page to which it was attached bore the man's name: Ed Harper.

"What's that supposed to mean? Who's Knuckle Head Ed?" Ethan pressed.

"It means it's an ongoing investigation and I'm not even supposed to be discussing it with you," Morris said curtly. He picked up the folder and gazed at it for a moment. "Knuckle Head Ed. Ed Harper. He's the leader of the Eighth Street Crushers. Everyone we speak to is protecting someone and we can't get squat. No-one's talking." Morris rubbed his forehead with the knuckle of his left thumb. "And we know it's him who's keeping everybody silent, but we can't prove it, and we can't get past him."

"So if you know who it is, why don't you just arrest him?"

"We got no proof he killed your brother, Ethan. But he knows who did, and he's smart. He's been around the block enough times to know how to keep himself clear of the law, but we'll get to him. It's just gonna take some time." Morris made a face as his gaze went to the files stacked up on his desk. Three piles of folders, each spilling with pages, occupied most of his desk. "We have to build a case. A conviction requires evidence. We need evidence, and right now we don't have much."

"Jesus, come on!" Ethan was frustrated. "It's no different to what you told me the last time."

"We're working the case, Ethan." Morris had detached the picture of Harper from its paper clip and was studying the image.

"Yeah, yeah." Ethan wasn't satisfied.

"You just leave this to the police, Ethan. Nobody likes a dead hero," Morris warned, shaking the picture in front of him as if Ethan were standing right there. "Least of all me, because then I have to do all the paperwork. Look, kid, do us all a favor. Leave this to the police, and stay out of trouble."

Ethan hung up. Morris stared at his phone and shook his head. He slumped into his chair, returned the picture to its paperclip, and flipped through the file on Carl Lynch. He stopped at the crime scene photos and laid them out on the table. The body of the young Carl Lynch lay face down in a pool of blood. There wasn't much else at the crime scene. Ballistics had matched slugs they'd pulled from the victim's car and the wall of a nearby building and confirmed that they came from .38 calibre, like an AK 47 or similar assault rifle, the kind that were illegally smuggled into the country from Russia. There was no prior record of this particular weapon in the database, and nothing linked to another case that could tie the shooter to the Eighth Street Crushers. The vehicle used in the drive by had left no tire tracks. There were no shell casings, no fingerprints. Nothing. Without the murder weapon, they had nothing to go on. There were no street cameras, and there were no private security cameras in the area either. The nearest traffic cams were six blocks from the crime scene. Morris' case was a dead end, but he couldn't tell that to the victim's family.

Detective Morris leaned back in his chair and called to his colleague who was over by the coffee machine.

"Hey Yank!" It was short for Jankelowitz.

"Yeah?" Yank turned holding a chipped coffee mug.

"When you gonna replace that cracked piece of shit?" Morris pointed.

Jankelowitz looked down at the mug. "My wife gave me this mug," he said defensively.

"Toss it already, will you, it's making the place look bad."

Yank looked around at the police precinct. The desks were at least thirty years old, every single one of them scratched and marked from their years of tireless service. Papers, files and folders were piled up on each one. There was clutter everywhere. Even the windows were grimy with age.

"It would take a fuckin' hurricane to make this place look any worse," Jankelowitz said.

"You think we can bring Ed Harper in?" Morris asked, looking down at the file.

"You out of your fucking mind? We got no cause," Jankelowitz said. He drank from his chipped mug, and Morris made a face. "What you gonna ask him anyway? He's not going to break. Even if he shot the kid himself, he's never given us anything except a hard time." Jankelowitz was slim, about the same age as Morris, but with short, thinning brown hair. He wore a suit well, unlike Morris, who looked like an overstuffed brown paper bag.

"Come with me for a ride," Morris said.

"You serious? You want to go question him in his own neighborhood?" Jankelowitz stared at his partner.

"Just wanna talk," Morris said.

"You *are* fucking crazy," Jankelowitz said. "Let me finish my coffee."

"That mug's probably carrying so many germs in those cracks. You got a better chance of dying from your wife poisoning you with that mug than getting shot at by the Crushers. In fact I think that's it. I think your wife gave you that mug so that it would poison you."

"Fuck you." Jankelowitz poured his coffee down the sink. He looked at his cracked mug with disdain and reluctantly dropped it in the bin with a loud thud. "You owe me a coffee."

"I'll get you a fucking medal, Yank. Come on." Morris was already at the elevator.

The early morning sun bore down brightly on the poor neighborhood as Morris parked his car a few blocks away from the scene of the Lynch kid's murder. He and Jankelowitz exited the car and walked towards a shabby building wedged between others just like it, with peeling paint and broken windows on the lower floors. People stopped their casual conversations to stare at the two white folk who were most probably police. They averted their gaze, backed inside doorways, and away from open windows.

"Nice neighborhood," Jankelowitz remarked. He drew a pack of cigarettes from his back pocket, extracted one for himself and one for Morris, and lit them as they approached the doorway. "Definitely think I'm gonna get me a place down here. Look how quiet it is."

Morris shook his head.

Three men stood outside the building and they turned to face the approaching pair threateningly. One had a black bandanna tied tightly around his head. The smallest of the group was over six foot tall, and the tallest was at least a head above that. Each must have weighed over three hundred pounds, most of which was muscle. The one with the bandanna stepped forward, arms folded and stood in the way of the two middle aged white men.

"Relax, Butch, I just wanna talk to your boss," Morris said causally as he approached.

"'Bout what?" the man called Butch asked.

"'Bout that kid that was shot a couple of blocks from here."

"We ain't seen nothing," he stonewalled.

"Like I said, I just wanna talk to your boss. Maybe he knows who saw something." Morris drew on his cigarette, and he and Butch engaged in a silent stand off. Jankelowitz stood alongside Morris, one arm hanging loose, close to his right hip and the gun holstered there.

They'd been here before more than once. Ed Harper owned these streets. He had no regard for the law, but Morris had established a kind of working arrangement with the leader of the Eighth Street Crushers. No-one else in the Department could get close to Harper. Morris and he had done each other favors that crossed the line many times over the years. Harper had given information about the Dragon Kings that had led Morris to some arrests, and in return, Morris had allowed Harper to run his empire undisturbed. As long as there was never any evidence against Harper. If that ever happened, the deal was off the table. Morris had made that clear from the start, and Harper knew his complicit adversary well. Plausible deniability all the way. There was never any evidence suggesting Morris had looked the other way when it came to accusations leveled against Harper because Morris had made sure there wasn't any.

"Wait here," Butch said. He left Morris and Jankelowitz under the watchful eye of the other two human obelisks, and let himself into the building by punching his access code into the panel.

Pretty tight security for a shitty neighborhood, Jankelowitz observed.

Butch appeared again a few minutes later and nodded to Morris. Jankelowitz stubbed out his cigarette but Butch waved a finger.

"Only him," Butch said.

Morris waved a hand to Jankelowitz. "I'll be fine. Wait here."

Yank shook his head as Morris followed Butch inside. He didn't move or shift even in the slightest as the two Obelisks folded their arms and glared at him. He was a cop on their turf, but still Jankelowitz feared nothing. He'd been right here, in this same position a dozen times. Maybe not with the same meatheads, but the feeling of *deja-vu* was overwhelming.

"You watch the Food Channel," Jankelowitz asked them as he withdrew the pack of cigarettes from his pocket and lit another one.

Both doormen glared at him, and then one of them said, "Yeah, I do." The other's eyes widened in disbelief, and the first one shrugged.

Inside the building, Morris followed Butch up the stairs to the second floor, then down a grimy hallway. Outside one of the doors stood another guard, about the same physique as the ones downstairs, but this one wore a sleeveless top revealing solid, glistening muscle. As Butch approached, the man's hand went instinctively behind his back. He watched Morris cautiously, ready to draw and shoot at the slightest sign of any threat. Morris held his hands far away from his body, palms raised. Harper's closest guard patted Morris down before he allowed the detective to enter the apartment while he watched him from the door.

"Detective Morris," the king of Eighth Street greeted him.

"Harper," Morris said.

"He clean?" Harper asked Butch. The guard nodded. "It's cool," Harper said. "Leave us."

Butch acknowledged silently and clicked the door closed as he joined the guard in the hallway.

Harper didn't get where he was by being shrewd. He was a fighter and he was ruthless. He'd maintained his position as leader of the Crushers by physical dominance. He stood a few inches taller than his inner circle of bodyguards, and he matched them pound for pound in muscle. He sat back in a leather sofa that definitely didn't belong in this part of town. It smelled fresh, and it looked brand new.

"What brings you here?" Harper asked. He stretched out both enormous arms and slung them over the back of the sofa.

"The shooting that happened in your 'hood last week," Morris said, sitting in the single couch opposite Harper. Ordinarily, anyone Harper allowed into his inner chamber would stand and wait to be invited to sit, but Morris behaved like an equal. Harper narrowed his eyes and pursed his lips silently, breathing in deeply to quell the rising anger at the detective's blatant disregard for his authority. "This new?" Morris asked, pointing to the sofa.

"Reupholstered," Harper replied.

Morris grunted. "Some Dragon Kings piece of shit that nobody cares about was taken out, and an innocent kid got caught in the crossfire. Now him we *do* care about, and I want the shooter."

"So?" Harper asked.

"Word is it was one of your guys pulled the trigger," Morris said.

"Don't know nothin' about that," Harper said.

Morris leaned forward. "Look, Harper, I ain't got time for bullshit. The Chief wants this case closed and I need someone to put away, *capisce*?"

There was more behind Morris' words, and Harper knew well what the detective was saying. *Give me anyone to nail for this thing, otherwise I'm coming after you.*

"Yeah, I feel you, but I can't tell you what I don't know," the King of Eighth Street said. His expression hadn't changed the entire time Morris had been in the room. It was deadpan, and completely devoid of emotion. Even the concealed contempt he felt for the detective didn't show.

"Ed," Morris leaned back to mirror Harper's gesture, "it was a hit on a Dragon Kings gang member. Who else would it have been? Don't throw me bullshit, man, I'm warning you. If there's a shred of evidence that it was you or one of your guys, I'm not gonna hold back. I'm comin' after you with everything I got."

Harper narrowed his eyes, the first sign of life from his stone face since Morris had entered the room. Only two people in the world had ever called him Ed, and they were both dead. His father, who had died in a stabbing in prison, and his mother, whom his father had beaten to death weeks before he'd ended up behind bars.

"You came all the way down here to tell me that?" Harper said.

"Nah," Morris said. "I was just down the corner getting fuckin' donuts and I thought I'd stop by. I came here to find out what you knew to save me the trouble of sending a dozen uniforms over here to tear this place apart. Tell me what you know, Ed."

"I told you. If it was one of my guys he did it on his own. Sure I know it was a hit on a Dragon King, but it never came from me. On my mother's grave." Harper held up his right hand.

Morris engaged Ed Harper in a stare down for a long few seconds.

"That's it? You got nothing for me?" Morris said, standing. Harper watched him from his seat.

"I told you, I don't know nothing."

"Ok, have it your way," Morris said heading for the door. He knocked twice, and the man in the hallway opened it. "But I swear to you, Harper, if I find anything that connects your gang to this shooting, you're going down."

"Have a nice day, officer," Harper said.

"Detective," Morris corrected him loudly as he was escorted

down the hallway, and immediately realized he'd just taken Harper's bait. "Fuck!" he cursed as he descended the stairs.

Outside the building, Jankelowitz was in conversation with the two Doormen. "I make mine with coconut oil," Yank said.

Morris burst through the door onto the street, followed by Butch.

"Really? Coconut oil?" one of the Doormen asked.

Morris stormed right past Jankelowitz, who followed immediately, leaving Butch standing behind them with the two Doormen, one of them about to say something, his mouth open.

"What the fuck was that about?" Morris asked.

"That?" Jankelowitz asked, pointing a thumb over his shoulder. "You left me with two of Harper's thugs, I had to find something to talk about. Did Harper give you anything?"

"Nothing," Morris said.

"Hmm," Jankelowitz grunted. "So what now?"

"Now the gloves come off," Morris growled. "I'm sick of this sack of shit."

Jankelowitz smiled.

Chapter 8

Riley waited anxiously. She moved a vase of red roses from the small, square table by the window and placed it on the kitchen counter. She clicked the kettle on, and it boiled almost immediately. She'd clicked that same switch several times in the last twenty minutes. She studied the vase for a moment and then moved it back to the window again, and finally placed it back in the center of the table. She straightened the four chairs around the table, and then sank into the sofa, chewing her nails. Jenna would berate her if she saw her, but Jenna was the last thing on her mind right now. She was more nervous at that moment than she had been writing her final exams at college. The silence was broken by the intrusive buzz of her intercom.

"Finally!" she breathed. She raised herself from the sofa as if her body were light as paper, and ran to the front door.

"Yes?" she said.

"It's Archer," the voice crackled through the speaker. Riley buzzed him in.

A few moments later she heard the light footfall as Archer

reached the top of the staircase and padded down the hallway towards her apartment. Riley was surprised to find both Martin and Archer standing outside when she opened the door.

"Riley," Archer greeted her, throwing a warm hug around her neck. She felt her apprehension lift almost immediately.

"Archer," Riley returned the greeting. "Martin." She moved to give him a hug too, but found him more rigid than the younger man. "Please, come in."

"Riley, nice to see you. Didn't think I'd hear from you again so soon," Martin said as he and Archer moved inside. "Nice place," he commented, nodding approvingly, like a parent stepping into their kid's neat college dorm for the first time. His gaze lingered on the vase of flowers.

"Thanks," she said.

"So me and Angel Martin arrived at the same time," Archer smiled, then laughed. "I just thought of something. Two..." he began, but he was laughing more and more as he spoke. "Two psychics meet outside a door," he said, and then looked at Riley laughing even more hysterically. Martin giggled modestly. Riley stared at him, confused.

"And then what?" she asked.

Archer burst into fits of laughter, louder and more hysterical than before, and Martin couldn't restrain himself. He joined in, laughing uncontrollably.

"What?" Riley asked, frustrated.

"If you have to ask, you're not a psychic!" Archer was doubled over with laughter. Martin slapped him on the back and the two of them laughed loudly. Riley just stared at them.

"I don't know what the two of you are on," she said.

"Sorry," Archer said, trying to control himself. His eyes were watering. "That was a medium joke."

"I thought that was a high," Martin said, and the two of them burst into fits of laughter again.

Riley left them by the door and moved over to the kitchen where she switched the kettle on again.

"When the two of you are finished, would any of you like some tea?"

After the laughter had subsided, Riley sat at the table with Archer on her right, Martin on her left, and three steaming cups of herbal tea in front of them, arranged around the vase of roses.

"Ok, Riley," Martin said. "Please tell me what's troubling you."

"Remember when I first came to see you," Riley began.

"How could I forget," Martin said warmly. "I'll remember that day for a long time. I've never experienced so many people wanting to pay tribute before. It was…" He searched for the word. "…special. Memorable."

Riley smiled humbly. "The angel that you saw after that," she said.

"I remember that too," Martin said. "The angel that carries the book?"

"Well, Archer has communicated with the angel you saw, and he's started communicating with me too."

"That's wonderful," Martin smiled broadly. "The angels are communicating through you?"

"Only the one," Riley said.

"If I may," Archer interjected. "I've seen this angel before, and for some time now. He would appear at random, and I could never figure out how to communicate with him until she showed up." He pointed a finger at Riley. Martin glanced at her, intrigued. "Well, he showed me what was in the book a few times, and every time, it was just before somebody crossed. And he would always show me the exact time the person was going to cross over. I never knew the person's name, just the time."

Martin took a moment to take in the news. This was a revelation he hadn't expected.

"And then when Archer figured out that he only ever saw the angel when he was near me, I started seeing him too," Riley broke the silence.

"You can see him?" Martin asked somberly. He was placing all of the pieces in his mind. "But only when Archer is around?"

"No. I've seen him without Archer too. But I don't see the pages in his book like Archer does," Riley said.

"No?" Martin waited expectantly. "What do you see?"

"You're going to think this is really strange," Riley said, nervously rubbing her hands together, "but I don't *see* what's in his book. I *live* it, as if it's really happening."

Martin cocked his head to one side. "What do you mean?"

Riley explained her experience with the car accident, and the woman she was destined to injure, and then she told him about Ethan and the flowers. Martin steepled his fingers beneath his chin, listening intently, looking at the bunch of flowers in the vase in front of them.

"Yes, I sensed something about the flowers. An unease." Martin was silent for a moment. "And while the angel was revealing this to you, you thought it was actually happening?" Martin asked pensively.

Riley nodded. "Both times. It was real. I only knew it wasn't real when everything rewound back to the present and I found myself back where I started." She looked up.

"What do you make of this, Archer?" Martin asked.

Archer pursed his lips tightly and shook his head slowly, staring at the roses. "I thought about this a lot," he began. "He's a gateway to the future, that's for sure." Both Martin and Riley nodded in agreement. "But he chooses his instrument. For a while there I thought I was his instrument, but then I realized I only saw him when Riley was around. And then the way she experiences his message…" Archer rocked his head from side to side. "Man, that's … that's something entirely different. Have you ever experienced anything like that?" he asked.

Martin shook his head. "Never."

"Me neither." He fixed his gaze on Riley. "You've got a special connection to this angel, that's for sure."

There was silence for a moment, then Riley spoke. "I must have some connection to this angel, but what's it all for? Why? Why me?

What's so special about me that he…"

Martin placed a reassuring hand over hers. "Angels don't choose you because you're special, or deserving, or worthy." He tapped his chest briefly with his fingertips. "There's nothing special about me. I studied accounting, for heaven's sake." Martin chuckled. "How many accountants do you know, about whom someone would stick up their hands and say, *that man is special, and worthy?* I live in an apartment on Eighty Fourth. If I walked past you in the street you wouldn't even notice me. Yet here I am. I see angels. And they communicate through me."

Riley considered his words for a moment.

"The angels choose you for reasons we'll probably never understand," Martin concluded.

Archer nodded. "I never did anything to deserve the gift I got. It's like being artistic. Or musical. Or good with numbers. If you listen to your gifts, they multiply. If you ignore them, they suffocate and die."

"So," Martin smiled warmly, "shall we see what your angels wish to tell you today?"

Riley shuffled in her chair for a moment. "Ok," she said.

Martin extended his hands towards Riley and Archer. They each took a hand, and to complete the circle Archer wrapped his hand around Riley's, who squeezed tightly.

"Gently," Archer said.

"Sorry." Riley loosened her grip on both Martin's and Archer's hands.

"That's better," Archer said. "He's here."

Martin nodded in agreement, and then Riley saw the angel standing in the gap between Martin and Archer. He looked majestic, and radiant. And fearsome.

"Angel," Martin began. "Thank you for being here. Will you tell us by what name you are called?"

Archer looked at Martin with a furrowed brow. He wouldn't have used as many words had he asked the question.

"I am Lucca," the angel replied in a voice all three of them could hear. Riley's pulse quickened, and she squeezed both hands so tightly that both Martin and Archer turned to her at the same time. She loosened her grip again, mouthing an apology.

"You reveal the future," Archer said. "You showed me pages in your book. Each time, it's been just before someone crosses over."

"And me," Riley said, her words rapid as the heartbeat thumping inside her chest. "You've shown me what's going to happen to me."

Before either Riley or Archer could get their next words in, Martin phrased the question they both wanted to ask more diplomatically than either of them would have, had they chosen their own words.

"Will you help us understand why you have chosen these vessels for your message, and how to understand the message you have given each one?" Martin asked. Riley and Archer nodded their agreement.

"People cannot change their future," Lucca said simply. "The future can only be understood. For you, Archer, that is the message. Simply to understand and accept."

"And for me?" Riley asked. "Why do I see the future so vividly?"

Riley found herself staring into Lucca's eyes, green, like a pair of emeralds held up against a bright light. It was as if his eyes were the gateway to another world, as if, beyond their brilliant green she might find eternity. She felt dizzy, as though she were going under anesthetic, drifting away from her body. She couldn't fight it, nor could she control it.

"You will understand in time," he said to her.

"But why me?" Riley wanted to know.

"You will understand in time," he said again, and Riley knew immediately that no matter how many times she asked the question, this answer was the only one she was going to get. The lightness faded, and she was aware that Archer and Martin were staring at her.

Riley's phone vibrated. Martin and Archer looked at her

disapprovingly. She ignored the noise, but the disturbance had interrupted the communication with Lucca, and he was gone.

"Sorry," Riley apologized.

"You may as well get that," Archer said, releasing Riley's hand.

She reached to the kitchen counter behind her and picked up her phone. "It's the hospital," she said. "I have to take it."

Martin and Archer exchanged glances, each one's expression showing their disappointment. They heard only Riley's side of the conversation.

"Hello, this is Riley...Yes...What? When?" Her eyes were wide open, and her hand went to cover her mouth. "I'll be right there!"

"What is it?" Martin asked, placing a hand on hers.

"It's Ethan," she said. All the color had drained from her face. "He's..." Riley gathered herself while Martin and Archer waited in anticipation. "He's just been brought in to the hospital. He collapsed."

"What?" Archer said. "But I saw him yesterday, he was fine."

"Did they say anything more?" Martin asked.

"He's critical," Riley said. "I've got to get to the hospital!" She stood, and searched for her car keys.

"Let me drive you," Archer said. Riley was in shock. The keys were on the kitchen counter alongside her phone, but she hadn't seen them. Archer scooped them up and guided Riley to the door. "You coming?" he said to Martin.

"Of course."

Fifteen minutes later, the SUV pulled into one of the parking bays reserved for medical personnel at the hospital. The three of them peeled out of the car, and Archer and Martin fell in behind Riley as she ran to the admissions desk.

"Where's Ethan Lynch," she asked abruptly. "He was brought in by ambulance in the last hour."

The reception clerk brushed the girl's curtness aside. He'd encountered dozens of people in a similar state to the woman in front of him. He'd learned to accept that when people who had been given bad news about a loved one bolted into the hospital, he was not a person, but merely a function. A source of information. They were bereaved. They wouldn't see him as a person until their questions had been answered. He searched for the patient's records on the screen in front of him.

"He's in Trauma One," the clerk said, but Riley was already darting off in the direction of the ward as he looked up from his screen. "You're welcome," he said.

"Thanks, man," Archer said loudly over his shoulder as he and Martin followed at speed. The clerk smiled and nodded.

Riley arrived at the trauma ward and burst through the doors.

"Where's Ethan Lynch," she asked the nurse at the trauma station. The woman scanned the list in front of her then looked up.

"There." She pointed to a bed around which a team of trauma personnel worked furiously. Two doctors worked on the patient, calling out rapid instructions, while the nurses handed them instruments and supplies, and scurried back and forth between the storage shelves and the bed.

"What happened? What's wrong with him?" Riley asked. Archer and Martin had caught up and stood beside her.

"We don't know yet," the nurse explained. "He was brought in at 11:38am unconscious. Apparently he collapsed at the supermarket. The doctors are working on him right now." The nurse placed a comforting hand on Riley's shoulder. "Why don't you take a seat over there. There's nothing you can do right now except wait, and give the doctors room to find out what's wrong. We'll let you know more as soon as we do." Riley felt the lightness return to her head, except this time Archer caught her as she fell backwards into his arms.

"Whoa," he said catching her. "Let's get you to a chair." The nurse came around from her station, slung Riley's arm skillfully over her shoulder, and helped Archer escort her to the row of chairs in the waiting area.

"Get her some tea with sugar," the nurse said to Martin. "You can take it from the kitchen over there." She pointed to a doorway a short distance down the hallway.

"Ok," Martin said taking off down the passage.

"Riley?" Archer said, tapping her face. She opened her eyes, and looked around her.

"Wait here," the nurse said again. "Are you ok, Miss?"

Riley nodded. Martin returned a few minutes later with a cup of hot, sweet tea, and placed it in Riley's hand. "Here," he said. "Drink this. Doctor's orders."

The next twenty minutes stretched out into what felt like hours as they waited, watching the hive of activity around Ethan's bed until finally, one of the doctors came towards her, peeling off a pair of blue latex gloves. Riley sat upright.

"Are you Riley?" the doctor asked her, crouching onto his haunches in front of her.

"Yes?" she replied.

"I'm Dr Jansen," he said extending a hand. Riley shook it, nodding, waiting. "Yours was the last number dialed on Ethan's phone. I had the trauma ward call you when he was brought in." Dr Jansen was in his late fifties. His receding hair was grey, and his face creased form long, arduous hours of physical work and little rest. He removed his silver framed glasses as he spoke. "I'm afraid it's not good," he said. Riley stiffened. "Ethan's in acute liver failure."

"What? How?" Riley asked. "I was with him yesterday. He was fine."

"Could be secondary Budd-Chiari." The doctor rose, stretching his aching limbs. "Unless he gets a liver transplant soon, like in the next twelve hours…"

"What?" Riley said in disbelief, rising to her feet. "What?" she said again, cupping her hand to her mouth. She began to shake as she was overcome with tears that made her entire body shudder.

"I'm sorry," he said. "He's AB Negative. It's going to be nearly impossible to find a donor liver …"

"I know," Riley said. The doctor looked at Martin and Archer with a frown.

"She's a transplant co-ordinator," Archer explained. The doctor nodded.

"We're going to do all we can for him…"

Riley looked at her watch. It was just before 12:00 midday. Then she felt that familiar sensation once more. The feeling of being sucked backwards in time, where everything moved rapidly in reverse. She felt herself moving backwards to the trauma reception. Saw the frantic activity around Ethan's bed. Running backwards to the hospital admissions desk. Running backwards to the car, and driving rapidly backwards to her apartment until she was back at the table in her apartment. She gasped.

"Riley!" Archer stood in front of her, holding her by both shoulders, with Martin crouching next to him. "Riley, are you ok?" Both of her guests were staring at her, concerned.

"How long have you been here?" she asked. They both stared at each other for a moment.

"What are you talking about, we haven't left. Are you ok?" Archer asked.

"What happened?" Martin asked. Riley found his voice comforting. It was deep, and he spoke in measured, soothing tones.

"I saw the future again," she whispered.

"What did you see?" Martin asked, frowning. He had a premonition it wasn't going to be good.

Riley was silent for a moment. "Ethan's dying. What time is it?"

"10:40am," Archer replied.

"He collapses and gets brought into the hospital with acute liver failure. The doctors give him twelve hours. And he has a rare blood type. AB Negative."

"What does that mean?" Archer asked.

"Little possibility of finding a donor," Riley whispered.

"Damn," Archer straightened up, and paced a small circle with his hands on his hips. "So what now?" he asked.

"Sit down," Riley said.

"What?" Archer tilted his head.

"Sit. You too," she said to Martin. They both moved back to their seats. "Give me your hands." They formed a circle.

"What are you doing?" Archer asked.

"Lucca," Riley called. "Lucca?"

There was silence. Riley looked at the gap between Martin and Archer, but no one appeared.

"Come on!" Riley shouted in frustration.

"Allow me, please?" Martin said. Riley nodded. "Lucca," he said. His voice was calm, the complete opposite of Riley's. "Lucca, will you show yourself to us?" After a few moments that felt to Riley like hours, Martin's face lit up with a warm, radiant smile. "He's here," Martin said, looking over Riley's shoulder.

"You can see him?" Riley said, about to turn her head, but Martin raised a finger, and shook his head.

"He's here, right behind you," Martin said. "Angel Lucca, Will you tell us the meaning of Riley's vision?"

"Ethan's going to die," Riley begged. "Can't you do something?"

"People cannot change their future. The future is only to be understood," Lucca repeated.

Riley felt the sensation of drifting away from her body again, and saw the angel's piercing emerald green eyes in front of her. Then he turned and she found herself following him into a long, dark tunnel. She felt cold. A brilliant light illuminated the far end, but all she could see was Lucca's silhouette against the brightness, his magnificent wings moving slowly ahead of her. She followed.

As they approached the end of the tunnel, Riley noticed how the light danced and sparkled as if someone were shining a powerful spotlight through a curtain of diamonds. All the colors of the rainbow lit up the world in front of her as she stepped out of the tunnel. Riley held her breath.

Of all the pictures people have painted of heaven, all the stories she'd heard about what it must be like on the other side, what she experienced at that moment made them all pale into obscurity. She floated, suspended in a cloud of dancing light that sparkled and radiated all around her. Riley was absorbed in their brilliance like a child, watching the tiny circles of light move across her skin.

She was floating, like a feather caught on a breeze, so high above the world, completely surrounded by the brilliance of the refracted light all around her, for as far as she could see above her and below. She noticed the distinct absence of fear and anxiety, and the overwhelming, overpowering sensation of a deep rooted peace, the likes of which she had never known.

"Where are we?" she asked.

"In a place where only you can hear me, and only I can hear you," Lucca said.

"How?" Riley asked looking around her. She felt weightless, floating in the dancing light. "Where are the others?"

"You are still with the others. It is only your spirit that is here," the angel said. "They will not realize that I have taken you away. When I return you, it will appear to them as if nothing has happened," Lucca said.

"Return me?" Riley looked around her. She saw only light, sparkling, dancing, bursting with vibrant color and felt peace flowing throughout her soul. "What is this place?" Riley asked. She reached out, and watched the light do its colorful dance on her hands. "This feels so real," Riley said. "Is this a dream? Like the visions you've shown me?"

"This Dimension is real," the angel explained. "As real as the one you know. It exists on the same plane as the one you can see, but only spirits exist in this Dimension."

"Then how am I here?" Riley asked.

"I am one of the few angels that has the power to bring people here from the Dimension of Time," Lucca explained.

"The Dimension of Time?" Riley asked.

"The world you know. The world you live in before you cross over," Lucca explained. "The Dimension where Time rules everything."

"People can only see this Dimension when they cross over? You mean die?" Riley asked.

"No soul ever dies. Your physical body exists in the Dimension of Time, and when your spirit is free from your mortal body, you will cross over to this Dimension." Lucca extended a hand around him. Riley looked at the endless light all around her.

"What exists here?" Riley asked.

"Everything," Lucca explained. "And nothing. No physical form, but every soul that has ever lived exists here."

"Where are they? All the other souls?"

"This place is not like the world your mortal mind can comprehend. This Dimension has no boundaries. We are at the doorway to a world no mortal soul will ever comprehend," Lucca explained.

"Is this Heaven?" Riley asked. She could see nothing but dancing light.

"Call it what you will," Lucca smiled. "Heaven. Utopia. Nirvana."

"Are my mom and dad here?" Riley asked, wondering what she would say to them if she were able to meet them now. They were little more than a distant memory to her, but she longed for them.

Lucca nodded. "Every soul that has crossed over is here."

"Can I talk to them?" Riley asked hopefully, looking around at the dancing light. Even Lucca, adrift close to her, was obscured by its brilliance.

"You cannot see them here," Lucca said.

"But people talk to spirits," Riley insisted.

Lucca smiled patiently. "While you are still in the Dimension of Time, you can only communicate with spirits through those who are in tune with this Dimension."

"What about Ethan?" Riley pressed. "What happens to him? You showed me his future for a reason, didn't you? Why else would you show me?"

Lucca looked deep into Riley's eyes. "People cannot change their future. All lives in the Dimension of Time have a beginning and an end. There must be balance."

Riley considered his words for a moment. "Balance?"

"A life must end when its time has come," Lucca said.

"I don't understand how that relates to Balance?" Riley said.

"All physical life exists in balance. A life must end when a new life begins."

"And Ethan's life must end so a new life can begin?" Riley asked. "Does Ethan's have to end so soon?" she begged. "Does it have to all balance?"

"That question is not mine to answer," Lucca said. "I do not write the future of the Dimension of Time."

"What do you mean?" Riley asked. "Who does?"

"Our time here is over," Lucca said. "Come."

He led Riley back into the tunnel. Enveloped in the darkness, she felt cold and alone. "What do you mean?" she asked again, but Lucca was gone.

"What?" Archer stared at Riley.

She looked into the confused faces of Martin and Archer.

"Did you not hear any of that?" she asked.

"We heard you saying, *what do you mean*," Martin replied. "Riley, are you alright?"

"No!" Riley blurted. "No, I'm not alright. Did you not see any of that?"

"The last thing you said was *Ethan's going to die. Can't you do something*?" Martin explained. He cocked his head to one side. "Why? What happened to you?"

"He took me away. Somewhere. There was light. Dancing light everywhere," Riley stared beyond Martin and Archer as she spoke. "He said Ethan had to die. There had to be balance."

"Where'd he take you?" Archer asked enviously, glancing between Riley and Martin.

"Into another dimension," Riley explained. She could still see the radiating light, and feel the sense of peace even now.

"The Dimension of Eternity," Martin said. He smiled as he nodded. "It's where the spirits of everyone who has ever lived on earth continue to exist. You saw this place?"

"He took me there," Riley said.

Martin shook his head slowly, smiling broadly at Archer, who seemed to understand.

"Spirits communicate with us mediums from the Dimension of Eternity," Martin explained. "We never get to visit them on the other side. They only communicate with us when they choose to. But you..." Martin held his arms out towards Riley as if she were a prophet, a spiritual marvel to be revered and awed. "He took you there."

Riley stared at Martin.

"Do you know what that means?" he asked her. Riley shook her head slowly. "It means that you're more special to the spirit world than anyone I've ever known."

"Me too," Archer agreed. "I've always been able to communicate with the spirits, but I've never been taken into their world."

"No one has been taken into their world," Martin continued. "No one that I've ever known. Riley, this is amazing!" For the first time, Martin's voice rose in excitement. "Do you know what this means?" he asked again. Riley shook her head. "It means you can answer questions we've never been able to before. You can visit places we've never had access to before."

Riley was suddenly aware of the way Archer and Martin were staring at her and she felt uncomfortable. "Stop it, you two, you're scaring me." She rose, gathered the mugs from the table, and moved to the other side of the kitchen counter where she flipped the switch on the kettle. She placed the mugs in the sink and took three fresh ones from the cupboard.

"Riley," Martin continued. "We only get to talk to spirits that come to us." His face was beaming.

"Yeah. So?" Riley said. She scooped coffee powder into all three cups, and added boiling water.

"So this means that you get to go to them. You can call on anyone you want to," Martin said excitedly. "Don't you see?"

"But there was no one else there. Just Lucca. And this incredible light everywhere."

Riley added milk and sugar, and pushed two steaming cups over to Martin and Archer, who ignored them in the wake of the most exciting spiritual discovery of their lives.

"Still, you can answer more questions than either of us could ever ask, and boy, do I have a lot of questions I want to ask," Martin beamed.

"Me too," Archer joined.

"But that still doesn't help me. Ethan's going to die." She looked at her watch. It was 11:05am. "There has to be something I can do!"

"What exactly did Lucca say to you?" Martin asked.

"The same thing he said to you. That people can't change their future, they have to understand it. That there has to be balance. One life ends, another begins."

"The Sum of the Universe," Martin said.

"What?"

"Everything in the universe exists in harmony. For every action there is an equal and opposite reaction. You cannot create matter," Martin said. "It's the Sum of the Universe."

"I don't follow?" Riley said. She leaned both elbows on the kitchen counter and breathed in the steam that wafted up from her coffee.

"It's a theory that my clan have believed in for generations. And many other medium circles, for that matter. It has to do with Balance and the Universe. It holds that there is an equation of equilibrium that keeps the world in balance. The sum of all life and death, the sum of all growth and decay. All must be in balance. A new life cannot be created without taking something away in return." Martin mirrored Riley from the opposite side of the kitchen counter. He spun his coffee mug around by the handle slowly.

"But that doesn't make sense. The world's population has been increasing," Riley said.

"Yes, and to the detriment of the planet. More people live, but the planet is dying," Martin said.

"So your equation for Balance in the Universe – its not only

177

human life for human life, it can be anything?"

"So it would seem," Martin mused. "But nothing new comes into existence without something making way for its birth."

Riley's phone buzzed and her heart sank. "It's the hospital," she said without looking at the phone.

"It begins," Archer said.

"When can I see him?" Riley asked Dr Jansen. He replaced his glasses and pushed them up on the bridge of his nose.

"As soon as we can get him stabilized," he replied. Riley nodded. "I'm sorry, Riley. I wish I could give you happier news."

"We've called his parents," Dr Jansen said. "They'll be here soon."

Riley looked at Archer and Martin. "I don't want to be here when they arrive. I haven't ever met them before. Meeting them like this will be …I don't know…wrong."

"Sure," Martin said.

Riley felt empty inside, as if she'd just been hit in the solar plexus, and all the breath had been knocked out of her. "I need a moment," she said.

"Sure," Martin said again.

Riley left the two mediums and ambled through the hospital corridors. She found herself entering the elevator, and pressing the button for the top floor. A few minutes later, she stood alone on the roof of the building, staring out over the familiar view below. The hospital parking lot was full. An ambulance reversed into its allocated bay. A never-ending stream of people moved back and forth between the cars and the hospital building. Visitors making their way in to see loved ones. People leaving the hospital in their pajamas, accompanied by friends and relatives who escorted them into waiting vehicles. Hospital staff taking private calls outside the main building, and wandering up and down the shaded parking with cigarettes between their fingers, leaving a thin trail of smoke hanging in the air. She was beginning to understand the Equation of Balance that Martin spoke about. The Sum of the Universe. This

178

place seemed to be a hub of balance.

"There must be something, Lucca," Riley said out loud, leaning her elbows on the parapet wall. "Can't you save him and take me instead?" Riley felt helpless and desperate. "Are you there? Are you even listening?"

Riley stared at the activity going on three stories below, feeling like her life had been ripped out from inside her. Her longing for love and her fear of loving had kept her from allowing anyone near her. Now that she had found her soul mate, she was about to lose him. She felt empty and alone.

Lucca's voice broke the silence. "I do not write the future."

"What do you mean?" Riley asked, face to face with the angel. He turned.

"Come," he said. "It is not me you seek."

Once again, Riley found herself following Lucca through a dark tunnel, moving slowly towards the brilliant light at the far end. Immediately Riley felt the overwhelming sense of peace.

As they reached the end of the tunnel, Riley found herself floating in what felt like a fine mist of tiny particles that refracted the bright light, causing bursts of colors everywhere she looked. It was like floating amidst hundreds of mirror balls decorating the world around her with thousands of tiny pinpoints of light constantly changing color.

"The Writers are the ones you must ask." Lucca said.

"This place feels so real," Riley said. "Why have you brought me here?"

"Because of what you ask," Lucca said. "And because another has interceded for Ethan."

"Who?" Riley asked, but then immediately thought of Ethan's parents. Maybe angels listen to people when they pray, she thought.

"I cannot tell you who has been interceding for him," Lucca said. Riley understood, and she already had a pretty good idea who it must have been. Ethan had mentioned that his parents were Catholic. It had to have been them. "When you first spoke to me about the future, you said the future was only to be understood. You said that people cannot change their future."

"It is true," Lucca said. "People are destined to the fate that has been written for them. The Sum of the Universe exists so that the Equation of Balance is maintained. If people were allowed to change their future, the Equation of Balance would be undone. The Writers maintain the Balance. They write the future of each person so that Equation of Balance is upheld."

"The Writers?" Riley asked.

"The angels who maintain the Equation of Balance. They write the fate of every human being," Lucca explained.

"Can the Writers change the future?" Riley asked hopefully.

Lucca nodded. "The Writers are the only ones who can change the future. They maintain the Equation of Balance. The future cannot be changed except by the Writers."

"But you said people can't change the future," Riley said, confused.

"*People* can't," Lucca said, half smiling.

"The Writers can change the future?" Riley asked, but Lucca remained silent. "They can, can't they? The Writers can change the future. That's why you brought me here. Can you take me to them?" Riley asked, excitedly. "Can I ask them to change Ethan's future?"

"I brought you here because I know it is on your heart to ask them. But you cannot approach them," Lucca said. Riley felt her hope slipping away.

"So how can I see them? Is it even possible?" she asked.

Lucca nodded. "If an angel presents a request such as yours to them, they will decide amongst themselves, and if they choose, they will summon you."

"So it is possible?" Riley exclaimed. "Will you ask them for me? Will you ask them if they will see me?"

"That is why I have brought you here," Lucca said. "I have asked them, and they have summoned you. They are already here," Lucca announced, drawing back his arm.

The fine mist that enveloped Riley O'Connor began to thin and the dancing colors faded, giving way to a bright light that was everywhere all at once.

Riley gasped, feeling completely insignificant as she looked around her. Hundreds up on hundreds of angels floated weightlessly around her, moving this way and that. Angels drifted up to a glistening, glass ceiling far above her that undulated as if she were looking at the surface of the water from beneath.

An angel passed by close to her, holding in his hand what looked like a sphere, like a diamond the size of a tennis ball, from which all the colors of the rainbow radiated in bright shafts of light. The angel waved a quill pen across its surface, and a trail of gold dust followed the movement of the writing implement, then converged on the diamond-like object. For a moment, Riley saw a face in the globe. A child's face, that became an adult's face, and then an old man's, and then the image melded with the shafts of colored light emanating from the diamond before it turned clear again. When the gold dust had all disappeared inside the orb, the angel opened his hand, and the sphere drifted upwards. Riley watched it rise, growing smaller as it climbed higher and higher.

"What is that?" Riley asked, looking up at the dancing light far above her. The entire expanse above her was composed of thousands upon thousands of multi faceted orbs through which the light refracted and sparkled. The object that the angel had let go of drifted up to join the others, becoming part of the ocean of floating, sparkling gems.

"That is the fate of a new soul," Lucca explained. "There, look!" Lucca pointed towards a throng of angels, clustered together. "New souls waiting to be born," Lucca explained. There were thousands of them, waiting patiently. Another angel in the distance released a similar sparkling orb, and as he did so, a soul waiting to be born moved forward, and floated upwards, higher and higher, into the glistening sea of floating crystals, and then disappeared from sight.

Riley was speechless for a moment. "They say you already know everything you'll learn on earth before you're born. Is that true?"

Lucca smiled. "There are some things you can only discover when you return here to stay," he said simply.

The more Riley looked around her, the more she saw angels waving quill pens, trailing gold dust across orbs, cut like spherical diamonds, letting them go so they drifted up like balloons that had slipped out of the fingers of children at the fair. Hundreds upon hundreds of them everywhere she looked. And as each orb rose, so a new soul was born, following the object in which their future was written up into the massive sea of the fate of the world, until they disappeared from view, and went to begin the journey of their lives.

"What about the Equation of Balance?" Riley asked, mesmerized. "If a soul has to die for each one that is born, where are they? The ones who die?"

"Cross over," Lucca corrected her. "There," he pointed beneath her feet.

Far below her, at the limits of her vision, tiny forms drifted upwards towards them, growing bigger and bigger as they drew nearer. Souls, just the same as those who had risen upwards to be born, but these ones ascended from a different place.

Riley watched as an angel greeted one of them, and held out his hand. An orb from the sea above descended slowly, as if drawn by a magnet into the angel's hand. As soon as it reached the angel's hand, the orb disintegrated into a fine mist that sparkled as the bright light caught the tiny particles.

"That is the end of a life on earth," Lucca explained. "Their fate becomes tied to them when they cross over into the world as you know it, and dissolved when they cross over again."

Riley watched beneath her feet as one after another, souls returned from the world to this place, and their fate, the story of their lives, etched into an orb of clear crystal, cut and honed like a diamond, descended from its place in the vast ocean above her, and dissipated into a shower of light when the two were reunited.

Riley thought of her mom and dad again, and wanted to ask the angel if she could see them, but remembered his words. As if reading her mind, Lucca spoke. "You are here to see the Writers. They are ready for you now."

Three angels approached from behind Lucca. They were similar in appearance to the emerald-eyed one, graceful in their movement, omniscient in stature. Each of them held a quill pen like the ones Riley had seen the other angels using to etch fate in the curious objects that floated above her. One of them moved forward. He wore a white robe with gold braiding that sparkled as the light from the undulating ceiling of gems above them caught its shiny surface.

"Riley O'Connor," the one in front greeted her, while the other two waited patiently behind him. Riley nodded unsteadily. "You may ask your question," he said to her.

Riley felt her heart pounding in her chest once more. How many times had she felt this sensation in the last twenty-four hours, she wondered. So many new discoveries in such a short space of time. She had learned so much about a world she never knew existed.

"My friend is dying," she began. "Ethan Lynch. He's dying. Can you change his future? Can you save his life?"

"You love this man?" he asked. His face was deep with wrinkles that made him look hundreds of years old.

"Yes," Riley nodded. "He's the only man I have ever truly loved. He doesn't deserve to die. He's already lost his brother."

The Old Writer smiled. "His suffering would end and he would be reunited with his brother here, in the Dimension of Eternity. Why do you wish that he should live?"

"His family have gone through enough," Riley pleaded. "They've just lost one son. They couldn't bear to lose another so soon. It would finish them."

"Your compassion is touching," the Old Writer said. "But if Ethan is to be spared, another life must be taken in his place."

"Take mine," Riley said without thinking. "Take mine. I'll go in his place."

"You would give your life for his?" the Old Writer asked.

Riley nodded. The Old Writer turned to the other robed figures around him and conferred. Riley couldn't hear their words, until the Old Writer turned to face her again.

"You must know before I grant your wish that once this is done, it cannot be undone," he warned. Riley nodded. The Old Writer held out both hands, and moments later, two sparking gems from the crystal sea above them descended and settled in his palms. "It will be done," he said. "Ethan will live. You will die in his place. You cannot ask, nor beg for this to be undone once it has been written. You cannot ask the Writers to change his future a second time. Are you sure you are willing to take his place? There can be no turning back."

Riley stared into the Old Writer's eyes. They were neither warm, nor cold. They appeared to extend into the very heart of the Universe, as if, beyond the surface of those dark brown eyes, the entire sum of every living being and every living thing existed.

"I am sure," Riley said.

"Very well," the ancient angel said. The other two Writers raised their quill pens, one at each orb, and wrote in gold dust, symbols Riley had never seen before. The gold dust swirled in the air, converging on each orb, and then disappeared inside.

"It is done," the Old Writer nodded. As soon as he had spoken, all three of the Writers vanished. Riley found herself moving through a dark tunnel, alone, and aware of the light waning behind her.

She found herself standing on the roof of the hospital staring at the people down below. A man and a woman ran across the parking lot and into the main building, and Riley knew somehow that they were Ethan's parents. She could picture them running through the corridors, frightened for their son's life. But she had just bought it back for them with her own. Ethan would live. She would die.

Somehow dying didn't seem so frightening any more. There was a sense of overwhelming peace up there, wherever Lucca had just taken her - the Dimension of Eternity.

She glanced at her watch. It was 12:30pm. She had a little over eleven hours.

By the time Riley returned to Trauma One, Ethan had been moved to a ward. Doctor Jansen caught Riley just as she was about to leave to find him.

"Riley," he called after her. She turned, and he spoke excitedly as he approached. "I don't know what just happened, but I tell you, I've never seen anything like it. He's making a full recovery. He stabilized about half an hour ago. It's as if nothing was ever wrong with him. He's going to be fine." The doctor smiled, and his eyes sparkled, nestled in deep creases. "We're going to keep him here overnight, but I'm sure he'll be well enough to go home tomorrow morning."

"Thank you," Riley said. She tried to force a happy smile, but her emotions were deeply conflicted. Ethan's life for her own.

Ethan was awake, his mother on one side of the bed, holding onto his hand as if letting go would cause her son to drift away again. His father pinched the bridge of his nose, his eyes red and glistening as he tried to fight back the tears.

"Riley!" Ethan smiled as his girlfriend put on a brave face and came closer.

"You gave us all a big scare," Riley said.

"It's nothing," Ethan said. "I'm fine. Look." He held out his arms. "It was just low blood sugar, that's all. Mom, Dad – this is Riley, my girlfriend." He smiled proudly, looking between the three of them.

"Pleasure to meet you, Riley," Carol said. She rose and gave Riley a hug, while Ivan leaned over the bed and shook her hand awkwardly.

"Pleasure to meet you too," Riley smiled.

"They said he had liver failure," Ethan's mother said. "But it looks like a misdiagnosis. Thank god."

"Thank god," Riley repeated. "You're going to be fine," Riley said. She wedged herself in front of Ivan and embraced Ethan tightly.

"Hey," Ethan said as she drew back. He sensed her fear. "I'm fine. I promise."

"I know," Riley said, wiping a tear from her eye. She looked around for Lucca, in case he'd accompanied her to Ethan's bedside, but she was alone.

Ethan held on to Riley's hand tightly. "Don't you go anywhere," he said. "Stay right here." He patted the bed next to him, and Riley edged onto the narrow space. Ethan's father moved around to the other side of the bed and stood next to his wife.

They made a happy couple, Ivan thought, looking at his son and the new girl in his life. Ethan hadn't made good choices in women, but this one looked to be the right one for him, he thought. Ivan smiled at his wife. She seemed to have read her husband's mind.

"You two make such a perfect couple," Carol Lynch said.

"Oh stop it, Mom," Ethan retorted. "But we do make a perfect couple, don't we?" He kissed Riley and held her as she leaned against him, resting on his chest.

Feeling Ethan beside her gave Riley strength. She looked at Ethan's parents, standing beside him, and gave herself comfort knowing that her life would be traded so they could keep their son. Ethan would be heartbroken. Why did the Balance of the Universe have to be so unfair?

Riley waited at the hospital until long after dark. She could sense it was time. She wanted to stay there, locked in Ethan's arms forever, but she knew that she had to leave. She stood, and turned to kiss him.

"I'll see you tomorrow?" Ethan asked.

Riley nodded.

"Good bye, my love," she leaned over and kissed him, long and slow, breathing in every scent, taking in every sensation, knowing it would be the last time she would see him. "I love you."

"I love you too," he said. "Drive safe."

"I will."

She let their hands touch for as long as she could before pulling herself away. She left without looking over her shoulder. Her life for his. That was the deal. It was 11:58pm. She had only moments left. How was it going to happen, she wondered. Would she simply cease to exist? Would she too fall unconscious?

She left the hospital building, and walked through the parking lot towards her car.

There was a loud noise behind her. A screech, like the skid of car tires, and instinctively she froze, turning to the source of the noise. Not too far away from her, a small blue Mazda had just entered the parking lot, and its engine roared loudly. The car lurched forward, gathering speed, and slammed into the back of another car that had just begun to reverse out of a parking bay. The impact changed the trajectory of the speeding vehicle, causing it to veer to its left on a direct collision course with Riley. She saw the lights of the approaching vehicle as it hurtled through the air. Then darkness.

Chapter 9

Riley felt that feeling again. The feeling of moving rapidly backwards in time. The car that had hurtled towards her moments ago moved backwards through the air, until it was at the entrance to the parking lot. Riley found herself in Ethan's arms in the ward, and then she was moving backwards through the ward, and back into the elevator. She found herself on the hospital roof, looking down at Ethan's parents as they ran across the parking lot and into the hospital. She'd never met them before, but she recognized them from her vision.

It was 12:30pm. She had eleven and a half hours.

"I have to find Archer and Martin," she said. "At least if they know, I can still reach Ethan from the Dimension of Eternity."

Riley took the stairs down to the Trauma ward. Doctor Jansen approached her excitedly, just as he had in her earlier vision. But instead of going to the ward after he had told her the good news, she called Archer.

"You still in the building?" she asked.

"Just about to leave now," he said.

"Wait for me!"

She found Archer at the entrance to the hospital.

"What is it?" he asked.

Riley hesitated for a moment. "I made a deal with the Writers," she began.

"The who?"

"Lucca showed me a way to change Ethan's future," Riley explained.

Archer's expression brightened. "What? But he said the future can't be changed, that we only saw the future so we could understand it."

"The future of the world, yes. The future of one person can be changed as long as there's balance," Riley explained.

"Balance. Martin's Sum of the Universe?"

"Exactly," Riley looked down, and Archer immediately sensed her sadness. He looked at her questioningly.

"Wait a minute. What did you do? Riley? Did you do something stupid?" Archer held her by both shoulders, staring into her eyes. Riley nodded.

"I told them I'd go in his place," she whispered.

"What?" Archer blurted loudly, drawing stares from passers by. Realizing what it must look like – a black man holding a white girl by the shoulders as if he were harassing her – he let go of her and paced his trademark small circle, hands on his hips. "What?" he said again. "But how is that possible? Lucca?"

Riley shook her head. "He doesn't have the power to change the future, but he took me into his world, and I saw the ones who do. They're called the Writers. They create the future. They maintain the Balance."

Archer was silent as he took this all in. "I've been a medium all my life, and I never knew about them. Not the Writers. The Equation of Balance. The Sum of the Universe. This angel with the book. None of it. Here you come, and in a week, you've already crossed over and come back again without having to die first, and now you're giving it all up? For one man? Riley, you don't know the gift you have! What did you do?" He closed his eyes and arched his head back, looking up at the cloudless sky for a moment. "What did you do, girl?" Archer's eyes welled with tears. "I only just met you, and there's so much..." He shook his head. "Girl, you really are something. To give up everything for this guy."

Riley forced a smile. There was no rational answer as to why she volunteered to take Ethan's place in death, except that she loved him in a way she'd never loved before, in a way she never thought possible. Love like this was rare. None of her friends spoke of love the way Riley had experienced it. Even if it was only destined to be fleeting, this love was worth dying for. And her act was the ultimate sacrifice of love. It wasn't heroism. She hadn't thought of it as self-sacrifice. Just an act of which only she was capable, an act that would save the life of the man she loved. She simply nodded, and said nothing.

"I saw how it happens. Here, at the hospital. Ethan stays here overnight. I leave his bedside at midnight. And then it happens, right about there," she pointed to the place she had stood in her vision. "A stray car. Random accident." Riley gave Archer the kind of smile people make when they're neither happy nor sad, the kind that visitors at a wake give the grieving family, accompanied by the rote words, *I'm so sorry for your loss.* "I'm going back inside, to spend the rest of ..." What was she to say? The rest of *the day?* The rest of *her life?* "...I'm going to be with Ethan until they kick me out."

"Riley," Archer said, his words an attempt to dissuade her, to make her change her mind.

"You can't change the future now," she said. "Remember the woman I saw in my vision? The one I was destined to injure in a car accident? Even though I managed to avoid the accident, I still sent her to the ER. If it doesn't happen one way, it will happen another. I'm dying tonight. At midnight. You can't change that, Archer." Riley embraced him, and felt the damp of his tears against her cheeks. "Don't cry, Archer. Ethan lives in my place. Be there for him. Watch over him. And listen out for my voice at the doorway to the Dimension of Eternity."

Archer nodded, and wiped his tears away on his sleeve. "I will," he promised. "You'd better be there," he said through a teary smile. "I'm gonna miss you, Riley."

"Me too, Archer. Fate brought us together for a reason," she shrugged. "Whatever that may be."

"Yeah," he said as Riley turned and disappeared through the main entrance and into the hospital.

"Yeah," he said again, as he stood alone outside the hospital. This building, he thought. Everything seemed to have happened here. His first encounter with the angel with the book. Lucca. At least now he knew the angel's name. And meeting Riley and Ethan. He looked down at the glossy white floor tiles. They had all stood right here, together. And now, Riley's life traded for Ethan's. "This is one messed up place," Archer said to himself as he turned. He looked up and froze. In front of him, was Lucca, and in his hands, he held a book. Lucca opened it and showed Archer a page which had only one line of text that made Archer's body run cold.

12:00am

"Can't we stop this?" Archer begged. "Please, if there's a way, show me!"

But Lucca disappeared, just as he had always done after showing Archer what was written in his book. His was only to understand.

"Martin!"

The man who called himself Angel Martin heard the panic in the Oracle's voice over the phone.

"Archer? What is it? What's wrong?" Martin said.

"Give me your address. I'm coming over. It's urgent, we have to meet now. We don't have much time."

Martin gave Archer his home address. "What's wrong?" Martin asked again.

"I can't tell you over the phone. I'll be there in ten minutes, I'm not far away. Cancel your appointments for the rest of the day," Archer instructed before hanging up.

Martin looked apologetically at the young man opposite him.

"I'm afraid I have an emergency I have to attend to, Allan." Martin looked perplexed, as if he himself didn't understand what he was saying. "Can we reschedule?"

Allan was in his late thirties, and wore a manicured, long hipster beard, with neatly styled short hair framing his face. "What kind of emergency?" he asked with a frown. It wasn't as if the medium was a medical doctor.

"I don't usually get spiritual emergencies," Martin said, rising. As he did, Allan stood, disappointed that his session had been cut short. "But when I do, you can be sure it's the kind that means the difference between life and death. Can you come back tomorrow, same time? I won't charge you for today."

"Sure," Allan said. "Sure."

Martin sensed the man's disappointment.

"Someone else's current problem needs my gift right now. Your problem, important as it is, isn't time critical. This one is. You understand?" Martin had a gift for diplomacy. He could defuse any situation with his soothing voice and carefully chosen words. Allan was appeased by Martin's final explanation.

"Of course. It's no problem, really. Mine isn't desperate. Go help your other patient," Allan said at the door.

"Client," Martin corrected.

"Yeah," Allan smiled. "Client. See you tomorrow."

Martin heard footsteps approaching rapidly. Archer came bounding down the corridor at speed. *How had Archer gotten through the front door, he wondered.*

"Hey," Archer greeted Allan on his way out.

"Hey," the hipster greeted him. "Hope you get your thing sorted, man," he said to Archer as he made his way down the hallway to the staircase. Standard practice for all of Martin's clients.

"Martin," Archer greeted him. "Oh, I used your access code at the door."

"But…" Martin began, shaking his head. "That's against the rules."

"Come on, we don't have much time." Martin ushered Archer inside and closed the door.

"What's all this about?" Martin asked as they moved to the small table by the window. Archer sat, and Martin stood opposite him, and began packing away the Tarot cards that were still laid out on its surface. He cleared the ones that had been upturned during his session with Allan, and was about to clear the remaining two, which were still face down.

"Wait," Archer said, placing a hand on Martin's as he was about to lift one of the face down cards. Martin searched Archer with an inquisitive stare as he sank into the chair opposite his fellow medium. The older medium removed his hand allowing Archer to turn the card.

"Death," Martin looked up at Archer. The card bore the number thirteen, and an image of a hooded figure whose face was a shadowed skull. In his boney hand he carried a long scythe. Archer's heart sank. "Ethan," Martin nodded slowly.

"Not Ethan," Archer said. "Riley."

"What?" Martin stared at the Oracle.

"She crossed over with Lucca, and she made a deal to trade her life for his," Archer said. Martin stared at him in silence. "She told me Lucca has the power to bring her over to the Dimension of Eternity. She said she met the Writers, the ones who write the future, and she made a deal with them. Her life for his."

"The Equation of Balance," Martin said, looking down at the upturned card. "But Lucca said you cannot change the future."

"He means the future of the world. The future of one person apparently can be changed, as long as there's still balance," Archer said, looking down at the card.

"So Riley agreed to die in Ethan's place?" Martin thought out loud. The cards were never wrong.

Archer's reached across and turned the remaining card.

"The Wheel of Fortune," Martin smiled. The card was colorful, featuring an orange circle containing various symbols in the center. There were clouds around the circle, and on them were four winged creatures. "You will recognize the coming tide and be able to make the most of it," Martin looked up at Archer.

"Martin, she can cross over to the other side and converse with the angels and the spirits. She's special. I've never known someone with her gift," Archer shook his head, feeling inside the weight of Riley's imminent death. "We can't lose her Martin. We just can't."

"But there isn't anything we can do. You know that," Martin said in his deep, measured voice.

"Lucca seems to be the key to all this. Lucca and the hospital," Archer said, turning the Wheel of Fortune over and over in his fingers. "He showed me Riley's book. She dies at midnight. We have to do something, Martin. Can we summon him? Can we summon Lucca?"

"We can try," Martin said, extending both hands. They had summoned him before, with Riley. Archer took his hands, and Martin spoke. "Lucca, we call on you. Will you speak to us?"

They waited, but there was only silence.

Martin beseeched the Angel to speak to them several more times, but still, they heard nothing. Archer's heart sank. He was certain that Lucca would speak to them.

"We have to go back to the hospital," he said. "There's something about that place. Everything seems to be connected to the hospital."

"Archer," Martin said solemnly, "you have to accept that you can't change this. You have to recognize the coming tide and make the most of it. You can't change it. You have to accept it. Understand it."

"No," Archer said, rising. "No! I won't. She's too special, Martin, you know it too. We can't let her die. There has to be something we can do."

Martin remained in his seat. Young people, he thought. They have no regard for the rules. They do not respect the traditions of the past. They want a new world, a new way of doing everything. But there are some things you can't change. "You go, Archer. I'm not coming with you."

"Come on, man. Martin, she can cross over. Do you know what that means?" Archer pleaded.

"It means we're not supposed to cross over, Archer. Don't you understand? We are not supposed to cross over. There's a reason we've never been able to cross. There's a reason only some people come back. There's a reason you have to die to cross." Martin was enraged. "You can't change the very fundamental essence of our Dimension."

"I didn't make the rules, Martin. I didn't make her," Archer said, raising his voice and pointing towards the door. "I didn't choose her. She just is. I never gave her the ability to cross over and come back. This isn't me changing rules, it's him." Archer motioned to a gap between them. "Now I'm going to the hospital to see if there's something I can do to save her, because I'm not the Hanging Man. This," he held the Wheel of Fortune up for Martin to see. "This is a sign."

"You're wrong," Martin warned. "You're just wasting your time."

"Yeah? Well I'm gonna carry on wasting it till midnight tonight because I refuse to accept that there's nothing I can do. You coming or staying?"

"I'm staying," Martin said, still sitting at the table.

"Fine!" Archer said. He slammed the door leaving Martin one card short.

"Fine!" Martin said to no one.

Riley watched from the door of the small ward. Three of the four beds were occupied, but the only activity was around Ethan's, where his parents stood by their son. Riley understood the anguish they must be going through all too well. She'd seen parents of young children hold on desperately as they stood by helplessly watching their child slip away.

"I'm fine, Mom, honestly," Ethan reassured his mother. "The doctor said he must have missed something." His mother held on to his hand tightly, and his father pinched the bridge of his nose, trying to hide the tears. Then he noticed Riley. "Hey!" he called to her. "Riley! Come on in." Riley approached as Ethan spoke. Carol and Ivan looked up. "Mom, Dad, this is Riley, my girlfriend." It was just the way he had introduced her to them in her vision.

"Mr. and Mrs. Lynch," Riley greeted them as she approached.

"Oh, please, with the formalities," Ethan's mother waved a hand and stood to give Riley a warm hug. "Carol and Ivan."

"Pleasure to meet you both," Riley said, although she already felt like she knew them so well. She'd spend hours with them in anguish during her previous vision.

Ivan Lynch leaned across the bed and shook Riley by the hand awkwardly. Then he motioned to the place where he stood.

"Why don't you come around this side? It's awfully cramped in here." He shuffled around to join his wife while Riley moved to the empty spot he had left for her.

"Twice in one week?" Riley said as she leaned in and greeted Ethan with a warm hug, and a kiss that she wanted to last forever.

Ethan couldn't disguise his surprise. "This one wasn't my fault," he said. "Apparently I collapsed at the supermarket. But the doctors say I'm going to be fine. They thought it was something horrible at first, but it couldn't have been because look at me. I'm fine." He stroked Riley's hair, sensing her concern. "Promise. I'm going to be fine."

"I know," Riley said softly, nestling her head on his chest. She wanted everyone to go away so she could spend her last precious hours alone with Ethan.

The conversation became awkward since she'd joined Carol and Ivan at Ethan's bedside, yet neither of them picked up the cue to leave. The awkwardness was broken by a new arrival.

"Ethan!" Archer called as he entered the ward.

"Archer? What are you doing here?" Ethan said. Riley sat upright, and turned so she could see the Oracle.

"Mr. and Mrs. Lynch," Archer greeted the parents with a nod. "Riley."

Riley gave Archer a look that warned him not to tell of their earlier conversation. Aware of her nonverbal admonishing, Archer said to Ivan and Carol, "Would you mind giving us a minute? There's something me and Ethan need to discuss in private."

Riley's eyes smoldered, but Archer refused to pay attention to her warning.

"Uh, sure. Let's go get some coffee, Ivan?" Carol suggested. Her husband nodded.

"We'll be right outside if you need anything, Ethan," he said as Carol dragged him by the hand towards the door. When Ivan and Carol were out of earshot, Archer continued.

"Ethan, man. Sorry to barge in on you like this but ..." he began but Riley cut him short.

"Archer don't you dare!" she warned.

"Dare what?" Ethan asked, confused. Archer searched the room and found Ethan's clothes neatly folded on a chair.

"Here," he said dropping the pile of clothes on the bed. "Put these on."

"Archer, what's gotten in to you?" Ethan asked, staring at the clothes and then up at Archer.

"Why don't you ask her?" He motioned to Riley with his eyes.

"Archer, no!" Riley tried to stop him, but it was too late.

"Ask her what?" Ethan said, confused. "Riley, what's he talking about?"

"Maybe you'd better put some clothes on," Riley said, glaring at Archer. "I know a place we can talk about this." She cast her eyes at the other beds in the room. "Privately," she added. "I'll wait for you outside the ward." Riley turned off the machines that monitored Ethan's vitals, and disconnected the sats monitor from Ethan's fingertip before leaving him to get dressed.

Ethan and Archer joined Riley a few moments later and followed her to the roof of the building. The three of them stood in the afternoon sun, looking over the hospital parking lot.

"What's this all about, Riley?" Ethan asked.

Riley took a deep breath. "You know that angel that I can see? The one who tells the future?"

"Yeah?" Ethan said.

"Well he's shown me your future."

"Wait," Ethan stopped her. "I don't want to know."

"This is important," Archer insisted. "You need to hear this."

"No!" Ethan protested. "I don't want to know my future. It's wrong."

"But, Ethan," Riley begged. "What if knowing your future allowed you to alter its course? What if your life was going to end, and you could prevent it if you knew."

Ethan screwed up his face. "No!" he said again, waving Riley off dismissively with his hand. "No! If I'm supposed to live or die, then that's what should happen. If you know something about my future, keep it to yourself, I don't want to know."

"Riley dies tonight. At midnight," Archer blurted. "We don't have time for this moral high ground bullshit. She dies. Tonight. She swapped her life for yours. You were supposed to die."

Ethan stared at Riley in stunned silence for a long while before he spoke.

"Riley, is this true? Was I supposed to die tonight?"

Riley nodded, biting her lip.

"And you … what? You traded places with me?" He asked in disbelief. "How? How could you? Without even asking me?"

"You were busy dying, Ethan!" Riley exploded, surprising both Archer and Ethan. "I saw your future before it even happened. I didn't ask to see it, he just showed it to me. The angel, Lucca. You were admitted to the hospital with acute liver failure. Your blood type is AB Negative. There wouldn't be time to find you a donor. You were going to die, tonight at midnight."

Ethan stared at her for a long moment. "How did you know my blood type?" He was stunned.

"I saw it in my vision, Ethan. That's how it works for me. I see the future as if it's really happening. I saw you wheeled into

Trauma One. I saw the doctor trying to save you. He told me you had acute liver failure and without a donor liver, you didn't have more than twelve hours to live. And he told me your blood type was AB Negative. I knew immediately it was going to be impossible finding you a donor in so little time."

"Then how am I standing here?" Ethan asked, still stunned.

"I begged the angel for a way to let you live," Riley said sheepishly. "I asked him if there was a way to change the future and he took me into his world to meet with the ones who write the future."

Ethan listened as she spoke. Had it been anyone else telling him this story, he would have dismissed it as fantasy, but coming from Riley, he believed every word.

"I was there, Ethan. In the afterlife. Or the spirit world, or whatever you want to call it. The Dimension of Eternity. Where people go after they die. I was there. And I spoke to the Writers, the ones who write what happens to each one of us. They said in order for you to live, someone else had to die in your place."

Ethan listened, hoping he wasn't going to hear next what he dreaded Riley would say.

"And I told them to take me in your place," Riley said, tears welling up in her eyes. Ethan's world imploded around him. He couldn't believe what he'd just heard. He dropped to his knees in front of her.

"Riley, why? Why did you do that? Not you! You can't die in my place, I won't let it happen, I forbid it!" He clung tightly to her, weeping. She knelt too, and they held on to each other, their tears falling on each other's shoulders.

"I love you, Ethan," Riley said, wiping the tears from her face. "I couldn't let you die."

"I love you too, Riley. I would never have let you die in my place. You didn't give me that chance. How can I live knowing you had to die in my place? How can I live with that?" Ethan's eyes were red.

They held each other as they sobbed. Archer watched, turning away now and then to wipe the tears from his eyes.

"Ok, you two. Sorry to break up the party, but Riley, you have to call Lucca. We have to undo this thing. Together," Archer said.

"But it's done," she said to him.

"And I don't give a damn. Undo it. Ask him to ask them if there's another way. Call him. Now!"

Archer knelt and pried Riley's hand away from Ethan's neck.

"Hold my hands," he instructed. "Now!" The three of them knelt in a circle, holding hands. "Call him!" Archer commanded.

"Call him," Ethan echoed gently.

Riley hesitated, and then said timidly, "Lucca?"

Immediately the angel appeared in the center of the circle.

"Man, at last!" Archer breathed. "Lucca, please, man, you gotta help us here."

Ethan's face went pale and his eyes widened. "Are you seeing this?" Ethan whispered. Riley nodded.

"I cannot undo what Riley has requested. Only the Writers can affect the Balance," Lucca said.

"Can we talk to them? The Writers? Can we talk to the Writers?" Archer begged.

"Not from the Dimension of Time. They only communicate inside the Dimension of Eternity," Lucca replied.

"Can you take us there?" Archer asked hopefully.

"All of you?" Lucca asked.

"Yeah. She went and asked to die in his place, so her and him, they gotta go. And I wanna come too, 'cos I ain't never been. Please?" Archer begged. "Can you take us to them?"

"You may not request to see the Writers," Lucca said to Archer. The Oracle's smile disappeared.

"Will you take me to see the Writers?" Riley asked.

"They will not grant you a second audience." Lucca replied.

Riley felt hopeless. There was nothing more she could do. She had spent her one and only chance at saving Ethan, and the Writers had made that very clear to her. What she had asked them could not be undone. She would not be given another audience with them.

"What about me? Can I see them?" Ethan asked. Riley stared at him.

Lucca nodded. "They will see you, Ethan. Come. Follow me."

The angel turned, and Ethan found himself following him into a dark tunnel.

"Where am I?" Ethan asked, bewildered. He was moving, but he was neither walking, nor running. He was floating, following Lucca's silhouette towards a bright light at the far end of the tunnel.

When they emerged, Ethan was mesmerized by the lights all around him, glistening and sparkling. Everywhere he looked, lights of every different color sparkled here and there, constantly changing like a kaleidoscope. It was as if someone had taken every tiny light from every Christmas tree that ever existed and set them free to drift around him.

"Where am I?" Ethan asked. He felt the overwhelming presence of peace deep within his soul.

"You are in the Dimension of Eternity," Lucca explained. "The place where every soul exists."

"Is Carly here?" Ethan asked. Lucca nodded, but in his eyes was a warning that forbade any attempt to see his brother.

Three angels approached Ethan, drifting weightlessly in the sea of dancing light. The Old Writer led the group as he had done before.

"Ethan Lynch," the Old Writer said. "You wanted to see the Writers. What is your request?" he asked. The Old Writer's deeply wrinkled face radiated warmth and wisdom.

"Um, I'm kinda new to this all." Ethan hesitated for a moment, and then found the words. "Riley O'Connor is the bravest woman I know. She came to you to ask if she could die in my place. But I love her too much to let her do that. So I'm asking – is there a way to undo what she asked for before? So she can live?"

The Old Writer moved closer to Ethan. "You wish for me to undo what the girl asked me to do?"

"I think so, yes," Ethan said. "And if maybe there's a way I could live too, that would be nice."

Ethan stared into the Old Writer's wrinkled face, into the dark eyes that had seen centuries of lives come and go in the Dimension of Time.

"For you to live requires a sacrifice," the Old Writer said. "To live, you must choose who dies in your place."

"I can't do that," Ethan said. "I can't choose someone to die in my place. If I am destined to die, then let it be me."

"You are sure this is what you want, Ethan Lynch?" The Old Writer asked.

"I am sure," he said, looking across at Lucca. "I am sure. I won't let Riley take my place."

"Once I write your fate, it cannot be undone. You must be absolutely sure this is what you want. You will die at midnight tonight, Ethan Lynch. Is this your wish?" the Writer asked.

Ethan nodded somberly.

"Then it will be so once more," the Old Writer said. "Now that you have asked, you may not ask again. This is your one and only chance to change your future."

"I won't ask again," Ethan promised.

The Old Writer held out his hands. Two sparkling spheres of what looked like cut crystal descended from above and settled in the Writer's palms. The other two Writers waved their quill pens, and gold dust swirled around the orbs before disappearing into the glass-like objects. Without a word, the Writers disappeared into the sea of lights.

Ethan watched the lights move further and further away, as he was drawn into a tunnel. He saw the form of Lucca in the darkness, leading him back to his world.

Moments later, he was aware of the weight of his knees on the rooftop of the hospital building.

"Ethan?" Riley sobbed, her face streaming with tears. "Tell me you didn't do it! I can't lose you. I love you so much."

"I had to," Ethan said. "Because I love you too," Ethan began, but his eyes widened in agony as the intense pain returned to his abdomen. He doubled over in pain, then fell unconscious onto the rooftop.

"Ethan!" Riley called out. "Archer! Get a doctor, quickly!"

Archer rose, and saw Lucca hovering beside Ethan, holding a book. It was a different book to the one he had shown Archer earlier. He held the book open, and on the page was the same single line of text:

12:00am.

"Ethan dies at midnight," Archer whispered. The angels had condemned Ethan to die. Riley had willingly taken his place. And Archer had conspired to undo Riley's selfless deed, condemning Ethan to die once again.

Doctor Jansen looked perplexed. He raised his palms in a gesture of helplessness. "I don't know what's going on with this patient. He presented with acute liver failure. It looked like a case of secondary Budd-Ciari Syndrome. Then it looked as if he was making a full recovery, against all odds. And now he's right back to square one again. I don't understand."

His colleague studied the patient's file, and placed a reassuring hand Jansen's upper arm. "You didn't miss anything, Brad. I would have made the same diagnosis. Both times."

"He's fucked, isn't he," Jansen said.

"Short of a miracle, I'm afraid so."

Jansen nodded, and took the file back from his colleague. His face looked drawn as he came through the doors of Trauma One to deliver the bad news to the family a second time. This time, the patient's parents were there.

"Mr. and Mrs. Lynch," he began, "I'm afraid it's not good news. His liver has relapsed. It's as we thought before. We're going to put him on anticoagulation therapy to see if it helps. If not, unless we can get a donor liver in the next six to eight hours, we're not going to be able to save him."

Carol Lynch sobbed loudly, and turned to her husband. She threw her arms around his neck, and cried loudly. "No!" she cried. "You can't take our boy. He's all we have left."

"I'm so sorry," Jansen said apologetically. "I'm moving him back to the ward. We'll do all we can for him, but…" he hesitated, "don't get your hopes up."

Riley stood behind Ethan's parents. The doctor gave her an empathetic look that said *I'm so sorry for your loss*, before returning to Trauma One. She remained in the hallway as Ivan and Carol Lynch made their way to the ward. Archer waited, seated on a worn, padded chair a short distance away.

"We tried," he said. Riley nodded, looking at her watch. It was 4:08pm. In just under eight hours, Ethan would slip away from her. She had tried everything that was humanly possible, and beyond. She had called on the help of the angels and the Dimension of Eternity to save him, and even that was not enough. Ethan would die at midnight. She had done everything she could. It seemed that fate, no matter how she tried to change it, was determined to prevail.

"I still don't understand," Riley said, sinking into a seat beside Archer.

"What?"

"Why we saw all of this." She waved a hand towards the trauma ward. "Ethan being admitted here, right down to the time he would die. Why?"

"I don't understand either," Archer said.

"I think I do," a deep voice said.

"Martin?" Archer jumped to his feet. "What are you doing here?"

"Been doing a lot of thinking and consulting with angels," Martin replied. He greeted Riley with a gentle kiss on the cheek, and sat in the empty seat next to her. "May I?" he asked Archer.

"Be my guest," Archer replied. He stood in front of them as they spoke.

"I think we've been looking at this all wrong," Martin

suggested.

"How?" Archer asked, making a face.

"Whose angel is Lucca?" Martin asked. Both Archer and Riley were surprised by the question.

"Seems to be Riley's angel, for sure," Archer offered, but Martin shook his head.

"Riley's angel is Haniel. I've communicated with Haniel before," he explained.

"He's right," Riley agreed. "The first time I met you, you saw her."

"Then whose angel is Lucca?" Archer asked.

"Ethan's," Martin said. The answer took both Riley and Archer by surprise.

"Ethan?" Archer repeated, his head jutting forward on his neck.

"Think about it," Martin said. "The message he's been giving all of us – its all about Ethan, and Ethan's future. We get to communicate with him, and he shares his message in different ways, but it's all about Ethan's future."

"But what about the time I saw my accident?" Riley asked. "That wasn't about Ethan, that was about me."

"Was that the whole vision?" Martin asked. "Or was there more."

Riley thought. "No, there was more. On the same day, just after I had the encounter with the woman in the hallway, the one I spilled the boiling water over, I had another vision involving Ethan. He met me there at the hospital."

"And Ethan was in the hospital when you had your last encounter," Martin said to Archer.

"That's right," Archer thought out loud. "When I first met Riley, Ethan was in the hospital. And when I saw him today, one time he showed me the time of midnight in his book, because Riley had taken Ethan's place, and now he showed me Ethan's page. It's all connected to Ethan."

"So Lucca is Ethan's angel?" Riley said.

"That's what it seems like to me," Martin said.

"How does that change anything," Archer said. "He's still going to die tonight. She's used up her only shot at changing the future. Ethan went and used his one chance to change it all back again. We're out of chances."

"Maybe not," Martin smiled.

"What are you saying?" Archer asked, hands on his hips.

"Your angel is allowed to intervene for you," Martin said.

"We can ask Lucca?" Riley said, hope starting to rekindle inside her. Martin nodded.

"We can only ask. It's up to him, and him alone," Martin cautioned.

"But he told me he couldn't do it for me," Riley objected. "I asked him if there was anything he could do. He said only the Writers could."

"For you, no." Martin smiled. "But for Ethan..."

Riley looked up at the swing doors that led to Trauma One.

"But Ethan's unconscious," she said. "How will he ask Lucca?"

"The soul never sleeps," Martin said, interlocking his fingers beneath his chin. Riley looked puzzled. "Why do you remember your dreams?" he asked her unexpectedly.

"I don't know," Riley said. "Because they're dreams?"

"Because your soul never sleeps. Your body rests, but your soul doesn't need a physical body. When your body sleeps, your soul is still active," Martin said.

"Can you communicate with him while he sleeps?" Riley asked.

Martin looked up at his fellow medium. "Archer, you channel Lucca through Riley. I'll summon Ethan's subconscious while he sleeps. Lucca will be able to communicate with him. If Ethan hears us, he can ask Lucca to intervene on his behalf. It's our only chance." Martin glanced at his watch. "We have little under seven hours now."

"What are we waiting for? Let's go!" Riley beckoned the other two, already on her feet. Martin rose, and followed a short distance behind her and Archer.

Ivan and Carol Lynch had taken seats at either side of Ethan's bed, and each held a hand tightly.

"I don't understand what's going on," Carol wept. "You were fine just a moment ago." Gently, she combed her fingers through her son's hair. She looked up at her husband. "We can't lose them both," she begged, though she knew Ivan was as helpless as she was. "God help us."

"Carol, Ivan," Riley said as she approached them. Ethan's parents turned to greet her, and acknowledged her without words.

"I recognize you," Carol said as Archer approached.

"Yeah, we met last time he was in here," Archer replied.

"This is Martin," Riley introduced the other medium.

"If anyone can help us reach Ethan, these two can," Riley said.

"What do you mean?" Ivan said, skeptically. Carol turned her gaze back to Ethan.

"What if I told you that there's another reason why Ethan's condition has taken a turn for the worse?" Riley began.

"I don't understand?" Carol tilted her head.

"Ma'am, if I may," Archer interrupted. "Imagine the world was like looking into a two-way mirror. If you're standing on the one side, you can only see your reflection. That's us here, on earth. We can only see our reflection looking back at us. But, see, there's another dimension behind the glass that we can't see. They can see us, but we can't see them. That's the spirit world."

Carol went rigid, and her face turned sour. "Don't talk to me about spirits! You speak of the Occult!"

"Look, Mrs Lynch, I know how you must feel, and I respect your beliefs." Archer held up both hands defensively. "But he ain't got much time left. The doctors only gave him a couple of hours. Really, if your god's gonna do anything, now would be a good time."

All eyes were on Carol Lynch. Raised a Catholic, she had never been allowed to even contemplate any spiritual reality besides what was written in the Bible. God was supreme. There could be no other gods but Him. And communication with spirits was the work of the devil. But was her belief so strong that she would cling to it at the expense of her only remaining son? Where was God when Carly was being gunned down in cold blood on Eighth Street? Where was God when Carly was lying in a gutter, riddled with bullets, the life pouring out of his body. Where was her god then? All her years of faith and observance hadn't saved her son.

"What are you going to do?" she asked. Ivan stared at her, both shocked and hopeful at the same time. If Carol wanted it so, he would tell them to leave, but he was not one to stand on ceremony. If these two men who spoke to the spirits could save his son, he would let them do whatever they wanted, as long as it would save Ethan's life. Time and again, Carol had clung to her faith at the expense of logic, and Ivan had let her overrule him. Even now, he waited to see what she would do, and he would honor her decision, whichever way it went.

"We're going to ask Ethan to ask his angel to intercede for him. To beg for another way to save his life," Archer explained.

Angels and intercession. Both were spoken about in church. God had sent angels to many of the saints and Apostles. Angels were biblical, as was intercession. Praying for another on their behalf. Surely this wasn't blasphemous. Surely this was the will of God? Surely her own prayers were being answered. These men weren't of the devil. They were messengers from God himself.

"Do what you need to do to save my son," Carol pleaded, rising.

"Could you give us a minute?" Archer asked Ethan's parents. Carol nodded rapidly. She took her husband's hand, wiped her tears from her cheek with her sleeve, and led him through the ward doors, looking over her shoulder as she left. If these two men who spoke to the spirits managed to save her son, what would that mean for her entire life of devout observance, she wondered.

Martin drew the curtain around Ethan's bed, and took his right hand. Archer stood between him and Riley, who held Ethan's left hand to complete the circle. Martin nodded at Archer, and then leaned in to whisper in Ethan's ear.

"Ethan," Martin whispered, long and slow, almost eerily.

"Ethan, awake inside. Your body is dying, and you must speak with your angel."

At the same time, Archer whispered in Riley's direction, "Lucca, we call on you. Please speak to us now."

They waited for long moment, and then Riley was aware of the familiar warmth. She opened her eyes to find Lucca floating as if he were lying face down on an invisible hammock directly over Ethan's bed, his face inches above Ethan's, the angel's wings spread out as if protecting him.

"Ethan," Martin's eerie whisper echoed. "Speak to your Angel. Beg him for a way to spare your life."

They waited in silence that stretched on and on. Nobody said a word. Whatever was being said between Lucca and Ethan was happening in Ethan's subconscious. The angel stared at Ethan as he hovered, and then he looked over his shoulder at Riley. Then he disappeared.

"What now?" Riley asked. "Did it work? What happened?"

Martin and Archer exchanged glances. The older one shook his head. "I don't know. Now I guess its up to them." He motioned to Ethan with a tilt of his head.

"So, what? We just wait?" Riley asked impatiently.

"I'm afraid it's all we can do now," Martin said.

Chapter 10

Ethan called out to Riley but she couldn't hear him. None of the people gathered around his bed could hear him.

"What's happening? Why can't they hear me!" he said in frustration.

"That's you there," Lucca said, pointing to the bed. Ethan looked at the angel, confused.

"Where am I? Am I … am I dead?" Ethan asked.

"No," Lucca replied. "You're with me in the Dimension Inbetween. You're neither living, nor dead. Your spirit crosses into this Dimension often, when you sleep, or when you're in a trance, but most people are not aware that this dimension exists."

"I've been here before?" Ethan asked.

"Often," Lucca replied.

"Why don't I remember?"

"Your subconscious can access this Dimension, but you are not in control of your subconscious."

Ethan was more than a little bewildered. He watched as Riley sank onto the bed, buried her head on his chest and cried. He longed to reach across and hold her, to stroke her hair and tell her he was fine, but it was as if there was a transparent shield between them. Every time he reached for her she seemed to be further and further away. He could not touch her, and she could not see him.

"Is this what it's like? Being dead?" Ethan asked.

"No. This is the Dimension Inbetween where spirits can still see the Dimension of Time, and those in it, but the people in the Dimension of Time cannot see you. Only angels can return to this Dimension once the body dies."

"Where *do* you go? When you die?" Ethan asked.

"When the body dies," Lucca corrected him. "The spirit never dies."

"Fine. Where does the spirit go?" Ethan asked.

"To the Dimension of Eternity."

"The place you took me before? That's Heaven?" Ethan asked.

"It's where your spirit goes when the body dies," Lucca repeated.

"Why is there no-one else here?" Ethan looked around. "No other spirits?"

"You are always alone in this dimension. Never with another soul. The only ones that can join you here are angels. Your angel, and the one that summoned you here." Lucca stood patiently alongside Ethan. He spoke calmly, devoid of urgency, as if there were no consequence to standing here for eternity watching the people before him grieve and worry.

Carol and Ivan came back into the ward and joined Riley.

"Mom! Dad!" Ethan reached out, but as he did, they moved further away from him.

"You cannot touch them," Lucca explained.

"Why am I here?" Ethan asked.

"You are dying. It was your wish to resume your own destiny and free Riley from her sacrifice."

"I remember that," Ethan said. "I asked the Writers to undo what Riley had done, and let my own future unfold as it would have. Without Riley suffering." He cast a longing glance at the woman who had turned his world upside down.

"You are here because your friends seek to save you still."

"How? The Writers said that was the only time they'd change my future," Ethan said.

"Riley has asked them once and you have asked them once," Lucca said. "But they will still entertain a request from one other."

"From who?" Ethan asked. Lucca was silent. "Who?" Ethan insisted, but still Lucca said nothing. Ethan stared at him, about to shout one more time, but then he felt a tingling in his being, as if all his senses were connected to an electric power source that sent pulses through his being. "You?"

Lucca looked at him, still not saying a word.

"You can ask them, can't you?" Ethan pointed to the gathering around his bed. "That's what all that was for. What do I have to do to get you to ask them? Will you? Can you? Will you ask them for me?"

Lucca nodded. "I will ask them," the angel said finally. "What do you want me to ask the Writers?"

"If there's another way," Ethan turned to the tabloid around his bed. In his moment of bravery when he had stood before the Writers, he hadn't fully considered what it would be like to leave Riley and his family. What it would do to her, and his parents. Watching his mother and father grieve, and Riley collapsed in tears on his chest made it harder for him to accept death. "I don't want to die," he begged Lucca. "I love her."

"That in itself would not persuade the Writers to change your fate. Life in the Dimension of Time is not of the same importance to the Writers as it is to those who live in it. In the Dimension of Time, you know of only one life. But once you have crossed into the Dimension of Eternity, the concept of life changes completely. There is no beginning, and there is no end. You always were, and you will continue to be."

"What can I tell the Writers? To make them listen?" Ethan asked.

"They seek balance. They are not concerned with your reasons, nor with what you have done, or what you will do. I will take your request to them. Wait for me here."

Lucca disappeared, leaving Ethan on his own in the Dimension Inbetween. He felt more alone in the moments that followed than he had ever felt before. In front of him, he saw everyone he loved, but he could not reach them.

He watched as Riley lay awkwardly on the hospital bed, her arm draped over him, and her head on his chest. Her tears ran down her cheek, and formed a growing damp patch on the sheet. His mother stared ahead of her, her expression vacant, holding onto Ethan's left hand. His father looked broken, holding tightly to Ethan's right hand with both of his own, shaking his head.

"I can't lose my boy," he whispered so softly that Carol couldn't hear him from the opposite side of the bed, but to Ethan, the sound was as loud as if Ivan had bellowed it in his ear.

"I'm right here, Dad," Ethan said, but his father could not hear his son's words. Ethan held a hand up, as if resting it on an invisible pane of glass that separated them. "I'm right here."

This encounter with Lucca made him remember Carly's funeral service, sitting in the church feeling like a fraud, as if everyone around him could see through his pretense, knowing he didn't believe. He'd never given much attention to his own religious convictions. It was one of the things he'd left unattended. As long as he neither believed nor disbelieved, he wasn't in danger of eternal damnation, but Carly's death had made him angry with the god his parents had raised him to believe in. It was then that Ethan had decided there couldn't be a god who preached love and redemption while allowing so much pain and suffering. Carly was a good kid. He was one of those people that everyone loved. He followed in Ethan's tailwind. Ethan was the one who was always causing conflict with Mom and Dad, challenging their traditions and beliefs, while Carly was left to sail calmly through the debris left by their heated exchanges. Ethan was the trailblazer. Carly had it easy. And because of it, he was an easier child.

Alone in the Dimension Inbetween, Ethan smiled. "I miss you, li'l brother. Maybe I'll see you again real soon."

Death.

He hadn't really thought about dying. He was young. Why concern himself with something that wasn't supposed to happen for decades? He had his whole life ahead of him. His whole life. It wasn't supposed to have ended so soon. Ethan felt his spirit slump. He wanted to cry, but in this state, there were no tears. It was a strange sensation. To be disconnected from everything he knew to be real. No sense of touch. No tears to cry when your soul feels like crumbling inside you. No senses to breathe in the scent and taste of Riley. He tried to remember, to recreate the sensation. There was a sweetness to her, but here in this Dimension of limbo, he could feel nothing, he could only remember that there had been a feeling. A sensation. He wasn't ready to die.

But looking at his own unconscious body, he was in no state to live either. What would happen when his world suddenly ceased to exist? He hadn't ever written up a will. He hardly had anything to leave to anyone. In material terms, he'd hardly made a difference to the world. There was little legacy to his name. He'd worked as part of a greater team on a number of buildings, but all of it was the work of someone higher than he was in the company hierarchy. He'd contributed little of value to the world he was about to leave. Except for meeting her. Riley. She'd somehow made living worthwhile. What was the purpose of his life, Ethan wondered. What was the purpose of any life? Look at how little he'd accomplished, how little he'd left behind. Was that how the value of life was measured? By what you leave behind? It couldn't be so shallow. What about those who never get the chance to do something great? It can't be that life only has meaning for those blessed with opportunity. So what was it all for anyway?

Lucca returned as silently as he had disappeared. One moment he had been there, and the next he was gone. Now he'd returned just as suddenly, and as stealthily.

"What did they say?" Ethan asked. He was apprehensive. What if the Writers said *No*? He would be condemned to die, to accept his fate, the fate of a life cut short. A fate that was a curse to his parents. For the one who had to die, the pain was brief. For those left behind, the pain could be endless.

"There is a way," Lucca said.

"There is?" Ethan was not expecting to hear anything positive. He was elated.

"Another must die in your place," Lucca said.

"What?" Ethan said, not sure he heard Lucca correctly.

"To maintain the Balance, the Writers will let someone else die in your place. Someone who was not meant to die at midnight must die in your place. That will maintain the Balance."

"Who?" Ethan asked.

"That is not for me to decide." Lucca looked at Ethan.

"What? I must *choose* someone?"

"If you are to live, another must die. It's the only way," Lucca said.

"That's not right," said Ethan, his elation replaced immediately by a sense of hopelessness. How could he condemn someone else to die? "I can't do it."

Lucca turned to Ethan. "You have not yet met your angel. You should meet her."

With that, Lucca vanished once more, and Ethan felt himself drawing closer to his unconscious body, merging with his own form until he felt the familiar sensation of waking from a deep sleep. He felt the weight of Riley's head on his chest, and the cool damp of her tears.

"Ethan!" Carol shouted, startling everyone around her. Riley shifted, raising her head and stared into his sleepy eyes.

"You're awake!" She kissed his lips tenderly, while Carol and Ivan came closer. Archer and Martin hung back, standing at the foot of the bed, giving the family some space.

Ethan realized that one thing had been notably absent during his brief time in the Dimension Inbetween. He was about to speak when the pain from his abdomen spread through his body like tendrils of fire.

"Ow, fuck that hurts!" he said, his hands reaching just to the right of his mid line.

"Ethan!" Carol said again, but her tone was very different from a moment earlier.

"Sorry," he began, but grimaced.

"No, I'm sorry," Carol apologized. "You say whatever you like."

"We were so worried about you," Riley said.

"I know," Ethan breathed as a fresh wave of agony coursed through his body. Then he whispered close to Riley's ear, so that only she could hear, "I saw." Riley shot a glance at the two mediums standing at the foot of the bed, but they simply looked back at her with friendly smiles.

After the nursing staff had tended to Ethan, and filled his drip with more pain medication, Martin crouched beside Carol.

"You can stay for this, but I'd like to speak to Ethan about angels, and I don't want to offend you, Mrs Lynch," the older medium said in his gentle, deep, soothing voice.

Carol smiled. "It's ok," she said, placing a hand on his. "A couple of months ago I might have had a lot to say, but right now..." She looked helplessly at her son, and tears welled up in her eyes. "Right now, I don't know what I believe any more." She let the tears fall as she looked to Martin for comfort.

"Whatever your religious convictions, it's never easy to watch someone you love suffer," Martin said. "It's never easy to lose someone. And every person wrestles with the same questions. Where do we go when we die? Where do my loved ones go when they die? How can I bear the pain of losing someone I love so much?"

Carol nodded, and dropped her head, sobbing uncontrollable tears that rolled from her cheek and splashed onto Martin's hand. Ivan came over and stood behind her. He felt in his pockets, and produced a crumpled tissue, which he passed to her with one hand whilst placing the other reassuringly on her shoulder. Carol wiped her tears, and gathered herself.

"You can say what you want to say, Martin. I'll stay," Carol said.

"You sure?" he asked. "There can't be any negative energy in the room."

"I want my son to live. If you can help him, I'll do whatever it takes to save my son."

Martin nodded, and he and Archer stood on either side of Ethan, with Riley leaning in from behind Archer.

"Ethan, did Lucca speak to you?" Martin asked. Ethan nodded. His eyes were heavy from the effects of the pain medication that fed slowly into his body through the drip, one droplet at a time. "What did he say?"

There was silence filled with apprehension and expectation before Ethan spoke.

"He said there was a way. Someone has to die in my place," he said softly.

"Who?" Archer asked, but Ethan just shook his head.

"I can't make somebody die in my place," Ethan said.

"Didn't Lucca say?" Riley asked. Again Ethan shook his head, and tapped a thumb on his own chest feebly.

"I have to choose."

Riley stared at Martin and Archer.

"I can't," Ethan whispered. "I can't choose someone to die in my place."

Riley buried her head in her hands. She had tried to be that sacrifice, but Ethan had reversed that. She would give anything for him to live. But to choose someone else to die, that was a different situation entirely. Volunteering to die was one thing. Choosing someone else to die for him would be no different to committing murder. Riley's heart sank. As soon as Ethan uttered the words, she knew there was no more she could do. The Writers had set the scene for Ethan's Final Act, and Ethan had chosen to enter the stage, and play his part. She couldn't persuade him to do otherwise.

"My angel," Ethan whispered.

"Yes, my love?" Riley said, lifting her face from her hands. Ethan shook his head, looking at Martin.

"Lucca said I must speak to my angel," Ethan said.

"Isn't Lucca your angel?" Archer asked, surprised. "I thought we figured Lucca out."

Ethan shook his head. "He said I must speak to my angel."

Carol exchanged glances with Ivan, looking up at him over her shoulder. Was this going to be a séance? A ritual that was ascribed to the dark arts, and one that was strictly forbidden by the Catholic doctrine. She knew she should leave the room, but something kept her rooted to her chair.

"Let's find out who that is," Martin said. He glanced at Archer who immediately, turned his palms upwards, waiting for hands to clasp his to form a circle.

"Carol? Ivan? Will you join us?" Martin asked.

Ethan's mother looked petrified. She was about to suggest that she and Ivan wait outside, but her faith had been shaken since Carly's death. Everything she had believed in her entire life had been turned upside down. At church she'd been part of committees and women's groups that had stepped in to help grieving families at the loss of a loved one. They had organized someone to stay at the family home, and look after the ones who couldn't fend for themselves. They had arranged a roster of church members to make meals, and help with shopping and chores. But she had never been on the receiving end of the grief she had helped alleviate until Carly's tragic death. Even then, her faith had been strong. She had welcomed the words of comfort from her community. Words suggesting it was God's will. That He would bring her comfort. That this was a test, and He would also give her the strength to endure. That God had allowed Job to be tested beyond what any human could possibly endure. She should get up and leave, Carol thought. Right now. This was wrong. This was all so wrong.

"Yes," she heard herself saying. She held out her right hand towards Archer, and with her left, she held onto Ivan's. "We'll join you."

"You sure?" Ivan asked. He knew Carol well enough to know

exactly what must have been going through her mind.

"I'm sure," she nodded squeezing Ivan's hand.

The five of them joined hands around the bed, with Martin holding Ethan's right hand and Archer at Ethan's left.

As Martin began to speak, Ethan's head rolled to one side and the monitors beside his bed started beeping. Moments later, two nurses came darting into the ward. The circle around Ethan disbanded as everyone moved back to allow the medical staff room to move.

"Ethan!" Riley called, her hands cupped over her mouth, as Archer moved her away from the bed. "We're too late, aren't we?"

Martin looked at her with sadness in his eyes. "I hope not, Riley."

Carol broke down in tears, clinging tightly to her husband. "He's punishing us for what we did. I know He is."

Ivan shook his head, but there were no words he could say to comfort his wife. Their son was drifting in and out of consciousness, and they both knew the end was approaching quickly. Too quickly.

As the small gathering shuffled into the hallway outside the ward, Ivan's mind drifted into its own recess. His son was dying. He felt a deep sense of remorse and guilt for the way their relationship had ended up. He smiled as he recalled Ethan's first moments in the world, right here in this very hospital. Ivan had been in his late twenties, and he and Carol were among the last of their friends to have children. It was a time when there was always to be too much to do, and neither enough time, nor money. It wasn't a good time to have kids for the Lynch's, but then, Ivan thought, when was it ever? There were always other things to do, expenses to pay, places he had to be other than at home, and when Ethan was born, life was at its most chaotic.

He had just broken away from his job as a project manager in a large construction company, and had started out on his own. Ivan had been running a number of small projects simultaneously for customers he'd managed to pry away from the big company, and things were going well for his new startup. On paper. In reality it was a different story altogether. He found himself constantly torn between being with his family, and finishing all the work he had created for himself. That was his job, of course. Being a project manager. Delivering everything on time was what people employed him for, and being a new business with new customers, Ivan didn't want to let any of them down. The first job he did for any of his new customers was the most important. If it succeeded, they'd spread the word, and he'd slowly pick up new referrals. If it bombed, word would spread like wildfire, and he'd be dead in the water. He wasn't going to let that happen. No matter how much work it took.

As people breezed casually up and down the hallways around him, Ivan relived some of those moments during Ethan's early days. The new baby took up all of Carol's time, and attention. She would take the night shift, letting him sleep, although he recalled never getting enough rest. He'd work until the early hours of the morning, and wake at 6:30am to get on top of things so he could make sure all his projects would run smoothly. Every day brought new urgent issues, urgent problems. It wasn't as if things were falling apart. They were just incredibly busy.

Ivan remembered sitting with Carol one Sunday after lunch on a day that wasn't completely taken up with work, sipping on a beer. Ethan was already walking, and he recalled vividly watching the toddler moving about unsteadily but continuously. He remembered that moment, but not the time between bringing his newborn baby home from the hospital, and that moment when he was already on his feet. The time in between was a blur.

His mind drifted to Ethan at the age of sixteen, taking a sip of his dad's beer. Life was less chaotic for Ivan then, but no less busy. The challenges of the new startup had given way to the challenges of running an established business. Different challenges, but no less demanding. Ivan had been able to take afternoons away from the office to watch Ethan play sport now and again, but work always managed to plague him at home. He would always arrive home with something to do before the next day. Something was always urgent. Something always required his attention. And sometimes he resented the fact that he couldn't finish his work until late in the evening when Ethan had either gone to bed, or had drifted off to his bedroom to play video games. Ethan had somehow managed to finish high school with a couple of awards for art, and a life outside school with his friends that saw him getting into bars and clubs with a fake ID. Ivan was aware of Ethan's antics, but let it slide, playing off in his mind the disruption of a confrontation versus maintaining a relationship with his son. He had erred on the side of non-conflict, giving Ethan free reign under the guise of responsibility. Ethan had demonstrated a need to be independent, and Ivan had allowed it, hoping his lenience would result in an uncomplicated childhood for his son. He wanted the boy to grow up with the self-confidence to believe he could be anything he desired. He had withheld discipline where it wasn't absolutely necessary, choosing instead to treat Ethan as a grown up from the first moments he showed signs of maturity and independence.

Ivan realized now what a mistake that had been. His unwillingness to rein Ethan in had resulted in an adolescent who chose to use that freedom to socialize with his friends at every opportunity at the expense of his relationship with his father.

With Carol hovering beside him now, her expression vacant, Ivan's mind was a mess of emotion and regret. His son was dying. He'd slipped into unconsciousness again, and there was no telling how long it would be before he woke up, or if he'd even wake up at all. He was slipping further and further away. The doctors were not optimistic. He was helpless, filled with a swirling swarm of emotion that made him feel like he was being sucked into a maelstrom. Fear of losing his son, remorse over all the time and opportunities he had already lost, guilt that this was all his own fault. He pulled Carol closer to him and kissed the top of her head.

"He's going to pull through. Pray for a miracle. We need one," he said.

221

"See how much shit he's going through?"

Ethan stood beside an angel. She looked similar to Lucca in that she had the same kind of ethereal glow about her, wings of the same grey feathers, but her expression was far more worldly. She had long brown hair, and was adorned in a long, flowing garment, similar to the one that Lucca wore.

"Are we in the Dimension Inbetween?" Ethan asked.

"He learns fast," the angel said.

"Who are you?" Ethan asked apprehensively, trying not to sound rude or abrupt, but he managed neither.

"Silica," she replied. "Your angel."

"*You're* my angel?"

"Suck it up if you don't like it, it's not up for debate," Silica replied, visibly offended. She glared at Ethan.

"No, I didn't mean it like that," Ethan stammered. Silica folded her arms and faced him threateningly.

"What were you expecting? A man? An archangel? You got me. That doesn't change," Silica glared.

"No, I really didn't mean it in a bad way," Ethan tried to appease her. He continued, hoping to soften her anger. "I thought Lucca was my angel until the last time I saw him, and he told me I should speak to my angel, and now you're here, so I said, *you're* my angel, as in, it's *you*. You're here. I'm finally meeting you. Like that."

"Oh," Silica said. She turned away from Ethan and stared at the small group of people in the hallway outside the ward. "Well your dad's going through a lot of shit right now. Recriminating how little time he spent with you while you were growing up."

Ethan watched his dad squeezing Carol, kissing the top of her head.

"I never knew," Ethan replied. He raised a hand as if pressing it against the bubble he felt like he was trapped in.

"You can't touch them," Silica warned curtly.

"I know," Ethan said. "Just habit."

"Hmm." Silica regarded Ethan suspiciously, and he dropped his hand to his side.

"Why did Lucca say I should speak with you?" Ethan asked.

"You don't want to be here?" Silica asked, instantly offended once again.

"No, that's not what I meant," he stammered. "I mean, Lucca said I should speak with you. Do you know what he meant?"

"Oh. Sure," the angel replied. Ethan waited for her to elucidate but she remained silent, standing beside him with her arms folded.

"Will you tell me?" Ethan asked cautiously, afraid that he might set her off again.

Silica smiled wryly. "Lucca wouldn't listen to me. I told him you'd want to know."

"Want to know what?" Ethan asked.

"Who killed Carly."

Her words knocked the wind out of Ethan's sails. "You know who killed my brother?" he asked. Silica nodded.

"But I can't tell you. It's against the rules."

"What? Why's it against the rules to tell me...?" Ethan began asking, but Silica cut him off with an imperious wave of her long, elegant hand.

"Oh, please," Silica said, waving her hands as she spoke. "Do you think we're allowed to tell you what everyone around you has been doing? Imagine how that would pan out. Imagine if I had a grudge against someone, and I went and told their friends or family or enemies what they'd been up to? It would create chaos. It's an abuse of my position. Just because I can see more than you doesn't mean I can tell you everything I see."

"So what was Lucca thinking?" Ethan asked, and waited for the backlash, immediately aware of how his words might be misconstrued. Silica narrowed her eyes, glaring at Ethan in a way that made him think he might be vaporized at any second.

"When he said you should talk to me?" she asked.

Ethan nodded, grateful she hadn't taken his meaning the wrong way.

"Because I don't always follow the rules. I thought you'd want to know who killed your brother."

"I do," Ethan begged. "I really do."

Silica folded her arms again, and turned to look at the people in the hallway. "Problem is you're not waking up any time soon, so I can tell you but what good's it going to do. You'll find out when you die anyway."

"Maybe I can tell *them*," Ethan looked at his grieving family, and at Riley nestled between Martin and Archer.

"Can't," Silica said. "You can't contact anyone from here."

"*You* can, can't you? You can communicate through Martin and Archer. You can tell them," Ethan said hopefully.

Silica bobbed her head side to side. "I guess," she said. "But they have to ask me. I can't just knock on their door and say, yoohoo, hey guys, I know who killed Carly, wanna play show and tell? It doesn't work that way. They have to ask."

Ethan felt despondent. If his physical body regained consciousness long enough, he could tell Martin and Archer to ask Silica. All he needed was a moment of consciousness long enough.

"Will you tell me then?"

"This is sounding a bit like *Hu is the new leader of China*," Silica said, shaking her head. "Knuckle-head Ed."

"What?" Ethan asked, completely lost.

"Hu is the new leader of China? You never heard that one?" She asked.

"No not that," Ethan waved a hand. "I mean, yeah, I heard that. Everyone's heard that one. Knuckle-head Ed?" Detective Morris had mentioned his name before.

"Knuckle-head Ed. Ed Harper," Silica said flatly, "the leader of the Eighth Street Crushers. He was going after some bottom of the pile Dragon Kings messenger kid, and Carly got caught in the crossfire. There," Silica said, "now I don't have to go through that awkwardness of having to spell it out to those two." She circled a long finger in the direction of Archer and Martin. "I hate séances and making appearances."

Hearing the name of Carly's killer brought no peace to Ethan.

He thought it would bring him some sort of comfort, but instead he felt more restless. Morris had said he suspected Harper had something to do with Carly's murder, but he had no evidence.

"Thanks," he said. Who would bring Ed Harper to justice, he wondered? What good had it done knowing who killed Carly? Why did Lucca want him to speak with Silica? This all made no sense. "I don't understand why Lucca wanted me to talk to you. I'm going to die at midnight. What good does it do knowing any of this?"

Ethan felt deflated. He had searched for love and had abandoned hope just before he'd met Riley. Now that he'd met her, he was destined to die. For a moment it seemed that Lucca might offer Ethan some hope, a way to change his future, but the answer Lucca gave him dampened any hope he may have had. He could never live knowing he'd chosen someone to die in his place. And then Lucca dangled a new hope in front of him when he told him to speak to his angel, but Silica appeared to be all attitude and no solace whatsoever. If anything, she'd succeeded in making Ethan feel more hopeless and more anxious than he was before.

"Will you look after Riley?" Ethan asked. "When I die?"

"Not mine to say," Silica said. "I'm not her angel."

"Thought as much." Ethan couldn't help himself. This angel was stroppy, arrogant, and entirely unhelpful.

"What?" she turned on him.

"You've been nothing but rude and full of attitude!" Ethan exploded. "I'm dying here. Lucca said to talk to you. I thought you'd be able to help!"

Silica's eyes widened, and she cocked her head. "What did you think this was? A concierge service? A shot at redemption? It doesn't work that way."

"So how *does* it work? What exactly is *this*?" Ethan demanded.

"*This* is bigger than you, or me. It's bigger than anyone, and it's bigger than everyone. And you need to realize that. You could have never lived at all, and the world would still have been the same, with or without you!" Silica said cuttingly.

225

Ethan wanted to cry, but in this state there were no tears. The feeling was one he had not felt for a long time. Since he was fourteen years old. The feeling of being betrayed by someone he trusted. Someone he thought to be a friend had embarrassed him in front of everyone at school, and Ethan was right back in that fourteen year-old boy, feeling embarrassed and hurt. He nodded, unable to speak.

He looked up to find Silica right in front of his face. Her eyes were sparkling pools of bright, radiant blue.

"Look, sorry, kid, but I've been doing this a long time. There's no place for false kindness that protects the feelings for a moment but damages the future forever. I tell it like it is. There's no emotions and there's no feelings in this Dimension. You bring with you what you can't let go of. You can't let go of that scar you've been carrying around with you since you were fourteen."

Ethan was surprised.

"Yes I know what you're thinking," she said it for him. "That's how it works. *That's* what this place is. It's like nothing on earth. There's no living and dying once you cross over. Whatever you think is your biggest problem right now doesn't even exist after you've crossed over. You'll shit yourself when realize how little everything you've been worrying about all your life matters here."

Ethan stared into her blazing eyes, which burned like two dancing blue flames.

"Lucca wanted you to speak to me so you could start dealing with dying. They're not going to see you again for a long time." Silica motioned to the gathering in the hallway. "To them it will feel like a long time. But to you here, time doesn't exist. One day is like a week is like a month could be a decade. To you it'll seem like you kissed everybody goodbye and went to school, and you'll see them all again when you get home for dinner."

"Will she still love me? When I see her again?" Ethan asked, staring longingly at Riley.

Silica smiled. "Now we're asking the right questions. Finally!"

Ethan looked at the angel, still confused.

"You still don't get it, do you?" she asked rhetorically. Ethan shook his head. "None of the stuff you've worked your whole life on earth to build, to save, to protect – none of it matters except one thing." Ethan gazed into her eyes expectantly. "What you're feeling right now, that's all that really matters." Ethan continued to gaze at Riley. "That's it, Ethan. There's your answer."

"What answer?" Ethan was still confused. "Will she still love me when she gets here? She'll find someone else, won't she?"

"Oh for the love of god," Silica said in frustration. "We were so close."

"What do you mean?" Ethan said, exasperated. "Just tell me, will you?"

"No lesson you've been taught is as effective as the ones you discover for yourself," she said, the dancing fire returning to her eyes.

"Why do I have to learn any more? I'm not staying here long," Ethan pouted. Silica glared at him, arms folded. "Am I?" Ethan tilted his head. This angel was making his brain ache.

"I'm going to tell you two things, Ethan Lynch, then I'm going to make you wake up one more time, and I'm going to leave you," Silica said. In a way, Ethan was relieved. This had been one of the most fearful encounters he'd ever experienced in his life. "Beneath the sofa in Ed Harper's apartment is what Morris is looking for." She enumerated on her fingers as she spoke. That was item one. "And two," Silica said, waiting a moment for dramatic impact, "There is a way, and you have to find it. Love will find it."

"A way for what?" Ethan asked, but Silica was gone. "A way for what?"

Chapter 11

"He's awake!" the nurse shouted as Ethan's eyes flickered open.

"A way for what?" Ethan mumbled.

"Welcome back. We didn't think we'd see you again, Ethan," the nurse said, "How you feeling? You ok?"

Ethan was aware of the sensation of pain again, and groaned involuntarily. He nodded. His soul knew that it wasn't up to them whether he lived or died. There was another power at work, forces neither they nor the doctors could stop.

"I need to see them now. Call them, please," he said, pointing to the hallway.

"You need to rest," the nurse said, the expression in her eyes conveying how serious she was.

"Call them for me, please," he insisted.

"Look, Ethan…" the nurse began, but the patient pulled the nasal cannula away from his face, and held on to the nurse's wrist.

"I know I haven't got long," he said. "Please. Before I die. I want to see them."

The nurse nodded. "Ok," she conceded. "I'll call them." She

turned, leaving Ethan alone for a moment.

"Silica," Ethan called, looking around. "Don't leave me." He expected to hear her voice, and her cutting remarks, but there was no noise except for the rhythmic pumping of a ventilator somewhere in the ward, and the occasional bleeping of monitoring apparatus.

Ethan's entourage filed back into the ward and apart from the two mediums, everybody looked emotionally drained. Riley placed her head on his chest within moments of returning to the ward.

"Don't leave me," she begged. "I don't want to lose you."

"Listen," Ethan said feebly. "Everybody listen. I haven't got long."

"What are you talking about, you're going to be fine," Ivan Lynch tried to convince himself.

"Dad?" Ethan extended a hand, and Ivan drew closer.

"I'm right here, Ethan."

"Dad, I'm going to die soon," he began. Ivan's face welled up with tears as Ethan spoke. "But, Dad, listen to me, ok?" He looked up into his father's eyes, glistening with tears that began to roll down his cheeks. "I know I didn't show it much, but I love you. You need to know that."

Ivan Lynch felt weak. He wavered, and Martin steadied him, sliding a chair in from behind.

"Here, Ivan. Sit, please," Martin's soothing voice resounded in the quiet room.

Ethan's father sank into the chair. It was as if Ethan had read his mind, as if he understood his unspoken thoughts and fears.

"I know you were there for me right from the start. I know you were just trying to keep it all together for all of us," Ethan said.

His father could only manage a nod as his sobs racked his body, and Ivan Lynch broke down and cried, sobbing loudly. Four hands found a space on his shoulders and back, and Ethan found himself looking up into a portrait of his father surrounded by his mom, Riley and the two mediums.

"I love you, my boy," his father sobbed.

"I love you too, Dad," Ethan echoed. "I love you too." Tears rolled down Ethan's cheeks. He and his father had never told each other in words, but rather had assumed, silently, that each loved the other. In his final moments, Ethan realized the power of love. That love, although it exists, and is real, needs to be loud, and clear. That there are no unwritten, assumed feelings. If it isn't spoken often, love melds into the plasterwork, and becomes one of those things that people see but don't notice, like a sign that was read when it was new, but over time becomes invisible in its blatant visibility.

Riley too was overcome with grief and emotion, her cheeks were wet with tears.

"Riley," Ethan called moving his hand from his fathers', and extending it to her.

"Ethan!" Riley took his hand, and smiled through the tears.

"I saw her. My angel. I saw her," Ethan said. Riley nodded.

Carol smiled behind Riley, but immediately felt a pang of guilt and denial.

"What did she say?" Riley asked, hopefully.

"She said there was a way, but she didn't tell me what that was. Only that love would find a way."

Riley nodded. She had come to accept that the world beyond her world was greater and more powerful than she could ever have imagined, and that people were mere players in a bigger and grander picture. Whatever way this angel of Ethan's had in mind, if it was meant to be, it would happen. She glanced down at her watch, and then looked up at Ethan.

"What time is it?" he asked.

"6:22pm," she replied.

"There isn't much time," Ethan observed. "Less than six hours."

Riley nodded, while Carol and Ivan exchanged glances behind her.

"Listen," he said to Riley. She fought back the tears, and squeezed his hand. "You know I love you, right? I love you more than anyone has ever loved anyone, ever."

"I love you too," Riley said. She leaned in and kissed Ethan tenderly.

"The angel. She said two things. She said that love would find a way. That was the second thing. And the first thing was that Morris would find what he was looking for. His card. I've got Morris' card. In my pocket." His eyes searched the room briefly, but there was no sign of his clothes. They must have been packed away in cupboard next to the bed.

Riley nodded. "I'll get the card," she said.

Ethan continued. "She said Morris will find what he's looking for under knuckle..." Ethan's eyes widened, and he gasped. His head rolled to one side. The machine that was connected to him by narrow cables and diodes beeped. Moments later, the nurses raced to his side.

"Out of the way!" they shouted. "He's crashing! Doctor! I need a doctor here, now!" The doctor on duty appeared seconds later.

"Get them out of here!" he instructed. The nurse ushered everyone to the door once again.

"Please, we need you to wait outside," the ordered.

"What's happening?" Carol asked.

"We'll tell you as soon as we know," the nurse replied.

In the hallway once again, Carol and Ivan Lynch clung to each other while Riley gathered with Martin and Archer.

"It seems that he spoke to his angel," Martin said. Riley nodded. "But what does he mean?"

"He said his angel told him two things – that love would find a way, and that Morris needed to look under his knuckle? That doesn't sound right," Martin thought out loud.

"No, he was mid sentence. He said Morris would find what he was looking for..." Riley continued, but Archer finished her sentence.

"...under knuckle something. He didn't finish what he was saying."

"Who's Morris?" Riley asked. Martin shrugged. Carol overheard and turned to join the conversation.

"Morris is Detective Morris. The detective investigating Carly's murder," she said. Carol Lynch was too empty inside to cry another tear.

"What did he mean?" Archer asked.

Carol shrugged. "I don't know. Why don't you call Detective Morris. Here, I have his card." She rummaged through her purse and found a plain, white business card, and handed it to Riley. "Here's his number."

Martin took it from her. "Let me call him." He dialed the Detective's mobile number, and waited while all eyes were fixed on him.

"Morris," the detective answered the call.

"Detective Morris? Hi, I'm Martin. I'm a friend of Ethan Lynch," Martin introduced himself.

"Yeah?" Morris said impatiently.

"Um...I'm with Ethan now. He wanted to tell you something, but he's in hospital, hardly conscious."

"Oh, hell. What did the kid do now? Did he go down there again? To Eighth Street?" Morris asked.

"No, no. It's worse than that," Martin explained, searching the eyes of everyone watching him as he spoke. He turned his back to them and spoke quietly. "He's dying, Detective. Something wrong with his liver. It's bad. Really bad."

"Oh. I'm sorry," Morris said diplomatically.

"I don't know if this is anything, but he said to tell you that you'd find what you were looking for under knuckle... and then he passed out." Martin tried to explain.

"Knuckle? Knuckle-head Ed?" Morris frowned on the other end of the line. "What the hell's the kid been up to?"

"Nothing," Martin explained. "He was admitted to hospital today, so not much except trying to live. Who's Knuckle-head Ed?"

"Dammit," Morris cursed. "He means Ed Harper, leader of the Eighth Street Crushers."

"Any reason why he'd want to tell you look under Knuckle Head Ed?" Martin asked, hoping the words would mean something to the detective. He turned back to face the small gathering in the hallway.

"Listen, thanks, Martin. I'll take it from here. That's all he said?" Morris said curtly.

"Yes. That's all he said. Does it mean anything?" Martin asked hopefully. The entire gathering held their breath as Martin listened.

"Doesn't mean shit, I'm afraid," Morris said. "Anything else you wanna tell me?"

"No, That's all he said," Martin relayed, looking at the disappointed faces of everyone around him.

"Ok then. Thanks for the call. Good night." Morris hung up.

Martin shook his head. "Didn't sound like he knew what that was about at all." Looking into the faces staring at him he added, "I'm sorry."

"He was going to say more," Riley said. "We have to find out what he was going to say." Archer and Martin looked at her. "We have to ask his angel." Martin looked at her apologetically. "Don't tell me we can't!" Riley insisted. "Find a way!"

"Lucca must know," Archer suggested. "Come on." He led Riley and Archer to the stairwell. They climbed the stairs to the third floor, and exited through the doorway that led to Riley's secret hideaway on the roof. Without saying a word, they formed a circle and joined hands.

"Lucca, can you hear me?" Archer asked. "We need you, man. Please!"

Martin looked up disapprovingly. That wasn't the way to talk to angels. Yet moments later, all three of them were aware of Lucca's presence.

"Lucca, we need to speak with Ethan's angel. What's her name?" Archer asked.

"Her name is Silica. But she doesn't communicate with everyone. Only those with whom she chooses," Lucca replied.

"Got it," Archer cut him short. "Silica? Silica, I beg of you, please, talk to us. You had a message for Ethan, but he never got to give it to us."

They waited in silence, hoping to feel her presence, to hear her speak to them, but all they heard was the sound of traffic in the distance, and the faint ring of an ambulance siren.

"Silica?" Martin tried, but still there was nothing.

"Silica, Please!" Riley called out to the surprise of the two mediums. "You have to tell us what Ethan said. It must have been important. You told him to tell us but he wasn't strong enough. Please, Silica, if you believe in love, if love means anything, please?"

"I see her," Martin said, looking over Riley's shoulder. "Are you Silica?"

The others watched Martin as if he were having a phone conversation in front of them. Only he could see and hear the angel.

Silica glared at Martin. "I'm Silica," she said.

"You told Ethan something about Morris and Knuckle Head Ed? Will you tell me what you told Ethan? He's lost consciousness again."

"Morris will find what he's looking for under Ed's sofa," Silica replied.

"Thank you," Martin said, and then thought for a moment. "We tried to tell Detective Morris, but he didn't want to listen. How do we get him to look under Ed's sofa?"

"Kick his door down," Silica replied.

"Ed's?" Martin asked, surprised.

"You don't even know who Ed is," Silica said, visibly irritated. "Morris."

"You want us to kick Detective Morris' door down?" Martin asked, drawing confused stares from Archer and Riley.

"Must I do everything for you?" Silica folded her arms. "It's a figure of speech. Figure it out. Oh, and tell Ethan's friends he's in a critical condition. They might want to know."

"Ok. Ok. Thank you," Martin said slowly trying to process what this angel with attitude had just told him. "Ok."

"Anything else?" Silica asked curtly, like she had somewhere else to be, and this interview was wasting her time.

"Uh, unless you have anything else to tell me?"

Silica disappeared instantly.

"Boy was she pissed," Martin said to Archer and Riley, letting go of their hands.

"Pissed? An angel, pissed?" Archer was intrigued.

"This angel was not like any angel I've ever seen. It was as if she was irritated at being summoned, like she was doing something she didn't want to," Martin explained.

"I've heard about angels like that before. They're camera shy," Archer explained.

"Camera shy? Angels can be camera shy?" Martin asked.

"They hate doing appearances. Prefer to do their thing and not engage with people."

Martin pursed his lips and nodded.

"What did she say?" Riley asked, impatiently. She'd given them long enough to ruminate about angels and cameras.

"She said Morris will find what he's looking for under Ed's sofa," Martin said slowly, repeating Silica's words precisely. "But when I asked her how we get Detective Morris to listen to us, she told me to kick his door down, although she did then say it was a figure of speech." Martin looked at Archer. "Angels don't use figures of speech, do they?"

Archer shook his head. "They're usually quite literal."

Martin's face lit up with a smile. "This Silica is a bit of a renegade. I wonder what she was like when she was alive." He turned to Riley. "She also said that we need to call Ethan's friends and tell them he's in a critical condition."

"I supposed we'd better do that soon." Riley looked at her watch, as Ethan's seconds ticked away slowly. "Let's get his phone. Maybe they're under his emergency contacts, or his last chats. You two should do that. I don't want to go through his phone. Feel like

I'm invading his privacy."

"Sure," Archer said, placing a hand on Riley's shoulder. "Come on, let's get back down to the ward. His parents must know who his friends are."

They found Ivan and Carol sitting beside Ethan's bed in silence. Both seemed to be lost in thought. Ethan's parents acknowledged the three of them with a feeble smile as they re-entered the ward.

"Do either of you know where Ethan's phone is?" Archer asked. "We need to contact his friends, and tell them Ethan's in hospital."

Carol withdrew her phone from her handbag. "Just Abe and Dan," she said. "They're his closest friends. Here, I've got their numbers. They've been friends with Ethan since they were kids. Let me call them."

After Carol had called Abe and Dan and told them about Ethan, the five of them resumed their vigil around Ethan's bed. Carol prayed silently for a miracle. Riley prayed to her angel for strength as she watched the love of her life waste away. Martin mumbled some chant over and over again, and Archer stood solemnly, waiting.

Ivan tried to recall every memory he'd had with his son, but could only remember moments here and there. If only he'd known then that those moments, the ones he remembered now, would be the collective sum total of his life with Ethan. Those moments seemed so insignificant at the time, yet some of them etched deeper into his mind than others. Moments he wished he could do over. Moments he remembered with fondness. His memories were made of moments that came and went with no fanfare, no warning that those would be the ones he would carry with him forever. What he'd give to have those moments again.

Abe arrived about half an hour later. He found Carol and Ivan at Ethan's bedside.

"Carol, Ivan." he greeted Ethan's parents. They both rose as he hugged each of them. "What happened?" he asked.

"He went into liver failure," Carol began, but she couldn't say more. Fresh tears began to stream down her face.

"The doctors don't hold much hope," Ivan added.

"I'm so sorry," Abe said, looking down at Ethan.

Dan joined them a few minutes later, and followed the same ritual of greeting Ethan's parents, and taking in the news about his friend.

Riley returned to the ward, followed by Martin and Archer, each carrying hot coffee and Carol introduced everyone as cups were passed around.

"Can I talk to you guys for a second. Out here?" Martin motioned to the hallway.

"Uh, sure," Abe said. Dan nodded, and followed Martin out of the ward.

"I'm coming too," Archer said, joining them.

"Wait for me," Riley called, and followed after Archer. They huddled in the hallway.

"I'm a medium. I talk to spirits," Martin explained to Dan and Abe, who exchanged glances with each other. Abe was intrigued. Dan was skeptical. "So is Archer. Both of us have a strong connection to the spirit world. We've been communicating with Ethan's angel. I know this sounds strange to people who don't believe in this, so forgive me if I'm treading on delicate ground with you two."

"I'm Jewish," Abe held up a hand. "No delicate ground here."

"You can go on," Dan said uneasily. He wasn't about to open up to strangers in the hallway of a hospital about his religious convictions.

"Ethan's angel is called Silica. I'm sure she was helping us get closure for Ethan. She told us who killed Carly," Martin continued.

"What? You know who Carly's killer is?" Dan said. Martin, Riley and Archer all nodded. "So let's tell the police!"

"It's not that simple. We tried. She told us who did it, and that the detective investigating the case, Detective Morris, would find what he was looking for in a certain place. We tried to talk to the detective, but…" Martin took a breath. "You can imagine how this sounds to him. I call him up and tell him I know who killed Carly, and he asks how I know. Telling him an angel told me…"

"Yeah, I can see how that's a problem," Dan said.

"So what did this angel say?" Abe pressed.

"She said that the only way we're going to get the detective's attention is by kicking his door down," Martin said. Dan's eyebrows rose. "Figuratively," Martin continued, motioning with his hand as if pressing the air down in the center of the huddle. "She said the only way to get the detective's attention is to go to him personally and make him listen. Now I could go, but it looks like Ethan's angel implied that it has to be the two of you. She told us to go to the detective, but then she immediately said we need to call Ethan's friends. The two of you."

Abe felt a wave of numbness pass through his body. It was the sensation of extreme panic, and it made him freeze. He found himself unable to move.

"You ok, man?" Dan asked. It took Abe a while to reply.

"Um, no, not really." Abe's gaze darted between Dan and the huddle of crazy people around him. "Is he serious? Do you believe this?"

"I don't know, man," Dan said. "But come on, what harm can it do. We go to this detective's house, we tell him to go take a look. We'll do it together. I'm in. For Ethan, man, I'm in."

"I can't," Abe shook his head vehemently. He began hyperventilating.

"Come on, man, why not?" Dan had never seen Abe this afraid.

"Because I had a dream about this last night," Abe said, silencing everyone. "I dreamed about this last night," he said again. "And somebody dies. One of us."

"What?" Dan stood back, shaking his head. He looked into the faces of the people around him. "Ah come on, man, it was just a dream."

Abe grabbed Dan's arm, and stared at him with a look of desperation. "I'm telling you man, I dreamed we were in this place, this huge, empty room, like a warehouse, together, you and me, but we were tied up, back to back, just like in the movies. And it was dark. Then the lights came on, and there were men with guns, and then bam!" The last word exploded from Abe's mouth, and was accompanied by a loud clap. Riley started back. "Then I woke up. You know how you always wake up before you die in a dream, because if you actually die, you actually die," Abe said, looking around at everyone. "Well it was like that. I woke up just before I died."

"What's this detective's address?" Dan asked. Martin handed Dan the card that Carol had given him. He'd written his address on the back, in case Ivan or Carol needed anything. "2325 East Thirty Fifth," he read. That looks like a house address. Abe, this definitely isn't a warehouse. Come on, man. I'll go with you. It's for Ethan. He would want closure on this. If our friend is dying, lets do this for him." Dan lowered his head, and looked deeply into Abe's panicked eyes. "For Ethan," he said again.

Abe nodded. "Ok," he said. "Ok."

"We'll take my car," Dan said.

"You feeling ok?" Dan asked as Abe buckled himself in.

"Yeah," Abe said, embarrassed at his earlier outburst. "Feeling a little stupid."

"It's ok, man. You wanna tell me about that dream again?"

It was dark as they left the hospital parking. Traffic was light, and they drove through the city streets freely. Abe watched the lights sail by. "It felt so real. And I knew it was just a dream when I woke up, because, when am I going to go to a big, dark, empty warehouse, right? So I just let it go, but as soon as that guy said we had to go bashing down doors, it just brought that dream back like it was, I don't know, a prophesy or something. I just wasn't expecting to hear that. And I panicked. I froze."

"Hey, man. It's me and you. We've been through everything together, since high school. You, me and Ethan," Dan reminded him.

Abe smiled. "Yeah," he said. A smile returned to his face. "Feels like yesterday, doesn't it? Where did the time go?"

"You speak like you're a hundred years old. You're not even thirty, man. We still got a lot of time left," Dan said.

"You think? Look at Ethan. I'll bet he didn't think he was going to be ... like this ... dying, when he woke up this morning."

"Yeah," Dan said somberly. "I guess."

"We don't have a lot of time in this world. A hundred years if we're lucky, and the last part of our lives we're probably going to be too frail to enjoy. I don't want to end up like that," Abe stared out the window.

"Like what?"

"Too old to wipe my own ass," Abe said watching the lights. "Too frail to get in my own car and go wherever I want to go. I think I want to die when I'm like, seventy. That seems to be a good age. You're still healthy enough to be independent, and you haven't started to degenerate to the point where people have to look after you."

"I want to live till I'm a hundred and twenty," Dan said. "That will piss my kids off." He laughed out loud.

"You don't have kids."

"Yeah," Dan said, smiling, "but I know how I'd feel if I had to look after my dad till he was a hundred. He's crotchety enough now and he's only fifty five."

"Got any idea what we're going to say to this detective guy when we kick his door down?" Abe asked.

Dan shook his head. "Not a clue."

Detective Morris' modest house was located in a neighborhood that could only be described as unremarkable. Dan parked across the street, and a few houses down. Together, he and Abe approached Detective Morris' porch.

"It'll be ok," Dan reassured Abe.

His friend nodded bravely. "Yeah, yeah, I'm fine," he waved off Dan's concern. "Press the bell." Abe thrust both hands deep into his pockets and shifted his weight from left to right as if trying to keep himself warm. Dan rang the doorbell.

"Christ!" they heard an angry male voice curse inside, followed by the pounding of footsteps on a wooden floor. The door swung open. "Yeah?" Detective Morris glared at the two visitors. He was still in his work clothes, although he had loosened his tie.

"Detective Morris?" Dan asked. Morris nodded impatiently. "I'm Dan. This is Abe. We're friends of Ethan Lynch," Dan said.

Morris waved a finger at him, visibly irritated. "What do you want?"

"Look, I know this sounds a little weird, but you'll find what you're looking for under Knuckle Head Ed's sofa," Dan said.

Morris stared at him. "This some kind of joke?"

Dan shook his head. "No sir. A guy named Martin called you earlier to try to tell you."

"Your guy Martin called me earlier to ask me who Knuckle Ed was, he didn't say nothin' more." Morris was agitated. "Listen, you got something on Ed Harper or the Eighth Street Crushers I can work with, bring it to me. Preferably during office hours." Morris cast a glance behind him, back into his house. Clearly, the two visitors were interrupting something he wanted to get back to. "You don't go after the king pin of the Eighth Street Crushers without something solid. If Ed's hiding something under his sofa, I need a warrant. To get a warrant I need probable cause. To get probable cause I need evidence. You got evidence?"

Dan and Abe stared at each other blankly. Abe considered mentioning that he'd heard it from a medium who'd heard it from an angel, but was sure that the detective wouldn't consider that to be evidence.

"Didn't think so. Have a good night." Morris closed the door, leaving Abe and Dan staring at each other. They turned and walked slowly back to Dan's car.

"We need evidence," Dan said.

"What are you talking about?" Abe said. "I'm going back to the hospital."

"You go," Dan said. "I'm gonna see what's under Ed Harper's

sofa."

"You don't even know who Ed Harper is," Abe said.

"You heard him," Dan said. "Ed Harper is the king pin of the Eighth Street Crushers."

"Are you absolutely insane?" Abe pleaded. "Look at what happened to Ethan last time he was even in the neighborhood. We're not going anywhere near there. You don't just go looking for the head of the Eighth Street Crushers!"

"No you don't," Dan smiled. "But you can if you're the head of their biggest rival."

"The Dragon Kings?" Abe was flabbergasted. His friend was losing his mind. The panic Abe had felt earlier at the hospital started to consume him again.

Dan nodded.

"You've lost the plot. Dan, you're a financial analyst, not a fucking undercover CIA agent," Abe reprimanded him sharply.

"That would be FBI," Dan corrected him.

"Whatever, man. No!" Abe protested vehemently. "No!"

"Look," Dan said, "we just go into China Town, and we ask around. We drop the word that we have information that the Dragon Kings would want to know that might bring the head of the Eighth Street Crushers down. Then we back off and leave it to them. They just have to bring us whatever's under Ed Harper's sofa." Dan was grinning. Abe was silent. "Come on, man, it'll be fun. When last did you and me have some real fun?" Dan insisted.

Abe took a deep breath. "Ok," he said reluctantly. "China Town. That's it. We find someone we can give the information to and we split," Abe insisted.

"We find someone and we give them the information, and then we wait for them to bring us back whatever is under Knuckle-head Ed's sofa," Dan said. "We'll wait out on the street. Promise," Dan said, still grinning ear to ear like a kid watching his first superhero movie.

"Ok," Abe said pointing a finger ahead of him. "China Town."

"China Town!" Dan sang. "This is gonna be fun!"

Abe didn't share his sentiment.

China Town ran all the way along Twelfth Street, just four blocks East of Eighth. They parked somewhere along Eleventh, and walked a block until they joined the buzzing activity that characterized China Town. It was as if a chunk of another country had been scooped up by some giant crane and dropped into the center of Western Civilization. The streets were packed with pedestrians, all of them Oriental. Shops and restaurants were all open for business as if it were midday on a Saturday. Mini Market stores were filled to capacity with produce shipped in directly from China, carrying everything from five liter jugs of soy sauce to a dozen varieties of noodles, dried mushrooms, and hundreds of packs of exotic foods, spices, and other ingredients that were completely foreign to the people who lived just one block away. Inside the shops, residents of China Town filled small baskets, talking loudly to one another, waving hands as they discussed cooking methods and recipes. The shop counter was manned by the owner or a member of their family, while other family members busily stocked shelves, or swept floors with a sense of urgency and pride. Fresh produce stores spilled their baskets of fresh vegetables onto the sidewalk. Huge root vegetables, long legumes, and baskets of varied green and purple leaves and mushrooms lined the length of their storefronts, both inside and out. Restaurants that looked like carbon copies of one another stretched as far as they could see, each one packed full of locals gathered around family tables of eight to twelve, with some Western visitors here and there who stood out like drops of cream on top of a butternut soup. And just a few blocks away, was the Western way of life. Sedate late night supermarkets with a handful of customers aimlessly wheeling trolleys down aisles they'd visited dozens of times before, picking groceries off shelves they perused regularly in solitude, while minimum wage employees manned the checkouts and stocked shelves with empty expressions on their faces.

"How the hell do we find the Dragon Kings?" Abe asked.

"Seemed like a good idea at the time," Dan replied looking around. "Let's start there. Feel like a spring roll?"

Dan led them to the restaurant nearest them, a functional establishment with bright lighting, and crates of drinks piled up on either side of the doorway. Outside the restaurant, a trolley stood unattended with some ingredients stuffed into plastic containers balanced on top.

They made their way to the back of the restaurant, past tables of Asian families, talking and laughing loudly, passing bowls of food, and rotating the central table piece back and forth to reach more rice, sizzling beef, and bowls of soup. A man wearing an apron stood at one of the refrigerators at the back of the noisy room.

"Can I help you?" he asked, wiping his hands on a dirty dishtowel.

"We're looking for the Dragon Kings," Dan said. "Do you know where I can find them?"

The man stared at them, then spat at their feet. "Out!" he pointed to the door, immediately drawing stares from nearby patrons. Men seated at the tables within earshot looked up, and set their chopsticks down on the table, as if they were all getting ready to join the man with the apron.

"It's cool. Ok, we're leaving," Dan said, holding his hands up defensively. He ushered Abe towards the door as the men at the tables glared at them threateningly. Out on the busy street, Dan pointed to another restaurant. "Let's try that one."

"Let's find someone nearer the door this time," Abe suggested. He was beginning to feel panicked again.

"Good point," Dan said, peering through the window of the next restaurant they came to. They waited till a young waitress with long, black ponytails, was just about finished laying food out on a table near the entrance before they entered. She turned and greeted them.

"We're looking for the Dragon Kings," Dan said softly, so only the waitress could hear.

She shook her head, and turned back towards the kitchen.

The two of them moved from restaurant to restaurant, and repeated the exercise again and again, but each time, they were met with the same response.

"We're not getting anywhere," Dan said.

"How about that spring roll you promised me," Abe said. "I'm hungry. There," he pointed to a street vendor half a block away from them. Abe hoped that the distraction might dissuade Dan from continuing with this insane idea of his.

Abe ordered a combination of chicken and vegetable spring rolls from the man in the food cart who looked to be close to seventy years old, wrinkled, but agile. The old man moved swiftly inside the cart, preparing their food.

Abe glanced across at Dan, and then found himself acting on an impulse he couldn't control, surprising himself with his boldness. "Hey," Abe called to the old man, who leaned through the window to hear the Occidental. "I need to get a message to the Dragon Kings. Do you know..."

The old man held up a finger to silence Abe. "What you want with Dragon Kings? You no belong here," he warned.

Abe leaned closer and whispered to the old man, "I have a message I need to deliver to their leader. It's important. Just a message, that's all."

The old man narrowed his eyes and studied the two men in front of him, then curled a finger, beckoning Abe closer.

"You wait," he said. He turned and busied himself at his fryer, and then turned back to the young man, holding out a crispy paper wrapper containing piping hot spring rolls. "Six Dollars," he said, holding out a hand. Abe handed over a crisp ten Dollar note, and the old man took it, then closed the shutter.

"Hey, my change," Abe said. He heard the rear door of the food cart open and shut, then lock, and before he and Dan could peer around the cart, the old man had disappeared.

"What now?" Dan asked.

"We wait," Abe said, handing him a spring roll. "Here, eat

something, I'm hungry."

"Ouch, this is hot," Dan exclaimed, tossing the hot, crispy spring roll from one hand to the other. "Give me a napkin or something."

They waited, leaning against a nearby trash can for what felt like ages before the old man appeared through the crowd, approaching his food cart. Without a word, he slipped behind it, unlocked the rear door, and reopened the shutter. Abe and Dan looked around, but saw only the old man.

"You looking for the Dragon Kings?" a heavily accented voice behind them asked.

Both of them turned to find a small man in front of them. He was an entire head shorter than Abe, and almost two shorter than Dan. He was slim, and wore a white shirt and a black jacket, but exuded the confidence of someone untouchable.

"Yes," Dan said. "We have a message for your leader. It's about the Eighth Street Crushers. We can help your leader bring their leader down."

The man flared his jacket and rested his hands on his hips. He regarded them suspiciously. "You cops?"

Both Dan and Abe shook their heads.

"Why seek the Dragon Kings?" he asked.

"Would you believe me if I told you an angel sent us?" Dan said.

The man thought for a moment. "No," he said, and then with lightening speed, he slammed a fist into each of their jaws. Dan and Abe fell unconscious at the small man's feet. Immediately, three men in similar black and white attire appeared from the shadows, and dragged the two unconscious men into a waiting van. The doors slid closed, and the small man in the black jacket slipped into the passenger seat. He nodded at the driver, and the van pulled away slowly. It was the only vehicle on a street meant solely for pedestrians, yet nobody objected to its presence. The van slipped off Twelfth Street at the first intersection.

Chapter 12

Abe opened his eyes. His head hurt. He found himself looking down at his boxer shorts. He tried to move, but his hands were bound tightly behind him. His torso was bare. Abe looked around, petrified.

"Where am I?" he shouted. "Dan? Dan!"

Abe heard a groan behind him, and felt something move.

"Abe?" Dan said groggily.

"What the fuck happened? Where are we? Where are our clothes?" Abe was petrified. His heart started pounding in his chest. "Dan! Are you tied up too?"

Both of them were stripped down to their underwear, and tied to chairs that were arranged back to back.

"Yeah," Dan said from behind Abe.

"It's my dream!" Abe was beginning to hyperventilate. "It's my dream! It's the same big empty room! It's my dream, Dan, it's my dream! Oh, god, we're gonna die!"

"Hey, man, just breathe, ok. Breathe!" Dan tried to calm Abe, but his mouth was dry as he looked around the dark room.

"Hello?" Dan called. "Anyone out there?"

Lights flickered on, and the voluminous, empty room became instantly bright. Five silhouettes moved towards them from the doorway. They walked slowly, confidently, just like the small man that the old food cart owner had brought to them.

"They're gonna kill us!" Abe whined. "They're gonna kill us!" He pulled hard at his restraints, but was unable to move. He jolted his body up and down, trying desperately to free himself, but only succeeded in raising the chair a few millimeters off the concrete floor, each time thumping loudly.

"Stop!" one of the men shouted. Abe froze immediately, looking down, frightened. "Who are you?" the man demanded.

Dan spoke, but his frightened voice faltered as he did. "My name is Dan Attridge. This is my friend, Abe Diamond."

"What do you want with the Dragon Kings," the man demanded, crouching so his face was level with Dan's.

"We just came to tell you something that might help bring down the Eighth Street Crushers. Ed Harper, you know him?" Dan stammered.

The man in charge turned to look at his colleagues.

"Why?" he asked turning back to Dan.

"My friend...our friend," Dan corrected himself, "Ethan. His brother was killed the other day in that drive by shooting."

The men spoke rapidly to one another in Chinese.

"You friends with that kid's brother?" The interrogator's tone changed immediately. Dan nodded rapidly.

"We didn't kill your friend's brother, that was Eighth Street Crushers going after Little Li," the interrogator said.

"All we know is that our friend's brother was killed in the cross fire," Dan said. "Carly. That was his name. He was our friend Ethan's little brother."

"So what do you want to tell us?" the interrogator asked.

"We've been told that there is evidence under Ed Harper's sofa. Evidence that the cops could use to bring Harper down. You find that evidence, I take it to the cops, they arrest Harper," Dan said.

"You said you weren't cops!" The interrogator straightened to full height threateningly.

"We're not!" Dan protested. "I swear. We're just friends of Carly's brother, looking for justice. If this guy Ed Harper killed Carly, and there's evidence in his apartment, underneath his sofa, the cops will use it put him away."

"If what you say is true," the interrogator said, leaning in again, "if we find evidence that Harper killed Little Li, we'll take care of Harper. There'll be nothing left for the cops."

The five men walked back to the door.

"Wait!" Abe called. "What about us? You can't just leave us here."

"If your information is true," a different voice said, "we'll come back and release you. If it's not, we'll come back and kill you. Either way, you stay." The five men turned and walked towards the door in the far corner. As the door clicked closed and Abe and Dan were left alone in darkness in the echoing, empty room.

"Dan?" Abe said.

"Yeah?"

"I told you this was a bad idea," Abe said.

"Yeah," Dan agreed. "This was a bad idea. But they didn't have guns so we're probably gonna get out of this," he tried to reassure Abe.

"Do you believe that shit about angels?" Abe asked.

"If it isn't true, we just took one hell of a gamble," Dan said.

"When I get out of here, I'm gonna kill that medium myself."

"Me too," Dan agreed.

"I'm killing him first," Abe insisted.

Five slim figures in dark jackets and white shirts strode down Twelfth Street. They disappeared into one of the fancier restaurants on the strip. Moments later, they emerged back onto the street, and waited. Within minutes, their number had grown to a small army, each wearing a similar uniform. Dark jackets, white shirts. They formed a semi circle around their leader, who gave orders in Chinese, and the band of Dragon Kings dispersed like vapor into the crowded streets, just as quickly as they had assembled.

The leader looked at his watch. It was 9:25pm. They would make their move at 9:30pm. He waited together with his four Lieutenants. At 9:28pm, the five men left Twelfth Street and strode towards Eighth Street, crossing a boundary that meant instant war under any other circumstance.

Outside Ed Harper's apartment building on Eighth Street, two sentries radioed their leader.

"Boss? We got company. Dragon Kings. Looks like five of them," Butch reported.

"What do they want?" Harper spoke into the radio.

"They don't look armed," the sentry said. He reached behind him, and gripped the butt of the firearm he kept in the small of his back. He was joined moments later by the two men whose job it was to guard this doorway with their lives. They stood behind the sentry like mountains, arms folded, as the five Dragon Kings approached.

"What do you want?" the sentry barked.

"We're unarmed," the Dragon King leader said, holding his hands in the air. "I want to talk with your boss."

"Boss, you hear that?" the sentry relayed into the radio.

"Yeah, I heard," Harper said. "Say what you want to say, Chen."

The leader of the Dragon Kings shook his head. "In person. Not like some dog through the radio."

"Fine, send him up, alone," Harper instructed.

"Two of my men go with me. We are unarmed," Chen insisted.

"How do I know this isn't some trick?" Harper asked.

"Because if we wanted you dead, your three men would already be lying a pool of blood on the street, and there would be a blade at your throat," Chen replied.

There was a long pause. "Make sure they're unarmed. Only Chen and two of his guys," Harper instructed.

Chen allowed himself and two of his Lieutenants to be patted down thoroughly before Butch led them into the building, leaving the remaining two Dragon Kings out in the street with Harper's guards towering over them, while unseen, in the shadows, a small army of Dragon Kings gathered and waited.

Morris' phone rang from an unknown number. "Jesus, what!!" Morris blurted.

"Sir, this is Peters. We've just seen five Dragon King guys arrive at Harper's building. It looks like one of them is Chen. Three of them are going inside now." Peters watched from inside his unmarked vehicle, parked a short distance from the entrance to Harper's apartment building.

"What the hell are they up to?" Morris asked.

"Not sure yet, sir," Peters replied.

"That was rhetorical, you fucking idiot," Morris shot back. "He's determined to fuck up my night, isn't he?"

Peters was silent. Morris sighed. "Dammit!" the detective cursed. "Call it in to dispatch. Get me a SWAT team, but tell them quietly! No sirens. I don't want any of those dumb motherfuckers to know we're coming. Get a team of paramedics there too, I've got a bad feeling about this."

"Yes sir," Peters confirmed.

"No sirens!" Morris barked, looking at his dining room table. On it, a model of an Amerigo Vespucci sail ship stood proudly, next to an empty whiskey glass. The ship was almost complete now. Around it, spilling out of the box, were the remaining pieces of miniature wooden boards, rigging, and the sails, which still needed to be assembled. So close to completion after months of painstaking work. Morris looked at the piece and cursed.

"Got it, sir. No sirens."

Morris hung up and dialed another number. "Yank?"

"Yeah?" Jankelowitz replied.

"Get dressed, and kiss that floozy good night. Meet me at Harper's apartment. Looks like shit's going down. I got a SWAT team on the way. Looks like Harper and Chen are going head to head."

"Jesus!" Jankelowitz exclaimed. He looked at the girl lying naked in his bed next to him. "Hey, how did you know...?" Jankelowitz asked.

"Because I'm a fucking detective." Morris hung up. "Fucking Harper!" he cursed slipping into his bulletproof vest. He pulled his jacket on over it, took one more longing look at the Amerigo Vespucci, and headed to his car still cursing.

Chen followed Harper's elite guard up the stairs and down the hallway. They approached the doorkeeper, who wore denims and a white vest, which revealed his muscular upper arms and shoulders. Chen held out his arms, as did his two aides. The Doorkeeper patted them down thoroughly. He opened the door and stood aside for them allowing Chen and his two Lieutenants to enter.

"You can leave us," Harper said. The Doorkeeper closed the door took up his position outside, with his arms folded.

"Chen," Harper said, not rising to greet his visitors. To Chen it was an instant sign of disrespect. To Harper, it was habit. Harper never got up for anyone. The king of the Eighth Street Crushers slung a bare, muscular arm over the back of the sofa as Chen and his two aides stepped in front of him. "What do you want?"

"This talk is long overdue," Chen said. "Little Li was gunned down not far from here."

"You think I don't know that?" Harper said, tilting his head. "Two of my guys were turned into chop suey on Twenfth Street the week before that."

Chen was silent for a moment. "Your men crossed into my territory," he said at length.

"And your guy was on mine." Harper's tone conveyed his lack of patience.

"There are rules," Chen said. "Territorial rules which you broke first." Chen pointed a finger threateningly at Harper. At the sound of raised voices, the door opened, and the guard stepped inside, reaching behind him for his weapon, but didn't draw. Harper held a hand out to stop him.

"Easy there, Carter. No need to shoot these three men. Yet." Harper kept his gaze firmly on Chen and his two Lieutenants.

Chen didn't stir. He remained poised, standing with arms at his sides, casually, as if he were waiting for a hand roll at the local sushi bar. Harper waved, and Carter nodded. The Doorman retreated to the hallway, and closed the door.

Harper spoke. "If my guys were in your territory I didn't have anything to do with it. Maybe they wanted some noodles. Fuck, how should I know?" Harper said defensively.

"You had no business going after Li," Chen hissed.

"Li was a snitch," Harper spat. "I heard he was a CI. And I ain't got no restraint when it comes to snitches. Somebody wants to be an informant, that's outside the rules." Harper glared at Chen.

"Li was no snitch!" Chen retaliated.

"Yeah?" Harper leaned forward. "Then what do you call this?" He held his phone out for Chen to see. It showed a photo of Li talking to a man, looking over his shoulder. "That there's one of Morris' guys. You know Detective Morris? That's one of his guys, and that there…" Harper pointed to the phone, "…is your guy talking to their guy. So what do you call that? Cops suddenly ordering Chinese take outs from your guy Li?"

"Li is none of your concern," Chen dismissed his adversary, staring down at the photo, clearly enraged. He looked at Harper. "You should have come to me with this information. If Li was an informant, I would have dealt with him. In my own way."

"Yeah, well coincidentally, the next day, two of my guys got arrested on narcotics charges, which your guy said my guys got from suppliers in your neighborhood. So your guy snitched on my guys, and that makes it my business. And apart from that, word is that the two of my guys that got sliced and diced on Twelfth Street – Li was the one who told your guys they were in your territory. That's a double motive for me."

Morris arrived at the apartment block just after 10:00pm, and pulled up behind the SWAT van. Despite his frustration, he closed his car door with little noise, approached the unmarked police vehicle and leaned into the window.

"Anything?" he asked Peters.

"Nothing sir, they've been up there in Harper's apartment for about half an hour now," Peters reported. "SWAT is here. Sergeant Fredericks is the man in charge."

"Thanks," Morris said, moving over to the van. "You Fredericks?"

"Yessir," the man replied. Morris extended a hand.

"We've got a possible shitstorm about to break up there," he said looking at the apartment building. "Two ganglords in the same room. Harper, kingpin of the Eighth Street Crushers, and Chen, leader of the Dragon Kings. I don't know what's about to go down, but I don't want a bloodbath up there, or it'll end up in outright war on the streets."

Fredericks nodded, studying the building, then he called his men and formed a huddle. Seven men in combat gear gathered around Fredericks and Morris. "Listen up," Fredericks said with authority, but quietly. "We've got a potentially explosive situation in there. I want two of you to cover the rear of the building, two at the front, and three with me and the detective." He opened Morris' jacket and nodded. "Ok, you got a vest on. I'm assuming you're coming with me. Stay behind Corporal Lance," Fredericks pointed to a strawberry blonde man in the huddle. Morris nodded. Both he and Fredericks looked up as Jankelowitz joined the huddle.

"Good of you to join us, Yank!" Morris chided his partner.

"Fuck you," Jankelowitz replied. The SWAT team chuckled. Fredericks checked Jankelowitz's vest.

"You coming too?" the SWAT leader asked. Jankelowitz nodded. "You stay with your partner behind Corporal Lance, got it?" Jankelowitz nodded again.

"Listen up," Fredericks said to his team. "You keep it together out there. The only body bags I want to use are for the bad guys, you understand? I don't want to have to talk to any of your families, got it?"

"Yessir," each of the SWAT team responded.

"Detective, on your mark," Fredericks said.

*****

"Li was family!" Chen insisted.

"Yeah, all you Chinese folk are related," Harper laughed.

"I didn't come here to be insulted!" Chen shouted.

"I didn't ask you to come. In fact, I didn't invite you. According to the rules, you're trespassing on my territory." Harper stood slowly. At his full height, he measured over a foot taller than Chen, and was double his width. Harper's chest was all muscle, and his neck disappeared into his over sized trapezius muscles at his shoulders. Chen stood his ground.

"What are you hiding, Harper?" Chen said pointing at the king of the Eighth Street Crushers.

"'Scuse me?" Harper's eyes went wide. His head craned forward, inches away from the leader of the Dragon Kings.

"What's under your sofa?"

"You come into my house and accuse me?" Harper's eyes were ablaze with anger and indignation.

"Let's get up there," Morris said. Fredericks signaled his team into position. Four men wearing black combat gear filed past Morris, weapons drawn, moving towards the front of the building. Two of them peeled away towards the rear entrance. Morris and Jankelowitz followed Corporal Lance as he fell in behind Fredericks and the rest of the team.

"Police!" Fredericks shouted as they approached the sentries at the front entrance, weapons at the ready. Harper's sentry opened fire, and was gunned down instantly in a hail of bullets. The other two muscle bound men, together with Chen's two aides raised their hands in surrender. The two men tasked to take the front entrance restrained them while Fredericks and his detail entered the building and climbed the stairs, with Morris and Jankelowitz following behind Corporal Lance. As they arrived at the second floor, Fredericks signaled the team to halt. He peered around the corner, and signaled one hostile. He moved first, and his team followed as they peeled out from the stairwell and into the corridor.

"Police!" Fredericks called out. "Drop your weapon!"

The man in the white vest raised his gun to fire on the approaching men, but was thrown back by two shots from Fredericks' rifle, which hit him in the chest. He stumbled back, and slumped against the doorframe.

Inside the apartment, Harper and Chen both turned at the sound of gunfire.

"What was that?" Chen snapped. "Police? What is this?"

"Easy now, I didn't call no cops!" Harper insisted.

Chen shouted something in Chinese, and one of his aides launched at Harper. The two men tumbled over the rear of the sofa, and crashed to the floor, grappling and punching at each other. They slammed against the small table behind the sofa, knocking glasses and empty beer bottles to the floor.

Fredericks heard the sounds of the struggle as he and his team took up their positions outside Harper's apartment door.

"Go! Now!" Fredericks called. He stepped forward and kicked the door once, with enough force to shatter the lock and swing it open.

"Police! Freeze!" Fredericks shouted. Chen and his remaining aide darted off into the kitchen. Two of the SWAT team gave chase while Fredericks and Lance went to pull apart the two men entangled in close combat on the floor.

Harper landed a punch that sent a trail of blood from the Dragon King's mouth onto the SWAT team leader's boot, and the Asian responded with an elbow strike to Harper's temple.

"Enough!" Fredericks shouted. Harper looked up into the

barrels of two rifles. The Dragon King landed another swift punch to Harper's jaw while he was distracted.

"I said, enough!" Fredericks slammed the heel of his boot into the Dragon King's face bringing an abrupt end to the scuffle. Harper rolled onto his back, blood dripping from his mouth and nose.

Ed Harper knew when to back down. Taking on police when he was outnumbered was plain stupidity, and besides, his clandestine deal with the local Police would mean that whatever charges they might find to bring against him would soon fall away. A couple of nights in a jail cell was part of the deal as leader of the Eighth Street Crushers. A small price to pay for getting away with all the other offences he had committed.

Fredericks looked around the apartment. Two of his team members had given chase to Chen through the kitchen window and down the fire escape. Morris came over to join Lance and Fredericks, while Jankelowitz hung back a few feet.

"Get up," Morris said, standing over Harper. The big man groaned and stood, towering over Lance and Fredericks.

"You bust into my place and arrest a man trying to defend himself?" Harper hissed, wiping blood from his face.

Morris stood his ground. "We got word that you and the Dragon Kings were meeting in here. That in itself isn't good. Then your guy opened fire on us in the street, and so did your guy at the door. Not good, by the way. Not good. And then we heard fighting going on inside."

"It was self defense. He came at me!" Harper insisted, looking down at the unconscious Dragon King on the floor.

Morris leaned in close and whispered in Harper's ear, "Remember, Harper. Any evidence against you and our deal is off the table."

The two of them stood facing each other. Morris regarded the huge gang lord for a moment. In his job, justice was a grey line. His idea of right and wrong had become blurred since his squeaky rookie days, when pissing on the sidewalk was grounds for arrest.

Over the years he'd learned to trade one evil for another, realizing that getting a case in front of a judge didn't guarantee justice, and criminals with lots of money could always afford better lawyers than those on government salaries working for the State Prosecutor. The more money you could throw at a case, the more the line between right and wrong blurred. Getting caught was just a game to men like Harper. He'd played the system, and he was smart. Morris eventually realized Harper would be more valuable as an ally than an enemy, knowing what he knew about this part of the underworld. Still he detested the man, and he would wipe his deal off the table the minute he could come up with a watertight case.

"You got nothing on me, Morris," Harper said. "They came into my house."

Morris shrugged. Harper may be able to squirm his way out of this one yet again, and Morris wouldn't lose any sleep over it. The gang lord would slip up somewhere along the line. It was only a matter of time.

"You hiding something in here, Harper?" Morris asked, studying the objects in the room.

"You got a search warrant?" Harper asked.

"Don't need one," Morris said without looking at the big man. "We heard a struggle. That gives us probable cause." Morris went through to the kitchen and started opening cupboards, leaving Harper in the company of Fredericks, Lance and Jankelowitz. "You know, for the king of Eighth Street, you sure live like shit, Harper." The kitchen was cluttered. Empty beer bottles stood on the counter together with dirty glasses, and a greasy pizza box lay open somewhere in between them. The kitchen fittings were old, probably installed forty years ago when the building went up, and had never been upgraded since. Morris picked up a can of coffee and shook it. He opened it, sniffed, and replaced the lid. He checked the bottom of cereal boxes, examined the contents of containers, opened the refrigerator and looked for anything out of place, but found nothing. He pulled a drawer open and lifted the plastic cutlery holder, looking beneath, but still found nothing. Harper was keeping it clean. There was nothing here that would break the deal he and Morris had made.

Then Morris remembered the phone call he'd received from Ethan's friend, and the two visitors who'd showed up on his doorstep earlier that evening. He may as well follow up since he was here, and had free reign to snoop around. He kicked the sofa back a few feet. Harper followed Morris' movement with his eyes. Morris looked over at Harper, aware that the big man was watching his every move.

"What you hiding, Harper?" Morris repeated. He crouched and tapped the floorboards. One of them moved slightly as he touched it. Morris looked up at Harper and saw the miniscule movement in his eyes. The detective reached into his jacket pocket and withdrew a blue latex glove, which he slipped onto his right hand. He pressed down along the length of the floorboard until the opposite end lifted. Again, Morris looked up at Harper.

There's a moment when a man knows he's beaten. When a fighter can't last the round. When a fugitive runs out of places to hide. When a man knows he's been caught in a lie. It registers in the eyes, no matter how hard the conscious mind tries to cover it up with bravado or false confidence. For a brief moment, Morris saw that look in Harper's eyes. A microscopic movement of the eyebrows, barely discernable. A slight widening of the pupils. The quickening of the heart. The release of adrenaline in the brain. The onset of fear. The body preparing for fight or flight. Morris lifted the floorboard and laid it aside. He took a small flashlight from his inside jacket pocket and shone the beam into the cavity beneath the floorboards. At first he felt a sense of disappointment as the light revealed an empty, dusty cavity, but then he saw something stuffed away deep inside the hollow space. Morris reached in with his gloved hand. He felt something hard, cold and heavy.

"Hah," Morris said as he pulled the AK-47 from beneath the floorboards, and held it up for Harper to see. "This what you been hiding?" Harper stared at Morris. "Kalashnikov assault rifle. Same caliber as we pulled out of Carl Lynch and Little Li. I'll bet we find a ballistics match on the slugs we pulled from both bodies too." He stood and carried the rifle over to Harper. "If they match, that makes our deal null and void, Harper. This is murder one, and you're going down."

For a big man, Ed Harper moved with the agility of a leopard. He grabbed hold of the muzzle of Lance's assault rifle, and whipped it out of his hands, catching Morris on the jaw in the same movement. Morris reeled back, and before Fredericks could react, Harper slammed the butt of the rifle into his face, and using the rifle like a paddle, whipped the muzzle across Lance's face before he could launch himself at the gang lord. Fredericks recoiled and fell backwards as Harper darted out of the front door and down the hallway. Jankelowitz was already in pursuit by the time Morris recovered. Morris heard his partner shout, "Freeze!" He heard the sounds of rapid gunfire. By the time he stepped into the hallway, still dazed, Jankelowitz was lying on his back.

Morris shouted into his radio. "Officers down. Officers down!" He crouched beside his partner. Jankelowitz groaned, holding his chest. Morris moved his partner's hand aside, and breathed as he saw the shining piece of metal lodged in the black vest. "You're a lucky son of a bitch, Yank," Morris said, then spoke into his radio. "Peters! We got a runner!"

Harper took the stairs three at a time, until he reached the basement. He knew there'd be a detail waiting at the front and rear entrance. Carefully he moved between the parked cars until he was near the roller door that secured the parking garage. His eyes fixed on a white SUV that stood in a corner bay.

Glass shattered as Harper smashed the butt of the rifle through the passenger window. He reached in and opened the door, before sliding into the passenger seat. Next, he smashed the plastic covering at the steering column to expose a collection of wires, and pulled and tore at the sheath surrounding them until he had exposed the copper strands. He touched two of them together.

Sparks flew as the engine hummed to life. Ed Harper slid into the driver's seat, and steered the car towards the exit.

The metal shutter rolled slowly upwards. Harper knew what was coming. Before the roller shutter door reached the top, two members of Frederick's SWAT team blocked the entrance, weapons drawn, trained on the white SUV.

"Police! Get out of the vehicle!" one of them shouted. Harper leaned over and pressed his body flat against the passenger seat, flooring the accelerator. The car lurched forward. It connected with one of the policemen, who tumbled along the bonnet and slammed into the windshield. The other dived off to the left, and rolled twice before rising to his feet. By that time, Harper had pulled himself upright, and twisted the steering wheel, turning the SUV away from a collision course with the cars parked on the opposite side of the street. He swerved as the policeman behind him opened fire. The rear window shattered, then the front as bullets ripped through the vehicle. Blood spattered across the splintered windshield as a bullet hit Harper's right shoulder. His arm slumped to his side and he screamed in agony, trying to control the vehicle with his left hand. The SUV gathered speed, and swerved as Harper tried to regain control, but his hand was shaking as adrenaline coursed through his body, trying to fight the pain, and drive him on to survive. The white SUV raced towards an intersection, and collided with a BMW coming from the right sending it careering across the street and into a lamppost. The SUV spun a complete circle, and was now on the opposite side of the road, right in the path of an oncoming cargo truck. The truck's horn blared as the monstrous machine bore down on the SUV. There was an almighty crash as they collided.

Abe was frightened. It had been hours since the Dragon Kings had left them tied up in the dark room.

"Do you think they're coming for us?" he asked.

"They'll come for us," Dan reassured him, but his hope was waning.

"I'm scared, Dan," Abe confided.

"Me too, man."

"I don't want to die like this. I'm not ready to die. I still want to get married. Have kids. See the world. I want to swim with the whale sharks. I still want to taste my mother's *babke* one more time," Abe rambled.

"We're not going to die, Abe. Have faith," Dan said.

"Faith? Faith in what? Do you really believe any of that?" Abe had fasted just a few days ago, but he hadn't really prayed for forgiveness of his sins. He'd gone through the motions, followed the instructions on the outside, but what was it all for? He regretted not being more observant all his life. If he were to die now, he didn't know where his soul would end up. Heaven? Hell?

"Man, I'm tied up in a dark room in my underwear. Right now I'll believe anything if it gets us out of here," Dan replied.

"You know, I've been brought up a Jew my whole life. Followed all the traditions. Fasted on Yom Kippur. Ate *matzoth* on *Pesach*. Had my bar-mitzvah when I was thirteen. Went to shul on Shabbos. Lit candles on Chanukah. Ok, not so much in the last couple of years. I haven't really kept kosher. But I've been a good Jew. I followed the Ten Commandments. I've been a good person. You think that counts for anything?" Abe asked. He felt like he was bargaining for his soul. "Does any of this mean anything? What did we do it all for?"

Dan was silent for a moment. "Because it was right," he said. "At the time, it made sense. Made you feel good."

"Made me feel less *guilty*," Abe corrected. "That's all it was. Things you do to make you feel less guilty, because the alternative is to not do them and feel guilty for not doing them."

"Maybe," Dan thought out loud. "Us Christians too. It's riddled with guilt. The whole thing. You don't go to church on Sunday, you feel like you should have been there. You give in to temptation, you do something you know you're not supposed to and you feel this immediate sense of guilt. You're right, we do it to avoid the guilt. I mean, is there really someone out there keeping score?"

"Do you believe in God, Dan?" Abe said.

"Yeah," Dan said. "Yeah."

"Where's he then?" Abe asked.

Dan was silent. "All around us."

"You really believe that? The Bible is full of stories of miracles. Did God go on vacation after the Bible? What happened to all those miracles? Do you think they were lying? The people who wrote the Bible? Do you think that stuff really happened? The miracles. The signs and wonders? That shit hasn't happened in two thousand years." Abe was beside himself.

Dan was going through his own crisis of belief. If God really did exist he could use some evidence of that now.

"Hey, do you believe that stuff about angels?" Dan said, trying to change the subject.

"That seemed pretty real," Abe said. "Except look where it got us."

"Yeah," Dan said. "Doesn't make it any less real though."

"When I get out of this place," Abe said, "I'm gong to find a nice Irish girl and ask her to marry me."

"You serious?" Dan smiled. "I think you're suffering from stress disorder. Post traumatic stress."

"How can I, we're still mid stress, we're not post anything. What are you going to do?"

Dan thought for a moment. "I'm going to go home to my nice apartment, all by myself, and I'm going to start writing a book."

"What?" Dan's remark caught Abe totally by surprise. "You? A book?"

"Yeah. I've always wanted to write a book," Dan said. "And if I die today, I'm never going to get that chance. I'm going to start writing a book. That's what I'm going to do when I get out of here."

"You never cease to surprise me," Abe said. "What you going to write about?"

"Being tied up in a basement with you."

Both of them laughed, but the reality soon killed their

momentary escape. They were tied up in a basement, and nobody was coming for them.

"I need to pee," Abe said.

"Don't you dare!" Dan warned.

Fredericks and Morris regrouped at the SWAT van. The paramedics had managed to get a dressing on the SWAT leader's face before being called away to the accident scene involving a white SUV, a BMW, and an eighteen-wheeler. The two men heard the sound of distant sirens as more EMT's joined the accident scene nearby.

The army of Dragon Kings hiding in the shadows had dispersed when the police had shown up.

Seven men sat on the curb, hands cuffed behind their backs, under the watchful eye of three SWAT members. Five of the captives wore black jackets and white shirts, one of them badly bruised and beaten. Morris paced before them, and then stopped in front of Chen. He crouched so he could look the man in the eye as he spoke.

"What were you doing at Harper's apartment, Chen?" Morris asked. The Dragon King leader looked up, but said nothing. "I got two dead Crushers, and Harper's in the wind," he lied. Chen didn't know that Harper was in an ambulance. "So what were you doing there, Chen? You and Harper don't strike me as drinking buddies. Was this about the shooting on Eighth Street?"

Chen diverted his eyes for a fraction of a second. Long enough for Morris to know he was right.

"It was, wasn't it?" Again, Chen looked away. "So what were the two of you talking about? I know that shooting on Eighth Street was a revenge killing. Your guys took out two of his guys, so Harper's guys took out one of your guys."

"Harper did it himself," Chen said looking up at Morris. "It wasn't one of his guys. Harper killed Li."

"Ah?" Morris pursed his lips, and nodded with the same expression he'd give a toddler, pretending to be was interested.

Playing along. "You got evidence?"

"That's' what we were doing there. We got a tip off."

Morris frowned. "You got a tip off?" He'd received a tip off about the same thing that night. Twice. "From who?"

"Two guys," Chen replied. "Said they were friends of the kid that Harper caught in the crossfire."

"What exactly did these two guys say?" Morris had lost the sarcasm and was suddenly keenly interested in Chen's response.

"That we should look under …"

"…Harpers sofa." Morris said in unison with the leader of the Dragon Kings. Chen tilted his head.

"How do you know about Harper's sofa?" Chen asked.

"Because those same two guys came to my house earlier tonight and I told them to get lost." He looked up at Chen. "So they must have gone to you instead. Where are they now?"

Chen looked to his aides, and sighed. "If I tell you, are you gonna let me and my men go?"

"That depends," Morris said. "On what you've done with them."

"Just kept them safe in case their information was a trap," Chen said.

Morris eyed the Dragon King leader for a moment. The deal he'd made with Harper was dead. He could use a new information source.

"Fredericks, get this one on his feet, will you?" Morris said to the SWAT leader. "Let's take a walk, you and me," he said to Chen.

Riley couldn't bear to watch Ethan fade before her eyes. It was after 11:00pm, and the clock was ticking down. She and Archer had left Ethan's parents at his bedside to give them some time alone with their son. Martin had stretched out on some chairs in the waiting area, which was now mostly empty except for a few people in the queue for treatment. Riley and Archer had walked the hallway several times, and were now heading for the main entrance for the seventh time.

"He's going to die, Archer," Riley said.

The medium nodded. "Lucca showed me the time. It was clear as day, and it was definitely Ethan's book. We tried," he attempted to console her. "Heck, we all tried. We went further to save Ethan than anyone's ever gone for anyone ever before. We crossed over to the Dimension of Eternity. Without having to be dead first. And we all came back." He stopped momentarily, and looked Riley in the eye. "You even offered to die in his place. That's real love, Riley. And he's going to die knowing how much you love him. What you did to try to save him. He knows that," Archer said. They continued their stroll along the empty hallway.

"But why now?" Riley asked. "Why give me the chance to find real love only to take it away again?"

"It's only for a short time here on this earth, and then you will be with your true love for eternity," he said.

"You think so?"

"Yeah," Archer said. "I've seen it before. Your soul mate on earth is your partner for eternity. If he's your soul mate, you'll be reunited with him in the after life."

"Thanks," she said. "It feels like I've known him all my life, and yet we've hardly had time to get to know each other."

"That's the thing with soul mates. You knew each other before this life."

"In another life?" Riley asked.

"Maybe," Archer said. "Some people believe you get a few turns here on earth. To me it doesn't all make sense. I don't believe that you get to write this test over and over again till you get the answers right. Whether you believe in reincarnation or not, the idea of the soul mate is the same in different belief systems. It's a predetermination. You knew each other before your time together on earth. Whether that was in a previous life here, or in another dimension before this one. Whatever the case, you and your soul mate knew each other before you were born, and you loved each other before. Not everybody is so lucky, Riley. Not everybody gets to find their soul mate."

Their conversation was interrupted by the sound of footsteps as a team of trauma staff ran past them. Moments later they heard the sirens, and saw the flashing red lights. An ambulance came to a stop outside the hospital entrance. Riley and Archer watched as the ambulance doors opened, and paramedics hoisted a gurney to the ground. The trauma team wheeled the patient into the hospital, followed by two uniformed policemen.

"Single gunshot wound to the shoulder, massive trauma to the head," the paramedic told the doctor on duty as they moved quickly down the corridor. "Patient is non responsive. He's lost a lot of blood."

"Get him to Trauma One, now!" the doctor ordered.

Riley and Archer watched as the gurney rattled past them while a second ambulance pulled up at the entrance. Another trauma team raced off to receive the next casualty.

The first patient they'd brought in was a tall black male. The right side of his shirt was soaked in blood, and his head was badly lacerated at the forehead. He was bleeding from his mouth and nose. Riley noticed his left hand cuffed to the gurney railing. They stood in the hallway, watching as the doctors wheeled the gurney through the doors to the trauma unit.

"That's why you gotta wear a seatbelt," Archer said.

"You two, wait outside," the doctor ordered the police escort, who were relieved to obey his command.

Riley and Archer stood back as the second casualty was wheeled past them. It was a white male in his early thirties, and he looked a mess. His head was in a brace. There was blood all over his white shirt and blue suit. His frightened eyes searched around him and for an instant, they stared right into Riley's as the gurney trundled past.

"Get him stabilized, and then get him to CT," the doctor instructed. "Possible C4 fracture."

"Yes, doctor," the nurse said.

Riley had seen those eyes somewhere before. The face looked familiar. Where had she seen him?

267

"This is it, isn't it?" Ethan said. "This is where I die." He watched from inside his bubble, unable to reach out to the people who were right in front of him. "I guess there are worse ways to go."

Silica gave him a reassuring smile. "Trust me, there are worse ways to go. You're surrounded by your family. People who love you. You're not suffering any pain. Its about as good as it gets."

"Will you help them? When I'm gone? They're going to need a lot of comforting."

"Sure," Silica said. "I'll make sure they're comforted."

"Thank you." Ethan watched his parents as they sat vigil next to his bed. "Did they get him? Did they get the guy who killed my brother?"

Silica smiled. "Come see for yourself."

A moment later, they were in the trauma ward, watching the doctor trying to save the life of the man in bed three.

"Did you get his blood results?" the doctor asked as one of the nurses ran back into the trauma ward. It was Doctor Jansen, the same doctor who had treated Ethan.

"AB Negative," she replied.

"Dammit," the doctor cursed. "Hang one more unit of O Negative. He's lost too much blood."

"AB Negative," Ethan said. "That's my blood type."

Silica smiled. "Yep," she said.

"That's the guy who killed my brother?" Ethan asked.

"Yep," Silica nodded.

"So that's it then. Is he going to die?"

Silica shook her head. "I don't know. I'm not his angel. But if you ask me, its not looking too good for him."

Doctor Jansen stopped working for a moment. The patient had suffered a massive head trauma. His pupils were dilated. In order to stabilize him, Jansen had him on a ventilator, but he knew the patient was most likely brain dead. He would need to perform an EEG to confirm, but all the signs were there.

"Doctor Jansen?" the nurse from reception called from the

doorway.

"Yeah?" Jansen looked up. His face betrayed his exhaustion. He'd been at it since midday, and although his shift was nearly over, he still didn't see himself leaving the hospital any time soon.

"Detective Morris wants a word."

Jansen sighed, and left the patient in the nurse's care before walking wearily into reception.

"You Detective Morris?" Jansen asked.

Morris looked around. He was the only one waiting at the reception, apart from the nurse at the front desk.

"Yeah," Morris said, biting back his natural sarcasm. "The guy they just brought in, Ed Harper – how's he doing?"

Riley and Archer made their eighth turn towards the hospital front doors, and were strolling past the reception desk as Morris spoke to the doctor.

Jansen shook his head. "Not looking good. Massive head trauma. Massive blood loss. His blood type is rare. AB Negative. Makes it harder to find donor blood, but we've managed to stabilize him."

"He gonna be able to stand trial?" Morris asked.

Jansen shook his head. "Doubt it. I don't think he's ever going to wake up."

Morris sighed. "He gonna die?"

"He's on life support. Unless his heart gives in, he could stay this way for a very long time."

"There's justice for you," Morris said. "A guy like that deserves to live every day regretting what he's done, and he gets off just like that." Morris snapped his fingers in the air.

Riley and Archer had stopped within earshot at the mention of the man's blood type.

"He's the guy that killed Carl Lynch," Morris said. "We finally got proof. I think."

"I'm sorry, did you say Carl Lynch?" Riley said, approaching Morris.

"Yeah. Who are you?" he asked.

"This is Ethan Lynch's girlfriend. Ethan's in a critical condition here at the hospital." Jansen explained. "He doesn't have long. He's in liver failure."

"My name is Riley," she said.

"Jesus, what is it with Ethan Lynch tonight? The guy's everywhere! Is his family in there?" Morris asked. Riley nodded. "Let me give them some good news."

Riley and Archer led Morris to the ward. It was 11:28pm. The hospital was silent, except for the sound of footsteps as the three of them entered the ward and moved over to Ethan's bed.

"Mr and Mrs Lynch?" Morris greeted them quietly.

"Detective Morris?" Both Carol and Ivan were surprised to see the detective.

"I'm really sorry about your son," he said, "I thought I might have some good news for you, but under the circumstances," he motioned towards Ethan, "at least it might bring you a little comfort. We caught the guy that killed Carl. And if its any justice, it doesn't look like he's gonna make it."

Ivan nodded. He had wanted to stare his son's killer in the eyes, and watch as whoever took his son from him was condemned to a life behind bars. Hearing that the man was close to death brought him little comfort. He nodded slowly. Carol's response was similar.

"Thank you, Detective," she said, forcing a smile.

"Just thought you might want to know," he added. There was a long silence, and then Morris said, "Well, good night. It's been a long day." As soon as he'd spoken the words he realized how hollow they must sound. To the family of the guy in the bed, a long day was the least of their worries.

Morris turned and left.

"Wait here," Riley said to Archer suddenly.

"Where are you going?" he asked her.

"To break a few laws," she replied, running after Morris.

"Wait!" she called to the detective. "I need to ask you something."

*****

Moments later, Riley, Morris and Jansen stood in Trauma One, looking at Ed Harper hooked up to a ventilator, with monitors registering a regular but weak heart beat. Jansen had dismissed the nurses.

"Well this is convenient," Jansen said looking up. "Is this for real?"

Neither Riley nor Morris said a word. Morris looked at Riley through narrowed eyes. Riley had just forged a document which could see both her and Morris imprisoned, and Jansen barred from medical practice.

"You sure you wanna do this?" Morris asked.

Riley nodded. Morris had turned a blind eye to Harper's indiscretions in the name of justice. What Riley was asking was no different, but it was in the name of love. Or insanity. Either way, it would make no difference to Morris.

"I could go to jail for this," Jansen said.

"Relax," Morris said. "Nobody saw nothing, right?"

Riley looked up at Doctor Jansen.

"Ok," Jansen said. "Marie!" he called. "Book me an O.R. now, get this patient moved, and get a surgical team together right away. Tell them I'll meet them down there in five."

"Yes Doctor Jansen," Marie replied.

"I'll call you when it's done," he said. "Wait out there." He pointed to the reception area.

Morris and Riley went out to wait in the reception area.

"Detective Morris?" Riley said as they walked. "Do you believe in fate?" she asked him.

After the bizarre coincidences he'd seen that night, he'd believe damn near anything. "Before tonight, maybe a little," Morris said. "After tonight," he looked at her and nodded.

Riley closed her eyes. "I hope I did the right thing," she whispered. Morris placed a hand on her shoulder.

"That makes two of us," Morris said.

Riley waited in silence, pacing up and down the corridors of Trauma One. She heard the rattle of a gurney as a nurse wheeled it towards her. Lying on it was the man she'd seen earlier, the one who was brought in right after Harper.

"I know this man," she said to the nurse as the gurney approached her. The nurse stopped.

"You know him?" the nurse asked.

"I think so," Riley said. "I recognize him from somewhere. I've seen him before."

"You know who he is?" The nurse asked.

Riley shook her head. "Not exactly."

"Well that doesn't help much," the nurse replied. "The only ID we found on him belonged to a woman."

"What happened to him?" Riley asked.

"Apparently he got caught up in that big car crash earlier. Him, a guy the cops say is a one of the big gang lords, and the driver of a freight truck. The truck driver was the only one who came out of that whole mess without a scratch. So, you recognize him?" The nurse asked.

Riley suddenly remembered where she'd seen him. The man from the bar. Grant. The man in the blue suit. The one who stole Jenna's car.

"What was the name on the woman's ID you found on him, do you know?" Riley asked.

"It's here with his personal stuff," the nurse said. She reached in to a laundry bag at the foot of the gurney and pulled out a purse. Opening it, she withdrew the ID card, and read the name. "Jenna Harris."

"Oh my god! Jenna's a friend of mine. Did this guy have some jewelry on him? A gold necklace, some rings, and a pair of diamond earrings?" Riley asked. "This guy ripped my friend off. Stole her car, her wallet, and her jewelry."

"What? You're kidding right?" The nurse said, but looking at Riley's expression it was clear that she wasn't. "Oh my god!" she said, hand over her mouth. The nurse looked down at the man in the neck brace distastefully. "Let me check," she said, looking over her shoulder cautiously. She rummaged through the laundry bag and retrieved the man's trousers and searched the pockets. "My god, look!" she exclaimed. In her hand she held a gold necklace, some rings and a pair of diamond earrings.

"There's two policemen over there," Riley pointed to the two cops waiting outside the ward where Harper had been. "And that guy there is Detective Morris. Let's go tell him what we found."

Riley accompanied the nurse as she wheeled the gurney towards Trauma One, and the waiting policemen.

"If you believe in Karma," the nurse said as they walked, surprising Riley, "this guy got it good."

"How so?" Riley asked.

"Fractured C4. He's never going to walk again, let alone steal someone's car."

Riley couldn't stand the waiting any longer. She stepped outside into the parking area in front of the hospital to get some air. The place was empty this late at night, except for a few parked cars. She heard the distant hum of an approaching vehicle far in the distance as she slumped heavily onto a bench. There were only a few minutes left till midnight. Did it work? Did she save him, she wondered. Riley heard a noise. A feint meow. She craned her head to see where the sound came from. In the dim light she saw movement on the other side of the parking lot. She heard the sound again. Crossing the parking area, she saw two kittens in the flowerbed. She crouched.

"Come here," she beckoned. "Where's your mommy?" Riley looked around for the mother, but saw nothing. She picked up the two tiny kittens and headed back across the tarmac towards the hospital entrance.

Jansen was scrubbed up, standing in the operating theatre. Two scrub sisters stood by, ready to assist, and the anesthetist, sat quietly at his machines, monitoring the displays and gauges. On the table in the center of the room lay Ed Harper. Jansen called for the surgical tools he needed, and began opening Harper up.

Twenty minutes later, Jansen stepped back.

"It's done," Jansen said.

The anesthetist nodded. "You ready?" he asked in a strong Romanian accent. Jansen nodded. The anesthetist flipped the switch, and turned off the ventilator.

"Time of death," the anesthetist said checking his watch. "Twelve Midnight."

Outside the hospital, a small blue Mazda had just entered the parking area. It suddenly revved loudly and lurched forward. The car collided with the rear of another car that was reversing out of a parking bay, changing the trajectory of the speeding vehicle, which hit a curb and became airborne, hurtling towards the entrance to the hospital.

Riley looked up to see the lights of the airborne vehicle heading straight towards her, and froze. Instinctively she held the two kittens close to her, protecting them with her body.

"Riley!"

She heard Archer's voice moments before he tackled her to the ground, and pushed her out of the way of the oncoming vehicle. The car came down hard where Riley had stood moments earlier, sparks flying at it hit the asphalt, and collided with a bench just outside the main entrance. Seconds later, an ER doctor and several interns burst through the hospital doors to see what had happened. They ran to the crumpled car, and pulled the door open.

"Archer?" Riley said looking up.

"I remembered what you told me," he said, lying on the sidewalk alongside her, breathing heavily. They stood slowly turning their attention to the wrecked car.

"That was close," Riley said. Archer dusted himself off. "Where are the kittens?"

"The what?" Archer asked.

"They must have spooked when I hit the ground." Riley looked for them, but the two little fluffy creatures were long gone.

The doctor was a young woman in her late thirties with short dark hair. She and one of the interns pulled an old man from the driver's seat, while the other two pulled a woman about the same age from the passenger seat.

"Sir?" the doctor said, examining the man's pupils using a narrow flashlight. "Can you hear me?"

"Where's my wife?" the man asked, confused.

"She's ok, sir," the doctor said loudly looking up at the intern that was tending to the woman. The intern nodded. She was ok. "Can you tell me your name, sir?" the doctor asked the man.

"William," he replied, looking up at her. "William Bennet," he said.

"William, you've been in an accident. Do you remember what happened?" the doctor asked, checking his pulse.

"My shoe got stuck under the accelerator," he said. "I was trying to brake."

"He shouldn't have been driving," his wife's voice came from the other side of the car. "He doesn't even have a license."

"Somebody had to bring you to the hospital," William said.

"Tammy was on her way, you idiot," his wife whined.

"Thank god nobody was injured," the doctor said, looking up at the interns. "Get them inside, let's make sure they're ok." She stood, and looked at the wrecked car. "And somebody get this mess out of here."

The interns stared at each other.

Riley and Archer returned to the ward just after midnight. Carol and Ivan sat holding one another at the empty space where Ethan's bed had been.

Carol looked up at Riley, her eyes red and swollen with tears.

"Where is he?" Archer asked, suddenly panicked.

"In surgery," Carol managed before the tears took over again.

"Have they told you how he's doing?" Riley asked. Carol shook her head.

"What's going on?" Archer asked.

"You don't want to know," Riley said.

"What do you mean?" Archer looked at her. "It's after midnight. Ethan's still alive?" Archer was elated.

"It worked," Riley whispered.

"What worked?" Archer asked suspiciously. "What did you do?"

"Remember what the Writers said to Ethan? That the only way he could live would be if someone else died in his place. Someone that wasn't supposed to die tonight."

"What did you do?" Archer asked again, slowly.

"The guy who killed Ethan's brother was on a ventilator. The doctors said he was brain dead," Riley explained. "I just sped things up a bit."

Archer stared at her wide-eyed.

Abe stiffened as he heard the door open. "They're back," he whispered to Dan. "They've come back for us. Do you think they're going to kill us?"

Moments later, they saw flashlight beams sweeping the room. They saw silhouettes of figures against the bright light. They were armed. Abe could see the outlines of rifles.

"Oh my god," Abe whispered. "They've got guns!" He tried to free himself from his chair, wriggling rapidly, bouncing the chair against the hard floor again and again.

"There they are!" they heard a voice shout. Suddenly all the flashlight beams converged on the two of them, and Abe froze, petrified.

"You're alright. We're police. You're safe now," one of them said as he approached the two men who were bound to chairs in the center of the room. "Help me untie them," the policeman said to his team.

They heard voices off to the left and right shout, "Clear!"

"What's that smell?" one of the policemen said.

"Dan!" Abe said. "Did you just piss yourself?"

It was close to 2:00am when Riley returned to her apartment to get a little sleep before returning to the hospital. Emotionally and physically exhausted, she set her keys down next to the photo frame in the entrance. She saw the picture every day, but hardly noticed the faces in the photo, even thought they were always right there, in that same place. Were it ever to go missing, she would notice that something was out of place, but day by day, she would place her keys next to the frame, and pick her keys up every time she left without really noticing the faces.

Having been in the Dimension of Eternity, and coming so close to losing Ethan, Riley felt a renewed appreciation for life. Like the photo itself, life was something she'd taken for granted. Now, she stopped and picked up the frame, taking a moment to relive the few memories of her parents that she carried with her. Her mom's gentle voice, and her dad leading her around the garden on the pony at her sixth birthday. If only Lucca had given her a chance to meet them, she thought with a longing smile.

Riley set the photo frame back in its place, and went through to the kitchen where she dropped her bag on the granite counter.

So much had changed in the last twenty-four hours. She'd discovered so much about life, and death, about love and angels. Ethan was alive. He would live, and they would be together. Her soul mate. She felt peace within her, just like the deep peace she'd felt in the Dimension of Eternity.

"Lucca?" she said, turning to find the angel hovering in front of her. "Thank you," Riley said immediately. "For saving Ethan."

Lucca nodded. "There was something else you asked me that I could not do earlier," he said. Riley frowned. "You asked if you could see your parents in the Dimension of Eternity."

Riley felt a tingling in her core as Lucca spoke.

"Yes?" she said, hopefully.

"You cannot see them in that Dimension until you yourself have crossed over," he began.

Was this an apology, Riley wondered.

"I understand," she nodded.

"You can speak to them from the Dimension of Time," he continued. It took a moment for the words to sink in. "Mediums, people in tune with the Dimension of Eternity can communicate with those who have crossed over."

"Are they here?" Riley asked. "Can I speak to them now?"

Riley heard a familiar voice. A voice warm with love. A gentle voice she had last heard when she was six years old. A voice she'd carried in her heart since then.

"Riley," the voice said.

"Mom?" Riley's cheeks immediately became wet with tears that flowed from deep within. "Mom? Is that you?"

"My beautiful little girl," Riley's mother said.

"Mom!" Riley cried, holding out her hand in the empty room. "I've thought about you every single day since…"

"I know. And I've wanted to tell you for so long how sorry I am that your father and I had to leave you. That we had so little time with you as a child. That we had to leave without saying goodbye."

"I remember that day like it was yesterday," Riley said through her tears. "My sixth birthday."

"It *was* only yesterday," her mother said.

"It was twenty one years go," Riley said.

"Being here, in the Dimension of Eternity, twenty one years feels like a day," her mother's voice said.

Riley hugged herself. "I've missed you so much."

"I know," her mother replied. "I have been there, with you, through every moment of your loneliness, and every moment of your despair, I was there. I held you while you cried, and I watched over you while you slept."

"Why couldn't I feel you?" Riley asked.

"You weren't ready," her mother said. Looking back, Riley could see what she meant. "You wanted to change the world. Set things right that couldn't be changed. The world is full of good and bad. They happen together, inseparable, like light and dark. You can't have one without the other. But over time, you learned the wisdom of life. That you can't change the past but you can change what happens as a result of it."

"That's why I joined the Organ Donor program," Riley said.

"Yes. To try to set things right," her mother added. "I know."

"Did you have anything to do with that?" Riley asked.

"No. That was all you. Everything you've done in your life has been all you."

"I miss being a family," Riley said, still hugging herself.

"You'll make your own family. Soon, I'm told."

"You know about Ethan?" Riley smiled.

"He's your soul mate. Just like your father and me are soul mates."

"I nearly lost him, you know," Riley said.

"I know," Riley's mother said. "That's why I sent him."

"Sent who?" Riley frowned.

"Lucca."

"*You* sent Lucca?" Riley felt a tingling throughout her entire body.

"I sent him so that the two of you would find a way to be together, just like your father and me found a way," Riley's mother explained. "We couldn't be apart from each other, not for a moment. We had to cross over together."

"That's why you had to die together?"

"Yes," the gentle voice said. "Even if it meant leaving you behind."

Riley felt a fresh wave of tears. "But I miss you so much. Why couldn't one of you have stayed with me?"

"Because neither of us could have lived without the other. If one had crossed over, the other would have died of a broken heart. You would never have understood until now. You yourself were ready to trade your life for Ethan's."

"It's true," Riley said, nodding to herself. "I love him so much, I would have given my life for him. I tried, but he changed everything back again. So *you* sent Lucca?"

"Yes," the gentle voice replied.

"Why?" Riley asked.

"Lucca was my angel."

Chapter 13

Ethan's eyes flickered open. His throat was dry, and he shivered. His mother was asleep, curled up in a chair next to him. Riley was in a similar position next to her. "Riley. Mom." He tried to speak, but found it difficult. He coughed, and Carol woke immediately.

"You're awake," she said. Her eyes were red and swollen and it was clear that she'd been crying.

"What happened? How come I'm not dead?" he asked, but the dryness in his throat prevented him from asking any more questions. He broke into a coughing fit, and Carol handed him a glass of water.

When he'd stopped coughing, Carol spoke. "Ask Riley," she said reaching over to shake the sleeping girl next to her.

Riley stirred. Seeing Ethan awake she smiled, stood, stretched, and came over to the bed and leaning over, kissed him gently. Her breath tasted sweet, like a bouquet of freshly cut roses.

"Your angel is one hell of a character," Riley said. She held Ethan's hand.

"I know. She's a feisty little thing. With attitude. A little bit like you, but with wings," Ethan said in a scratchy voice.

Riley smiled, and Carol looked uncomfortable.

"It's ok," Carol said. "I've seen enough in the last day to make me think very differently about ... everything I've ever believed in," she conceded.

"So what happened," Ethan said. "How did you...?"

"Save you?" Riley asked. Ethan nodded. "Now *that's* a long story," she smiled. She looked up at Ivan. "Tell the others he's awake?" Ivan nodded and slipped out of the room.

"You still owe me a long story. The last one was pretty disappointing," Ethan said. He began coughing again and Riley helped him drink some water.

"Do you remember the message you had for us from Silica? That we should tell Detective Morris he'd find what he was looking for under Ed Harper's sofa, and that love would find a way?"

Ethan nodded. Right now, that whole encounter with his angel felt like a hallucination. "That was real?" he asked. Riley nodded. "Felt real, but like a dream at the same time."

"It was real," Riley confirmed.

"He's back!" Abe said as he and Dan entered, followed by Ivan, and then Archer and Martin.

"Jeez, what is this? It's getting a bit crowded in here," Ethan said, looking at all the faces around him.

The newcomers greeted him one by one, but Ivan waited till the excitement was over.

"Glad to have you back, son," Ivan said, stepping forward.

"That you, Dad?" Ethan said.

"It's me, son," Ivan said, coming closer. He placed a hand on Ethan's shoulder and gave his son a squeeze. "Glad to have you back from the dead." Carol gave him a look of admonishment, but it was lost on him. He had another chance with his son, one he thought he'd never get again. Ethan looked up at his father and took hold of his hand.

"Good to see you, Dad," Ethan smiled. "I didn't think I was

going to make it."

"You weren't," Ivan said. "If it wasn't for your friends here, I don't think you would have made it. Honestly." Ivan looked at Riley and smiled a note of gratitude. Riley acknowledged with a warm smile of her own.

"So, tell me what happened?" Ethan looked back at Riley.

"Abe and Dan were the real heroes. They literally beat down Detective Morris' door," Riley looked up at them.

"Aw, it was nothing, really," Dan said. "We just nearly got ourselves killed."

"What?" Ethan sang. "You're kidding right?"

Abe shook his head. "I don't know if I'm ever going to listen to him again. He's fucking crazy!" Abe looked down at Carol. "Sorry," he apologized. Carol shook her head, and waved a hand. Abe continued. "So, wait, before we tell you what happened, I have to tell you that the night before, I had a dream that me and Dan were tied up in a warehouse, and next thing these men with guns came in and bam!" He clapped both hands loudly. "So when Riley told us to go tell Detective Morris that he had to look under Ed Whatever-his-Name-is' sofa, I literally had a panic attack."

"And I had to talk him down." Dan clipped Abe on the back of the head.

"Ow!"

"So what did you do?" Ethan asked.

"We went to Morris' house and told him that he had to go look under Ed's sofa, and he told us to get lost. Said he needed evidence before he could search the guy's apartment, and we told him that we were trying to give him evidence," Dan explained.

"Yeah, so then this crazy lunatic," Abe pointed a thumb over his shoulder at Dan, "came up with the clever idea that we should go tell the Dragon Kings, and let *them* look under his sofa."

"The Dragon Kings? The gang? You went to find the Dragon Kings?" Ethan recalled how his visit to Eighth Street had panned out.

"Not just the Dragon Kings," Abe said. "This guy went looking for the *head* of the Dragon Kings."

"You're insane!" Ethan said in disbelief. "I thought I was crazy going down the wrong end of Eighth Street."

"Oh, it gets better, believe me," Abe said, but Dan put a restraining hand on his chest.

"Let me, please?" He looked at Abe. "So we went to China Town, and I started asking around to speak to the Dragon Kings, and we stopped to buy a spring roll at this food cart."

"Wait," Abe interrupted, "Before that, we'd been in and out of like, a dozen restaurants asking for the Dragon Kings, but nobody wanted to speak to us."

"Yeah, one of them actually spit on my shoes," Dan continued. Ethan made a face. Dan continued. "So we ordered some spring rolls at this old guy's street cart, and Abe asked him if he knew where we could find the Dragon Kings. He made us wait there, and a few minutes later, this little Asian guy, like this big," Dan held his hand, palm down, at his chest. "He came to talk to us, and then, bam!" Dan clapped loudly once more. "Next thing we know we're tied up, in our underwear, in a warehouse somewhere."

Ethan's mouth dropped. "What?" he said, trying to raise himself to a sitting position, but he winced in agony. "Ow, fuck! What did they do to me?" He looked up apologetically at Carol. "Sorry, Mom." She waved a hand. "It hurts."

"Later," Riley said. "We're getting to that. She squeezed his hand as Dan continued excitedly.

"So then the leader of the Dragon Kings came in, with four of his bodyguards, and we told him to look under Ed's sofa, and he kept us tied up there for hours. Said if the information checked out, he'd let us go, and if it didn't he'd kill us."

"That's just like your dream," Ethan said pointing at Abe. Abe nodded, and then Ethan smiled waiting for everyone else to laugh with him but no-one did. "You're kidding?" Ethan said, expecting them to tell him none of it was true. "This is all a joke, right?"

"He's telling the truth," Abe said. "We were tied up in there for hours."

Dan looked at Abe threateningly. Abe smiled, but Dan held a hand firmly over Abe's mouth. Abe doubled over, laughing so hard his shoulders shook.

"What?" Riley asked.

Abe motioned to Dan with a thumb, resting his other hand on his knee. "Dan wet himself," he laughed. There was a chuckle throughout the room.

"We'd been in there for hours," Dan said defensively.

"So then what happened?" Ethan asked when the laughter had died down. Dan glared at Abe.

"I was waiting here at the hospital," Riley continued. "They brought in a gunshot victim, handcuffed to the gurney, accompanied by a police escort. It turns out it was Ed Harper. Detective Morris arrived at the hospital later and told me what had happened. Apparently, the Dragon Kings had gone over to Ed Harper's apartment to check out what Dan and Abe had told them, and the cops stormed the place. They found the gun that killed Carly under Harper's sofa."

"They found the gun?" Ethan asked. "It *was* him?"

Carol nodded. "Detective Morris called me this morning to say they'd tested the gun they found, and it matched the bullet that killed Carly. They found his fingerprints on the gun. Everything. It was him, Ethan. They found Carly's killer."

"Thank god," Ethan said. A tear rolled down his cheek. He squeezed Riley's hand. "What happened to him? Ed?" He tried to move again, but stopped immediately as sharp pain spread from his abdomen. He looked down. "What did they do to me?" he asked.

"Lie there and don't move," Riley smiled.

"I wish you'd said that to me when we were at my place," Ethan grinned. Carol pretended she hadn't heard.

"You've just had a major operation," Riley explained. "This is where everybody should leave the room," Riley said, looking around at the gathering.

"We're not going anywhere," Archer said. "We're as much a

part of this as you are." He folded his arms and stood resolute.

Riley took a breath. "I remembered what the Writers had said to you." She looked at Carol, who avoided her gaze and looked down. "That you were to die at midnight unless someone who wasn't destined to die at that time took your place."

Ethan narrowed his eyes. He felt a hollowness in the core of his being. He wasn't prepared to condemn anyone to die in his place. Riley continued.

"Morris said Harper tried to escape when they found the gun. Harper stole a car, and ended up in a car wreck. When they brought him in to the hospital, he was brain dead." Riley placed a hand on Ethan's arm. "He wasn't going to recover, Ethan. Detective Morris was there too. He was with me when I did it."

"Did what?" Ethan asked.

"I forged Harper's signature on an Organ Donor form."

"You forged his signature on an Organ Donor form? But that's illegal," Ethan insisted.

Riley nodded. "They salvaged his liver and turned the machines off at midnight. I couldn't let you die, Ethan. I love you too much to let you die. It was a choice between you or him, and I chose you," Riley said, tears rolling down her face. "He was dead anyway. The machines were keeping him alive."

Ethan winced as the pain spread through his abdomen once more. "What did they do to me?" he asked, looking at Carol.

"You were in liver failure," Carol said. "And you have a rare blood type." Carol looked up and smiled at Riley.

"Harper was AB Negative," Riley said softly. "You got his liver."

There was silence in the room. A long silence as Ethan looked down at his abdomen as if it were some offensive curse.

"Morris checked Harper's records. He had no family. His body would have been unclaimed. I filed the paperwork," Riley said. "It would have all happened anyway, in time. His body would have been cremated. I just sped things up."

"I shouldn't be alive," Ethan said, looking around. "Someone had to die in my place. I shouldn't be alive." His face contorted as he broke down and cried.

"All of this happened for you," Martin said, his deep voice soothing Ethan's anguish. "Think about it."

Ethan looked up, his eyes red with tears. "What do you mean," he said, wiping his face with his forearm.

"From the minute the angel first showed Archer what would happen in the future. Everything happened so you wouldn't die." Martin had a kind of prophetic look on his face. "Archer saw the angel here at the hospital which led him to Riley. You met Archer, and through that, Archer led Riley to you. Lucca chose Riley to see the future. And Riley was the one who saved you in the end, because of what your own angel told her. *Love will find a way.*"

Ethan was dumbfounded as everything Martin had just said slotted into place. Riley had seen the future, and she was the one who had tried to change it. She had even volunteered herself in his place.

"And everything is linked, Ethan, or it wouldn't have been allowed to happen. Harper took your brother's life, and in the end, he had to give his life so you could live," Martin continued. Ethan looked up at Angel Martin. "Of all the things Silica could have told you in your final hours, she chose to tell you two things. One led to Harper right here in this hospital at death's door. And the other led the one person who loves you more than life itself to find a way to save you. Silica knew this would happen. This was what she wanted for you. *This* was your future."

"Do you think so?" Ethan asked.

"Ethan," Carol spoke, "you know what I've believed all my life?" Ethan nodded, and Carol continued. "This has tested my faith more than anything I've ever gone through. More than losing Carly. This thing with angels and nearly losing you has been the hardest thing I've ever had to go through. Not only because I almost lost both my boys," she squeezed Ethan's hand, "but because I also almost lost the very thing that helped me get through all of this. My faith has been the one thing that I've turned to through all of life's troubles. But this is all real. These angels that you've seen. Angels that have spoken to you and shown you the way. It's rocked my very foundation." She looked up at Martin and Archer for a moment, and then turned back to Ethan. "But I prayed for a miracle. I prayed over and over again for a miracle. And now look at you. You're alive. My boy is alive. And I don't know if the miracle came from God, but you're alive and my prayers have been answered." She looked up at Ivan. "But maybe *my* miracle is that I've seen another side to my faith. That there's more to my faith than I've always believed." She looked up at Archer and Martin. "I can't deny that what the two of you see is real. That there are angels, and they speak to us. Through you. So what does that make of my faith?" She shook her head. "I don't know what it all means, but I guess what it means for me is that I might listen more to other things." Carol smiled at Ethan. "If these angels brought you back to me, then I'll listen to them, Ethan. I'll speak to them too if it keeps my son alive." Carol wiped the tears from her eyes. "My faith couldn't save Carly, but her faith saved you." She smiled at Riley. "I can't thank you enough, Riley. Thank you for bringing my boy back to me." Carol Lynch let go of Ethan's hand, and threw her arms around Riley's neck, and wept so deeply that her tears touched everyone in the room. All who were gathered around Ethan's bed wept with her, through the smiles of happiness on their faces.

Everyone had finally gone home, leaving Ethan to rest. It was late, and though he hadn't moved from the bed all day, he was exhausted. Mentally and emotionally. Inside his body he carried the liver of the man who killed his brother. He lived, but at what cost? So much had happened since he had lost consciousness the day before. So many people had been working to save him. Fighting to save him. Dan and Abe literally put themselves at the mercy of one of the most ruthless gangs in the city to save him.

"Silica?" Ethan whispered. "Silica, can you hear me?" He waited in the dim light of the hospital room. Beside him, the monitors registered healthy vital signs, and a steady heartbeat. "Silica? Can I talk to you even when I'm not dying?"

"What?" he heard the familiar voice. Was she inside his head, he wondered. She sounded like she was irritated with him, like he'd called her away from her dinner.

"I think I figured it out," Ethan said.

"Figured what out?" Silica asked impatiently.

"What you were trying to tell me the last time."

"Go on," Silica urged.

"The purpose of life," Ethan said.

"I'm waiting," the angel said. She had a way of making Ethan feel uncomfortable, as if he were keeping her from something more important.

"The purpose of life is to love," he said. Ethan waited, expecting some sort of confirmation or acknowledgement.

"Oh, you want me to congratulate you for getting something so obvious. We were so close last time," Silica said.

"When you die, you can't feel pain, or anger," Ethan said, hoping Silica would give him some sign of approval. "The only thing I felt when I was with you was my love for the people who were waiting for me to get better. There was no pain. No anger. Just love. It's the only thing you bring with you when you cross over, isn't it? The only thing anyone can do, no matter where they're born, or how little money they have, is to love. If we're all judged by the same standard, then there's only one answer to the question. It's the only thing that makes sense."

"If you think you've got the answer, let me ask you another question," Silica said. "What is love?"

"It's that feeling you have for someone else that makes you put them before yourself," Ethan said.

"It's not a feeling," Silica said. "Feelings are created by hormones that make you do stupid things. Try again."

"It *is* a feeling," Ethan insisted.

"Then how come people can love each other even when they're mad at each other?" Silica asked. "How come a mother can love her child while she's so angry with them she could literally rip their head off in that moment? How come a husband and wife can argue and yell at each other, and still love each other in that moment? Try again."

"I don't know, tell me," Ethan surrendered. "You're not a very easy angel to talk to, you know."

"This isn't about me," Silica said. "You called me. You said you had the answer."

"What were you in your last life?" Ethan asked. "A drill sergeant?"

"I was a wife, and a mother," Silica replied.

"Then how come you're so bitter," Ethan asked.

"I'm not bitter," Silica responded. "You can't feel emotions like that once you die. You're right about the love part. It's the only thing you bring with you when you die."

"So if you're not bitter, what are you?"

"This is my way," Silica said. "Like your way is gentle and encouraging, my way isn't."

"So you're not pissed at me?"

"No," Silica replied. "Just wish you were quicker on the uptake."

Ethan laughed, and then grimaced in agony, holding his right side.

"You haven't finished your answer," Silica pressed. "What's love if it isn't a feeling?"

Ethan thought for a moment. Would he say that his mom and dad loved each other? They seemed to. They were still close, but it wasn't a rush of hormones that kept their love going.

"I don't know, is it the way you behave towards someone?" Ethan suggested.

"You're getting there," Silica said.

"The things you do for the person you love?"

"You can't use the question in the answer," Silica said flatly.

He thought about Riley, and how she had been prepared to sacrifice herself for him. The ultimate act of love.

"It's when you put someone else before yourself. When you act selflessly towards another person," Ethan thought.

"Do you have to love someone to act selflessly towards them?" Silica asked.

"Oh, now you're just messing with my head," Ethan waved a hand dismissively. "You know I've got the right answer," he said smugly.

"Would you put Riley before yourself? Your mom and dad? Abe, Dan, Martin and Archer?" Silica continued.

"Maybe some more than others," Ethan said. "I'd do anything for Riley without thinking. Mom and Dad – I might hesitate a little. Maybe add a condition or two. Abe and Dan – they nearly got themselves killed for me. Would I do the same for them? I guess, yes, maybe. And Martin and Archer? Not as willingly. Does that make me a bad person?"

"There are degrees to love," Silica explained. "Real love isn't doing those selfless things for the people closest to you. That's the easy part."

"It's doing those things for the people you don't feel that way about?" Ethan said.

Silica smiled at him approvingly. "But to go back to your question. What is the purpose to life?"

Ethan thought about the people in his life. "So what matters more than the work I've done is how I've acted towards the people around me."

"Finally," Silica said. "*Now* you can rest."

"Wait," Ethan said. "Why me? Why all this to save me?"

"I told you before, this is bigger than just you," Silica said.

"No, you said that everything was much bigger than me and my life. Why? Why did you do all this to save me?" Ethan asked. He felt as though Silica were hiding something from him.

"Ask a different question," she said. "I can't answer that."

"I don't know what else to ask," Ethan held up both hands in surrender. "Lucca wasn't this cagey. How come they thought he was my angel?"

"He's not your angel," Silica said defensively. "I am."

"So who's angel is he then?"

"Lucca is no one person's angel any more. He was someone's angel until she crossed over. He belongs here now. At this hospital. I guess you could say he's the hospital's angel," she said.

"So you still haven't told me. Why me?" Ethan tried again.

"That's not the right question," Silica said again.

"So what is the right question then?" Ethan said in frustration. He thought for a moment. Lucca was the angel of the hospital. He'd started all this, showing Riley her future. "Why did Lucca show Riley her future and my future in the first place?" He asked, but Silica said nothing. "You did it, didn't you? It was you?"

"What was me?" Silica said.

"You made Lucca show Riley the future. So she'd do what she did to save us both," Ethan reasoned.

"I did," Silica agreed.

"So what's the deal with you and Lucca then?" Ethan asked.

"Now *that* would be the right question, Ethan," Silica said. "When souls are created, they're created in perfect pairs. Soul mates. When you enter the Dimension of Time, you begin your search for your one true soul mate. Not everybody finds theirs. In fact, most people don't."

"Riley is my soul mate," Ethan said.

"Yes," Silica replied.

"And ..." Everything seemed to finally make sense to Ethan, "...Lucca is your soul mate."

"Yes," Silica said again.

"What happened between you and Lucca then?" Ethan asked.

"We found each other only moments before I died," Silica said, sadly. "My husband had died in the War, and I was left widowed, with two children. Lucca and I met after the war ended. We fell in love, and we knew we were soul mates form the first moment."

"And?" Ethan asked.

"I developed Tuberculosis. I died only weeks after we met," she said. Ethan heard a tone of sadness in her voice. A feeling of longing.

"So when I met Riley…" Ethan began.

"You were soul mates," Silica said simply. "I couldn't let you die so soon after meeting her."

"You let us live because you and Lucca…"

"…never had the chance to," Silica said.

"Thank you," Ethan said. "For giving us a chance to live this love we found. Thank you."

"Love will find a way," Silica reminded him. "Remember your true purpose in the Dimension of Time."

"I will. Silica? Will I be able to speak to you again?" Ethan asked. "After all this. Once I'm out of here."

"Any time," Silica replied.

"Will you always be so hard on me?"

"What do you think," she replied.

Ethan found himself alone in the darkness of the ward. It was quiet except for the odd click and beeping of machines elsewhere in the room. He felt a tickle against his cheek and moved his hand to his face. He found something that warmed his heart, and made his eyes well with tears. A single white feather, soft as silk, lay against his skin.

Loved Lips of an Angel?

Write a Review

If you enjoyed Lips of an Angel by Adam Alexander, pop onto Amazon.com and post a review about this book to help other readers choose their next read.

Other Titles by Adam Alexander

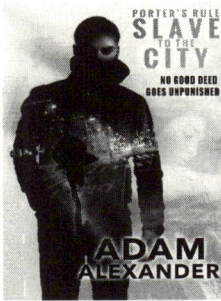

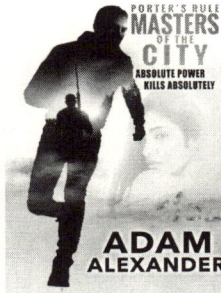

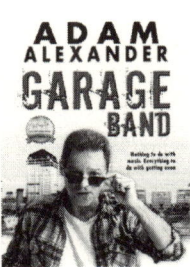

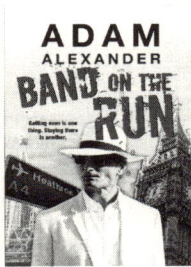

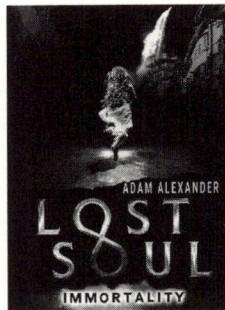

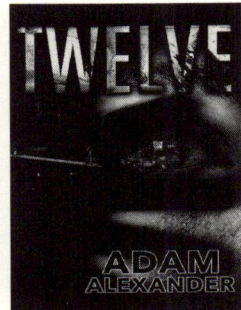

Lips of an Angel

What if you could know how your story ends, right now?

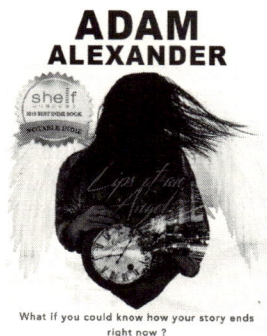

**ADAM
ALEXANDER**

*What if you could know how your story ends
right now ?*

Are the whispers of your guardian angel a blessing or a curse?

Riley's just come out of a relationship torn apart by lies. While nursing her bruised heart she's avoiding men at all cost.

Ethan's brother's murder is still unsolved, and he's convinced the cops aren't even trying to find the killer. He doesn't have time for love, not when his brother's killer is still free.

When Riley meets a medium with a direct line to the angels, she's intrigued. The more she listens to the voices of angels the more she learns about a dimension few know about.

But there is one angel that has a message only Riley can hear...
A message that will change her world forever...
Riley wants to know even more...

When Riley and Ethan meet the attraction is instant, the romance undeniable. Regardless of being burned by love before they can't ignore the connection. As their newfound love is explored Riley realizes her angel has one more message for her.

A message that will change everything.

If your guardian angel had something to tell you, would you listen?

"Intense yet so refreshing, …. This is a real entertainer!" - Reader's Favorite

***Winner of a Notable Indie Badge in the Shelf
Unbound Best Indie Book of the Year
Competition 2019***

Porter's Rule: Slave to the City

No good deed goes unpunished

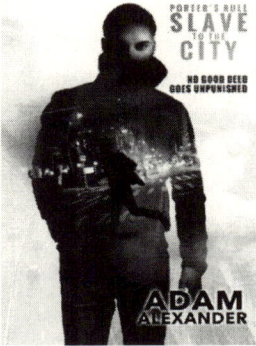

Porter's way. Porter's Rules. You can be a good cop all your life. But it only takes one bad decision to bring it all down.

All women are trouble. No exceptions. Rule #2. But when he sees her sitting in the Diner, her green eyes deep with sadness, Matt Porter has to be the hero. No good deed goes unpunished. Suddenly his career is in ruins, someone is trying to kill him, and there's a conspiracy that goes all the way to the office of the Governor.

Everyone's a victim, and no one can escape the grasp that's suffocating the City. Matt Porter won't give up. He's the only one that can release the stranglehold.

Can he save his own life, and his career as he struggles to stay alive and find out who really controls the city? Who is the girl with the sad green eyes, and why did it all start to unravel the day Porter met her?

Slave to the City is the first book in the Porter's Rule Detective Series. The series follows the challenges of Matt Porter, a stubborn, witty and cynical detective trying to survive in a world of power and crime. If you love detective novels, this one has it all; romance, suspense, thriller, drama... Porter will have you re-evaluating your own rules.

Adam Alexander

Porter's Rule: Masters of the City

Absolute power kills absolutely

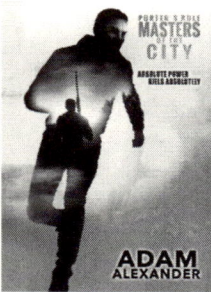

Will an old flame make Porter forget his rules?

Matt Porter is a freelancer... but not the usual kind. He dedicates his time and effort to helping victims of the rich and powerful. When he receives a plea for help from Christine Walker, he doesn't hesitate to step in.

After overhearing a conversation in the boardroom late one night, Christine's life is in jeopardy and only Porter can help her. Porter has his own rules, rules that have kept him alive, rules that have kept him sane. Helping Christine reminds Porter of rule nr. 2. All women are trouble, no exceptions. Will he remember this rule when an old flame returns?

As Porter delves deeper into the company threatening Christine's life, he opens a tin of worms he never anticipated. A conspiracy bigger than anything he's ever experienced before. Porter finds himself in a maze of danger and pitfalls and needs to navigate through it to save both his life and Christine's.

Will Porter save Christine, or will he go against his own rules? Join Porter in this action packed, nail biting detective thriller as he reveals a conspiracy big enough to change the world forever. Will he manage to save the world in time?

Masters of the City is the second book in the Porter's Rule Detective Series.

"fast paced, action packed ... left me anxiously chewing my nails ...master writing if ever I saw it. An absolutely fantastic read that I couldn't put down. Twists that knocked me for a six"
  - Blithering Bibliomaniacs

Porter's Rule: Lords of the City

Your house. My rules.

Can Porter save himself in time to save the world?

Matt Porter, ex-cop, is kidnapped after his father's funeral. When he wakes up he's no longer in familiar territory, the only familiar face, a dangerous escaped convict he put away only months ago.

He knows he's on his own; he only has his wits and experience to help him escape. Even as he plans his escape, he realizes something bigger is at stake.

It soon becomes clear to Porter that he was kidnapped to help the convict with a bigger plan. A plan big enough to threaten the fate of an entire country.

It isn't just his life on the line this time.

Porter must single-handedly pursue his nemesis, outsmart him enough to escape and save the world before the clock runs out.

Will Porter find a way to outsmart the devious convict? How will he escape if he needs to stay to help save the nation? Enjoy another jam-packed action novel from Adam Alexander as Porter is faced with challenges bigger than ever before.

Lords of the City is the third book in the Porter's Rule Detective Series.

Garage Band

Nothing to do with music. Everything to do with getting even.

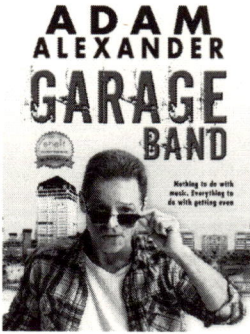

Lanthus Trilby worked for Eastland Insurance for seventeen years when he finds himself retrenched with no warning. He is about to be replaced by younger, brighter, more dynamic people as Eastland merges with its newest acquisition. Enraged, the passive, back-room actuary seeks revenge on his ex-boss for his unfair dismissal.

A random meeting one night in a bar leads Lanthus to his grand plan for revenge. The once-shy and quiet actuary must now transform to become a criminal mastermind as he plots an event that will cripple Eastland, and send a message to his ex-boss, Charles. Lanthus assembles an unlikely team – a hacker, and explosives expert, a cage fighter and a pair of acrobats to pull off the most daring hostage situation the world has ever seen and hold Eastland to ransom. But can he stay one step ahead of the relentless Detective Muller and the entire police force in his single-minded quest for revenge?

Garage Band is a witty, light-hearted comedy/suspense that keeps you in stitches while you balance on the edge of your seat.

Also available as an Audio Book on Audible

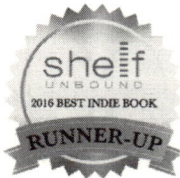

Garage Band was a runner up in the 2016 Shelf Unbound Best Indie Book of the Year competition.

Band on the Run (releasing 2020)

Getting even is one thing. Staying there is another.

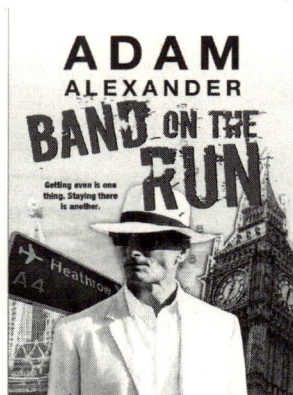

A global chase. An international fugitive. And hundreds of millions of dollars. He'd give it all up to see his kids just one more time.

He got his revenge, but he had to disappear from everyone, including his kids. To get them back, Lanthus Trilby has to come out of hiding, and that's exactly what Detective Muller is counting on.

Lanthus Trilby desperately wants to make contact with his kids, but the relentless Detective Muller has never given up his search for the fugitive who held Sandton City to ransom.

Muller is cunning and relentless and will do whatever it takes to bring Lanthus Trilby to justice, even if it means chasing him halfway across the world. With little time to plan, Lanthus has to do the impossible to avoid getting caught.

The Garage Band is back for one more thrilling, edge-of-your seat caper, even bolder and more daring. Everything is at stake for the Band on the Run.

301

Adam Alexander

Lost Soul – Immortality

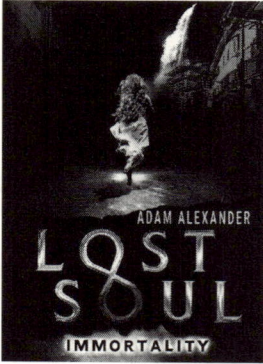

What would you do if you discovered your soul was worth killing for?

On holiday with a group of friends, Cassandra discovers a shocking secret about herself. She is the Pure Soul. According to myth and legends the Pure Soul holds the key to immortality, and only walks the earth once every thousand years. Cassandra is hesitant to accept her fate until she realizes she is being hunted by sorcerers from the dark ages with evil intentions.

If her pure soul is conquered the sorcerers will attain the one thing their magical powers cannot conjure - immortality. When they learn that the Pure Soul has been reincarnated into an innocent girl, they will stop at nothing to devour her soul.

Cassandra can only survive by seeking help from the bloodlines of ancient ancestors. She must call on the forces from the spirit world to defeat the powerful enemies who want to destroy her to increase their own power.

Enjoy this fast-paced urban fantasy novel filled with magic from the dark ages as Cassandra flees for her life in modern day Italy. Will she and her friends survive the dangerous chase? Can Cassandra find love while she's running for her life? Lost Soul builds suspense, keeping you glued to the pages as Adam Alexander takes you on a journey to amazing destinations while Cassandra tries to outsmart her evil hunters.

If you enjoyed the Hunger Games and Percy Jackson, then you'll definitely be thrilled by **Lost Soul – Immortality**.

About the Author

Adam Alexander is a multi-talented author who manages to capture audiences across a diverse range of genres including Fantasy, Suspense / Thriller, Comedy and Romance/Supernatural. He describes his brain as "not normal" as he always finds himself looking for the hidden story in the things that most people see as just a normal day.

"I love to entertain people when I write. There's enough shock and horror in the news. I write to carry my audience away and put a smile on their faces, even if it's just for a few minutes of their day."

There's a story behind every story, and his own story is both entertaining and inspiring. He is big on vision and dreams, and as a motivational speaker, he tells his powerful and inspiring story to encourage people to do all the things they've always wanted to do. He certainly has, and continues to do so.

Apart from being an accomplished writer and entrepreneur, he draws, sings, and plays guitar. Adam is a devoted husband and father, and lives in South Africa in a house overrun by emotionally unstable Boston Terriers and a Ragdoll cat with an identity crisis.

Join Adam Alexander's Mailing List

for updates, news, free e-books and giveaways:

www.adam-alexander-author.com

Follow Adam Alexander:

Facebook: Adam Alexander Author
Twitter: @AdamAlexBooks
Instagram: @AdamAlexanderAuthor
Bookbub: https://www.bookbub.com/profile/adam-alexander